THE GLASS REPUBLIC

TOM POLLOCK

Jo Fletcher

BOOKS

First published in Great Britain in 2013 by

Jo Fletcher Books
an imprint of Quercus Editions Ltd.
55 Baker Street
7th Floor, South Block
London
W1U 8EW

A CIP catalogue record for this book is available
from the British Library

ISBN 978 1 78087 010 6 (HB)
ISBN 978 1 78087 011 3 (TPB)
ISBN 978 1 78087 012 0 (EBOOK)

10 9 8 7 6 5 4 3 2 1

Typeset by Ellipsis Digital Limited, Glasgow
Printed and bound in Great Britain by Clays Ltd, St Ives plc.

For my sister Sarah,
who always finds me at the end of the day.

I

THE GIRL WHO LOOKED BACK

CHAPTER ONE

Laughter burst out over the playground. Like a lot of weapons, laughter had two edges, and the tall girl in the green hijab was intimately familiar with both. She listened to it carefully, even while she joked, wary in case it turned.

'Honestly, I spent a week in training, then I was plunged into this network of underground cage-fighting clubs. The face came from this one girl, vicious little thing half my height – she hid these tiny nails under the knuckles of her gloves. It was totally against the rules, but nobody cared. Every time she hit me it was like getting a facial from a wolverine.'

A handful of students, bundled up against the February cold, clustered around Pen. She resisted the urge to draw the headscarf closer around her face under their scrutiny.

One of her audience, a superior-looking blonde in a fake-fur coat hissed impatiently, 'But seriously, Parva . . .'

'Seriously, Gwen?' Pen shrugged. '*Seriously*, it was a jealous lover, said if he couldn't have me, no one could.'

Laughter again, but more hesitant this time, and it quickly

petered out. Gwen Hardy's eyes widened slightly and she said, 'What . . . actually?'

'Sure,' Pen deadpanned. 'Or maybe it was an angry cat – mutantly big – Catzilla, basically. Had claws out to here,' she mimed. 'I can't quite remember, mind. It was a while ago—'

'It was four months ago.'

'Yeah, but it was only my face, it wasn't like it was important . . .'

'*Parva!*' Gwen's smile was achingly wide. 'Will you just tell us already?'

Pen licked her uneven lips, wishing her current strategy involved a little less playing court jester to Gwen's little crew. Still, she had disappeared without warning for three months and returned with a reconstructed lip and a tangled thatch of scar tissue over her cheeks. If you wanted back into school society with all that baggage, you needed the backing of somebody influential.

She made a show of sizing the three of them up, as though deciding how much truth they could take: Gwen Hardy, whom Allah in his loving wisdom had made pretty and bright and hard-edged as a diamond-cutter, stood next to her boyfriend Alan Jackson, who was just as smart, but given to speak only in soft monosyllables. Everything about him was as lean and efficient as the muscular frame zipped into his football team jacket. Next to Alan, and trying not to be too obviously excited about it, was tiny, freckled Trudi Stahl. Trudi had replaced recently graduated nightmare Harriet Williams at the crank-handle of the school's rumour-mill, and still seemed to be catching her breath at finding herself in such exalted company.

Pen beckoned them forward and they shuffled in, obscuring the shapes and muffling the noise of the younger kids who were kicking tennis balls across the asphalt until a breathless kind of intimacy enveloped them.

'Well?' Gwen demanded.

Pen drew in a deep breath and said softly, 'I was kidnapped by a living coil of barbed wire – the servant a of a demolition god whose fingers were cranes. I was its host, and it sent me to kill Beth Bradley, but she freed me from it instead. I held the monster down with my body while she cut it off with a sharpened park railing.'

There was a long moment's silence, then Alan made a *tchk* sound in the back of his throat and laughed. Gwen actually stamped her foot and puffed out a little condensation-cloud of frustration even as she grinned, but it was Trudi who spoke.

'Damn,' she said. 'I actually thought we were going to get something there.'

The bell sounded the end of morning break and, chatting, whooping and swearing, Frostfield students converged on the doors to the main block. Anyone under sixteen was at least nominally in a blue and grey uniform. From above, Pen thought, it must've looked like a tide of dirty water streaming towards a plughole.

Gwen shouldered her satchel and slung an arm around Alan's neck. She pulled him in and kissed him ostentatiously. At length she broke away and asked, 'What's now?'

'Maths,' Alan replied.

She rolled her eyes and Trudi, taking her cue, groaned along.

'Eff. Eff. Ess,' Gwen said. 'With the new woman? Foreign-Chick?'

'Faranczek.'

'Whatever. Can any of you even understand a word she's saying with that accent? I never thought I'd say this, but I seriously miss Salt. Did you get anywhere finding out what happened to him, Tru?'

'Nothing solid, but a couple of the year 7s are spreading it that he's been suspended,' Trudi replied. 'Apparently some girl said he touched her up.'

Pen felt her stomach muscles clench. 'Really?' She managed to keep her voice even. 'Who?'

Trudi looked a little crestfallen. 'They didn't know.'

'Selfish, lying bitch.' Gwen snorted in disgust. 'Whoever she is, she's just out for attention, and she's going to screw up our exams while she's at it. Now, if some *boy* had said Salt went for him . . .'

She left it hanging and everyone laughed, including Pen, even though it wasn't funny and her ears and chest were burning, even though she could feel the laughter pressing its blade against her stomach, because sometimes that was what you had to do.

'You not coming, Parva?' Gwen asked when Pen didn't follow them towards the door.

6

Pen shook her head. She pulled a cartoon-mournful face and drew an invisible tear down one cheek with a finger.

'Still playing the trauma card?' Gwen said with a good-humoured *tut*. 'Lucky cow. Still, I don't blame you. If I could get away with skiving it, I would.' She tucked her arm through Alan's, and the untouchable pair sauntered inside. Trudi hung back with Pen. She tucked a coil of red hair behind one ear. 'You will tell us, though, Parva,' she said, her voice kind; concerned. 'The stories are fun and all, and Gwen's cutting you some slack, but sooner or later you *will* tell us how your face got so fucked-up.' She tilted her head and studied Pen's cross-hatched cheeks. 'I just wanted to make sure you knew that.'

Pen forced a smile. She felt her scars bend: a dozen mocking, mirroring mouths.

'Sure, Tru,' she said. 'It'll be good to talk to someone.'

'That's what friends are for.' Trudi rose onto tiptoes, kissed her on the cheek and headed in through the doors.

Pen walked against the tide of the students into the play-ground. Something cold landed on her eyelash: snowflakes were drifting from the yellowing clouds. She pulled her headscarf tighter around her and shuddered.

You will tell us.

She should have known that was coming. Pen was hanging around with Gwen because her . . . *patronage* – she couldn't think of it as anything other than that – kept the rest of Frostfield off her back, but Gwen didn't do charity. She wanted to be seen to be the one the damaged girl opened up to, the one who could get the answers to the questions the whole school was buzzing with.

Where did Pen go for those three weeks last autumn?

What was it that had mutilated her face?

And where on earth had Beth Bradley, Pen's best friend, a girl she never used to be seen without, *gone*?

Buried in her thoughts, Pen almost walked into the school perimeter wall. She shook herself and bent double against the snow. The wind had started up and now it shrieked up and down octaves and stripped her face raw. She was grateful for it – everyone else would have hurried indoors and there was less chance of being seen.

The old junior block jutted out into the playground in front of her, bandaged up in hi-vis tape like an injured brick limb. Some workmen had found asbestos in it while Pen had been gone and the whole structure had been cordoned off. Orange cones marked out the edge of the forbidden zone.

Secret spaces can open up so fast in the city, Pen thought.

Wary of the CCTV, she squeezed herself in behind the tangle of spiny evergreen bushes that grew by the wall and edged her way towards the fire escape at the back.

The air inside was dank and cave-like, but out of the wind it felt warm. What little light penetrated the muck-smeared windows silhouetted little funeral cairns of bluebottles. Pen picked her way along the corridor, climbing over a couple of toppled-over lockers, and ducked into a doorway on the right.

It had been the girls' bathroom once. Toilet-stall doors stood open, plastic seat lids down and covered in dust. Sinks jutted from the wall like pugnacious chins, with a long frameless sheet of mirror-glass still screwed in above them.

Just to be sure, Pen checked inside the stalls, but she was alone in the room.

Anxiety bubbled in her throat as she stepped up to the mirror. She saw herself up close: the scars criss-crossed her cheeks like cracks in broken glass. Luckily Dr Walid had owed her father a favour from their university days, so he hadn't charged when he rebuilt her nostril and her lower lip using a graft taken from her thigh. Camouflage, carefully applied, could conceal the border between them and the surrounding tissue, but it left a flat texture, a *wrongness* that couldn't be disguised.

There was only so much you could hide from people if they got too close.

'It's all you, Pen,' she whispered. 'They just rearranged you a little bit.'

Gradually her gorge subsided. It helped to be here, in this mildewed, tumbledown bathroom, the only place in the world she could find someone who understood.

She leaned over the sink and rapped on the mirror with her knuckles. 'Hello? Hello?'

Her voice echoed hollowly off the tiles.

Hello? Hello?

'Hello.'

In the mirror, Pen saw a slender girl walk out of one of

9

the toilet stalls; the same stalls Pen had looked into and *knew* were empty. The interloper stepped up behind her, put her arms around Pen's waist and settled her chin on her shoulder. Pen felt the pressure from the girl's hug and the comfortable heat from the cheek next to her own, but she didn't bother looking sideways; she knew she'd see nothing there. She kept her eyes on the glass, studying the reflection that appeared not to be cast by anyone at all.

The clothes were different; the girl in the mirror had obviously been shopping. She wore tighter jeans, a stylishly cut leather jacket and a pair of heels that meant she had to stoop slightly to hug Pen. The girl's headscarf looked new too, an expensive-looking raw silk in pigeon-grey.

The face though – the face was identical: fine-featured, brown-skinned, even down to the intricate asymmetry of the scars.

Pen looked into the mirror and saw her reflection doubled. Two copies of her looked back.

The girl next to her reflection broke into a grin and the slashes that framed her mouth became something quite beautiful. 'You look good, girl,' she said.

CHAPTER TWO

Pen's new face was like a bully: the unstable, manipulative kind who sticks close to you like they're your needy best friend, demands constant attention and care and then ridicules you the moment anyone else shows up.

After she came out of hospital, Pen spent hours at her dresser, skin camouflage cream open before her. She patted over the little ridges of twisted, discoloured skin with the sponge, the way she'd been taught, trying to change what she saw in the mirror back into someone she recognised.

The first week, she hadn't worn any makeup at all. Burning with the energy of what she'd survived, she'd tried to catch the eye of total strangers and started conversations at the Number 57 bus stop about the weather or *Downton Abbey*. She'd been pugnaciously cheery, *daring* them to look at her.

It hadn't been worth it.

Only little kids would let themselves gape openly; adults just became fascinated with the their own feet, not wanting to be caught staring, and more and more Pen had started to hide her new face.

She took to running in the middle of the night, keeping her eyes on the pavement so she wouldn't see the Sodium-ites dancing their burning dances inside the streetlamps. She ran until the freezing air turned to fire in her lungs and sweat drenched the scarf tied around her hair. She looked up strength-training regimes on the internet and practised them in her bedroom until calluses armoured the inside of her fingers and she could do chin-ups on the lintel over her door. The thrill as her body responded to her felt like defiance and she watched in satisfaction as her ribs emerged through her tightening skin. She became a little more careful about what she ate, then a little more, then a little more. Food felt risky; it could unpick the changes she had willed on herself. She'd chop and mix the chickpeas and spinach on her plate, prod at them with bread but take very few bites. Every refrained-from mouthful burned in her chest like another victory. She did her best to ignore the worried looks from her parents.

You know best, Pen, she told herself. *It's your body.* Yours. *Everything's going to be fine.*

Prayer had become almost impossible.

It wasn't as though she'd never missed Salah, back in the time that she was beginning to think of as simply 'Before'. She'd often overslept, or been out with Beth, or been so busy she'd just forgotten, but this was different. At first, she was careful to make the time: she wanted prayer to be something she could hold on to. But the familiar words of the *rak'ah* felt awkward in her mouth, and she faltered before she finished, feeling horribly, *intimately* insincere. Eventually she'd stopped trying. When her dad tried to lead prayer at home, she told him she was going to pray in her room instead; she'd just stared at him, using her scars, until his protestations had faded away.

Once she had her morning makeup routine down to forty-five minutes and her hands no longer shook when she held the sponge, she went back to school.

The 57 drove her past a building site on Dalston High Road. From the upper deck Pen glimpsed cranes, spindly as winter trees, through the chilly fog. They were still, their motors stopped and voiceless, but she shrank back in her seat anyway. There was a flicker of movement inside the bulb of one of the still-lit street lamps and for an instant she saw a hand silhouetted against the glass.

Her phone buzzed in her pocket. She pulled it out and read, *Look left.*

Outside, something darted across the mouth of an alley, human-shaped, hooded and impossibly fast.

Her phone buzzed again.

Too slow. Look right.

Through the far window, Pen saw a figure fly across the gap between two rooftops.

Pen! This is harder than it looks, you know. Try and keep up! Look behind you.

Pen rolled her eyes and then, very slowly, craned her neck to face the back of the bus.

Upside down, hanging *somehow* by her toes from the roof,

her nose pressed to the glass, a teenage girl with skin the colour of concrete blew her a long, slow kiss.

Didn't think I'd miss your first day back in the madhouse, did you?

They stood at Frostfield High's metal gates. It was still early. A few uniformed kids, hunched like Sherpas under their rucksacks, made their way in from their parents' cars. A couple of them looked, but no one recognised Pen. She glanced back over her shoulder and took in the landscape. East London's terracotta roofs overlapped like insect-chitin in the long shadows of the tower blocks.

Beth leaned with one foot against the gatepost, hood up, head down, thumbs flickering while she texted. The spiked iron railing she always carried now rested in the crook of her elbow. She showed Pen her screen. *Sure you're ready?*

Pen exhaled. 'Nope,' she said, 'but I'm not sure I ever will be, so I might as well do it now.'

Hardcore, Pencil Khan. I'm proud of you. Pavement-grey eyes met Pen's.

Beth held her gaze and typed blind. *I'll come in with you if you want, you know that, right? Screw 'em. I'm still enrolled. Just give the word and we'll be sitting together in French.*

Pen looked at her curiously. 'When I suggested that before you didn't seem so up for it.'

Beth shrugged, a little shyly. *Just for me, no. But I'd line up next to you in front of a firing squad if that's where you wanted me.*

She would too.

Pen touched her cheek. 'No thanks, B. I could use a bit of

14

upstaging, mind, but I think you might draw a bit *too* much focus.'

Be all right. Got a spear.

She was joking. Probably. Nevertheless, Pen winced at the thought of Beth prodding the railing into anyone who looked at her funny. There was a wild edge to her friend now and she couldn't entirely rule that out.

'Still,' she said, 'I think it might put a bit of a dent in Operation Normality.'

She caught the guilty flicker in her friend's eyes, but her own voice echoed back to her.

No further down the rabbit hole, B. She'd said it and she had to hold to it; she couldn't look back.

Beth stretched out her hand, Pen pressed her palm to hers and they interlaced fingers. She felt the uncanny texture of Beth's skin graze over her own, warm and rough as summer pavement.

Beth texted one-handed, *I'll find you at the end of the day.*

The street-skinned girl kicked herself off the gate, tucked the railing under one arm and sauntered into the slowly thickening morning crowd. Pen caught a couple of disapproving glances from older, stuffier-looking pedestrians. Hooded head bent as though against the cold, Beth could have been any teenager who'd eyed up a Monday morning at school and decided she couldn't be arsed.

'You're still you,' Pen muttered to herself turning back to the gates. 'And school's still just school.'

Like that wasn't the problem.

Gripping the straps of her rucksack like it was an escape parachute, she pushed past the gate.

Frostfield's hallways were the usual cacophony of laughter, shouts, phone-speakers leaking bass, trainers, squeaky lino and slamming lockers. Under it all, Pen heard the muttered snatches and the cut-off gasps. She saw the hurried looks away.

'—look who's back—'

'—what *happened* to her?—'

'—where's her punky little mate?—'

'—She got kicked out for that graffiti stunt, remember?'

'Nah, Salt never made that stick . . . where is Salt, anyway?'

Pen knew exactly where Dr Julian Salt was: out on bloody bail. The DI in charge of her case had called her the day before to tell her. The same brown-haired, tired-eyed woman had spent four hours a week ago asking Pen painfully blunt questions in a gentle voice.

'No,' Pen had answered, feeling small and resentful, clutching her mum's hand while she spoke. '*No we never did . . . that. But he touched me. No, he never physically forced me. No, it was – it was blackmail. He said he could get Beth put in a foster-home. She's my best friend. No, she doesn't know. No, I don't know why you can't reach her.*

And, '*No, the scars were something else. An accident.*'

And she'd trotted out the same ridiculous plate-glass window lie she'd sold her folks – because how could they ever, *ever* come close to believing the truth?

It had taken Pen a long time to recognise the black, choking feeling in her throat for the anger it was. Even though she was assured that things were 'progressing', even though 'action was being taken', the fact that Pen had screwed up her courage and made the call and that Salt was still free for Sunday lunch at home with his wife blistered her with rage.

'Hey, Parva.'

Pen looked up in surprise. Gwen Hardy's smile had the voltage of West End signage. Pen blinked and faltered and stammered, 'G-Gwen.'

Gwen had nodded approvingly, as if Pen deserved a prize for remembering her name. The hallway was silent now. Everyone was watching. Pen felt their scrutiny like an icy wind. She braced herself for the question she was sure was coming . . .

'*What the hell happened to your—*'

'Beth not with you?' Gwen asked. Pen shook her head, more in confusion than in denial. It was probably the first time that name had passed Gwen's glossy lips, but she used it with casual intimacy, as if Beth was *her* best friend, not Pen's.

'Too bad. Good to have you back anyway. If you want to catch up at lunchtime, you know where we usually sit?'

Pen inclined her head slowly, trying not to let her puzzlement show. The oh-so symmetrical lines of Gwen's face creased as her smile grew wider, but the expression never reached her eyes, and it was only when Pen looked past her to the shocked expressions of the other students and heard the scandalised whispers, that she understood what had just happened.

Pen was marked out, ugly and untouchable. She was ready for that, she'd geared herself up to fight it.

Gwen Hardy had just undercut it all, and she'd done it on purpose. She'd stepped out and offered the poor unfortunate a refuge, just because she *could*. Gwen was the only one who didn't need to fear the social taint the wounded girl carried with her. She was untouchable in a different way, and she'd just used Pen to rub everyone's faces in it.

. . . she'd just used Pen . . .

Without warning, the trembling started.

Everyone was looking at her.

Her fingertips started to drum on her thigh; she tried to stop them, but she couldn't.

Hot and cold shivers rippled her skin.

—used Pen—

She blinked fast and images came: a face carved in the collapsed masonry of a building site, cranes like metal claws, metal barbs hooked in her skin. Her chest was tight, as though bound by a wire tourniquet. She remembered blood drying on her cheeks. She fought to still her muscles and hot shame flooded through her as she failed.

She ran from the hall.

The banned junior block was the only place she knew she could be alone. She found herself in the bathroom by accident, sitting on the chilly floor and hugging her knees until she stopped shaking. Unsteadily, she stood and gulped chalky water from the tap.

'So,' she muttered to herself when she'd gathered her breath, 'that's what a flashback feels like. Well, okay, we coped, didn't we? We'll just have to cope *better* next time.'

She'd turned away from the mirror on the wall and instead snapped her compact open. That was the ritual, and rituals were important.

'It's all still you,' she whispered. 'They just rearranged you a little bit.'

She looked at herself, caught between the tiny round makeup mirror and the massive frameless slab screwed to the tiles: an infinity of scarred, headscarved girls with smeared makeup stretched back into the reflection, as if there was one for every choice that had brought her here.

And then, suddenly, all those images of her concertinaed hard together into one.

An instant later the compact mirror shattered, pain shot through her skull and she cried out. It felt like a fault-line was shaking open right down the middle of her head.

The world shuddered and blurred around her.

The tiles were cold against her palms and her knees hurt. She didn't remember falling. Nausea swelled up, but she fought it back down.

Her fast, shallow breathing was the only sound in the silence. She rose unsteadily and reached back to steady herself on the sink behind her.

'Pen.'

It was her own voice. It sounded a little weird, the way it did when she heard it recorded on her answerphone, but still it was unmistakable.

Except she hadn't spoken.

'Pen—' The voice came from behind her, where there was only a tiled brick wall and mirrored glass. It sounded confused, and very, very frightened. 'Pen, *please* . . .'

Pen sucked her reconstructed lip between her teeth and bit it.

She looked back.

CHAPTER THREE

'Gwen's not so bad,' Pen said, stretching out on the cold concrete floor. 'At least, not next to the crowd she runs with. They're . . .' She groped for the right word.

'Toxic?' the girl behind the mirror put in. For reasons of mutual convenience, they'd agreed she was 'Parva' rather than 'Pen'.

'I honestly think that if Iran stockpiled Gwen Hardy's friends, the Americans would invade. There's probably a UN convention just against Trudi Stahl.'

Parva laughed, the sound echoing through the glass. 'Well, here's to your new crew—' The reflected girl rummaged around in her ostrich leather handbag and, to Pen's astonishment, pulled out a bottle of wine. 'I hope they make you happy.'

'You're *drinking* now?'

'Pen,' Parva said patiently, 'in the last four months I've been kidnapped by a barbed-wire monster, ridden to war at the head of an army of giant scaffolding wolves *and* rejoined school in the middle of term. There's only one girl I know who deserves a drink as much as I do, and I'll happily share.' She unscrewed the cap and swigged straight from the bottle before offering it to the lips of Pen's own mortified reflection.

Pen shrank back. 'But I *never—*' she started.

Her double grinned at her through the mirror and said, 'But I'm not you any more.'

Pen knew that. She'd plied Beth with careful questions, feigning idle interest, and learned as much as she could about the mirrorstocracy and their city behind the mirrors. The girl on the other side of the glass had come from her – she was composed of all the infinite reflections of her that had been caught between the two mirrors – but that was when their coexistence had ended.

Pen and Parva had diverged from that moment in time like beams of refracted light; now Parva had her own feelings, her own *life*, built up in the weeks since she'd first stepped into whatever lay outside the bathroom door in the reflection. She drank wine, ate meat and swore like a squaddie with haemorrhoids. Much to Pen's chagrined envy, she'd even managed to land herself a job, although she wouldn't say doing what.

But still, she *had been* Pen: for nearly seventeen years they'd been one. Parva had seen everything Pen had seen, felt everything Pen had felt. It was like having a sister, a bizarre twin – a twin who understood *everything*. Not even Beth could do that.

'I want to show you something.' Parva blew softly over the

neck of the bottle and the liquid pipe-sound echoed through both bathrooms. 'Give me your hand.' In the mirrored bathroom she extended her own hand towards Pen's reflection.

Pen reached into the empty space in front of her and felt warm, invisible fingers close over her skin.

'What are you—?'

'*Shhh.*' Parva was digging in her handbag again. She pulled out a phone and earbuds and put one bud into her own ear and the other into the ear of Pen's reflection.

Pen heard the crackle of an old-fashioned waltz and felt her double's ghostly hand on the small of her back.

'Come on,' Parva said, 'one–two–three, one–two–three!'

And then they were off, dancing to the creaky music. Pen followed the rhythm uncertainly, her feet stumbling a little, her arms curved around empty air. In the mirror, she saw her expensively dressed double leading her.

'One–two–three, one–two–three – that's it.'

Pen felt her arm lifted over her head and she spun under it as Parva whooped. Pen found herself laughing as they pirouetted around the tumbledown toilets like they were in a nineteenth-century ballroom.

'Where did you learn this?'

'One–two–three. It's the job, they're teaching me all kinds of things, it's—'

'Ow!' Pen abruptly broke away. She hopped in a circle as pain spiked through her foot.

'Sorry!' Parva winced. 'I'm not used to leading, and, uh . . . the shoes are new too.'

'Yeah, I noticed them.' Pen slid down the bathroom wall and tugged off her trainer and her sock. The impression of Parva's vertiginous heel had gone all the way through to the skin, but at least there was no blood. 'You have to go back to Reach to hoist you into them?'

Parva smiled from the mirror. Jokes about the slain Crane King were part of their routine. They felt weirdly daring, disarming the memories of their abduction.

'I managed by myself,' she said. 'Just.'

'Pretty fancy. Are they from the new job too?' Pen clutched theatrically at her heart. 'That's it: that's the lethal dose. I am now officially too jealous to live. Fancy new shoes, fancy dancing lessons – at least say your new boss is a slave-driving creep.'

Parva shrugged. 'Sorry, sis. The new boss is really sweet, actually. Everyone is – well, most of the time.'

'Most of the time?'

Her mirror-sister frowned. 'It's nothing really, just . . . the very top people here – only *some* of them, mind, and only some of the time – but . . . The way they look at me. I feel like they're watching me when my back's turned. Sometimes – sometimes I can't shake the feeling they mean me harm.'

Pen sighed. That sounded familiar. 'I reckon, after everything, maybe feeling like that's normal for us, you know?'

'I guess.' Parva chewed her reflected lip. 'They just look at me funny.'

'Hate to be the one to break it to you, hon,' said Pen, 'but you are toting three-fifths of the western world's total supply of scar-tissue around on your face.' She smiled gently. 'So, are you actually going to tell me what this magic new job is?'

Parva was about to speak when the distant sound of the period bell carried through the closed window.

'Tell you next time,' the girl in the mirror said. It was what she always promised, like Scheherazade, keeping back one last story.

Pen pouted and headed for the door. 'Whatever. Have fun at work.'

'Pen, wait.'

Pen paused in the doorway. The lonely note in her double's voice was stronger now.

'How's Beth?'

'Chatty,' Pen said drily. 'Supposedly she's still living at home, but I don't think Paul sees her much. Things are okay, but a bit . . .' She struggled to phrase it. 'She thinks I—'

'—blame her,' Parva finished quietly. 'You do, a little. I do. It'll take time.'

Pen didn't reply.

'Listen . . .' Parva hesitated. 'Do you think . . . do you think she'd come here? I get why you haven't told her about me yet, but – well, it would be good to see her, you know?'

Pen imagined leading the silent, grey-skinned girl here; letting her in on this one last secret, and a resentful flare ignited in her throat. She loved B, but this was *her* sanctuary, her respite from the life she was living because of Beth.

The resentment burnt out fast. She loved B, and so did

Parva. And unlike Pen, Parva hadn't seen their best friend in months. 'I'll ask her.'

'Thank you.' Parva smiled in relief. 'What you got now?'

'English: Richard Three.' Pen mimicked a movie-trailer voice: *The hunch is back!*'

Parva snorted at the weak pun. 'With jokes like that, it's a good thing you're pretty.'

'Narcissist,' Pen countered.

Her double laughed. 'Get out.'

CHAPTER FOUR

Beth pulled her hood up and crossed the threshold into the sewers, gripping her iron railing like a spear. She fed on the city around her with every step she took, drawing power and information through the bare soles of her concrete-grey feet:

A railwraith clatters across Blackfriars Bridge like an iron heart attack. A pair of streetlamps flicker angrily at each other across Electric Avenue as an argument between Sodiumite sisters flares up into insults and duelling challenges. Masonry Men move through the walls of an old house in Hampstead, rippling the brickwork and making it groan, while in an upstairs bedroom, a mother reassures her frightened daughter, whispering, 'Old houses just creak a bit, sweetheart.' Pylon spiders race along cables beneath the pavements, whispering to each other with white noise, static and stolen syllables.

Underneath the distortion there was a familiarity to the arachnoid voices that made Beth's chest ache.

It was a typical London night, only not *quite* typical, because deep in the tunnels ahead was something very unusual, and so subtle that had she not been within a hundred feet of it and listening intently for that very thing, she would have missed it utterly:

A tiny sphere of perfect silence.

It was no bigger than her clenched fist, but she could hear the way London's other sounds contorted around it. It *had* to be what she was looking for.

Beth had been trawling London's sewers for five straight nights now and this was the first sign she'd found. Her pulse quickened. She tightened her grip on her spear and picked up her pace, all the while straining to listen past the swish of the water across her ankles.

The stream widened and deepened and she began to wade. The rich sewer gases fugged around her and she shook her head, trying to clear it. To her right, two vaguely human-shaped lights, one orange, the other white, flitted across the mouth of an access tunnel, safely away from the water. There was a flushed excitement in their glow which made Beth smile. Mixed-spectrum couples were still rare, but more and more had got together in the months since the war – those few brief days when Blankleit and Sodiumite had fought side by side against the Crane King had unlocked something. She wondered just how many of them were sneaking around down here while their disapproving elders dozed in the daylight. These two were late getting back.

Lamp-crossed lovers, she thought, and her smile stretched to a grin.

The last of their light faded and the darkness crowded back. A few months earlier Beth would have been blind down here, but now she saw the brick tunnels in new colours: bruise and thundercloud hues. She remembered the boy, cocksure and scrawny and loose-limbed, who'd possessed the same spear she now carried.

Is this how you saw the city, Fil? she wondered. *Is this how you saw me?*

The thought was like being stabbed in the heart with a safety pin.

She took another corner, and came face to face with her prey.

The lizard didn't look like much, but, to be fair, it seemed equally unimpressed with her. It clung to the bricks, an inch and a half of greenish-brown leather. It rolled a black, liquid eye to track her, but otherwise didn't move.

Without realising it, Beth held her breath.

Slow now, B, she told herself, *slow as a sloth with a hangover. Remember what Candleman said: don't piss it off 'til it's pinned.*

She didn't so much walk as allow herself to accrete towards it. The hairs were standing up on her neck and her forearms and she was aware of every single one of them.

The unimpressive lizard blinked slowly. Not only did it make no sound, but Beth could hear the sounds in the tunnel bending themselves around it. Dripping water and scurrying rats struck countless echoes from the sewer's brick walls, but none of those echoes penetrated the tiny reptile's cocoon of silence. Its tongue glinted like metal as it tasted the air.

Just stay there, just a few more seconds . . .

She reached over her shoulder into her backpack and drew out a lidless glass jar. The lizard stared at her.

She stared back.

It blinked again.

Beth lunged.

Glass clinked on brick and she pressed the jar down hard. The lizard scrambled around the inside of it.

Got you! Beth crowed inside her head. She could hear the clicking of its claws now its sealed bubble of gas was broken. She clung to the base of the jar. Her fingers were sweaty. The muscles in her arm felt as taut as guitar strings and she realised she was actually trembling.

The creature froze. It glared at her through the glass with a single, furious, magnified eye.

Well, she thought, *thank Thames for th—'*

A heavy guitar riff crackled from the phone in Beth's pocket and she jumped. Her fingertips slid greasily over the glass; she tried to clutch it again, but it was too late. The ringtone cut off just in time for her to hear the jar splinter on the floor.

Beth just had time to wonder how in Thames' name she had a signal all the way down here, and then the lizard dropped off the wall.

Oh shit.

The reptile fell for a split second, and then it stopped in mid-air. It lashed its little tail in a corkscrew-like propeller motion and lazily, like a crocodile in the water, the lizard began to spin.

Double shit.

It spun faster and faster until it blurred. Beth felt the foetid air in the sewer begin to move. The edges of her clothes rippled. The atmosphere thickened, clinging to her lips as the sewer gases flew in. The lizard's tail dipped and twisted, mixing methane and ammonia like an artist mixing paint. Beth tried to reach for it, but her hand kept slipping off the air currents. The tendrils of gas were flowing so fast around her that they were dragging vacuum. Beth couldn't smell anything; she couldn't hear anything. She was caught in skeins of silence. She gritted her teeth and hooked her fingers, but she was trapped in the coils of swiftly moving gas and couldn't even lift her arm.

Not coils, she thought, uneasily eyeing the spinning lizard. *Claws.*

Her stomach lurched as her feet left the floor.

Supersize buy-one-get-one-free bargain buckets of shit.

Abruptly, it stopped spinning and hung motionless in the air, though the gas continued to rush around it, pummelling Beth even as it held her suspended. The lizard bobbed gently in the eye of the miniature storm it had created. It tasted its handiwork with a flick of its tongue. It rolled an eye to look at Beth and she could've sworn she saw a self-satisfied smirk on its reptile face.

It cracked its tail once and shot down the tunnel like an arrow from a bow. Beth's stomach plummeted as she was dragged in its wake.

Bricks whipped past, skinning her fingertips where she

touched them. Pain flared, oily blood bubbled out and coagulated with cement speed. She could barely breathe. Her internal organs felt like they'd been crushed to the back of her ribcage.

They were flying too fast and the light was too meagre for her to see anything. Desperately she clicked her tongue, but the rushing air stole the sound and she got no echoes back. As they twisted and jack-knifed around corners her spear struck the walls, jarring her arm, but she clung to the iron railing – drop it here and she might never find it . . .

. . . *I don't know where I am.*

The realisation shuddered through her. London was *her* city – she could touch any inch of it and know right where she was. But she wasn't in contact; she was cut off, trapped in empty space. Disorientation welled up in her like nausea.

A little more light bled into the tunnel and glimmered in the lizard's eye. The floor dropped away suddenly and Beth saw the sewer stream crash into a waterfall beneath her feet, its base lost in darkness. She craned her neck upwards, but she couldn't see the roof of the tunnel either. They were flying down the centre of a brick-sided gorge, capped and shod in shadow. Light shone from tiny alcoves gouged into the wall on her right – thousands of them, irregularly spaced embers, networked like stars in constellations. Beth peered into one of the crevices as they passed and saw a stoppered glass flask, shining with a queasy phosphorescence.

Something flapped past her face and she recoiled sharply.

The winged thing settled on the lip of the one of the alcoves and cooed softly. *A pigeon, down here?* Beth thought incredulously, craning to watch it as it shrank behind them. It cleared its ragged wings – its feathers were coated in some liquid that gleamed in the dim light. An acrid smell stung Beth's nostrils: *oil.*

Memories surged up, triggered by the scent: her, immersed in a polluted pool, where the chemicals and city essences clawed at her skin, invading her and changing her while oil-soaked men in oil-soaked suits waited for her on the bank.

She thought of the price those oil-soaked men had exacted for granting her that transformation: the scrawny, city-skinned boy they'd mined for the essence that made him human. Panic stabbed her in the gut as she imagined falling into the darkness below her, and wondered what price those men might extract to guide her out of it again.

At last she knew where she was. But this was not her place; this place belonged to the oil-soaked men of the Chemical Synod.

Away. Away. The thought pounded urgently around the inside of her head. *We have to get away.*

But she had no voice to sound her plea for she'd already sold that.

The lizard kept its diamond-shaped head pointed straight as it flew, dragging her at breakneck pace. Beth thrashed, and she felt its claws of ammonia and methane flex around her. *Take us—*

She kept wriggling, and managed to free an arm. She

flailed, and without even meaning to, she brushed the belly of the tiny lizard itself.

—*away!*

Its head twitched and it looked upwards, as if it had scented something: only a tiny movement, but Beth saw it.

Hardly daring to hope, she stretched out her fingers again – but it was no good; she couldn't reach. Straining every joint against the flowing gas that held her, she just managed to lay a finger on the little reptile's skin.

In the wall above them she made out the mouth of a tunnel.

Please, she thought again, *please, take us away from here.*

Something like a static-electric shock rippled from her forehead to her fingertips. The reptile's head swung upwards and she felt its invisible methane wings beat as it fought to gain height. Beth's heart leapt in incredulous relief, but then it stuttered.

The lizard couldn't get enough lift . . .

I'm too heavy. A hot shiver broke over her skin. *It can't climb—*

The lizard banked to the right, hard and sudden, and Beth's stomach flipped. Its metallic tongue lashed out and struck sparks from the brick walls. The heat as the gas ignited was like a punch.

Beth screwed up her eyes against the glare. Beads of oily sweat stippled her forehead. Every muscle clenched as she waited for the flames to engulf her, but no coruscating tide consumed her. Seconds passed until, slowly, she eased her eyelids apart.

For the first time, she saw *the whole* of the creature that held her.

The little lizard was swimming through the boiling air at the centre of a far vaster ghostly reptile, an exo-self, outlined in blue fire where the methane burned. The zephyrkinetic creature wriggled its muddy toes and Beth saw massive fiery claws curl in answer beside her. It swayed its head and the burning muzzle swung, puppet-like, with it. It twitched the little nubs on its back and the fiery wings responded.

Talons like torches pincered Beth's waist. The flames burned holes in her hoodie and left sooty marks on her arms, but they didn't hurt her; her concrete skin was equal to the flame.

The sewermander beat its burning wings, the updraught took them and they surged into the tunnel mouth. Beth crowed silently, cocooned in blue fire in the tunnel's confines. They zigzagged through junctures, left, right, left again, then a different kind of light permeated the space. Fresh air washed over her as they burst from an archway in the riverbank.

They soared straight up. Beth risked a look over her shoulder and saw the industrial porcupine of the Millennium Dome shrinking into the distance. Night-time London stretched out below them, streets lit like rivers of magma running between rooftops.

Beth's fingers were still on the soft scales of the lizard's underbelly. An idea struck her.

Left, she thought at it, and the sewermander dipped its left wing and they banked westwards.

Right. The long neck curled the opposite way. The heat of the fire washed back over Beth's face as the drake corrected. She stared at the reptile, unnerved and awed by its obedience.

Okay, why are you doing what I tell you?

Her pocket buzzed – then again, and again: three messages. Only one girl was likely to be texting her in the middle of the night.

Beth tucked the spear under one arm and tugged her phone out. She scrolled down and read, *Can you come tonight?*

Then, *I want to ask you something.*

Please . . . ? Tonight. P

Beth grinned wickedly and felt the flames on her teeth.

Yeah, Pen, she thought, *I can come. I've got a ride.*

The sewermander banked and twisted on its own thermals, finding its new heading. Beth looked down into the dark mirror of the Thames and saw a winged streak of fire, heading north.

Pen was just beginning to doze again when her phone went off. Blearily, she checked the display.

Pen? The one word was all Beth had texted. Pen frowned.

Beth, she thumbed, and hit 'send'.

An instant later, the device buzzed in her fist. *Pen?* it buzzed again and again, in quick succession, like an insistent child:

Pen?

Pen?

Pen?

She sighed. For a girl steeped in all the strange powers and essences of the city, Beth loved to abuse an unlimited text package.

What? Pen texted back irritably. It was five a.m. She'd stayed awake, trying out the conversation over and over in her head, honing the words she'd use to reveal Parva to Beth, to explain why she'd kept her secret – but B had kept her waiting and she'd felt her concentration slip as the sky paled. Anxiety swilled around in her gut: she was sure she was going to screw this up. Part of her hoped Beth was texting to say that she was off chasing railwraiths on the other side of town and couldn't make it. Pen's phone buzzed once more:

Open your curtains.

Pen clambered off the single bed and stomped over to the window. She dragged the curtain aside—

The floor had jolted her tailbone before she'd even realised she'd fallen down. She stared upwards, wide-eyed and open-mouthed. Beth was squatting on the windowsill, impossibly balanced with only the very tips of her grey toes on the ledge. Hovering behind her, its wings spread like a heraldic beast, was a monster made of fire.

Beth grinned. She thumbed her phone, and Pen's own buzzed once more. Numbly, she lifted it between her eyes and the monster.

I ONLY WENT AND GOT A BLOODY DRAGON!

Pen shook her head like a fly was spinning round it. There

was a high-pitched sound in her ears. Slowly she leaned forward and slid up the sash window.

At last she found her voice. 'Um, B—? That – uh . . . Is it yours?'

Beth's grin widened. She shrugged, a happy '*Looks that way*' gesture. She texted rapidly, *Think I'm gonna call him Oscar.*

'Well, do you reckon you could back Oscar up a bit before it sets fire to my house?'

Beth's grin vanished, replaced with alarm. She turned somehow on that tiny ledge and reached into the fire. There was a dark shape in middle of the monster, like the little patch of black at the heart of a gas flame. As Beth's fingers brushed that shape, the fire abruptly flickered out. A tiny lizard scrambled up over her arm and perched on her shoulder. If flicked its tongue and blinked its little black eyes at Pen.

Beth was texting again.

He's a sewermander, he can manipulate gases . . . Like methane and stuff. I think he can suck them out of the mains too – play havoc with your gas bill. Isn't he cool!?!

Pen looked at her best friend. 'Sewer gases?' she said levelly. 'Seriously? You found a fart dragon?'

Beth's face fell a little, then she grinned. She showed off her hand with its concrete-and-oil complexion as if to say, *Who am I to judge?*

Pen backed away from the window and Beth wriggled inside. She moved differently now, *insinuating* herself around the corner like a street rat. She left oily thumbprints on the white paint. Once inside, she let the little lizard move from hand to hand, stroking it with her fingertip. The rasps of pleasure the reptile made were almost cat-like. As Pen looked at the two of them, she felt a pebble of frustration settle in her diaphragm.

Beth pulled out her phone again and Pen watched the screen over her shoulder: *It's amazing. I went for it in the tunnels and it totally had my arse kicked but the minute I touched it . . . It just changed – like it wanted to protect me. Like it wanted to do what I wanted it to do. It—*

'B.' Pen stilled Beth's hand with her own.

Beth lowered her phone and raised her eyebrows expectantly.

'Sometimes I just wish you'd use the front door, you know?'

Beth assumed an expression of mock scandal. She gestured to the lizard in her palm and out of the window at the city. *With all this at my disposal*, she seemed to say, *the front door would be criminally boring.*

'Yeah, I know,' Pen snapped, her temper rising. 'You're the princess of the city, you've got your fancy grey skin and your metal rod and your big chair on top of Canary Wharf and I'm happy for you, I really am, but I don't need it in my face every minute of the damn day.'

Perhaps she'd leaned a little heavy on the word 'face' – she wasn't sure. She didn't think she'd meant to, but Beth blanched, her pavement-skin lightening a couple of shades.

'I'm sorry, B.' Pen let her tone soften. 'I've just – it's been heavy at school, and what with . . .'

She tailed off before mentioning Dr Salt. Beth still didn't know what the maths teacher had done. She was all but nocturnal now, and with her out in the streets most of the time, the secret hadn't been hard to keep.

'. . . it's been hard, you know?'

Beth raised a hand to protest, but Pen gathered herself and went on, 'Listen, I know you'd come with me if I asked, B – I know you would, but you can't, can you? Not without bringing that world with you. It's who you are now, and I won't have it there, B. I *won't*. I carry enough of it with me every day.'

She touched her cheek. She'd stripped away the makeup. Beth held her gaze for a moment, a pained expression on her grey features, and then she went to the window. For a moment Pen thought she was going to leave, but instead she leaned out, hoisted herself up onto the sill and started rooting about under the eaves.

When she swung back inside, she dropped a fragile object into Pen's outstretched hand.

It was an eggshell, stippled white on red, one end of it crumbled away. For a second, Pen thought it was just a pigeon's egg, but then she felt the texture of it, coarse against her palm.

It was made of brick; the stippling was tiny flecks of mortar. Something rattled around inside as she turned it, and she shook it out onto her palm: a tiny wisp of feather nestled against her skin. It was made out of roof slate.

Beth picked up her phone, hammered out a message and turned the display towards Pen.

Tilequill pigeon. It was under your eaves, Pen. Your roof. There is only one world, and you live in it every day.

Pen stiffened slightly as Beth pulled her into a hug.

I'm sorry, Beth typed, after she'd let her go. *What did you want to talk to me about?*

'I wanted to ask you something,' Pen said. She braced herself to say Parva's name, to break the secret of her doppel, and then she stalled. *There's only one world.* Her mirror-sister's smiling face floated in her mind.

'Is there a way to go behind the mirrors?' It was only as the question left her lips that she realised how long she'd been thinking about it. 'To where the mirrorstocracy live?'

Beth frowned. She typed, deleted, and then typed again. Pen half expected to read a suspicious query, but all Beth wrote was: *I don't know. Fil never mentioned one, and neither did Gutterglass.*

She hesitated before adding, *The Chemical Synod might know a way, but the price they'd charge wouldn't be worth it.*

'Oh.' Pen deflated slightly. 'Okay.' Her head dipped, but pavement-textured fingers caught her chin.

Beth's grey face almost looked like it would crack under her concern. *You still writing?*

Pen blinked; she looked away, flustered. 'Yeah, B. I write all the time.'

Beth spread her hands, raised an eyebrow: *Yeah, but?*

It was true, Pen would jot down half-lines in her notebook, but she invariably scratched them out the next day. They looked so limp and inadequate on the page. She hadn't written a full verse since she'd left the hospital four months before.

Pen, are you okay? We never used to keep secrets.

Pen gently pushed Beth's phone away. 'I know, B,' she said. 'But maybe we should have.'

Out of deference to Pen, Beth let herself be guided down the stairs and escorted through the Khans' front door. She loitered on the frosty pavement, watching as Pen's slim silhouette returned to her window. She'd watched like this, from the street or the rooftops opposite, more than once over the last few months. She'd seen Pen throwing herself into exercise or holding herself with rigid discipline, demanding ever-greater control over her body. She thought she understood why and it worried her, but she didn't know how to intervene.

Tonight, though, Pen did something Beth had never seen before: her arm was crooked in the air as though around an invisible partner, and she danced.

CHAPTER FIVE

'Parva.'

As soon as Pen heard her name, she knew something was wrong. She felt the premonition of it curl tight up tight in her gut. Gwen had a tone she kept for members of the flock who had stepped out of line: a gentle tone, tinged with sadness and the promise of terrible correction.

She was using it now.

Pen eyed the sanctuary of the abandoned junior block, then turned around.

Gwen, Trudi and Alan stood amidst the playground's semi-frozen sludge, and they weren't alone. There was Harry Baker and Faisal Hamed and Leila Akhmal and Susie Thomas and . . . and— Figures bundled up in scarves and hats crowded behind Gwen's immediate entourage, all looking expectantly at Pen. Trudi smiled and nibbled on a lock of ginger hair. This wasn't impromptu. They'd arranged an audience.

'It's a real shame,' Gwen said. Her green eyes were tinged with what looked like genuine sorrow. Her voice carried clear in the winter air. 'I really wanted it to work out for you.' She reached out and laid a hand on Pen's cheek.

Pen flinched backwards, brushing up against Trudi, who had quietly stepped around behind her.

'I wanted us to be friends,' Gwen carried on, 'but what kind of friends can we be if we *lie* to each other, Parva?'

Puffs of condensation were suddenly coming too fast from Pen's mouth. She was snatching at breath. She tugged her hijab closer and dug into herself to try to find the bravado she'd faced Gwen with before. She came up with nothing.

Pen stuttered, her teeth suddenly chattering in the cold, 'W-w-what— what are you talking about?'

Gwen's expression didn't change. 'What am I talking about, Tru?' she echoed.

'We know it was you.' Like a well-trained pet, Trudi mimicked her mistress, even down to the air of patronising regret. 'We know it was you who said Salt touched you up.' She sighed. 'That's sad, Parva, really heart-breaking.'

A rumble of surprise went through the crowd, punctuated by a couple of startled laughs. The teenagers started to spread out, to get a better look at her. They stretched right across her vision, as though they were surrounding her. And then she twigged what the crowd had in common: they were all in her maths class.

Pen felt her stomach clench. Like any bully who had a shortlist of victims, Salt had been popular with everyone who wasn't on that list.

'We all know it's bullshit,' Gwen said. 'After all, Salt hated you – it was obvious; we all saw it. And you had it in for him, you and Beth Bradley and that graffiti stunt. Now that I think of it, you always were grabbing after *attention*, weren't you?'

She tailed off, looking solemn, then said, 'Don't you feel at least a little bad? Lying like that?'

Pen's chest was tight. For an instant she felt invisible metal barbs digging into her skin, inside her elbow, between her fingers, pricking her throat.

'Still' – Gwen's smile was positively beatific – 'we're not here to punish you, Parva. We're here to help. We understand it's not your fault. It's a compulsion.'

'All it takes is the truth,' said Trudi, but *she* wasn't smiling. 'All you have to do is tell the truth, here and now. Admit he never touched you, and tell us how you *really* got those scars.'

Pen's hand went to her face without her willing it. She could feel the panic like another too-tight layer of skin, just under the surface.

Trudi had to come up on tiptoe to speak into Pen's ear. '*Tell us*. You did it to yourself, didn't you?'

Pen recoiled. She tried to retreat, but there was nowhere to go; the crowd was hemming her in, trapping her like wires – like a metal cage. They'd all heard what Trudi said. They were all letting themselves stare at her now. Little black oblongs appeared in gloved hands: phones, filming her.

'You did it for attention. You did it so people would look at you.' Trudi snorted. 'So let us *look*.' Her wool-gloved hand flashed out towards Pen's hijab, but Pen snatched it tight around her. She could feel her pulse hammering where her fingertips rested against her neck.

'Yeah!'

Pen felt a sick little lurch at the first call from the crowd. It was Leila Akhmal. She'd always *liked* Leila.

'Tell us—!'

'Let us look—!'

'Tell us—!'

'Lose the scarf—!'

Another hand went to grab her hijab, then another, then another, rubbing over her scars through the thin fabric. Pen gripped the headscarf and hunched over, trying to twist away as they pressed in. She didn't say anything – she was scared of hearing her voice come out thin and squeaky and pathetic; she was scared of them laughing at her. She lashed out with one arm and felt someone catch the wrist and twist it. Pain flashed up her arm. Someone barked a laugh. Pen caught a glimpse of Gwen. She looked excited, nervous – she'd lost control.

'Let it go! Let it go!' Trudi was all but yelling it at her now. 'Let it *go*!' Pen shook her head dumbly, like a dog. Her head was ringing.

'No?' Trudi almost snarled. There was a clinking metal sound, and suddenly everything was still. A memory flashed into Pen's head: Gwen's boyfriend Alan, igniting a roll-up from a stainless steel Zippo, accompanied by exactly that sound. Her eyes found him, but he was patting his pockets in consternation. Pen looked sideways, and there was Trudi, her red face flushed and blotchy with excitement, a naked flame dancing wickedly above her fingers.

For a moment, there was total, breathless silence.

'Do it!' a voice called from the back of the crowd.

And then, as casually as if she was lighting a cigarette for a friend, Trudi Stahl reached out and set fire to Pen's hijab

The stench of burning hair and fabric rushed into Pen's nostrils. Heat touched her neck, and then a prickling pain rushed over her skin. She choked, gagged, and pulled her arm free. In her panic she struck out, and something fleshy cracked under the base of her palm.

She dragged the burning scarf off her head and flung it into the dirty slush.

The flames guttered out, leaving grey-black wounds in the green cloth. The cold wind balmed her neck. She bent over and gathered the scrap of ruined fabric. Then, trembling, she straightened and took in the crowd.

No one was laughing. Trudi sat on the frosted pavement, blood spilling from behind the hand which was clamped over her nose, but no one moved to help her. They just stared at Pen, and she stared back, letting them look. Her rebuilt lip curled of its own accord and she spat at them, like an angry cat.

And then she ran. They parted for her silently, and she rushed through them before they could see her cry.

'Parva!' Pen's voice echoed shrilly off the tiles, both in this tumbledown bathroom and the one behind the mirror. 'Parva!'

She folded in the middle like a hand puppet, hands on her knees, gulping down snotty, tearful breaths. There was a strange taste to the air, a metallic tang that mixed with the dust and the sour scent of her own scorched hair.

'*Parva!*' She knew someone would hear her – people had seen her run in. Someone would come, if they weren't coming already, to drag her out of this forbidden zone, away from her mirror-sister. A rat scuffled out of a cracked pipe and skittered over the floor, its tail twitching. It scampered back and forth over the same bare patch of lino, licking at it with quick stabs of its tongue and emitting little squeaks. There was no other sound, no familiar voice. Pen's gaze roved over the mirror, but she only saw herself.

Her scarred face was tear-swollen. Streams of diluted eyeliner meandered down the topography of her cheeks. Her hair was ragged and tangled where the scarf had been pulled away. The thin bald jags where the Wire Mistress' barbs had killed the follicles showed starkly.

'"You did it to yourself, didn't you?"' she echoed, a little hysterically. She had chosen to follow Beth into her strange city, after all. 'It's all you, Pen.'

She stepped up close to the mirror and the rat fled, chittering, from under her feet. She laid her hands flat on the cold surface and called again, 'Parva!' Her breath misted the glass, but there was no answer from behind it – of course there wasn't. Her mirror-twin would be at work now. They hadn't arranged to meet. It was just instinct that had driven Pen here; instinct, and sheer, blind hope.

She slumped, touching her forehead to the mirror,

And froze.

Directly between the feet of her reflection was a puddle of dark red liquid. Pen inhaled reflexively, and choked as she realised what the source of that metallic smell was.

Blood.

Numbly, Pen crouched down, and scraped her fingers over the apparently dry lino on her side of the mirror. They came away damp, and the invisible stuff that coated them was tacky when she rubbed her thumb across their tips.

She stood and looked back into the reflected bathroom. Next to the dark red pool, the floor was marked with a half-print of a hand, a familiar shape with its long, thin fingers. It blurred into a long streak that swept backwards across the lino, petering out long before it reached the door . . . as though the owner of that hand had been *dragged* out of the room. The lino beside that streak was torn, and underneath, she could see the concrete floor was rippled and puckered, almost as though it was scarred.

She hammered on the glass with her fist and shrieked, 'Parva!' Her voice echoed back off the walls behind the mirror, but her body had no way in.

She slammed her fist forward and the mirror fractured under the blow. Where the glass flaked away, only brick showed.

'*Parva! Parva!*'

'Parva?'

It was a man's voice: old, and abraded by cigarette smoke.

Pen spun around. Mr Krafte, her English teacher, was standing in the bathroom doorway.

'Parva – are you all right? Why do you keep shouting your name? Good lord, what happened to you—? You know you can't come in here—'

Pen didn't answer him. *You can't come in.* The thought went around her head, over and over: *You can't come in. You can't . . .*

. . . come in.

Mr Krafte recoiled as she barged past him into the corridor. She felt the invisible blood on her fingers soak into the headscarf in her hand.

CHAPTER SIX

A chill wrapped itself around Pen's heart as she rode the tube. She swayed with the motion of the carriage, barely noticing when the back of her head bumped off the little square window. She couldn't stop seeing that smeared, bloody handprint. She couldn't stop imagining being hauled across the floor, screaming at the mirror for help, or else, dull and muddled by blood-loss, watching her window onto her only friend disappear as she was dragged through the bathroom door. Pen pictured herself in Parva's place and felt the terror pick its way over her skin.

She's only there in the first place because of you.

Her mobile sat dark in her bag. She'd switched it off and even now part of her mind was screaming at her about that, but she ignored it. She knew with a cold certainty what she needed to do.

We never used to do secrets.

But maybe we should have.

Parva had been Pen's secret: the girl in the mirror, the little fragment of her universe she'd kept solely for herself.

But it wasn't jealousy that kept Pen from asking Beth for help: it was the fact that she knew with a bone-deep certainty that she'd get it.

In her mind's eye she saw it: the street-skinned girl, eyes gleaming like hubcaps on a summer's day, grabbing her railing spear and gesturing for her best friend to lead the way.

The Chemical Synod might know a way, but whatever they would want in exchange wouldn't be worth it. Beth's last encounter with the synod had cost her the boy she'd loved, and the price for their help now would likely be just as terrible. Pen couldn't ask Beth to pay that, not again.

The tube lights flickered and a memory welled up from the dark: an invitation scrawled on bricks in spray-paint. *Meet me under broken light.*

There was a cost when you asked someone you loved to follow you into this world.

The abandoned dye factory stood half collapsed on the south bank of the Thames. Patches of dark red lichen were eating the walls, looking like cold, gradual flames. Pen walked towards it, wading through her fear like it was chilly water. At each moment she expected black, oil-soaked figures to emerge and advance on her with symmetrical steps, but no one came.

She scrambled over the chain-link fence, ignoring the corroded warning signs. It took her a full three minutes of clenched teeth and muttered swearing to work herself up to squeezing past the barbed wire. The second-hand on her watch goaded her with every tick. The metal was chill where it brushed her neck, and she tried not to feel her skin crawling.

Mercifully, the rust had chewed out the lock. Pen leaned on the metal door and the only resistance came from the cobwebs as it shrieked inwards.

Inside, all was darkness. Pigeons fluttered high up, but she couldn't see any holes where they could have got in. The chill that blistered her skin felt old, as though the factory was a storeroom for years and years of past winters.

A prickle crept up Pen's back. She started to call out, but her throat was parched by dust, and anyway, there was no point: they already knew she was here. She could feel them watching her, their eyes blending into the dark. She fought not to tremble. She licked her lips and peered into the shadows, trying not to blink, trying not to show them she was afraid. The darkness had eaten her; she couldn't see her hands, or where she was putting her feet.

Something metal clinked behind her and she spun around, her heart thumping. The door was still there, a comforting rectangle of glare, but the daylight clung close to it and somehow didn't penetrate any further into the room. The factory darkness had substance, like liquid, like oil. Next to it the light felt weak.

She forced herself to turn back and keep walking, groping ahead with her hands. Something hissed, steam rushing from a punctured pipe, its source camouflaged by echoes.

Pen's eyes found outlines in the darkness, black on deeper black. Blood thundered in her ears like a tide.

A shape in the darkness solidified into something not-quite human, something thin and threatening and hungry. It *hated* her – Pen could feel its hate. Its jaw opened in a silent howl. It stretched out fingers made of shadow and lunged.

Pen shrieked and ran. She barely managed to stay upright as she threw herself forward. She could feel her feet wanting to turn towards the door, to make her flee, but she wouldn't let them: they were *her* feet, *her* muscles, and they'd do what she bloody well told them to. She felt invisible things reaching for her, slithering over her skin.

Her knees rose and fell, almost of their own accord. She couldn't not run, so she gritted her teeth and ran deeper into the dark. From the corners of her eyes she glimpsed nightmare things squatting fatly on heavy haunches with back-bent teeth and empty eye sockets. There were flickers of motion. Heads snapped on thick necks to track her. Even though there was no light, even though there was no way she could see them, she saw them anyway.

Something snorted and snapped by her ear and Pen flinched. She zigzagged, recoiling from the hands she could feel reaching for her, tugging at her clothes and sliding, chill and slippery, upwards to play in her hair. Cold snouts pressed to her neck. The hissing grew louder; there was a *plack plack plack* sound of some viscous liquid hitting concrete. She screamed into the dark again and broke into a headlong rush. Something firm snagged the collar of her T-shirt and her feet were jerked from under her. Her stomach tumbled in sickening weightlessness for an instant, and then the floor jarred her spine like a hammer.

She lay there, unable to move, wondering, for a horrified instant, if her back was broken, if she was paralysed. She listened to her own wheezing, panicky breaths and felt the slender, invisible things grasping for her out of the darkness. Would it be this moment? Or this? Or this, when they finally touched her? The steam-hiss was right beside her ear as it bled into words:

'Sssalutationss, Ssurvivor,' it whispered. 'Sssundered Sssisster and Insssubordinate Sservant. Misstress' lasst host. Greetingsssss.'

The voice paused. An amused note crept in. 'Ssorrry to aressst your progresss sso sssuddenly. I shudder to inssinuate that your wisssdom might be ssusspect, but your sssupremely asstute sstrategy of running blind in a darkened chemical worksss was sstarting to sstray a little clossse to sssuicide.'

The voice sighed. 'Lightsss, pleasse, Ssimeon.'

There was the clunk of a lever being thrown, and glare ruptured the darkness. Pen screwed up her eyes, then opened them gradually to make out a dark figure bending over her. He wore an immaculately tailored suit and had slicked-back hair and a broad, wicked grin. Every inch of him, eyeballs, fingernails and teeth included, was covered in smooth, black oil. A droplet fell from his forehead and splashed onto her lips.

Johnny Naphtha, unofficial voice of the Chemical Synod, London's Brokers of Everything, snapped the lid shut on the cigarette lighter he was holding and gestured with it. Pen lifted her head to look past her own feet.

She lay on a narrow spur of concrete. The stainless steel vat it jutted over was as wide as a tractor wheel, and half-full of colourless liquid.

'Well?' he whispered.

'Th-thank you,' she managed. She knew what she had to say, but it was hard to speak. Her heart was galloping like a routed cavalry charge.

'Yesss?'

'I – I owe you.'

Johnny Naphtha's grin grew even wider. He rummaged in one oil-soaked pocket and produced a shiny steel screw, which he flicked into the vat with his thumb. It entered the liquid with a tiny splash, at the exact same time as four other identical screws. Pen saw the other black figures standing on the metal gantries, leaning over her in poses that exactly mirrored Johnny's.

There was a bubbling hiss and a strange tangy smell as all five screws were dissolved by whatever was in the tank.

'We'll work sssomething out. Can you sssstand?'

He led her up a spiralling iron staircase. The other four oil-drenched men converged on them with synchronised strides. They reached the top and ducked through a doorway in the eaves.

The walls of the room beyond were more hole than brick.

Jagged gaps opened out onto the empty winter sky, and
pigeons cooed and groomed themselves in the crevices. The
birds were all soaked in oil, but that didn't seem to impede
them when they cleared their wings for take-off.

Pen looked down and her stomach plummeted. Most of
the floor had crumbled away too. The room, or what was
left of it, jutted from the back of the top of the factory, sitting on a spine of rusted iron pillars. Massive gaps yawned
either side of her feet, and through them she could see the
scrub grass and gravel of the factory yard a dizzying distance below. A narrow path wound between the gaps and
the synod trod it together, their footsteps leaving the floor
slick with oil. At the far end was a little island of concrete,
with two black leather sofas and what looked like an old-
fashioned drinks cabinet. The five symmetrical men turned
expectantly as they reached this island, each with a hand
on his lapel.

Pen swallowed hard and took a step. Her foot slid sickeningly under her and she threw out her arms, fighting for
balance. She hissed between gritted teeth and took another
step. Oil seeped into the fabric of her trainers. The black
birds flapped and called to her.

'Perhapsss it might go fassster if you didn't look down?'
Johnny Naphtha suggested.

A derisive laugh burst from Pen's lips, startling her almost
as much as it seemed to surprise them. 'Thanks, but since
down's where the path is, I'll look where I like and take my
own damn time.' She looked down again and saw the gaping

holes in the floor, the oiled slickness, the suicidal height. She took another step.

The synod didn't move until she was on the island with them, then, in identical time, they unbuttoned their jackets. Three of them, with Johnny in the middle, sat on one of the sofas. The other two stood behind, hands clasped, as if for an official photograph.

'Pleasssse,' Johnny gestured, and Pen sat opposite. She felt the slick black surface of the sofa soaking into her jeans. They looked at her, and she stared back, wild-eyed. Now that it came to it, she had no idea how to start.

'Ssstill in sshock,' Johnny Naphtha muttered to his neighbour, and the other four nodded in identical agreement. 'Hardly ssssurprising, ssince she burssst in on our experiment.'

'Experiment?' Pen said sharply.

'Of courssse experiment. It'ss been a marvellousss morning. We've jusst sssuccesssfully ssynthesissed sssscotophobia. And then' – he tutted – 'a tardy tresspassser tainted it.'

They leaned forward, and suddenly there was something shark-like in their faces.

'By rightss we sshould you make you brew the next batch.'

Pen gripped her knees until they hurt. *Act tough*, she thought, *like B would.*

'Scotophobia,' she said, her voice just about even. 'Fear of the dark.'

The Chemical Synod smiled as one, and Johnny Naphtha

said, 'Of coursse – the factory floor isss flooded with it. Why do you sssuppose we excised the light? The phobia wasss the product of the procedure, but to be perfect itss primer chemicalsss needed to be pure.'

Pen just stared at him. Beth had told her about the synod, but seeing them for real made everything feel off-kilter, like the little bones in her inner ear had come loose.

'Perhapsss a resstorative would sssettle you,' Johnny said, pointing to the floor. Pen glanced down to see a battered tin cup next to her foot, half full of a dark-red concoction.

Maybe, she told herself urgently, *that's been there all along, and I just didn't notice it. Maybe they* didn't *just conjure it there.*

'What's in it?' she asked.

Johnny pursed his lips. He rolled his black eyeballs as though consulting his memory. 'A ssselection of ssaltss, kerosssene, cyanide, a little ssad, certain ressolutenesss and cherry juice,' he said. 'But only in medicinal quantitiess. I'm quite certain it'ss ssafe.'

Pen pushed the cup politely but firmly away with her trainer.

The synod sighed as one.

'Sssuit yoursself,' Johnny said. 'Ass you ssso ssuccinctly sstated: *take your own damn time.*'

Pen watched the synod, and the synod, patient and inexorable as geological forces, watched her back.

'I need your help,' she said at last.

'Why elssse would you come?'

'So . . . How does this work?'

The five oil-soaked men shrugged, their shoulders rising and falling in an undulating symmetrical wave, starting with Johnny and rippling to the two taller figures on the flanks.

'You sstate a desssire,' Johnny said. 'We sset a price. It'ss esssentially sshopping.'

There was a little pebble of tension in Pen's throat. If they couldn't help her, she had nothing. 'I need to go behind the mirrors,' she said. 'I need to go to London-Under-Glass.'

There was silence, broken only by the ruffling of oily wings.

Johnny Naphtha hissed slowly through his teeth. He sounded like a bit like a plumber, just before telling you that the last guy was a total cowboy and that the cost of the parts would be roughly equal to the mortgage on a house in Hampstead and the price of a couple of kidneys.

'We ssseldom ssee that sside of the glasss. The cossst will be sssignificant.'

Pen drew a deep breath. 'I'll pay.'

A thin smirk spread over five pairs of lips. 'What makess you think you can afford usss?' Johnny's eyes were black on black, but there was a circular rainbow shimmer in the centre like an iris.

Pen focused on that patch of colour and straightened up. 'You trade in anything, right?' she said. 'So there must be something I've got that you want – something about me that's valuable, even if I don't know it. You can have it, but get me through that mirror.'

Five heads tilted in interest, and Pen felt herself shrink a little. 'Only I won't hurt anyone,' she added.

There was nothing cruel in Johnny Naphtha's voice as he said, 'Of courssse you will.'

The five men stood and buttoned their jackets. 'Thiss way, Ssteel Insssurgent.' Johnny reached out to Pen. 'We have a propossition.'

Pen swallowed, hesitated and took his hand.

She felt the wrongness instantly. The pads of his fingers squeezed between hers and the oil spread over her skin, chill and viscous. She tried to jerk her hand back, but his arm just stretched, strung out like chewed gum.

'What are—?' she started, but her voice died in her throat. Johnny Naphtha's face was melting, his features running in an oil slick off his neck. The others were doing likewise, their feet blending into an oily pool. Rivulets raced off the side of it and ran over the edge of the floor.

'Wai—' Pen tried to say, but her teeth felt as soft as candlewax against her tongue, and in front of her she could see her hand blending, emulsifying into what was left of Johnny's.

She felt a drunken kind of falling and all the colours in the world ran together into black.

She gasped, and her lungs drew in dust and she choked and coughed. She couldn't see, but there was brick, rough and solid under her knees and palms. She blinked and brought her free hand up to rub her eyes, but the blindness clung on.

There was a snap-click-hiss and five flames appeared, bobbing alarmingly over lighters in oil-soaked hands. The synod smiled down at her.

'I—' she managed at last. 'I thought you'd . . .' There was only one word that fitted the memory of the creep of oil over her skin. 'I thought you'd *eaten* me.'

'Why? When did we sssay we'd require payment in advance?'

The smiles remained the same; she couldn't tell if he was joking.

'Well then, next time d'you mind asking before you melt me?' Pen demanded.

'Excussse usss, Sssteel Inssurgent,' Johnny whispered courteously, 'we undersssstood you to be in hassste. It iss a sseven-hour desscent through the dark to where we sssstand by bipedal means. And ssome of the ssspaces you would need to traversssse would be, *disssquieting*.'

He offered her his hand, but Pen ignored it and pushed herself up. Vaulted brick tunnels stretched off in five directions. The walls were riddled with roughly shaped alcoves that gave off a sickly, variegated light, like the weird deep-ocean creatures she'd seen on the BBC nature documentaries her dad loved. She figured they must be in a sewer, but there was no dripping of leaking pipes, no scuttle of rodents. Instead, the tunnels were like the halls of a brick palace, long buried and forgotten. Their footsteps echoed as Johnny led down one of the halls, but that was the only sound. The whole place felt weirdly hermetic.

Johnny began to murmur, reciting nonsense in a terse, concentrated tone. He gestured vaguely to alcoves, as if naming them: 'Horssefly, wanderlussst, ssweat and ssusspi-cion, loathesssome allegory, Pylon Venom, charge, charm, charred bisscuit, an old noble-lamp'ss tearsss . . .'

They swung left, then right, then right again. Pen thought she could hear tension creeping into his voice – or maybe it was excitement?

'Pet'ss tooth, an old puzzle, comfortable bread . . .' He hesitated where the tunnel branched.

Claustrophobia clung to Pen, heavy as an oil-soaked blanket. She wondered how far this warren must reach if it could confuse even its master. She'd completely lost track of the turns.

'Falsssehood, falsssehood and hope – come on now, Naphtha, think, you ssubsssist on your recollectionsss – Falsssehood and hope, and . . . *time*, hah!' He put one hand on the wall and swung himself with gusto down the right fork.

'Falsssehood and hope and time leadss to memory.'

'Oh.' Pen said it in a small voice, but it echoed. A soft breeze fluttered a stray hair against her cheek. In front of her, the tunnel fed out into empty space. Opposite was a wall, perhaps only twenty feet from where the floor ended, but the *depth* of that gulf seemed immeasurable. The wall opposite was speckled unevenly with coloured lights. Pen nervously toed the edge of the precipice and craned her neck, but she could see no end to this ocean of bricks and gently glowing alcoves. It extended to vertical horizons on either side. It was like being up-close to the night sky. The sounds of wings echoed in the emptiness. Little flitting shapes crossed the wall, oil-soaked pigeons cooing as they tended the synod's stores.

'It's beautiful,' she murmured, in a stunned voice.

'It . . . hass itsss momentsss,' Johnny Naphtha admitted.

'What is it?'

He raised his lighter as he answered, 'Ssselfishnesss, greed, sssyrupy sssentiment, commemorationss of a few fumbling firsst romancess, an irrational love of peanut butter and an equally inssane loathing of arachnidss' – he pointed at individual lights as he spoke, naming constellations on the wall. 'Courage, compossure, a confection of courtesssy. Ssentiensse, or ass passsable a ssubbsstitute as we have thusss far ssuccceded in composssing. You are looking at our besst current sssynthessiss of a mind.'

'A mind?' Pen breathed. 'What's it for?'

'To patch the perceptionss of a prissoner – a client whose cognition iss sso corroded by hisss long languisshing, he doess not yet know that he needss it.' Johnny Naphtha grinned wickedly. 'Bussinessss development. It iss almosst complete. *Almossst.*' He looked at Pen with predatory appraisal. 'But not quite.'

Pen felt her hands flinch upwards instinctively, as if she could protect herself from that look, that possessive intent, with her fists.

Johnny's smile became almost pitying. 'Sspare yoursssself your anxiety,' he said. 'The ssupplementary ssubstancess we

64

need are not in your psssyche. Ssstill, for what you asssk, we will accept nothing lesss.'

'I won't hurt anyone else,' Pen insisted again.

Johnny inclined his head as if to say, *You said that already.* Four other heads mirrored his.

'We would not asssk you to. A long way behind ussss, at the intersssection of the sstoress of electromagnetissm and ephemerality there iss a ssubsstansse that might ssserve you, a compound fit to change *sseeing* into *doing*, a tincture to transsform a window to a door: a portal primer, if you will, or a doorway drug. It might even get you sssomewhere ass issolated as the mirrorsstocracy's republic. Our price for ssuch a prize is sssimple—'

He flourished his empty oil-soaked hand. 'A complete ssset of memoriess of a child, rendered from the mindss of her parentsss – not copiesss, you undersstand, but originalss.' He snorted. 'Even true memoriess degrade, copiess of them wassste like they're diseassssed.'

For a long moment Pen didn't understand, then something hot and painful sank slowly towards the bottom of her stomach as she realised what he was asking her for.

'You want my folks' memories . . . of me?' she whispered. 'You want them to forget me.'

'Mosst assssuredly no.' Johnny's tone didn't change. 'We do not *want* them to forget you. That iss an irrelevant ssside effect.'

Pen gave a little tight shake of head. 'Something else,' she said. 'Not them – not my parents. Something of mine—'

'Nothing you posssesss iss sso potent ass a parent'ss memoriess of thosse they have born. Ssuch thingsss kindle conflictss and are the ssseeds of sscience. They are the wellspringss of hope and obssesssions of even the sssanest of men,' Johnny said gently. 'We want nothing of yourss.'

'I told you I wouldn't hurt anyone!' Pen's cry echoed off the bricks. She stared back down the tunnel, but all she saw was a maze.

The flame from Johnny's lighter danced in his liquid eyes, and his voice was sonorous in her ears. 'Sssilly little pilgrim, that'sss precissely why we asssk thiss. We know your ssstory. You musst know, ass we know, that your mother and father blame themsselves for your pressent, parodic appearance. "If we'd only watched her better, or taught her better, or loved her better or fed her better".' He spoke with a calm viciousness, eyeing the sharp jut of her cheeks. '"If only we" – that'ss the ssentiment that sstrangless your parentss' sssleep. Would you like to know how poorly they sssleep now? How tenuousssly they are ssstitched to their happinesss? If you are sserious about not hurting them, your choice iss ssimple. Either sstay by their sside and ssacrifice whatever urgent quesst hass made you sseek uss out, or accept our price, and make ssure they won't missss you when you're gone.'

Pen felt the bricks of the wall in her back like the supporting hand of a friend, but rather than collapse against them she stayed stiffly upright.

Ssacrifice whatever urgent quessst . . .

She tried to imagine it. She tried to picture herself turning around and going home and hiding under the duvet. She tried really, really hard.

But she couldn't. She didn't recognise the girl in that picture. She wasn't her, and she didn't want to be. A strange kind of calm settled over her as she realised this wasn't really a choice after all: it looked like one, but it wasn't. She pictured the future where her folks had forgotten her, and it came clearly: her dad reading the paper, her mum engaged in her endless second-floor ballet with the Hoover. They'd be okay, they wouldn't miss her. They *couldn't* miss her. It was appalling, but it was true. That was the point. She wetted her lips to accept the inevitable. There wasn't another option here . . .

Unless she made one.

'You said you didn't go behind the mirror.' Pen's voice came out hoarse, a little crackly, but strong. 'Isn't there something better behind there than a few sentimental memories of my first steps? You're collectors, aren't you? There must be something. What if I could bring it to you?'

Each of the five members of the synod took a step forward, hemming her behind a wall of petrol-soaked suit. They looked even more predatory when they were intrigued.

'Interessting. Sssomething ssingular,' Johnny said. 'Ssomething of unique sssignificance – obtain that for usss, and we will find the memoriesss we need elssssewhere.'

Pen nodded hesitantly.

'And sssecurity?' Johnny whispered. 'You might run off,

after all; you might like it behind the mirror, or you might very well perissssh. How are we to be recompenssed if you do not return?'

Pen didn't flinch as she met his rainbow-irised eye. 'I'll bring you what you asked for,' she said. Johnny was right, she needed a way to spare her mum and dad, and this – this awful, gargantuan cataclysm of a way was at least *a way*. If all went well, she'd be buying her parents' memories back with mirrored coin. If not . . .

You want them to forget me?

They'd be all right.

'You will have ssseven dayss,' he said. 'After that we will put your pawned payment to ussse, and it will be irretriev-able.'

Pen's lip curled. The words sprang into her mouth auto-matically, as though she was haggling at Dalston Market. 'A month,' she countered.

'Two weekss—'

'Three.'

'Twenty-one dayss and nightsss,' Johnny confirmed. He didn't sound perturbed; rather, satisfied, and a little impressed, as though some crucial ancient formality had been observed. 'But Missss Khan? Bring uss sssomething ssspectacular, or they won't remember you at all.'

He held out a hand and Pen shook it slowly, feeling the oil ooze from between her fingers, but this time she didn't dissolve. 'Thiss way,' he whispered, and then the synod swept past her and back up the tunnel. Pen put her hand on the bricks as she followed, and, just before the light got too weak to see by, she made out the handprint she'd left: the outline of slim black fingers, shining wetly in the dark.

CHAPTER SEVEN

Three a.m., and in the narrow lanes behind Carnaby Street, the Blankleit market was in full swing.

The bulbs sat dark in the streetlamps, but the bricks flickered with light and shadow as the glass-skinned, tungsten-veined Lampmen bartered in semaphore on the pavements.

Beth moved casually from doorstep to doorstep, admiring the wares piled high on them: heaps of assorted remote controls, bales of copper and platinum wire, tiny glass birds fluttering in heatproof tungsten cages, glimmering with silent song. Along one wall, injured men queued patiently, some leaning on crutches of broken lamppost, their shoulders, elbows, wrists or knees ending in jags and powdery cracks. At the front of the queue, a heavy-shouldered Blankleit Street Surgeon worked over a brasier, delicately etching knuckles and fingernails into replacement limbs blown from white-hot glass.

Beth had been here a dozen times in the last few months, but she still felt a little fizz of awe at it, even if tonight that awe was dampened by toothache.

The pavement skin'll probably break a needle, and the blood'll set like cement, she thought, tonguing the offending canine. *Explaining that to the dentist's going to be fun.*

The heat from all the Lampmen's blazing filaments made her sweat, but still she walked with her hood up, her hands thrust into her pockets, the railing spear strapped into the little harness she'd made for it in her backpack. She paused at a doorway where a young Blankleit was lounging indolently. He was strikingly handsome, with a neon-bright smile. His cheeks and chest were patterned with rosy filter-paint to show off his crystal-clear skin. He flirted easily with the passing crowd in an easy semaphore patter, giving one or two of the more likely-looking glass gents a flirtatious tickle with his fields.

Beth pulled a torch from her rucksack and rapidly semaphored, *Where's Candleman?*

The painted glass boy started at the light in his face like he'd been yelled at. He swore dimly and snapped back, *Who?*

Don't play dull, Beth signalled. *Your line of work might not be exactly illegal, but Lucien dislikes it enough to restrict the number of places you can buy the slap.* She indicated the filter-paint on his rapidly darkening cheeks. *So, I ask again, where's Candleman set up shop tonight?*

The massage boy flickered some grumpy directions that Beth just about understood, and then decisively turned his back on her, redoubling the wattage in his blinding smile.

Beth's eyes adjusted gradually as she left the glare of the legitimate market stalls behind. She took a complicated series of turnings, vaulted over a back-alley skip and descended some metal steps to a basement-level courtyard. Filthy sleeping bags on heaps of mouldering cardboard occupied the corners. Bass thuds seeped through the walls from the club inside.

Hello, Candleman. Beth flashed the torch at one of the sleeping bags. *Looking prosperous. Business good?*

The zip of the sleeping bag was tugged down from the inside. The Blankleit voice that glimmered out from inside was dim enough to count as a whisper, but the shade was red with anger. *Bradley? In the name of all that's bright and holy, shut that thing off, or we'll both be staked out for the next rainstorm.*

Beth sat down cross-legged on the edge of the cardboard and peered into the open zipper. She saw a glass nose, jawline and lips, all outlined in the gentle white glow that the sleeping bag was there to cover.

There is a reason we call this the Dark Market, you know, he flickered huffily.

Beth glanced at the other sleeping bags. Conversation came in little flickers from gaps in the fabric, deals struck in whispers no brighter than burning matches. Every now and then glowing glass hands would emerge from the bags to exchange small valuable items, or seal deals with a magnetic handshake. The Dark Market – the Blankleit economy's literal shadow.

Sorry. Beth shaped the word exaggeratedly with her mouth, letting him read it.

You will be if Lucien or any of your Statue-wearing chums catches a glimmer of you here talking to me, the glass man strobed grumpily.

The Pavement Priests? Beth frowned. She couldn't think of any reason they'd have a problem with Affrit Candleman – after all, it was the repeat business of the stone- and bronze-armoured clerics that had made him the richest stall-runner in the Dark Market. He offered them a service they could get nowhere else.

'*I thought they were your biggest customers?*'

'*Some of them are,*' Candleman glimmered sourly. He shifted inside his sleeping bag and Beth saw one of his eyes burning like a small white coal. *But it's hardly as though everyone with a granite wardrobe thinks alike, is it? My customers are liberals; the more hardcore lot think I'm messing around with divine punishment.*'

Beth wasn't sure she'd read that right. She strobed a request for clarification.

'*When a Pavement Priest dies and gets reborn entombed in a statue, that's Mater Viae's will,*' Candleman explained. '*So if they grow up missing half their memories, well, that must be Mater Viae's will too – part of the sentence. According to them, my little interventions are sacrilege.*'

'*Mind you,*' he added, considering, '*The fact that they think a small-time crook like me could do anything to wipe the church-spire smile off their Goddess' face says maybe their faith in her's not what it used to be.*'

Beth sat motionless as the last embers of his words died.

73

Eventually she mouthed, '*It shouldn't be. She's dead.*' London's street goddess had committed suicide before Beth was even born, and she'd used the stolen and distilled deaths of her priesthood to do it, leaving them to pay the price – endlessly reborn into stone. Even now, months after she'd broken the secret, she felt anger hot in her stomach. '*She's dead. I proved it to them.*'

'*Oh, you "proved" it? Really? Oh well then . . .*' Candleman's sarcasm was a deadpan white. '*I can't imagine why they've chosen their faith in a Goddess they've spent a dozen lifetimes worshipping over the word of a seventeen-year-old girl.*' He glanced down at the soot-stained scar on her wrist: city tower blocks arranged to form the spokes of a crown. '*Especially when that girl's still wearing the Goddess' mark.*'

He shook his glass head, making shadows dance on the floor. '*The purists, the gravel-and-thunder lot? They'd grind me back into sand given half a chance, but Gaslamps alone know what they'd do to you. Apostate is about the politest thing they're calling you. The angel-skinned one in particular, Ezekiel? He's—*'

Candleman dimmed as he groped for the right word. Beth mouthed a suggestion.

'*Pissed off?*'

'*I'm not familiar with the term, but if it's anything like "would quite enjoy pulling all of your internal organs one by one out through your throat and squashing them into meaty jam with his bare hands" then it's close enough.*'

Beth stared at him. A shudder ran through her as she remembered fighting side by side with Ezekiel at Chelsea

Bridge, watching his stone gauntlets shred the Scaffwolves' steel hides.

'*It's close enough*,' she muttered. '*Do you have it?*'

A glass hand emerged from the zipper, selected a bulging orange plastic bag from the heap and passed it to her. Beth looked inside. It was full of assorted lightbulbs: fairy lights, screw caps, energy savers, all jumbled up together. She hefted it, and it clinked.

'*That's as close as I could get from what you told me*,' Candleman strobed. '*And that wasn't easy. Most of my clients have known the person they want ReMinded for multiple lifetimes, not just a couple of weeks. That boy must have made quite the impression.*'

Beth pictured 'that boy' – pavement-skinned like her, so scrawny that you could count every one of his ribs. Smiling grey eyes under a fringe of soot and brickdust-coated hair.

'He did,' she mouthed.

'*Remember*,' Candleman's words darkened to a more serious shade, '*I make no promises. Those lights aren't really his mind, any more than an A-to-Z is something you could actually drive a bus down. They're a map, a model, nothing more. But like all representations, they hold something of the essence of the thing itself. Growing up with that map, looking at it every night for years, it should help him remember who he was.*'

Beth pursed her lips. It felt like such a fragile hope. 'I understand.'

'*Do you have payment?*' Candleman's voice grew brighter in his excitement.

Beth nodded.

'*I don't see it.*'

'*I don't see your arse, but I trust that it's there without you talking out of it,*' Beth mouthed, but she slipped her hood back anyway. The sewermander's little claws pricked her skin as it ran over her neck. It perched on her shoulder, blinking at Candleman with black, liquid eyes.

With a startled flash, the Blankleit jerked backwards. His glass body chimed loudly off the drainpipe behind him. The sleeping bag slipped down to show curly fibre-optic hair and a disreputable face, both burning bright in desperate panic.

'*What?*' Beth mouthed, alarmed.

'*It's not caged!*' Candleman strobed desperately. '*What happened to the jar I gave you?*'

'*It broke,*' Beth mouthed with a puzzled shrug. '*I didn't need it in the end. Long as I'm touching it, it just sort of does what I want.*'

'*It just sort of—*' Candleman's glass jaw slackened. '*The Gaslight gatherer – the reptile herald of our ancestors – it does your bidding?*'

Beth shrugged again.

Candleman's eyes stretched. '*That's im—*'

'Over there!'

Beth jerked her head up. The voice that had shattered the silence was familiar, and more sounds followed it: footsteps, and the grind of stone-on-stone as heavy wings churned the air.

The Blankleit read her expression in perplexity. '*What is it?*'

As Beth opened her mouth to answer the air blurred and

the courtyard was suddenly crowded with statues, their stone bodies crouched for combat, their faces etched in rage.

She stood slowly and unslung her spear. She had no voice, so she let her gaze speak for her, letting it travel slowly over the Pavement Priests as though her heart wasn't suddenly slamming. She got ready to spring.

The sound of beating wings grew louder and a life-sized angel carved from granite descended at a stately pace into the courtyard. Ezekiel's neck churned against itself as he looked at her. Beth looked into the pinprick apertures in his hosanna-singing mask and imagined his pupils contracting in hate.

'The blasphemer *and* the black marketeer.' Ezekiel's voice was as dry as dust. 'Both at once. That's . . . almost disappointing. Take them.'

The statues blurred into motion, impossibly fast. Beth felt stone fingers grasping at her arm. She twisted from its grip and lashed out with her spear. Rock cracked and a dusty voice groaned. She spun around and swept legs from another. They were too quick for the eye, but she felt them through the street, moving on instinct. Her bare feet sucked up the rank energy of the city and she matched their speed, sliding between their unseen hands as though the air itself was oiled. She struck out for knees and elbows, only using the spear butt, but using it viciously. They fell around her with a sound like collapsing buildings, and for a fraction of a heartbeat she was back in the Demolition Fields, under the gaunt shadows of Reach's cranes.

A stone wing flickered into being, crunching into her jaw.

Her head snapped back and something sharp pierced her tongue. Blood filled her mouth with a taste like hot asphalt.

She stumbled and fell back. Statues hemmed her in, almost blotting out the glare of the terrified Candleman, who was sweating bullets of pure light as he pushed at the closing Pavement Priests with his fields. The statues parted and Ezekiel stood over her, wings extended in thin silhouette: Ezekiel the fanatic, Ezekiel who had followed her and counselled her and comforted her. Ezekiel whose faith she'd shattered when she pronounced his Goddess dead.

Beth spat blood. She bared her teeth in a silent snarl and braced herself for the first stone foot to come crashing down on her chest.

Nothing happened.

The Pavement Priests stood there as if they were simple statues – as if there was nothing between their bellies and their backs but solid rock.

Seconds ticked by.

Uncertainly, Beth rose to her feet. The statues' expressions were blank now, but she could feel the astonishment radiating from inside them.

What? she wondered. *What is it?*

A jolt of pain from her tooth made her wince and she touched the tender place instinctively with her punctured tongue. She faltered. The tooth felt *wrong* in her mouth, too thin, needle-like, and sharper than a fang.

'*Viae—*' The whispered oath came from a Pavement Priest with the mustachios of a Victorian gentleman. He tapped the stone on his wrist and it crumbled like chalk. On the pale skin beneath was an image in iron-grey ink: the Towerblock Crown. The arm blurred to his mouth as he kissed the tattoo.

Beth started forward and they parted for her. There was something horrified in Ezekiel's shape as he melted from her path.

A bathroom window with a fan in it was set into the wall. With Candleman's light behind Beth, it became a dim mirror. She peeled her lower lip back with her fingers until she could see the place where it hurt. She stared in astonishment.

A third of the way along her jaw, her gum had dried out, becoming rough, splitting and cracking – but the cracks were geometric; they turned at sharp right angles, outlining tiny rectangles of coarse flesh.

No, not flesh, she realised with a shudder, *brick*.

Where her canine should have been, the tiny bricks rose into the narrow cone of a church spire. The sharp iron cross that topped it was wet with her blood.

Candleman's words flashed again in her mind: *wipe the church-spire smile off her face* . . .

'*Mater Viae*,' the Pavement Priest breathed again.

From the depths of her hoodie, the strangely obedient sewermander blinked at her with black, liquid eyes.

CHAPTER EIGHT

Pen went through her house in the middle of the night, erasing herself.

It was surprisingly tricky. Johnny Naphtha had charmingly assured her that the clear, sharp-smelling liquid he'd supplied would wash her from her parents' minds like *ssso much light sssoiling—* But since when did people keep their memories solely inside their heads?

She'd scribbled a list on a bit of paper torn from the fridge-door pad: *Books, posters, photos (mantel), photos (stairway), Venka the Velociraptor, home videos, Facebook, Twitter, computer & phone-memory, laptop, school reports, birth certificate* . . . She crept up and down the hallways like a burglar carrying two massive zip-up holdalls, crossing items off as she dumped pieces of her life into them.

In the small messenger bag over her shoulder, the bottles Johnny Naphtha had given her clinked.

'Thisss potion iss highly proprietary,' he'd said as he'd placed it into her hand. 'Itss preparation iss a ssecret we have sssupplied to only one other perssonage. Were it to "accidentally" passs from your posssesssion to another'ss, it would occasssion ssome quite extreme action on our part.'

Pen had shrugged off the threat as irrelevant. Who could she possibly sell it to?

She paused in the doorway to the kitchen. A series of pencil lines scored the faded wallpaper, marking the young Parva's dizzying ascent to and then ultimate surpassing of five foot six inches: a frankly Himalayan height for a Khan woman. Her mum had had to balance on a phone book to see the top of her head.

She sighed, and set to work with her rubber.

A high-pitched beeping from her wrist made her jump. The digits on her watch burned green: 6.25 a.m. Mum's alarm would be going off in five minutes. What was left? *Food.* She raced into the kitchen, yanked the fridge open, scraped the leftover veggie patties she'd made a couple of nights ago into the bin. She hesitated. Nestled at the back by a couple of old onions were a pair of green-lidded Tupperware boxes. They were interlopers to the Khan family refrigerator, but Pen recognised them from her mum's cancer scare three years ago, when a legion of aunties, cousins and female friends had descended, filling their Dalston maisonette with home-cooked scents and distracting chatter. When Pen first came out of hospital, the fridge had been crammed with a rainbow of Tupperware, evidence of the same network's activity. Four months later, the green ones remained, half-full of her Aunt Sarita's special chickpeas. More than anything else, those green lids told her how much her mum was hurting.

Synod or no synod, she thought, swallowing on a suddenly dry throat; she nodded stiltedly to herself as she pulled the Tupperware out: *Maybe this is for the best.*

She turned and raced back through the living room, sweeping a handful of missed pictures from the top of the TV as she went, zipped the bag shut and bolted into the cellar.

Her mum was waiting when she came out, knotting her green dressing gown, patient suspicion on her face. Pen pushed the door closed behind her with a foot. Her mum frowned, but all she said was, 'Leaving early for school again? Would you like some breakfast first?'

Pen caught her lip between her teeth before she answered, stilling it as it threatened to tremble. 'Mum, I'd absolutely love some breakfast.'

She sat at the kitchen table and stared at her own steepled fingers while her mum pottered around behind her, clanging pots and running taps and banging cupboard doors, generating a racket fit to wake if not the dead, then certainly Pen's still-slumbering father. Pen had an uneasy sense that her mum was summoning her husband for moral support.

The meal laid out on the table bore the same relationship to Pen's normal tiny morning bowl of Sugar Puffs as the US Navy bears to a rubber duck. Dark golden paratha with crispy edges and chewy middles, two wobbly-yolked boiled eggs, fruit, yogurt and, because Samira Khan was a mum and therefore knew what her little girl liked, even if she didn't necessarily approve of it, a small bowl of Sugar Puffs. When she was done, she perched on the edge of a kitchen chair, sipping from a chipped mug of sweet tea and smiling in her faintly worried way.

Pen took in the feast. Her stomach pitched as she thought, *I'm busted.* Some deep maternal instinct had laid bare her plans, and this was her mum's way of helping: at least now she'd have one good meal in her when she ripped her folks' beating hearts from their chests by running away again.

But then she realised what her mother was really trying to say: *You're losing weight. Your wrists are too bony. Eat. Eat and be looked after. I'm worried about you.*

Pen hesitated, and then picked up a paratha. It felt awkward and unfamiliar in her hands. She tore off a piece and popped it into her mouth. It was delicious, and incredibly hard to swallow. The light coming through the window blushed gradually up into full brightness.

Her dad creaked his way down the stairs. He did a double take at the bounty on the table and grumbled that his wife never laid on breakfast like this for him any more. He helped himself to some bread before shaking out the morning paper.

Pen reached into her bag, tugged out a clipboard with a stub of pencil attached on a bit of string and set it carefully on the table.

'What's that?' her dad asked.

'Schoolwork,' Pen replied.

'"Survey on terms of residency",' her dad read from the form.

'It's for geography.'

'You mean colouring-in.' He harrumphed and turned back to his paper, but he was beaming. Her dad faked 'grumpy old man' less convincingly than anyone in living memory, but he loved to try.

'I remember the day we moved here,' he said. 'Your mother was eight months pregnant with you, and her belly went out in front of her like the big white spaceship at the beginning of *Star Wars*.'

'*Star Destroyer*.'

'Right! The place was more decrepit than our eighteen-year-old cat, but it had enough space for three, and we could afford it.'

Pen watched the levels in his and her mum's mugs covertly. When her dad drained his dregs with a noise like ancient plumbing, she said, 'More tea, Dad? Mum?' Her voice didn't even quiver.

Her parents made happy noises and held out their mugs.

Pen flicked the kettle on. While it was bubbling away, she pulled the synod's bottle from her satchel. The metallic liquid inside ran like mercury, laced with an oily rainbow sheen. She shook a couple of droplets into each mug, hiding them casually with her body. Only the tinkle of the teaspoon on enamel as she stirred in the sugar gave any clue that her hands were trembling.

'Thank you, dear one,' her mum said, accepting the mug

gratefully. Her dad raised his tea to his beloved of two decades, and she raised hers back. They both blew across the top of the scalding liquid, and then, with a synchronicity the synod would have been proud of, they sipped.

They hesitated. Their expressions became fugged and confused.

Pen jumped as if their uncertainty was a starting gun. She stepped smartly forward and prised the mugs from their rubbery fingers. She took the pair of empty flasks from her bag, spun off the lids and decanted the liquid that had been tea. It gleamed at her, malevolent and silver, before she screwed the flasks shut again.

Something sharp caught in Pen's chest. Her pulse was slamming but she didn't stop. *No time to hesitate. No time to think twice.* This was why there was a plan. *Control, Pen, stay in control.* She stowed the flasks and turned on her heel, sank back into her chair and nudged her plate with her elbow so it slid to sit before her mother instead. She lifted the clipboard in one hand and her tea in the other.

Her mug rattled on her teeth as she sipped. 'So,' she said, forcing herself to sound casual. *Look up, Pen, look up.* Her eyes were fixed on the grain of the table. The muscles in her neck felt almost paralysed. *Look. Up.* 'You were saying?'

The air felt as thick as quicksand as Pen drew her head up through it. For an instant her mum blinked at her in total incomprehension, and then she reacted.

It was a tiny motion. Pen's mum's manners were immaculate and her self-control peerless, so it was only a fraction of an inch, but it tore at Pen's heart. She watched her mum recoil from the scarred face of the girl she'd never seen before.

'You were saying,' Pen repeated, as though nothing was wrong.

'I— I was saying—?'

'How long you'd lived on this street,' Pen explained. She assumed a carefully practised smile, as though slightly puzzled at having to repeat herself. 'It's for my survey – human geography. Like I said, Mrs Khan, I'm going round the neighbourhood. It's really good of you and Mr Khan to help me out on my school project. Being new around here, I don't know many people to ask.'

'Ah – yes, of – of course—' Samira Khan clutched at this conversational driftwood as if she was drowning. She looked deeply upset that she couldn't remember any of this, but evidently she had decided to play along until a better explanation presented itself. 'I suppose,' she said, 'it must be . . . what, seventeen years now?'

'That's right.' Pen turned to her dad as he spoke. He kept blinking at her and then at the Olympian breakfast as though they'd both just erupted up through the floorboards.

'That's great, thanks, Mr Khan – and do you happen to remember what brought you here to Wendover Road in the first place?'

'Uh—' His teak-coloured face scrunched up earnestly as he fought for the memory.

Pen drew in a quiet, shallow breath.

86

'I'm afraid I don't . . . Work, perhaps? It was a long time ago.'

Pen nodded her understanding and her thanks, swallowing down a mix of relief and bile before it could choke her. 'Thank you,' she said, wrestling her voice into the shape of gratitude. 'That's really helpful, Mr Khan, Mrs Khan. I'm sorry to have interrupted your breakfast. It smells delicious. Mrs Khan, you must be a wonderful cook.'

Pen's mum's shy little smile battled bravely out from behind her confusion. 'Why thank you. Would you like some bread to take with you when you go?'

Pen's front door shut with a dreadfully familiar crunch. She clutched a faintly warm Tupperware box of paratha in her fingers. A chill breeze whispered inside her headscarf and stroked her eyelashes. She released a single, shuddering breath.

A hand closed on her shoulder, five slim fingers pressing in. There was a presence behind her that had not been there before. A pungent, oily liquid seeped through her jacket. Pen didn't look back; she fumbled in her bag and passed the flasks back over her shoulder. The hand released her and took them and a little shiver went through her as though some spindly insect were walking over her heart. She felt cold glass pressed into her palm: two slim vials. With an effort, she closed her fingers around them.

And then the presence behind her was gone.

'Okay,' she murmured to herself. 'Okay.' She said it over and over, but it didn't get any more true. '*Okay.*'

She stared at the patina-splotched brass numbers on her door. 47 Wendover Road. There was only one way back into that house now, and it led through a mirror – a window she would make into a door. Now she had two things to go through that door for: her mirror-sister, and a ransom for those pieces of her parents' minds she'd just given away.

Or else she could never go home again.

She stumbled backwards a couple of steps, skidding slightly over the frosty pavement, then she turned and ran, unable to look at the house any more.

CHAPTER NINE

Pen huddled up against the cold and watched uniformed figures jog up the steps of the police station across the road. She rubbed her thumb anxiously over the screen of her phone. She'd switched it on from reflex as she'd left her street and the voicemail tone had nearly startled her out of her skin.

'*Parva, it's Juliet, Detective Ellis, from Blackfriars Police Station here. I'm really sorry but the system's completely backed up and the earliest date we could get for hearing your case was June twentieth. Listen, I know it's a blow, but please try to stay positive. The gears grind slow sometimes, but we will get there. Call me back if you have any questions or if you just want to talk. Parva, I believe we can do this, if you stay strong, I believe we can put him away. Talk to you soon.*'

Pen started to worry at the skin on her thumb's cuticle. *I believe.* Three months ago, those had been the only three syllables she'd wanted to hear from the matter-of-fact policewoman with the gentle voice. Those words had been all that mattered, but they rang a little hollow now. She felt a choking frustration rise in her. Every delay made it feel more and more like they could delay her forever, like nothing would happen at all, and now . . .

June twentieth. She might never see that date.

A stocky woman in a leather coat peeled away from the commuter crowds and headed towards the station stairs, earphones in, singing under her breath in little puffs of condensation. Pen pushed herself off the wall and stepped off the pavement. If she was going to do what she came for, now was the time.

But halfway across the road she faltered. A black cab's horn jolted her and she danced back to let it pass. Inside her head, she recited once more what she wanted to say to Juliet, the desperate plea she'd come here to make.

I have to go away. I might not be able to come back. If I can't, please, you have to go after him anyway. You have to try.

She craved reassurance. The idea of Salt walking away from this filled her mind with a blank white fury, obliterating everything else. But now, facing the moment, she heard how it would sound to the policewoman, the unanswerable questions it would raise:

You have to go? Go where?

And worse, *Are you having second thoughts?*

More traffic hooted at her and she edged back to the pavement. She watched the trailing edge of Detective Ellis' coat disappear through the door. She thought briefly of following her, of making this an officially registered visit, but it would do no good, and there was no time.

You'll just have to come back, she told herself, surprised and a little scared by how hot her anger burned, almost stronger than the desire to see her parents again. It was as much, if not more, her need to see Salt fall that made her determined to return.

She curled her fingers into fists, released them very slowly, and turned and walked away towards the river.

To the east, across the water, she saw the Shard rearing over London Bridge Station, the narrow spike of the capital's new tallest tower puncturing the skyline like a broken bodkin. A crane perched at its ragged apex like a spindly bird, and Pen shuddered.

Her original plan had been to sneak back into the abandoned girl's bathroom and cross through the mirror there, right to where she'd last seen Parva. But she'd sent a menacing note to Frostfield on faked-up letterhead from an expensive-sounding law firm she'd found online, saying she was still recovering psychologically from what the school had 'allowed Trudi Stahl to inflict on her' and that Frostfield shouldn't try to contact her until the Khans said she was ready, on pain of bloody lawsuit. She couldn't risk being caught back there now.

The synod's vials clinked in her bag as she played with the zip. The winter sun etched her reflection starkly into the windows she passed, but there were too many people, even at this hour.

Where then?

An idea struck her, and she hurried down the slippery stone steps next to Blackfriars Bridge.

Her breath fogged the air in front of her face. Close to, the river looked almost cold enough to freeze. It surged sluggishly, a vast silver snake on the edge of hibernation. Pen watched the ripples in her murky reflection, the shadows cast by her raised scars. Riverside tower blocks rose behind her, warping and flexing slowly with the tide.

It was a mirror of sorts, and out of the way – and if this didn't work, at least she wouldn't be pulling fragments of broken glass out from between her fingers.

Before her nerve could fail, she unscrewed the cap on one of the vials and tilted her wrist, letting the clear fluid it contained splash onto the Thames. It spread like oil, stilling and clarifying the surface until the water beneath it was utterly invisible. The reflected buildings ceased their slow surging; their images were frozen in place, distorted, like in funhouse mirrors.

And *Pen's* reflection . . .

Her breath caught. Her reflection had vanished.

She craned forward, but where her reflected face ought to have been she saw only the steps and the railings above her. It was as if she was invisible. A couple walked arm in arm along the embankment behind her. Pen heard them chatting, but she didn't see them reflected either.

A wry smile touched her lips as she realised what had happened.

Tentatively, she reached down towards where the water's surface ought to have been. Her fingers brushed nothing but air.

There was a hole in the river.

It was the shape of the puddle she'd poured from the vial. The wavy, distorted buildings she was looking at weren't reflections, she realised, but real: solid mortar and masonry beneath her. It was as though she'd smashed a hole in what she'd thought was a mirror and found it was a window instead. The Thames lapped at the edges of the hole. Droplets splashed over and fell upwards into the reflected sky like inverse rain until they were lost to sight.

Pen's stomach clenched as she tiptoed to the river's edge. Down or up, whichever, it was a long, long way to fall.

A sudden burst of synth and bass from her phone made her jump, almost tipping her in.

The text was from Beth: *I need to see you.*

Pen hesitated, her thumb poised over the keys to send the automatic response. With her other hand she reached into her bag and touched the other thing she'd brought with her: an eggshell made of stippled brick, with a few slate feathers inside.

No messages, she told herself, *no clues, no cryptic comments.* She would leave no broken picture for Beth to piece together, no 'Fractured Harmony'. Beth was too smart. She'd work it out and come after her, and then it would be *her* in the synod's factory, paying the same awful price that that Pen had – or a worse one, because who knew what sacrifice Johnny Naphtha would extract from the new Daughter of the Streets if she put herself in his debt.

With a whispering sigh the hole in the river started to contract. The window was closing.

She put the phone back into her bag without answering it, braced herself and willed herself to jump. For a dreadful instant her legs wouldn't obey her. She watched the hole diminishing. In just a few more seconds the gap would be too narrow to fit through. She had a brief vision of getting stuck – her head and torso sticking up out of the Thames, while her legs waved up from the surface of its mirror river like some mad synchronised swimmer's.

The hole was shrinking more quickly now. She could see her own reflection returning in its wake. She concentrated and her knees bent agonisingly slowly under her.

'*Pen!*' she snapped at herself, and jumped. For a split second she kicked at empty air, and then she plummeted down through the hole in the river. The water at its edge splashed over her face.

What felt like a half-ton of paratha surged up into her throat as she gagged. The distance to the reflected buildings stretched away beneath her flailing legs. She fell, faster and faster, until the wind pummelling at her face snapped her head back. She stared upwards: she was plummeting through a tunnel in the water like some kind of aquatic rabbit. For a moment she glimpsed the towers of her home city gleaming in the bright winter light, an impossible distance above.

And then the tunnel-mouth closed over her—

Water roared down and the liquid walls crashed in towards her. She snatched a single frantic breath before the restored

Thames smashed into her like a giant fist. She jerked hard upwards as the water broke her fall. She tumbled, her blood drumming in her ears. Every beat of her heart made her head throb. She thrashed and floundered, kicking upwards, desperate for air, but the water around her stayed the same dank, uniform green, with no sign of the sun. She was sinking. She could feel some invisible force dragging her downwards. She flailed her arms frantically but sluggishly, the water feeling treacle-dense as, still kicking hard, she strove to rise. Her lungs felt like they were going to burst, but no matter how hard she squinted through the silty Thames she couldn't see the surface.

The remnants of her precious last breath puffed her cheeks out, straining to escape her mouth. She struggled to swallow it back, but a fat round bubble slipped treacherously between her lips.

It zoomed *downwards* – away past her feet.

Understanding was a white spark in her oxygen-starved brain.

Of course: it's a mirror! Up is down and down is bloody up!

Little stars exploded behind her eyes, leaving tiny black holes. She stopped struggling and sculled her hands, flipping herself over. She let the invisible force seize her and drag her sharply through the water. She screwed up her eyelids and exhaled hard.

CHAPTER TEN

Noise crashed back into Pen's ears as she surfaced. The air was full of shouts and the shriek of sirens, but she was too exhausted to care. She snorted water out of her burning sinuses and spread her limbs like a starfish. She floated on her back, dragging in breath after ragged breath, revelling in the miracle of buoyancy. She turned her head a little and realised she'd drifted out towards the middle of the river. She could see dark-uniformed figures hurrying agitatedly back and forth on the embankment and pointing at her. The crackle of radios whispered to her through the air.

A splashing sound disturbed the water and the sirens and uniforms clicked into place in Pen's brain. She was being rescued. The people on the dock and the swimmer must be cops. They thought she was drowning.

'I'm okay,' she tried to say to the swimmer, but all that came out was a croak.

She struggled to get her feet under her, patting at the Thames' choppy surface as she dragged her head up under her soaking hijab.

'I'm oka—' she tried again, but the words died on her lips. The man swimming towards her didn't look like any paramedic Pen had ever seen. He was toothpick-thin, and the soaking clothes that clung to his shape were ragged. His pale, knobbly elbows poked through holes in his sleeves as he windmilled his arms in a frantic front crawl. His hoodie, his hair and his wild, matted beard were soaked black and crusted with silt.

And his eyes . . .

They bulged wide with effort, or maybe it was fear. He was dragging himself through the water with panicky, inefficient strokes. When his gaze fell on Pen his whole face went slack with shock.

Behind him on the embankment, the uniformed figures had stopped rushing around. A barked command crackled on their radios and two of them raised rifles to their shoulders.

The swimmer stretched out a hand towards Pen. His fingers were like white twigs and his nails were blue with cold.

'*Help* . . .' He choked the word as water splashed into his mouth.

A rifle shot fractured the air.

The swimmer hissed sharply. Red spray blossomed from his shoulder. Pen felt warm mist on her face. The swimmer jerked and struggled, cried out and swallowed water. Pen kicked towards him on instinct. She got her arms under his, but his legs churned the river under them, tangling with hers. He was too heavy. Freezing water closed over her and she swallowed the Thames, tasted metallic blood in it. Struggling, kicking, her legs came free and she fought for the air only an inch from her face. Her ears popped as she broke surface, she heard the growl of a boat motor, a propeller chopping. She still couldn't breathe. Wet fabric clogged her mouth. She'd surfaced into her floating hijab. It covered her face like a shroud. Panicking, she tried to wrestle a hand from the swimmer to claw it away.

But the motor was loud now, close, and as it cut out strong arms seized her under her armpits. Pen went limp as she was dragged clear. Still blinded by the headscarf, she slumped in the boat. The motor sputtered and roared to life again. After a moment the boat bumped against something and moments later she was dumped bodily onto dry land.

'Down.' The voice was muffled and distorted, its instruction rendered unnecessary by the shove that drove Pen onto her knees on the wet flagstones. On her right, someone – she thought it was the swimmer – was emitting an agonised keening noise. There was a meaty *crunch* and the noise cut off, leaving only sharp staccato breaths. The sharp ammonia tang of urine stung Pen's nostrils. She still couldn't see, her drenched hijab clung to the top half of her face like a demented octopus. She tried to raise her hands to move it but they were wrestled behind her. There was a zipping sound and something plastic cut into her wrists, binding them. She could hear boots scraping over flagstones.

A cold circle of metal was pressed to Pen's neck, and she froze. There was a ratcheting click *exactly* like the sound a gun makes being cocked in the movies, only much closer and more horribly personal.

'Faceless filth.' The voice buzzed in her ear; weirdly electronic. 'I could execute you right now, you know that? I want you to know that. I want you to *know* I could blow your half-reflected scumbag head right off your shoulders and no one would say a word.'

Pen's jaw was rigid with terror, but she fought to work it loose: 'I . . . I d-d-don—'

'Shut *up*.' The gun barrel pressed harder into her neck, and Pen bit her lip. 'I don't want to hear you deny it. We caught you red-handed. Even if you weren't concealing your endowment it'd be obvious you're one of 'em.'

Concealing what? One of who? But the horrible cold pressure on her neck stopped her from saying it aloud. She could feel the man behind her bend over her.

'I bloody *loved* that girl. My bloody *kids* loved that girl. You people are *sick*—'

'Mennett,' another voice interrupted, 'are the hostiles secure?'

'Yes, Captain,' the man behind Pen said smartly.

'Then do you think we could get on and arrest them sometime this week?' The captain's voice had that same machine-like buzz, but was dry, almost bored. 'I'd like to be indoors before the weatherturn.'

Pen felt her captor straighten up behind her.

'Lesser reflected,' he addressed her in his chilly voice, 'I'm arresting you on suspicion of membership of a terrorist organisation, conspiracy to commit anti-aesthetic acts and the kidnapping of a member of the Mirrorstocracy.' He paused. 'And not just any member of the mirrorstocracy neither,' he added, his voice thick with disgust. He prodded her with a boot like she was something vile. 'But Lady Parva bloody Khan.'

Pen's involuntary jerk of surprise drew shouts from those around her.

'DON'T MOVE! DON'T FUCKING MOVE!'

Something slim but solid cracked across her cheek. The world went white for a split second and she slumped sideways. She tongued a loose tooth and the taste of blood filled her mouth. She was dazed, her head throbbed and she wanted to shake it clear.

'Pleathe—' It was only when she tried to speak that she realised she'd bitten her tongue when they hit her. 'Pleathe, thake off my hithjab—'

'Shut up,' Mennett snarled.

'The thcarf,' Pen mumbled, 'pleathe, jutht look at my fathe—'

'Go ahead, Sergeant.' The captain sounded amused. 'I'm not suggesting we get into the habit of taking orders from terrorists, but it is, after all, the *law*—'

'Move and I'll blow your head off,' Mennett said again, presumably in case Pen had forgotten in the last eight seconds. Fingers snared the clinging fabric and swept it clear of her face.

Pen couldn't see much beyond a circle of heavy black boots, but she could feel the atmosphere change.

There was a long silence.

'Mother Mirror merciful be,' Mennett whispered.

Pen turned her head to look at him. He and the four other figures around him were wearing body armour. It looked much heavier than even riot police wore at home, almost like a mediaeval knight's, only made of black Kevlar and carbon fibre rather than steel. The visors in their helmets were black holes of matte glass. Despite their anonymous outfits, Mennett's shape spoke of horrified embarrassment, as if he'd made a racist joke and then turned around to find Mike Tyson standing behind him. His head was turned towards his gun barrel, as though he could blame the weapon for the way he'd smacked her around the jaw with it.

Slowly and deliberately, Pen sucked her teeth and spat on the ground. Mennett flinched as the bloody mucus splattered onto the stones.

'Sergeant.' The commanding officer's voice was harpwire taut. 'Do you think you could cut the cuffs off the countess? And help her up?'

'Of course of course,' Mennett gabbled. 'I'm so sorry, Milady – I didn't— I didn't mean to – it's just you'd covered your *face* – I couldn't see your endowment. I thought you were an insurgent—' He gently lifted Pen onto her feet. He busied himself at her wrists for a second and the bindings fell away.

All of the black-armoured figures were facing her. She couldn't be sure, because of the visors, but it felt like they were staring.

One of them had shoulder-guards patterned with silver chevrons. He shook himself and pulled a radio from his belt. 'This is Corbin. We've found Lady Khan. Repeat: we have found Lady Khan. The suspect led us right to her. She's unharmed, but she has been in the river and has – er . . . sustained minor impact damage. We're taking her to St Janus' for medical assessment. Over.'

Pen clearly heard the answer crackle from the radio: '*Negative, Captain. Deliver the countess to the palace for immediate debriefing.*'

The captain sounded startled by the contradiction, but all he said was, 'Confirmed, proceeding directly to palace. Out.'

Pen rubbed feeling back into her wrists. Her mind was racing, desperately trying to keep up.

The guys with the guns thought she was her mirror-sister, that much was obvious, and since that appeared to be the only reason they were no longer pointing those guns *at her*, she wasn't in any hurry to set them straight. But *Lady* Khan? *Countess? Palace?* Who *was* Parva in this place?

Pen looked up. The buildings clustered above on the embankment were like fun-house reflections of those she knew from home. She recognised the art deco horses of the Unilever building over her, and the old power station that housed the Tate Modern on the opposite bank, but they were taller here, and their shapes rippled as they rose into the sky, their familiar outlines bent by strange accretions of brick and stone.

They look exactly like they look reflected in the river at home, Pen marvelled. *Here, that's how they actually* are.

A hacking sound dragged her gaze back to the pavement.

The ragged swimmer lay flat on his back, his eyes lolling, and flecks of bloody saliva erupted from his mouth as he coughed. A medical pad had been slapped on his shoulder, tape peeling half off, but a fat bruise was blossoming on his left cheek. He'd taken a heavier pistol whipping than Pen had, and she flinched at how painful it looked. His head slumped sideways, revealing another bruise on his right cheek.

Pen went cold.

That bruise was *identical* to the first, with precisely the same patterning of yellow and purple on the man's white skin. In fact, she now saw that the whole of the right-hand side of his face was the same as the left, even down to the direction of the curl in the hairs of his beard. He was *exactly* symmetrical.

Something on his face glinted in the sharp morning light. Bisecting his face from hairline to chin along the bridge of his nose was a dotted silver line, a fine thread stitched in and out of the skin like the anti-counterfeit strip on a bank note, marking the axis of his symmetry like the edge of a mirror.

Sergeant Mennett caught her staring. 'Are you all right, ma'am? Did the miserable terrorist bastard hurt you? Want to kick him a couple of times?'

'What? No!' Pen didn't take her eyes off the eerily symmetrical man at her feet. 'He didn't touch me – I've never seen him before just now.'

Captain Corbin turned to Pen. 'I'm sorry, My Lady, but are

you saying you don't recognise this man? But—' He left it hanging.

'But what?' Pen stared at him.

Mennett's next question came out careful and nervous. 'Ma'am, if he didn't force you in, how did you get in the water?'

'I—I . . .' Pen looked from one armoured figure to the next, but none provided any help. She seized on the simplest lie in the world. 'I don't remember.'

The captain spoke back into his radio. 'Command, Lady Khan appears to have sustained some loss of memory. Concern over possible head injury, over.'

'Oh, *frag*,' Mennett muttered fervently.

'*Confirmed. Medical staff will be waiting upon your arrival at palace. Bring her in now, Captain. Orders from Senator Case's office, over.*'

'Confirmed.' The captain stepped forward. 'Please come with us, My Lady. You're safe now.'

Pen didn't know what else to do but nod. Black gauntlets took her elbows and she was ushered gently towards the embankment. Sergeant Mennett's touch was so timid she barely felt it. As they guided her up the steps, she looked back at the scrawny figure lying prone on the flagstones. Blood trickled into his beard from cuts in the centre of his bruises, the red droplets progressing on identical paths down his cheeks.

Pen decided to take a chance. 'Sergeant,' she said quietly. Her tongue still felt huge in her mouth.

'Yes, ma'am?'

'That man,' she said. 'He didn't hurt me. Make sure you don't hurt him.'

'My Lady, I—' he began.

'*Sergeant*.' She leaned on the rank. 'I believe I made myself clear. I wouldn't want to have to make an issue of *this*' – she touched her jaw, where her own bruise was rising – 'at the palace. Make sure he's looked after. Now.'

The black-armoured figure stiffened. 'Yes, ma'am. I'll . . . I'll try.' Something in his voice suggested he didn't think much of his chances, but he let go of her elbow and went back down the steps two at a time.

A train rattled the railway bridge as the captain led her underneath it. A black SUV with tinted windows waited for them in front of the stuccoed edifice of the City of London School. Two police horses whickered next to the vehicle – at least, Pen assumed they were horses. They were horse-shaped and horse-scented and rigged with saddles and blinkers, but every inch of them, hoof-to-ears, was wrapped tight in black cloth. They were like horse-mummies, all bandaged up, except for the dark holes of their gaping nostrils. They snorted and tossed their heads and stamped. Both vehicle and animals were marked with the same emblem: a white coat of arms featuring a stylised chess knight with the letters GC reversed – mirror-writing – printed underneath.

The captain lifted off his black helmet to reveal a head of dense, closely cropped hair. His broad face was almost as symmetrical as the swimmer's, and like the swimmer, a row

of metal stitches glinted down the centre of it. The only difference between his left and right sides was that while his
left eyebrow was brown, the right one was grey and had
another ring of tiny stitches around it. The skin around the
right brow was different too, wrinkled and liver-spotted. It
looked like it had been transplanted from a much older man.

'My name's Corbin, ma'am' he said. 'I don't know what
happened with your last protection detail, but there won't
be any funny business with a Glass Chevalier escort. Scylla
and I'll look after you.' He patted one of the horses fondly
before opening the back door of the SUV.

'If you'll just climb in, we'll be off.'

Pen was barely listening. She was staring over his shoulder,
back towards the south end of the railway bridge. There
was a billboard there, hoisted against the side of a brutalist
slab of concrete apartments. At the bottom of the advert,
elegant silver reversed script on a black background read:
ƎƆNAHƆ ЯUOY ƎʞAM – MAKE YOUR CHANCE, she realised
– and listed a website: gl.yrettolssalggnikool.www –
www.lookinglassalottery.gl.

Above those words was an image, a photograph of a girl.

Pen barely felt the loosening of her jaw, or the cold air
that swept into her lungs as she inhaled.

Fifty feet high, every pore blown up to the size of a dinner
plate, immaculate dark makeup making her eyes luminous
and picking out each individual scar: Pen's own face smiled
back at her from the billboard canvas.

II

A CUT ABOVE

CHAPTER ELEVEN

Pen rested her forehead on the window and watched the city drift by under stony clouds. Men and women filled the pavements, hustling or strolling, laughing into mobile phones, shovelling sandwiches and fried chicken into their mouths from takeaway cartons or simply walking with their heads down and hands thrust into their pockets, lost in themselves. They could almost have been Londoners, had it not been for the eerie symmetry of their bisected faces. Where they passed windows, they cast no reflections. It was like being in a city full of vampires. They paid no attention to the Londoners who moved through the city caught in *their* mirrors, the city Pen called home.

Most of the pedestrians weren't *exactly* symmetrical though. Like Captain Corbin, they had stitched-in differences on one or other side, a scrap of lighter or darker skin, a mole or a scar, always quarantined from the neighbouring features with a border of silver thread. A few had several such patches, and Pen thought they walked a little taller than the others, a little more confidently. Behind the car, Captain

Corbin plodded along on his cloth-swathed mount, the clatter-clop of horseshoes just audible through the glass.

The buildings that loomed over them were all stretched and warped: distorted reflections of those back home. The old Blackfriar pub spiked up like a gothic nightmare; the Gherkin was elongated to a glass teardrop. Pen shivered. It was as though the London she knew had run in the rain.

There were supermarkets and cafés Pen recognised, their signs displaying London-Under-Glass' reverse script, but nestled amongst this unfamiliar familiarity were other shops she hadn't seen before. There was a boutique with silver-on-black signage displaying a disembodied smile. She worked to translate the backwards sign: *Fulcrum and Scroutt: Beauty Brokers*. The windows displayed photographs of women in glittering jewellery with crooked noses or big pink birthmarks on their cheeks. The centrepiece of the display was a miniature treasure chest, and nestled against the plush velvet lining were three elegantly arranged human right ears, all in different shades of skin.

They drove past a narrow alley and Pen did a double take, feeling her throat constrict. *Cuttner's Close, EC1*, the enamel sign read. The name wasn't familiar and neither was the street itself.

It should have been.

In her own London, Pen had wandered up and down these pavements a million times on her way to and from her dad's practice; they were an extension of her rat-runs, her neighbourhood. A chill spread through her, and she turned from side to side, peering urgently out of the car windows. More and more unfamiliar details struck her, more and more that was wrong: a missing shop, or a building razed to the ground where its equivalent in London still stood; a row of front-ages continued unbroken where Godliman Street ought to have been. This reflection of London wasn't just distorted; it had been rebuilt in places, its topography altered.

It doesn't match, she realised, her stomach sinking. She'd assumed that the London she knew would be a map for London-Under-Glass, but it wasn't. But without a map, Pen had no idea how to find Frostfield High – or if the school even existed here.

A city of eight million people, covering more than six hundred square miles, and the room with the bloody hand-print on the floor could be anywhere.

Twenty-one days and nights. Johnny Naphtha's silk-and-oil voice whispered through her mind. *Twenty-one.*

Her driver kept shooting illicit looks back at her and then snatching his gaze away again. He cleared his throat and opened his mouth like he was going to say something, then he bottled it. He scratched the back of his head and sighed loudly, then he tilted the rear-view mirror until it caught her. It never showed her him.

'Look, are you all right?' Pen asked.

'Oh, frag me!' he started. 'I was staring, wasn't I? Oh, Mirror of God, excuse me – I'm sorry, ma'am, I was just—' He groped for the words, and then sagged slightly in his seat.

'Forgive me?' he asked sheepishly.

Pen blinked. 'What for?'

'Well, my language, Lady Khan, for one thing – I shouldn't be talking to a Mirror Countess like that, I know that – it's just . . .'

'Yes?'

'Well, I'm just so relieved, ma'am.' His grin was furtive, as though smiling at her was a liberty he could scarcely afford to take. 'Everyone is, of course, but especially the wife and me. Thank Mago those Faceless scum didn't do . . . well, what everyone said they'd done.'

'Um . . . thanks?' Pen said.

'Oh, no problem, ma'am. We're such big fans. Not that I know anyone who isn't a fan of yours, of course.'

'Well, I'm sure there must be *someone*.' Pen's laugh was perplexed.

''Course not,' said the driver, beaming, 'Face like that? – If you don't mind me saying, ma'am, who wouldn't love you? It's not just the looks – though obviously they're important, and so refreshing, if you don't mind me saying. With all the stitch-cheeks and suturing that's been in vogue recently, it's grand to have someone looking a bit classier, but–' He hesitated.

'But–?'

'Well, we all feel like we know you.'

'You do, do you?' Pen had a sinking feeling that the driver *did* know the girl he thought she was, better than she did.

'Oh yes, ma'am,' he said. 'The Face of the Looking-Glass Lottery? Especially now, on the run up to Draw Night, with the amount you're on TV and such, I reckon I see more of you than I do my own kids! Not that we don't all love it, of course,' he added hurriedly. 'I mean, look at them.'

He jerked his thumb at the window and Pen looked out. Teenagers stood in a ragged queue that must have stretched a hundred yards back from a nondescript doorway. Neon tubes looped above the lintel spelled out the words Parlour Knife. An A4 printed photo of a smiling Lady Parva Khan was taped to the bricks beside the door.

'Been queuing overnight, some of 'em, to get the new look,' the driver said amiably. 'I saw 'em on the way out. And that's only a cheap place too, doesn't do the fine scarring, but they queue up for it anyway. My own little girl's been bugging me about it for weeks, but we can't really afford it, and anyway, maybe I'm old-fashioned, but I reckon nine's just a little young to have your face cut. I keep telling her, next year . . .'

Pen watched the knife parlour recede behind them. A long-haired girl in a puffa jacket emerged from the doorway. The girl was facing away from Pen, but Pen could hear the cheer that went up through the glass. The other teenagers in the queue high-fived her and slapped her on the back. A tall black boy stood straight from where he'd been leaning against the wall and hugged her so fiercely and joyfully that he lifted her off her feet and spun her around.

Seen over his shoulder, the girl's face was just a blank white space. It took Pen a moment to realise it was wrapped in bandages.

Her driver glanced around and beamed at her. 'Mago!' He murmured the name like it was a commonplace blasphemy. 'And all to look like you – what it must be to be a trendsetter!'

They drove over London Bridge and took a left in behind the station, under another billboard of Parva's face. The Shard reared over them as they pulled up to the sidewalk. In this distorted city it was a rippling glass stalagmite, its tip lost in the clouds.

'Back to palace life, eh, Countess?' Her driver turned and gave her a wink. Pen shrank instinctively back into the leather seat as Captain Corbin dismounted and opened the door.

Remember, she told herself, *you're an aristocrat. Walk like you own the place.*

She fixed on what she hoped was an appropriately condescending smile, feeling her scars tug at her mouth as she got out of the car.

The Shard's lobby echoed with the click of footsteps and the burble of elegant water features. Immaculately suited bureaucrats hurried this way and that clutching files, but when Pen looked down at the polished granite floor, hers was the only reflection. The place was like a weapons-grade library; no one spoke above a whisper.

Corbin escorted her to a bank of lifts. The last on the right was guarded by two bulky men, bareheaded but clad in the same black armour; they held machine-guns against their chests. The door was already open.

Corbin gestured, and Pen stepped inside. There was a

single, unlabelled button on the panel by the door. It was only when Pen looked up that she realised he hadn't followed her in.

'You aren't coming?' she asked.

Corbin frowned, his brow wrinkling symmetrically. 'You have lost your memory, haven't you? *No one* goes up to the ninetieth without an invitation from a senator. That's what Max and Bruno are here to ensure.' He gestured at the lift's guards, who blushed and beamed to have her august attention drawn to them.

'Don't worry, you're perfectly safe. She knows you're coming. Besides, I need to go and sweat the miserable scum who kidnapped you.'

'He didn't kidnap me!' Pen insisted.

Corbin eyed her sympathetically. 'With respect, ma'am, if you can't remember, how do you know?' He leaned into the lift, pushed the button and gave her a reassuring smile. 'Your ordeal is over, Lady Khan. Welcome home.'

The steel doors slid silently shut, leaving Pen alone.

Her ears popped as the lift began to accelerate. A sickly swirl stared in her belly. She exhaled. Her heart was fluttering like an insect's wing. *They've got no reason to doubt you,* she told herself.

It had been a spur-of-the-moment decision to pretend to be Parva. People here had assumed and she hadn't contradicted them. She realised now what that pretence might cost her, just as she also realised she had little choice but to keep it up.

Take stock, she told herself, fighting down her panic. *It can't be as bad as it seems.*

It was exactly as bad as it seemed.

Pen was in a metal box with no controls, heading for a private appointment with a woman who, given what the word *senator* usually meant, was probably one of the most important people in London-Under-Glass. *No one goes up to the ninetieth without an invitation.* She thought of Max and Bruno in all their muscular, gun-toting menace waiting at the bottom of the shaft. Now didn't feel like quite the right moment to mention she was there under false pretences.

But there was more than simple fear stopping her from owning up. Parva's voice drifted into her head: *They're always smiling at me, but sometimes I see the smile, and sometimes I see the teeth. I think they mean me harm.*

What if someone in the palace knew something about Parva's disappearance? What if they were involved somehow? These were obviously the people she'd worked with. Until she knew more, there were only two people she could trust behind the glass, and both wore her face.

Pen might be alone, half-drowned and sickeningly out of her depth, but 'Countess Parva Khan' had power here: her face decorated tower blocks and her name opened doors. To have any hope of finding her mirror-sister, Pen was going to need that power.

You're Countess Parva Khan, she told herself. *You're Countess Parva Khan.*

In the back of her mind, a voice whispered back, *It's still you, Pen.*

Pen shut that voice away.

She felt it in the pit of her stomach as the lift slowed. The doors opened and Pen gasped as she stepped out.

CHAPTER TWELVE

Birds chirruped and insects chittered. Leaves glowed vividly, green edged with white where the sun broke through the canopy. Pen gaped around herself, wrong-footed by the change of scenery. Had she just come outside? Was this a roof garden? She turned as she heard the doors close. The little building which housed the lift was so shrouded in ivy as to be almost invisible.

Peering through the foliage, she saw light gleam on something metallic and made her way towards it. Her feet shushed through damp grass. She pressed through the bracken and the carefully manicured bushes until a beam of light touched the back of her neck, warm and intense, focused through a glass window-pane, and when she looked up, she saw through the tree canopy a glazed wall sloping above her, shrinking to a point at the apex of the ceiling. The pinnacle of the skyscraper was a massive glass pyramid – the perfect greenhouse – and someone had filled this side of it with a English country garden.

The manicured lawns were surrounded by carefully

trimmed rose bushes and beds full of all sorts of flowers Pen couldn't even begin to name. An old lichen-covered statue stood beside a gravelled path that wound between the roses. Overhead the branches were in full leaf; she guessed they must hide some sort of sprinkler-system to keep the place hydrated. Pen inhaled, and felt the scents of blossom and grass lift her.

A pair of wooden doors screened behind a row of bushes opened and a woman stepped onto the path. Pen stood awkwardly, examining the newcomer just as the woman was taking her in. Her suit and her hair were the same winter-sky grey, the latter pinned in an austere bun. Her face was lined and creased as a lantern-fruit skin. It took Pen a moment to realise that there were no silver stitches on her face, and the wrinkles on the left side didn't mirror those on the right. For some reason, that sent a little shiver down her spine. This woman wasn't symmetrical. She was an exact copy of someone in Pen's London, composed of an infinity of reflections caught between two mirrors, with all the differences and variations that original woman had. She was a mirror-image of someone, just like Parva was of Pen. A member of the Mirrorstocracy.

So, thought Pen, *this must be Senator Case.*

The woman took a single step forward. Her gaze roved over Pen's face, as if itemising every detail. Her hand went slowly to her mouth, as though frightened her next breath might unmake the moment. She took another hesitant step, and another, and then with a *crunch crunch crunch* on the gravel, she ran the remaining distance and wrapped Pen in a fierce hug.

'*Oh Mago*,' she murmured in an awed voice. 'Oh, *thank Mago*, you're safe. You're *safe*.'

She fell silent then, and they stood like that for a long time. Eventually she straightened and moved her hands tentatively to Pen's shoulders, as though holding her was an addiction it took a multi-step process to break. Pen struggled for something to say. 'The garden's beautiful, Senator Case,' she managed at last. *Wow, Pen. Incisive.*

'Senator?' The older woman gave her a quizzical frown. 'When did we become so formal, *Countess*?' She laughed. 'You can call me Maggie when we're alone, Parva, you know that. And you can come up to the garden any time if you like it.'

'Thank you. It's . . . very peaceful.' Pen said, managing a thin smile. *Amazing. Brilliantly inane. Keep it up.*

Senator Case laughed again, a light, infectious sound.

'Peaceful? Yes, that's exactly the word. It helps keep me sane on days like today.'

Pen felt herself warming to the older woman; she had a sort of sternness edged in warmth, like a schoolteacher you really want to look after you.

'Why,' she asked. 'What happened today?'

The senator's smile twisted. 'Another attack: the Faceless raided Waterloo Station last night, just after the mirrorgration train came in. Fifty-two new immigrants were kidnapped – snatched right from the border checkpoint.

They'll be dead now, I expect, their faces stripped and sold off on the black market.' She sighed wearily. 'That's the fourth raid in two months – the terrorists grow bolder every day. Corbin's an excellent officer, and I know he's doing his utmost, but still . . .'

She shook her head as if to dispel the images and smiled at Pen. 'You being found was the best news he's brought me in a long time.' Then concern touched her features. 'I'm told you don't remember much.'

Pen felt herself tense as she shook her head, but Senator Case smiled encouragingly. 'Never mind. It's the shock, I'm sure. It will come back to you. At least you aren't hurt – at least we still have *this*, hey?' She lifted a hand and stroked Pen's cheek gently.

'Shall I tell you something exciting? We were so busy looking for you, we never actually got around to cancelling the photoshoot tomorrow. Are you feeling up to it? Of course I'll understand if not, but they showed me the dress you'd be wearing and it's *astonishing* – I mean, I'm a cynical old bag, but even my wrinkled heart started to beat a little faster at the thought of seeing you in it.'

'Photoshoot?' Pen asked carefully.

'The final promo shots for the Lottery, remember? It's been booked for weeks, and what with Draw Night only being a week away, I thought . . .'

Her enthusiasm drained away with her words and her lined face looked suddenly shrivelled. 'I thought they'd destroyed you, Parva,' she confessed. 'When I saw that video and then I heard you'd disappeared . . . I thought they'd destroyed *us*.'

Pen felt her stomach pitch and the image of the bloody handprint on the bathroom floor flashed into her mind. 'What video?' she asked.

Case held her gaze for a long moment. Pen watched the wattle on her neck move as she dry-swallowed. Then without another word she reached into her jacket and pulled out a touchscreen phone. Her fingers danced over it for a second, then she handed it to Pen.

A sound crackled from its tiny speakers, low but incessant: a human voice – groaning.

The video was dark and grainy, filmed on a single fixed camera in what looked like a cellar, or maybe an attic. Pen could make out three figures on the small display. Two of them faced the camera; they wore black sweatshirts with the hoods pulled up and dark bandanas covered their noses and mouths. They looked the way the kids from Pen's neighbourhood did when they were playing at being gangsters. One of them held a dark shape and Pen felt a jolt of shock as she recognised it as a gun.

Mennett's words when she was lying on the dock came back to her: *You'd covered your face . . . I thought you were an insurgent.*

The third figure sat between the other two with his back to the camera. As far as Pen could see, he was naked. He was tied down with blue nylon ropes, so tightly that his skin bulged between the wooden slats of the chair back.

Pen watched the phone's timer ticking off seconds in the bottom right corner. The thin moaning that emanated from the speaker was the only sound – the only sign that the video was playing at all, so still were the figures on the screen.

After a full minute, one of the hooded figures spoke. 'We are the Faceless.'

Pen could see his mouth moving beneath the thin fabric of the bandana. His voice was distorted, like someone had messed with the sound before releasing the film. 'We are unseen, but we will be heard. We could be *anyone*. We could be *anywhere* – and we *are* everywhere. This is not a demand.' The hooded figure gestured at the man in the chair. 'It is a *demonstration*.'

At the word 'demonstration', the man in the chair flinched, straining against the ropes. The speaker gripped his shoulder and the moaning stopped abruptly, giving way to wheezy, frightened breaths.

'The earl here used to believe that beauty was his birthright. We've taught him to look inside himself, and he knows better now. He has contributed – *generously* – to our cause.'

Pen's skin felt too tight on her. She was suddenly acutely aware of her scars, as though they were crawling like grubs over her face.

The hooded figure leaned in close to the camera. His eyes gleamed in the room's dim light, and Pen could see his irises were blue, flecked with hazel and gold. The pattern of colour was exactly symmetrical.

'The tyranny of the Looking-Glass Lottery *will* end,' he said. The chair legs shrieked against the floor as he dragged the naked man around to face the camera.

Pen wanted to scream, but the sound never quite made it out. It lodged in her throat – half-born distress – choking her.

Sweat plastered the naked man's hair to his forehead, gleaming in the light from the room's single bulb. But *below* that hairline – where the man's face ought to have been – was *nothing*.

The earl had no face.

Pale, bloodless skin continued unbroken, dipping shallowly over eye sockets and cresting gently where the nose ought to have been. There were no ears.

For a moment Pen thought they'd covered his head in some kind of skin-coloured fabric, but then the camera was dragged in close and she realised she could see sweat beading from the tiny pores.

The only feature in that nightmarish expanse of skin was where the man's mouth should have been: a dark lipless hole, rough-edged as though made with too blunt a knife. It was no larger than a child's mouth, and somehow its tininess was the worst thing in that massive adult unface. Its edges worked and stretched clumsily, and through it, the earl began to keen.

'We are the Faceless,' the hooded man said somewhere off-screen. 'And now, so is he.'

The screen went dark.

Pen felt the phone eased from her unresisting fingers. Slowly she became aware of the sunlight, the glass-housed garden around her, the fresh smell of the leaves. Senator Case's voice was tight. 'The poor man disappeared three days ago and this showed up online twelve hours later. When you vanished too, we . . .' Her voice sank for a moment, and then she recovered herself. 'We feared the worst. I showed it you, only because you could have found it yourself online in about four seconds.'

'Who was he?' Pen croaked, when she finally managed to find her voice.

'John Wingborough, Earl of Tufnell Park.' Her voice caught on the name. 'Jack. My nephew. Very handsome man. Or at least he was – Mago knows how many more bombs and guns *his* face will have bought them when they fenced it.' Her voice turned grim. 'I hope they've killed him. It would be kinder.'

Pen didn't bother stating the obvious: that kindness didn't appear to sit very high on the Faceless' list of priorities.

Senator Case lifted Pen's chin. 'Listen to me now,' she said. 'You are the face of the *Looking-Glass Lottery*. Nothing and no one in London-Under-Glass will be better protected, and that includes me and the other six sleepless old farts who run the place.' She leaned in and kissed Pen's forehead, and Pen just about managed not to tense up.

'I promise you,' the old woman told her, 'what happened to John Wingborough won't happen to Parva Khan.'

Pen nodded, but she felt chilly claws grasping at her stomach, because Parva Khan wasn't standing there. And in reality, the senator could promise nothing of the sort.

CHAPTER THIRTEEN

Senator Case's private lift serviced only her office and gardens on the top floor of the building, so Pen had to ride all the way back to ground level to go anywhere. When she stepped out into the cool granite expanse of the lobby, there was a third black-clad, chisel-chinned column of muscle standing next to Bruno and Max.

'Countess.' He inclined his head respectfully. 'My name is Edward. I'll be your bodyguard from now on.'

Pen took him in. He was like a cliff with a head on it. He had two small scars patched to one side of his perfectly symmetrical chin, just to the right of the silver seam that bisected his face. She blew out her cheeks. 'Okay,' she said. 'Why not?'

Actually, Pen was rather grateful for Edward. For one thing, he had the soldiers' habit of staring straight ahead when talking to anyone he believed to be his superior, which meant that he never actually looked at Pen's face, which was a relief because all the gawping by everyone else was making her want to hide in a cupboard.

More importantly, following her new bodyguard around let Pen hide the fact that she had no idea at all where she was going.

In a small sterile room in the basement, a mirrorstocratic doctor in round wire-framed spectacles gave her a clean bill of health and, to her embarrassed bemusement, a lollipop. Afterwards Edward took her up to the sixty-second floor. Pen looked left and right down the corridor. There were only two doors: polished dark wood, one at either end. If these were apartments, you didn't get many to a floor.

'I'm afraid the palace reassigned your lady-in-waiting to the Duchess of Deptford, ma'am,' Edward said as he led the way to the right-hand door and opened it for her. 'You know what her ladyship's like – she does go through them a little fast. We'll arrange a replacement for you as soon as we can, but getting security clearance for new staff takes time. In the meantime, do let me know if I can help you with anything.'

'Thanks,' Pen said. An unpleasant prickle ran over her skin. Was there something possessive in his tone, or was she just imagining it? Salt's face flickered briefly in front of her eyes. 'I'm sure I'll be fine.'

'Ah, Countess? One more thing.' Edward offered her something in the palm of his meaty hand. It was a black leather fob with a silver button about the size of a five-pence coin sticking out of it. 'A replacement panic button. I trust you don't need a refresher in how it works?'

'I panic, I push it?' Pen hazarded.

He nodded approvingly. 'Then stand well back and let me remove the cause of your panic from your life.'

'Via extreme blood-curdling violence?' Pen eyed the man's hefty build.

'Countess, please,' he tutted. 'Via *wholly proportionate* blood-curdling violence.' He smiled briefly, the smile of a man secure in his own lethality. 'Rest well, Countess. I'll be just down the hall if you need me.'

'Wow, Parv,' Pen muttered as Edward closed the front door behind her. 'Quite some gig you had going on, didn't you?'

The sitting room was as big as a stage in a West End theatre. The wall on the far side of it was all one vast window, and through it Pen saw London-Under-Glass, spread out before her.

Crest after crest of gables and rooftops rose like breakers on a slate ocean. Uncannily shaped tower blocks reached up to surreal heights, and the early-setting winter sun limned the clouds in orange. It was an Impressionist dream of a city realised in brick and stone and concrete and glass, rather than paint, and it was beautiful.

It took a long time for Pen to drag her eyes away. She blinked and shook herself, and explored the rest of the apartment.

Pen reckoned she could have fitted the total floor space of her Dalston home into half of one room. The dark floorboards were liberally covered in thick white rugs and there were several comfy-looking sofas, but the living space still felt cavernous, and the yawning fireplace didn't help. A brushed-steel staircase spiralled up to a mezzanine level, which turned out to be Parva's bedroom. Both bedroom and living room came complete with fully stocked bars. Apparently, Parva hadn't needed a fake ID to satisfy her newfound thirst.

Best of all, neatly tucked into a corner, was a desk with a keyboard and a flat-screen monitor.

Pen tossed the panic button onto one of the sofas, crossed to the desk and sat down. She hit a key and as the screen brightened she felt a little catch in her throat: Parva was looking out of the glass at her.

It was a video, paused. Judging by the angle, it had been recorded on the webcam set into the frame of the monitor Pen was now looking at. She moved the mouse and clicked 'play'.

'My Lords, Ladies and Gentlemen,' video-Parva said. The crackle of the speakers made her voice spectral. She looked focused, like she was practising a speech. 'Welcome to the Draw for the two-hundred-and-fourth Looking-Glass Lottery. I am Parva Khan, Countess of Dalston, and I am delighted . . .' She faltered, frowning. 'Damn, it's *honoured*, isn't it, not delighted . . . Bet this looks rubbish too.' Video-Parva sighed. 'Okay, let's start again.' Her face froze as the video hit the end of its playback.

'Countess of Dalston, huh?' Pen murmured. 'Check you out.'

She clicked out of the player and toured through the various folders on the computer's desktop, but there weren't any other files saved.

She sat back, drumming her fingers on the desk, watching the dim reflection in the polished surface. Then Senator Case's voice came back to her: *You could have found it online yourself in about four seconds.*

None of the icons looked familiar, so Pen just clicked through them at random until she found something that looked like a web browser.

—*two-hundred-and-fourth Looking-Glass Lottery*—

—*you are the Face of the Looking-Glass Lottery*—

—*the tyranny of the Looking-Glass Lottery must end*—

Pen looked down at the keyboard. The letters on the keys were reversed, of course. She pursed her lips and typed.

'gl.yrettolssalggnikool' appeared, right to left in the browser's bar, and she hit enter.

Parva's face materialised onto the screen. There was no header with the Lottery's name on it, no fancy banner. Apparently Pen's smiling, scarred mirror-sister was all the branding the event needed. Above it were three links in a graceful, backwards calligraphic font:

ɣɹoʇsiH ǝɥT

sǝlnꓤ ǝɥT

ɣnomǝɹǝƆ ǝɥT

It took her a moment to get her head around the mirror-font, then she clicked the 'history' link and read under her breath, 'Inaugurated one hundred and four years ago by Senator Howard Bramble, the Looking-Glass Lottery has become one of London-Under-Glass' most cherished institutions: more than more than a century of philanthropic tradition that makes the Simularchy such a beloved part of the city's heritage.

Read Senator Bramble's inaugural speech <u>here.</u>

Pen clicked. Under a painting of a man in a wig and a frock coat with a moustache that would do a yeti proud was a mass of inverse text. Pen had to concentrate hard at first, but reading in reverse began to feel natural surprisingly quickly.

'Fellow citizens, I come before you today burdened with a conviction that I know many of you share. I speak to articulate that feeling, but I wish to do more than give it a voice; I wish to give it form and flesh. I wish to give it a face.

The conviction I speak of is this: that those less fortunate in our fair city should not be doomed without hope by the circumstances of their reflection, nor their father's reflection before them. Mirrorborn or naturalborn, none of us chose how we came into this world, but we have taken this strange, miraculous city into our hearts and hands and made of it what we chose. Now we must do the same with ourselves.

'On behalf of the Silver Senate of London-Under-Glass, and with the full authority of the Simularchy, I hereby inaugurate a citywide lottery. On the anniversary of this day, one person from amongst the city's Plebeian class shall be raised to the Mirrorstocracy. One fortunate unfortunate – one lucky lesser-reflected man or woman – will have their aesthetics perfected by the State.

From that point on, they will be granted deed and title according to their newly attained beauty, and that beauty shall be theirs to pass on to their naturalborn children and from them to their children, for all time until the mirrors crack and the cloud-wrought towers crumble into dust.

This is London-Under-Glass, where we have always made our own choices. Now we shall make our own chances as well. I urge you, make yours well.

Good night, my friends.

May Mago bless you and bring you beauty.'

Pen finished reading and clicked back. She was just about to see what the 'Ceremony' link would reveal when an immense concussion rolled through the room.

Pen jumped to her feet, imagining the tower crumpling under the force of some powerful explosive, burning and crumbling beneath her.

Fourth attack in two months. No survivors.

The cold blue eyes of Faceless stared out from her memory.

The tyranny of the Looking-Glass Lottery will end.

The sound boomed again, Pen's teeth clattered together. A crystal paperweight was shaken off the desk and a tiny starburst fractured across its surface. The tremors subsided, and she tested the floor nervously. It still felt solid.

At the third echoing roar, Pen finally managed to place the sound: not explosives, but thunder, deafeningly near.

'Weatherturn!' the cry was outside, but it came clearly through the glass.

A myriad other voices took up the cry: Weatherturn!'

'Weatherturn!'

'*Weatherturn!*'

Pen went to the window. This high up, the clouds were impossibly close, looming taller and fatter than she'd ever seen them on her side of the Mirror, and they looked *jagged* somehow, pixelated like a digital photo in ultra-close up. As she stared at them, she realised the redness she'd seen on them wasn't reflected sunlight – it was the colour of the cloud vapour itself.

A scar of lightning flashed in the sky. With a final savage roar, the weird clouds opened.

Swollen drops began to streak past the windowpane in strange colours, red and black and silvery-grey. *The water here must be filthy*, Pen thought.

A dull reddish fragment of something thunked into the window and skittered away. Pen stared at the trail of dusty mortar it left, and then realised it wasn't raining water . . .

It was raining *masonry*.

Tiny chunks of brick and stone and concrete and glittering slivers of glass rattled down from the sky like a convocation of meteorites. They hammered the window relentlessly. Pen flinched, but the pane didn't take so much as a scratch. Marvelling, she straightened from her cowering and pressed her face to the glass, peering between the stone raindrops. The finer-ground bits of architecture clung to the roofs, piling up like epic dust. Thick dunes suddenly scores of feet high coated the gables.

Gradually the storm slackened. The drops grew finer, drifting on the breeze like brick snowflakes. The air cleared, leaving the roofscape covered in rubble. It looked like pictures she'd seen of London in the Blitz.

'Abatement!' a voice called from somewhere hidden.

'Abatement!' another voice cried.

'Abatement.'

Across the skyline, top floor windows opened. Hatches hidden under slates popped upwards, cunningly spring-loaded to propel the mounds of rubble lying on them down into the street below.

Figures swarmed out onto the roofs. They looked like polar explorers, clawing their way across the newly settled masonry with pickaxes and barbed boots. Most were armoured, some in snug dark Kevlar and fibreglass, others in a cheap-looking hodgepodge: scuffed leather and battered metal, helmets that might have been hammered from saucepans. A few went barefoot in vests and shorts, obviously relying on only their muscles for grip. No one covered their faces. There were sinewy old men and women, there were kids with dust in their hair. Some frowned and swore at handheld computer screens, or tapped the dials of the barometers they wore around their necks like oversized medallions. Only a very few had tied themselves off with ropes. Shouts rose above a burble of muted conversation.

'Voleskull Crew to me!'

'Shovelwights rally!'

'Clinging to a line now, Espel? When did you become such a pussy?'

Catcalls and laughter echoed from the roofs. Pen opened the window a crack and more words became distinguishable from the background hubbub. She heard bets being made.

'Three eyelashes says we build ours taller!'

'Chickenshit!' A coarse voice hollered down from the roof above her. 'Bet properly if you're gonna, or don't waste my time.'

'An eyebrow then!'

'Cocky, much?' a braying, raucous laugh. 'Done!

They unslung shovels and sledgehammers and trowels and went to work, shoving the rained rubble in localised avalanches to the pavements below. A boy began to sing. His voice was high enough that he could barely have been into his teens. Another voice joined in, then another, then another, until the entire city thrummed to the rough and ready choir.

> *'Oh, keep the brick and clear the brack*
> *That's the life of a steeplejack*
> *Work the rains and the snows that kill*
> *That's the life of a steeplejill*
> *We spit on slate and laugh at sleet*
> *Jacks and jills we can't be beat!*

A raucous cheer greeted the last line, and they started again. They scampered over the broken roof-terrain agile as squirrels. The burliest amongst them cleared rubble. The slightest and quickest figures scrambled over the moraine just before it fell, palming certain specific fragments and passing them back to the waiting chisels of their fellows, who smoothed them off. Yet more stood ready with quick-setting mortar, adding them to the existing architecture. Pen began to see how the buildings here had got so tall and so strange.

Astonishingly quickly, the towers grew.

But even as the steeplejacks and steeplejills worked, the sky grew dim. Another thick band of cloud blotted out the sun and the snow of brickflakes grew denser and darker. It began to fall straight until Pen realised it was no longer brick but wickedly sharp shards of roof-tile, lashing down as fast as hail.

'*Slate!*' cried a steeplejack in dismay as the slateshower started rattling into the towers. Jacks and jills danced as best they could between the lethal precipitation. Splinters of it shrieked over windows. Cuts opened on exposed skin, suddenly and shockingly red. Blood ran over the roofs. A lithe woman leapt from the head of a gargoyle to a balcony railing, but just as her toes touched metal a slate fragment caught her in the cheek. She flinched despite herself. Pen watched, her stomach clenching, as for a dreadful second the woman's arms wind-milled, fighting vainly for balance. Then with a single choked out 'N—' she tumbled from sight between the buildings.

'Steady now!' the voice from above Pen's head roared. 'Show 'em what it means to be Palace Crew!'

Pen stared in horrified incredulity. They were still *working*.

On and on they laboured, pausing only to wipe the blood and the sweat from their brows before they heaved their hammers again. There was no singing now; they needed all their concentration to dodge the most dagger-like pieces of slate as they fell. The towers rose, slower now but still climbing. There were no cheers. By a chimneystack just across the river, a man sagged under a hail of slate as though exhausted, his cheap tin helmet cut to ribbons, blood running freely from the gashes. The slate fell harder and he bled more freely, but he didn't move again.

Get inside, Pen thought furiously. *Take cover, you idiots!*

Something caught her eye: a billboard for the Lottery across the river, Parva's beaming face plastered across it. An idea struck her. *You're Countess Parva Khan. They might listen to you.*

She'd call out to them, order them to stop. She groped for the window latch, to open it wider, but knife-like shards rattled against the reinforced pane. She flinched, the remembered pain of metal thorns searing her skin.

'Stop!' she yelled, swallowing against thick fear. 'Get inside!' but no one heard her.

Again she reached for the window latch, but as she did, a shrill whistle echoed across the roofscape and a voice boomed out, 'That's enough! Get in.'

The sky opened on a seam of lightning. The slatestorm redoubled in ferocity. The jacks and jills stowed their tools and, cowering behind what was left of their armour, they turned back towards their hatches.

Pen let out a shuddering, relieved breath.

Something black smacked into the windowpane and Pen shrieked and leapt backwards.

It was a girl, boxed up in cheap tin and leather armour. She hung upside down, arms splayed, her left leg tangled in a rope umbilical. Blood and wet hair streaked her face. She wasn't moving.

She wasn't moving. Slate fell. She wasn't moving. For horrible long moments Pen watched fragments of the wicked rain erode her skin. Then she lurched for the latch, yanked the window open and let the storm into the room.

Needles of hot pain erupted on her cheeks, the backs of her hands, her forehead, but she ignored them and reached for the girl with one hand, trying to shield her eyes with the other. Tiny quills of slate embedded themselves in her skin. The girl was slight, fragile as a bird.

Pen shoved her face into the shredded leather jacket, away from the weather. A hot fug of blood and sweat and dust engulfed her as she wrapped her arms around the girl, taking her weight while she fumbled with the rope.

It wouldn't come – the snarl was too tight. There was a wide-bladed knife strapped to the girl's belt. Pen grabbed it and sawed dementedly at the nylon until it began to fray.

All at once, the fibres slithered apart and the girl's weight unbalanced her. Teetering backwards, she just managed to reach out and slam the window closed before she tipped over and smacked her head into the hardwood floor.

She lay there for a moment, simply breathing, the warmth and stink of the girl sitting on her like a blanket. Then through the skin of the girl's neck, pressed up against her cheek where they had fallen together, she felt a pulse.

'Are you okay?' she yelped, louder than she'd meant to. She scrambled out from under the girl and bent over her. 'Are you – bloody hell, are you *alive*?'

The leather-swaddled mass flopped over sideways. The girl's eyelids flickered in her red-smeared face and she drew in a shuddering breath. Her eyes opened, slowly focused on Pen and stretched in horrified recognition, then they went to the knife Pen still held.

Pen jumped like she was holding a live snake and dropped it onto the table. The girl's eyes rolled back.

'Oh, splintered fragging Mago,' the girl murmured. 'Not for much longer I'm not.'

CHAPTER FOURTEEN

'These are very shallow,' the doctor said, peering through her wire-framed spectacles.

The girl, the *steeplejill,* lay back on one of the white sofas, her hair fanning back over Edward's jacket, which had been laid down to catch the blood. The gore and grit and rooftop grime had been sponged away and her forehead and cheeks had been swabbed with a disinfectant that smelled like it stung.

The face that had been revealed was utterly symmetrical, split by a silver seam that ran from hairline to chin. The girl was strikingly pretty, but she'd gone out of her way to customise herself: dark roots and eyebrows showed beneath hair bleached white-blonde. A small tattoo of a thunderbolt sat just above each cheekbone. A row of studs stretched all the way up her left ear, and a ring punctured her left nostril. Unsettlingly, her *right* ear and nostril were dotted with small holes too, as though she regularly switched her piercings from one side to the other.

Strangest of all were the cuts. The slate shards had

opened a myriad tiny wounds in her face, and they mirrored each other perfectly, either side of the silver stitching. If the doctor found anything odd in this she didn't remark upon it; she just squinted into the lamp and threaded a needle.

Something Pen couldn't quite define kept compelling her eyes back to the girl's face. Maybe it *was* those cuts, and the knowledge that if she hadn't acted, they would've swallowed that face whole. She'd barely thought about it at the time, but now . . .

I saved your life. She tried the words out in her head and shied away from them, from the massive commitment they implied. One decision – a few brief seconds . . . It scared her that a connection that important could appear so *fast*.

'They'll need stitching, but they shouldn't scar,' the doctor was saying. Her needle hovered casually over the girl's left eye. 'Unless of course you want them to?'

The question didn't shock Pen as much as it would have done the day before – the memory of the queue snaking from the knife-parlour door was still vivid in her mind. What did shock her was that the question hadn't been addressed to the blonde girl on the sofa, but to *her*.

'W-why would I—?' she stammered for a moment, then noticed the way both the doctor and Edward, looming a couple of feet away so not to blot out the light, were looking at her.

'Why would I want that?' she asked, forcing calm into her voice.

'Well, it is quite usual for mirrorstocrats to require their staff to maintain certain standards of presentation, milady,' the doctor said. 'Normally those standards are the purview of a tailor's needle rather than a surgeon's, of course – but I thought with your *gifts*' – she gestured to Pen's own scarred cheeks – 'it would fit. I could make it rather chic,' she said, happily musing on the idea. She whipped a scalpel from her bag and slashed the air a fraction of an inch from the girl's face in hypothetical cuts. Pen's stomach muscles clenched as she watched.

'I'm sure the girl wouldn't mind,' the doctor added as an afterthought. 'After all, it is all the rage at the moment.'

Pen didn't know how the doctor could have missed how wide her patient's eyes were, but she had the distinct impression that the girl would mind, *quite a bit, actually.*

'Just put her back the way she was,' Pen instructed, forcing calm into her voice. The injured steeplejill relaxed fractionally. 'Besides,' she continued, 'she's not on my staff.'

The doctor gave a disappointed sigh and raised one wire-thin grey eyebrow.

Edward coughed uncomfortably. 'That's your prerogative, of course, ma'am,' he said, 'but I doubt Slater'll let her back into his precipitecture crew. Not after she let Your Ladyship get all cut up on her behalf.' He glared down at the steeple-jill, who didn't meet his eye.

Pen's own cuts had been cleaned and treated first, despite being minor enough to need only tape. Tiny white squares of the stuff dotted her cheeks and chin – she looked like she'd been trying to put her makeup on with a sharp rock while drunk.

She pointed to the older ridges of scar tissue. 'I've had worse,' she said.

'As you say, Milady,' Edward said with a harrumph. He'd crashed into the suite like a whipped ox when Pen hollered and had almost bundled the blonde girl back out of the window before Pen could explain she was an invalid rather than an invader. He'd insisted on checking the steeplejill's leather-and-tin armour for weapons before he agreed to call the basement for the duty medic. Even now, with the scrawny girl as frail as a sick hatchling and dressed in only a cotton vest and shorts, he eyed her suspiciously. Maybe he thought she was liable to explode.

Four attacks in two months, she thought. *That's liable to make people a little paranoid.*

'Caught in a slatestorm without a helmet,' he muttered disgustedly. 'Letting the tile cut your rope – and you yourself a steeplejill. Mother Mirror, how did you ever get on the Palace Crew with skills like that?'

Even lying bleeding on the sofa, the girl stiffened. 'Weren't nothing to do with my skills.' Her voice was tight, barely audible. 'Slater bet the Precipitect from the *Savoyeur* Crew an eyebrow. He didn't wanna lose it, so we kept working – that's all.'

Edward snorted. The doctor tutted and waved him out of her light. She leaned over the blonde girl with her threaded needle. 'Dextress or sinistress?' she asked.

'Sinistress,' the girl replied, her pale blue eyes never blinking, and never leaving the tip of the needle.

The doctor nodded, and with quick, efficient tugs began to draw closed the cuts on the left side of the girl's face. As she did so, the mirroring cuts on the right side sealed themselves in perfect synchronicity, as if by magic.

Pen felt her mouth dry out. She did her best not to show her astonishment.

When the doctor had finished, she packed away her tools and dropped a curtsey towards Pen. 'I meant to say earlier, ma'am' – she gave a delighted smile – 'it's an honour, truly. The images don't do you justice.' She let herself out.

'Come on, you.' Edward jerked his head at the unfortunate steeplejill. 'Let's find out what Slater wants to do with you.'

He bet an eyebrow, Pen thought, shuddering inwardly. *He didn't want to lose it, so we kept working.*

'Wait,' she said.

Edward froze bent over, halfway to picking up the blonde girl. Pen felt a curious satisfaction at arresting the big man's progress. It was like super-strength by proxy.

'I want to have a word with our guest,' she said. 'Alone.'

Edward frowned at the word *guest*. 'Ma'am? I really don't think that's—'

'No, you don't think, Edward,' she snapped. 'Not for me. I'm perfectly capable of doing that for myself.' The tone was imperious and harsh. It sat as awkwardly in Pen's mouth as a foreign curse, but the bodyguard recoiled anyway.

'Yes, *ma'am*,' he said, wincing, but his treatment of the wounded girl forestalled any guilt on Pen's part.

'I'll be right outside if you need me, ma'am.' He threw another full-bore glare at the interloper on the couch, and stomped from the room.

Pen exhaled hard. Her heart was still drumming. 'Oh,' she breathed to herself, '*kay*.'

She went to the bar. She didn't recognise any of the labels, so she picked one at random and poured out a neat shot of something that smelled like it was designed to scour plumbing. She offered it to the tattooed girl, who hesitated before taking it.

Just in time, Pen remembered to pour herself a shot too. *Get into character*, she thought. Her eyes watered at the fumes coming off the liquid.

'What's your name?' Pen asked. She kept her distance, leaning against the bar.

'Espel, ma'am,' the blonde girl said in that soft, brittle voice. Her eyes stayed fixed on a spot of carpet a few feet in front of her. There was a tension to her stillness. Without actually moving, she gave the impression of being fidgety.

'It's all right,' Pen said. 'You can look.'

The blue eyes blinked and flickered upwards.

Pen lifted her glass and tilted it gently against sealed lips. On the sofa, the tension in Espel's shoulders eased a little more and she sipped from her own glass.

'Is it true? What my bodyguard said?' Pen asked. 'Are you really going to lose your job over this?'

Espel shrunk a little further into herself. 'It's possible, ma'am,' she said.

'Why?'

Espel hesitated. 'Because it was . . . careless of me – getting blood drawn from so famous a face on my account.'

There was a moment when it looked like she was trying to smile, then, all at once, her brittle composure just snapped. Her face crinkled and folded in at the edges, symmetrical as origami. 'I only made the Palace Crew two weeks ago.' She uttered one of those little chokes that's supposed to be a laugh but doesn't fool anyone, and sucked at the lip of her shot glass.

Pen's heart started to trip a little faster. An idea came to her as the steeplejill was speaking. She winced inwardly at it, but it was the best she had. She sat down beside Espel; the girl's tears made identical progress down her cheeks.

'You know me, right?' Pen said. 'You know who I am.'

At this absurd question, Espel managed a small smile. 'Of course, ma'am.'

Pen piled ahead before her nerve could fail. 'Do you . . . *trust* me? Sorry, stupid question, you only just met me. Still, hopefully after I say this, you will, *trust me*, I mean.' She was gabbling; she always gabbled when she lied, as though she could make up for the paucity of truth in her words by supplying them in bulk. *Slow down.* She exhaled slowly.

'Right,' she said, 'I'm going to make a confession and then I'm going to make an offer. And hopefully you'll listen to both, because if you don't – well, I'll be honest, I'm screwed.'

Espel couldn't have looked more scared if Pen'd been tossing and catching a cut-throat razor while singing the theme from *Barney the Dinosaur*. The steeplejill drained the rest of her glass.

'You know I went missing a few days back?' Pen asked.

Espel nodded, her eyes still wide.

'Of course you do. It was probably all over the news. Well, the Glass Chevaliers pulled me out of the Thames this morning – maybe that was on the news too?'

Espel nodded again. She shot a betrayed look at her empty glass, as if to say *What have you got me into?*

'Thing is,' Pen went on, 'what I bet *hasn't* been on the radio is this: I can't remember who I am.'

Espel's voice came out as a dry croak. 'Ma'am?'

Pen spread her hands helplessly. 'I don't remember being kidnapped. I don't remember this place. I don't remember this room. I don't remember *being a countess*. Everything from when I came here, when I got reflected through, four months ago, to this morning, it's all *gone*.' Her voice quavered as she lied, and she hoped it would be mistaken for depth of feeling. 'It's this big white field in my mind. I've got no bloody clue why my face is decorating every other billboard and half the buses in this city. Maybe I got hit on the head or something, I don't know. But I'm scared.

'This morning Senator Case showed me a video. These people, these guys in the hoodies, they'd *taken a man's face away*. The senator said they wanted to do the same to me.'

Espel's knuckles paled slightly where she gripped her glass. 'The Faceless,' she said, her voice harsh as bleach.

Pen wondered if she'd lost someone in one of the attacks.

'They think the Faceless are after you.'

'And I don't know why,' Pen said. She didn't need to fake the fear in her voice.

Espel just stared at her.

'Even Senator Case doesn't know how much I've forgotten,' Pen said, her voice dropped to a conspiratorial whisper. 'She'd *panic* if she did. Draw Night's only a week away and you know how important that is.'

Espel nodded fervently. Her eyes had widened at the mention of Senator Case's name.

'Besides,' Pen went on, 'I know Maggie only wants the best for me.' She dropped the senator's first name, ostentatiously familiar. 'But she'll only tell me what she thinks I want to hear – what she thinks won't scare me. But I'm already scared, and I need someone I can trust to be completely honest. Someone I can keep close. And it just so happens' – Pen licked her lips and made her pitch – 'that I have an opening for a lady-in-waiting, and the way I hear it, you could use a job.'

Espel's eyes were wide and blue as tiny oceans. She opened her mouth and closed it. For agonising seconds, she said nothing at all.

And then, still wordless, she held out her empty shot glass in front of her.

Pen let herself breathe out. She grinned at Espel, grabbed the bottle from the bar and topped her up.

When at last Espel found her voice, it was barely audible. 'Um . . . Where do you want to start, My Lady?'

'How about the basics,' Pen said sheepishly as she poured. 'Who am I? Who do *you* know me as?'

Espel knocked the shot back in one. She looked shaken by the question, then, slowly, an incredulous smile blossomed onto her face. 'That's easy. You're Countess Parva Khan,' she said. 'You're the most beautiful woman in the world.'

CHAPTER FIFTEEN

Pen blinked. 'Say again?'

'You're the most beautiful woman in the world, ma'am.'

'Oh . . . okay.' Pen sat down sharply, missed the edge of the sofa and smacked her tailbone on the floorboards. 'Ow!' she cried, and Espel started forward in alarm.

'Are you all right?'

'I'm fine. I'm just—'

—the most beautiful—

The world blurred for a moment. The billboards, the way people had been looking at her, the queue for the knife parlour – she supposed she shouldn't have been surprised, but the words still left her throat dry and a hollow roaring in her ears like distant traffic.

'I'm— *Really?*'

Her new lady-in-waiting nodded. She traced her own pale cheek with the edge of her shot glass as if echoing the lines of Pen's scars. 'The other cities sulk about it, of course, but even Mirrorkech and Zerkalograd haven't got anyone *close* to your kind of asymmetry. You're the first Face of the

Lottery for forty years who wasn't from one of the three big families, the only first-generation mirrorborn to hold the position *ever*. Papers have been calling you "a triumph for diversity".' Her lip twisted in apparent amusement.

'You disagree?' Pen asked

'Oh, no, Countess. I'm sure you are, in your way. It's just—'

'Yes?'

'Well, you know.' Espel shrugged. 'Mirrorborn mirrorstocracy versus naturalborn mirrorstocracy—' She mimed weighing the ideas in her hands like sacks of flour. 'You're all *mirrorstocrats*. I'm just a half-faced kid from The Kennels. It's all a little out of my class.'

Pen frowned. 'What do you mean, "half-faced"?'

Espel stared at her like she'd just asked what a nose was. She gestured to the seam running down the centre of her forehead. 'It means what it says, Countess. I'm skin-flinted, visage-strapped – I'm a sinistress, a leftie. I've only got half a face.'

Pen shook her head blankly and Espel whistled. 'You *have* forgotten a load, haven't you? Mago, how to explain this?' she muttered.

For a moment she looked completely at a loss, then she set her glass down and put her fingertip behind her own left ear. 'When I was born,' she said, 'I was born with this' – she drew her fingertip down the length of her jaw – 'my own, natural face. But it stopped *here*.' Her finger halted on the point of her chin, where the silver thread flashed in and out of the skin.

'Everything to the right of there was blank as unused paper, same as my mum and dad, and their mums and dads, and my great-grandprofiles when they were reflected through from the Old City in the thirties. My whole family started their lives in this city with half a face.'

There was a fractional tightening in her voice. 'But you can't just walk around looking like that, can you? People'd lose their lunch looking at you. So the government gives you a prosthetic.' Espel's finger crossed the seam and continued its progress up the right hand side of her face. '*This*: it's bog-standard mass-produced mirrorskin, grafted on when I was a baby. It copies and reverses whatever's on your natural profile, so it always matches. "*Cosmetic, prosthetic, completing your aesthetic*",' she sang like it was a TV jingle. 'It's my id.'

'It?' Pen asked

'*Id*,' Espel corrected. 'Eye Dee, for "Inverse Depictor".' She touched her left cheek. '*Face*,' she said. She moved her finger to her right cheek. '*Fake*. Do you get it?'

Pen nodded slowly. She thought about the way the wounds on Espel's right cheek had closed when her left was stitched. *Reflections of reflections within reflections like a funhouse maze.* The idea brought a vertiginous swirl to her stomach. 'It's a reflection,' she murmured. 'Pure symmetry.'

At the word *symmetry* Espel winced and dropped her gaze. 'All right, all right,' she mumbled. 'No need to be so pointed about it. I never said it was *pretty*. I can't afford any original features for it, that's all. A genuine freckle or an eyelash are a fortnight's wages on a steeplejill's salary, even on Palace Crew.'

Espel was blushing furiously and Pen realised she'd been staring at the symmetrical girl the way that people back home had stared at her, the way she hated to be looked at. She hurriedly dropped her eyes. 'You been a steeplejill long?' she asked, eager to change the subject.

'Eight years, ma'am,' Espel said. 'I've been treading tile since the week after my ninth birthday. It's kind of a local business where I'm from, down in Kenneltown – sorry . . . I mean, Kensington. We get pretty heavy weather there: slate-storms, monsoon cement, even the odd chimneysquall. Makes for some interesting precipitecture.'

'*Chimneysquall?*' Pen muttered. 'Bloody hell.' She massaged her eyes. For a second she pictured entire chimneystacks falling fully formed from the clouds.

'Where does it come from?' She tried to make the unfamiliar word sound like it belonged in her mouth: 'The . . . precipitecture?'

Espel raised her eyebrows. 'The *sky*, ma'am.'

'Thanks,' Pen said, slightly acidly. 'I mean, *before* that.'

'The biggest mirror in the city's the river, and the biggest thing it reflects is the buildings – so loads of reflections of concrete and brick get churned and broken up in the tides, and then evaporated with the water. It condenses into clouds and falls down again.'

'You sound like you're a real expert.'

'Oh, I wouldn't say that,' Espel said, in the tone of someone who's often said that. 'But a jill needs to know a *bit* of mirror meteorology. Helps with the whole "not-getting-brained-by-a-falling-brick" aspect of the job tnat I've always been such a big fan of that.'

Espel knocked back the rest of her drink, looked up at Pen shyly and then burst out in a big sheepish grin. 'On which subject, by the way,' she said, 'thank you.'

Pen glanced at the cuts on her hand. 'Oh, any time,' she said drily.

Espel sat forward. Her expression took on something close to awe as she gazed at Pen's cheeks.

'I've got to be honest,' she murmured, 'I was one of the ones who thought they tweaked the pictures, but . . . *Mother Mirror*! They're just *so* intricate – it's like the details go on forever. You could get lost in those scars.' Her fingertips twitched, almost as though she wanted to trace the shapes of Pen's scars but was too shy to raise her hand. 'Even for mirrorstocracy you're a cut above.'

A cut above. It was a nasty, jagged burr of a phrase, and it snagged something in Pen's mind. 'That doctor wouldn't really have cut you, would she?' she asked. 'To look like me? Not . . . just because I said so?'

Espel peered at her, bemused. 'Why wouldn't she?'

'But it's *your* face.'

The curl of the girl's lip suggested Pen was being naïve at best and at worst disingenuous. 'Oh, *technically*, she'd need my consent. But honestly, ma'am, think about it. Who'd listen if I said I didn't give it? *Everyone* wants to look like

TOM POLLOCK

Parva Khan, and *everyone* knows it. No one'd believe me if I said I was any different. They'd think I was just making trouble.'

The sharpness in her voice struck Pen. 'You are though, aren't you?' she asked. 'Different, I mean.' She remembered the way Espel had eyed the doctor's scalpel: the fear in her face, and the hatred of the blade as it hovered over her.

'Espel?'

'Ma'am.'

'Why *don't* you want to look like me?'

Espel's blue eyes rolled to look into Pen's. The drunken giggliness had gone and just for an instant her expression was fierce and proud. 'Like you said, milady: it's *my* face.'

A little while later, Espel began to slur, and her eyelids started to droop. Remembering that the steeplejill was on her fifth shot, Pen sniffed her own glass. The fumes alone were like a chisel to the prefrontal cortex. Was it even *safe* to drink this stuff neat? The gaps between Espel's words grew longer and longer and she groped after them in the air in front of her face as though they were evasive butter-flies.

Eventually she asked to be excused. She put her hands on her knees decisively and braced herself to rise. Five minutes later she still hadn't got up. Her eyes weren't focused on anything in particular.

Pen gently pushed her shoulder and she toppled onto the sofa like a domino. Pen lifted her head and pushed a cushion

155

under it so her neck wouldn't crick. The steeplejill stretched languorously as a cat, then curled up, hugging her thin arms around herself as if she were cold.

Pen shut her eyes, but the space behind her eyelids flickered with billboards and bloodied floors and faceless men. She sighed. 'Sod it. It's not like I'm going to be getting any sleep tonight anyway.' She jogged up into the bedroom and returned dragging the duvet behind her. She slung it over her new lady-in-waiting and eyed her for a moment, trying to work her out: Espel was brave enough to run over rooftops through curtains of wicked slatedrops, but utterly tongue-tied when confronted by the humble personage of Parva Khan.

And the way you stiffened when I looked at you, Pen thought, *like a little hunted animal, like you didn't want me to see you at all.* Pen knew exactly how that felt – so much so that she wondered if she was just projecting.

She went to the window. The towers and spires outside were lit up against the night, and the city burned back at her like a mirror to the stars. Across the river, the Lottery billboard was doused in yellow floodlight, as though London-Under-Glass itself were refusing to let darkness claim that face. Pen eyed her missing sister's image, unease creeping over her.

You're the most beautiful woman in the world.

Where could you hide that face in a city where it was displayed on every street corner? A city whose inhabitants knew it even better than they knew their own?

In a coffin, a poisonous little voice inside her mind volunteered. *In the ground. In a sack at the bottom of the river, if the Faceless have taken her. Or maybe they've got rid of it entirely.* She shuddered at the memory of the empty expanse of skin in the propaganda video.

But isn't that the point? she thought. If the terrorist group really had claimed the face of the Looking-Glass Lottery, wouldn't they want to broadcast it? Where was the video of them crowing over Parva while they stripped her features away?

Somehow those terrorists as abductors didn't quite fit. There was something else – something she was missing. She tried to concentrate, to think it all through, but she was exhausted, and the thoughts dangled like lures on a stick, just out of reach.

It's easy, a voice in her head told her with brittle cheeriness. *You see this all the time in the movies. Reconstruct her movements. Find the bathroom with the bloody handprint. Track her down from there. Only you have to do it without asking anyone any questions that might give away the fact that you* aren't really *her.*

Easy, she thought with a pitching queasiness. *Fine.*

Of course, just because she couldn't wander around asking after her mirror-sister's movements, that didn't mean *no one* could. She glanced over at Espel, sleeping on the sofa. The lights from the city outside etched her cheekbones starkly on her endlessly symmetrical face.

A new lady-in-waiting: inexperienced, nervous and eager

to please, wanting to learn her new employer's habits? Yes, that might work . . .

'*What immortal hand, or eye,*' Pen thought, and chewed her lip, just the way Mum always told her not to—

—and homesickness hit her then, as sudden and violent as a heart attack. She felt perilously alone. She missed Beth and she missed her mum, and knowing her mum wasn't missing her back was no comfort at all.

Pen hesitated. She licked her lips and cleared her throat. Then, before she could lose her nerve, she spoke, just audibly, into the night:

'There once was a girl with scars on her face.
Only surgeon she needed was an inverted place.
She'd been turned in on herself, like a leaf, tightly
    curled
She opened out: the most beautiful girl in the world.'

She swallowed hard, eyeing her reflection in the darkened window glass.

The most beautiful girl in the world, she thought. *Tomorrow, Pen, that has to be you.*

CHAPTER SIXTEEN

Beth felt the statues' gaze on her. Their eyes didn't move behind their cataracts of moss and birdlime, but still she felt them track her as she picked her way between the gravestones. Winter had stripped the foliage from the trees and the cemetery felt open and naked. Distant figures, hazed by fog, watched through the thin dark branches as Beth kept walking. The lightbulbs clinked together in her plastic bag.

Beneath the traffic noise from nearby Church Street she could hear the Pavement Priests breathing.

She'd left their more orthodox brethren in the alley behind the market. She'd scowled at them, showing them her uncanny tooth, and they'd recoiled like threatened cats. Candleman and his colleagues had taken advantage of the their confusion and fled, glimmering dusky oaths of vengeance; he was lucky the stone-robed clerics probably hadn't understood them.

Ezekiel had watched her, agonised, caught somewhere between hatred and devotion. Beth hadn't waited for him to make up his mind; she'd run.

She'd shoved her way past a goggling drunk into the bathroom of a twenty-four-hour Burger King and looked full into the mirror for the first time in months. The difference from the face she remembered chilled her.

Under the fluorescent light, she'd seen the way her cheeks were cracked like hot concrete. Tiny paving slabs broke up her skin like lizard-scales. Strands of black hair came loose from her hoodie, rubbery and black like electrical cable.

Another jolt of pain in her jaw had made her open her mouth: as she'd watched, the enamel on her lower left canine cracked like an eggshell and crumbled away to reveal another spire.

And so here she'd come, to the Stoke Newington Cemetery where the free-thinkers and reformists of Mater Viae's former priesthood still gathered: those stoneskins who, in their beating flesh-and-blood hearts hidden deep beneath the granite and stone, had not been all that surprised when Beth had revealed to them the truth of their Goddess' betrayal.

She really wished Pen would text her back.

'Well, I've got to hand it to you.' A voice like gravel being churned in a bucket dragged her from her thoughts. 'This has to be the most comprehensive piss-take in the history of London.'

Beth jerked her head around. She hadn't seen the monk statue approach, but there he was anyway, standing by a frost-stippled elm. That was how it was with the more powerful Pavement Priests: the muscles hidden inside their stone punishment skins could move them with uncanny speed, The exertion cost them. though. Beth could hear the strain in Petris' voice as he continued: 'First, you show up out of the blue, recruiting for an unwinnable war in the name of an absent goddess. Less than a week later, you broadcast on every street corner that that same goddess really topped herself sixteen years ago and that we've been living a lie ever since. And *now*, after a few months' absence and *oh how we've missed you, Miss Bradley*,' – Petris' sarcasm was as heavy as his robes – 'you walk in here wearing her face like a carnival mask at Mardi Fucking Gras. I honestly don't know if you want me to pray to you or punch you, but I *do* know in which direction I am heavily leaning.'

Beth looked at him. Even in her shock, she'd known the provocation it would be to come here looking like this. She raised the carrier bag and jingled it at him.

Petris sighed and exhaled stony dust. 'All right,' he said. 'I'll take you to him.'

He crossed the space to a small mausoleum in a series of sudden dis- and re-appearances. His jerky, *here-now-suddenly-there* stop motion still unnerved Beth. His fingers busied themselves with the bronze lock in flickers too fast for Beth to see.

The doorway wasn't really made for full-sized people, any more than the mausoleum was a full-sized classical temple, and she had to squirm to enter.

Stone scraped on stone as Petris forced his way through

to join her. 'We brought him in here when the weather turned nasty,' the Pavement Priest rumbled in the gloom. 'It's dark, but it's a bit warmer and at least it's dry. It's . . .' The gruffness in his voice faded slightly. 'It's what we thought you'd have wanted.'

In the fine cracks of light admitted by the door's hinges, she saw a rough-hewn limestone statue lying on its back on the floor, its features effaced by rain and knife-point graffiti. She tapped the stone over its chest with the butt of her spear and watched it crumble like dry plaster. Inside the statue, a grey-skinned baby blinked at her. It wriggled and stretched out a pudgy hand. Tattooed grey on grey on the inside of his wrist was a tower-block crown, a miniature copy of Beth's own.

Hey, Petrol-Sweat, she thought, then, *that's not much of an insult any more, is it? Not given my architectural dental work. I'm going to have to come up with a new one for you – not that you can hear me, or that you'd understand me if you could. So basically, I'm talking to myself. Never reassuring, even if I have done crazier things in the last few months.* The humour sounded strained, even in her head.

So anyway, how's it going? The stoneskinned boys looking after you? They ought to be; after all, you're one of them now.

Filius Viae had suffered the same fate as the Pavement Priests, his mortality rendered from him by the Chemical Synod, leaving him to be eternally reborn inside London's statues. The difference was that the stone-robed clergy had had their deaths sold out from under them by their suicidal

162

goddess, while Fil had bargained his own mortality away. His price had been the very transformation that, if that Burger King mirror was anything to judge by, was still working its way through Beth's system like a slow drug.

Do you really want to be like me? Fil's voice was still crystalline in her mind, even when she was beginning to forget what her own had sounded like.

Yes. It had been the only answer she could give.

But I'm not like you, am I? she thought. *You never had church-spire teeth. What did you buy for me, Fil? What in the name of Bloody Thames did you let them turn me into?*

She licked her lips, as though she were speaking for real. *And why aren't you here to help me through it?*

Once again her fury at his oh-so-selfish selflessness boiled up inside her like pit-tar.

Memory rose with it: his last request, her incredulity, and his insistence. Setting the railing-spear against his skinny chest, her sweat making her hands slip on the iron. Then the three-second count that, no matter how hard she'd willed it, could never have stretched to encompass the future she was about to destroy.

Three, two . . .

Her shoulder driving forward; his ribs cracking, heels drumming as City blood leaked from a punctured heart.

I thought I'd killed you – I thought you'd gone forever. I might yet be right, she thought fervently.

Please, *let me be wrong.*

She upended the bag Candleman had given her and shook

it out. Instead of clattering onto the floor, the lightbulbs floated out into the air as though they were in zero gravity. For an instant nothing happened, then one of the tungsten filaments began to glow, bright in the mausoleum gloom as a tiny nova.

The glow spread, rippling through the glass cluster as individual bulbs contracted the viral light.

The cluster briefly resembled a frozen explosion, like the mushroom cloud over Oak Ridge, and then it began to move.

Beth watched, entranced, as the bulb-cloud bloomed in the air, flexing like a living thing, and prowled between Beth and Petris. Its charge lifted the fine hairs on her arms and she felt something like attention on her, but whatever the bulb-cloud was interested in, it wasn't her. The cloud of lights drifted on into the middle of the chamber, and a change came over it when it came to hover over Fil. It reconfigured itself, spreading and unfolding towards the edges of the room, and individual bulbs took up specific places in the network like stars in a constellation. Its lights began to ripple in a complex semaphore code that Beth couldn't hope to follow, but just feeling its light wash over her gave her a familiar prickle of recognition, like the presence of an old friend.

It's not really his mind. It's a map, a model, nothing more.

Beth thought of all the tiny synaptic sparks inside Fil's brain, the electrical impulses that had made him who he was. She looked at the dancing lights and wondered if they could really represent them.

There was, it struck her, something *familiar* about the apparatus – something she'd seen that *did* look like this, but writ larger, more complex. She frowned, trying to place it.

The grey-skinned baby was enraptured. He waved his stubby arms delightedly, his dark gaze swallowing up the show.

'Holy Hell and Riverwater,' Petris muttered. 'You went to Candleman?'

Beth nodded.

'*That* bright spark,' Petris growled. 'He's the bane of my existence. I'd be a fountain of song and sunny disposition if it wasn't for him. Don't look at me like that,' he said when Beth arched an eyebrow at him. 'He might not be a heretic, but he's still a parasite. His clients go to him grief-blind and grasping, missing those they've lost so badly, wanting them back, wanting them to *remember*. They're so obsessed with the idea that it *might* be possible, they never stop to think whether or not it's *kind*.'

He snorted. 'Growing up inside a punishment skin's hard enough without knowing you've done it sixteen times before. You—'

A commotion from outside cut him off. Shouts and curses from desiccated throats. Stone crashed against stone with a screech that made Beth's bones vibrate. Then a familiar voice called, 'Bring her out, Petris!'

Before the old High Priest could react, Beth ducked under his arm and shoved the door open.

The scene outside looked a bit like a game of oversized

chess: statues faced each other on the frosted grass, drawn up in battle lines, stone teeth bared, stone fingers hooked like claws. Some overeager pair had already clashed, for a marble scholar stood hunched, his arms still locked around the elbow of the sprawling Victorian bronze he'd just thrown over his shoulder. Both were motionless, but she could hear the rasping breath being dragged into their lungs.

In the midst of it, Ezekiel stood, hands and wings outstretched, his stone face beatific, as though he were calling for calm.

The words that came from his mouth however, were hardly conciliatory. 'Give her to me, Petris, or I'll pull the arms off your punishment skin and use them to beat you into bloody shale and take her anyway.'

'Why?' The stone monk kept his voice mild as he emerged behind Beth. 'Whatever are you going to do with her?'

'Well, first I'm going to make her a nice cup of tea,' Ezekiel said acidly. 'Then I'm going to rip that blasphemous lie of a face off the front of her skull and make her eat it, and then I'm going to kill her. Depending on time constraints, I might have to skip the tea.'

Well, Beth thought, her stomach pitching, *good to know you've made up your mind, then.*

'Careful 'Zeke,' Petris said. 'By the Scriptures you claim to hold to, it's *that* that sounds like blasphemy. You're sworn to protect her, after all.' His tone was insultingly offhand, a deliberate provocation, and it stripped the last vestiges of warmth from Beth's skin.

'*She. Is. Not. Mater. Viae*,' Ezekiel hissed. The priests that flanked him tensed: they didn't move, but there were suddenly lines carved in their stone muscles, as if they were ready to spring.

'I'm not giving her up, Stonewing,' Petris said. 'She's our friend. She set us free from a lie.'

'She's *bound* you in one!' Ezekiel shouted back, saliva spraying from his mask. 'But then, you were so quick to believe her propaganda, I wonder if it wasn't what you were secretly hoping for anyway. Reach himself could've shrieked it to you and you would have bought it.'

'*Reach!*' Petris laughed incredulously. 'The Crane King fell *because* of her.'

'Just like you will,' Ezekiel said, 'if you don't get out of our way.'

Beth swallowed hard. *If this was a movie*, she thought, *this is the bit where I give myself up to avoid bloodshed.*

Somehow, though, taking the noble route was harder when you couldn't see any way you'd go on breathing for more than twenty second afterwards.

She gripped her spear, wondering if she could fight her way out. She eyed the statues in front of her, trying to memorise them. When the stone ranks broke, there'd be precious few ways to tell friend from foe in the blur of the mêlée.

The ranks flickered closer together until the carved jut of Petris' cowl was almost touching Ezekiel's angelic face.

Beth's mouth was dry with the anticipation of violence.

Petris snorted derisively, dust puffed from under his hood. 'You're hopelessly overmatched,' he said.

'The Masonry Men will fight for us, and the Blankleits too,' Ezekiel boasted.

'Will they? And if they do, who do you think their Amber cousins will fall in behind?'

'My faith gives me my courage.'

'That's wonderful. My three-to-one superiority in numbers gives me mine.'

'Mater Viae will decide.'

'Mater Viae is *dead*!' Petris shouted.

Both clerics fell silent then, possibly in surprise at the razor-sharp railing spear that had been thrust between them. The gap from stone belly to stone belly was so small that the spear's blade was caked in dust, granite on one edge, marble on the other, where it had sliced fine channels in their armour.

Beth gripped the weapon in shaky fingers. Absurdly, her mind flashed to a classroom years ago: Mr Billings was choking on marker-pen fumes. The date *28 June 1914* was inked in the corner of a whiteboard. In the centre, ARCH-DUKE FERDINAND was printed in capitals and ringed in red, and around that name, a web of wonkily drawn lines linked the names of countries, standing for the web of distrust, paranoia and blind loyalty that had dragged the world into war. She pictured that spider diagram superimposed on a map of her own city.

All she knew was that she could not let these men lay a gauntlet on each other.

Ezekiel's head ground slowly around to face her.

'What's that face then, a trophy?' His voice was bitumen-black. 'Can you actually hear yourself, Petris? How can you tolerate her parading Our Lady's likeness around like that? I mean, what is she even supposed to *be*?'

Inside his carved open mouth, Beth saw Petris' real flesh-and-blood lips move to answer and then hesitate as he wondered exactly the same thing.

Beth swallowed against her parched throat. The world shrank. *What is she supposed to be?*

That was the question that was driving Ezekiel, she realised, the question that was very nearly driving him mad. Whatever he might protest, he wasn't certain; he didn't know what to make of her, so reminiscent was she of the Goddess she'd pronounced dead. Part of him wanted to despise her for it; another wanted to grasp at her like a drowning man. He couldn't bear being torn like that, so he had to destroy her.

Beth did have a choice: she could fight Ezekiel, or she could try to help him understand.

With numb fingers, she let the spear fall and as it clanged off the stones she pulled a black marker pen from her pocket and dropped to one knee. The Pavement Priests watched her uncertainly.

On the pavement beneath them she wrote:

I don't know. But I know who to ask.

CHAPTER SEVENTEEN

Pen's attempts to put on her makeup would probably have been going a lot better if she could have stopped her hand shaking.

'I must say, My Lady,' the courier who'd turned up at six a.m. that morning had said, 'I'm really looking forward to seeing today's shots. I hear they're going for immediate syndication, so they should be out in time to make the evening papers.'

'Papers?' Pen had said hollowly. 'Lots of people will see them, will they?'

'Oh, a fair few. About three million, I should think, Countess, plus the folks who'll look online, of course—'

'Three . . . *million*?' Terror threaded itself through Pen's throat and pulled it closed.

'At least.' The courier had beamed as he'd handed her a large black box tied with a silver ribbon in an elaborate bow, then he ducked his head and backed away down the corridor, delaying looking away until the last possible moment.

The box had been lined in velvet. Pen had emptied it out and found foundation, blusher, lipliners and lipsticks, eyeliners, mascara, Touche Éclat and eyeshadows in every conceivable shade, along with an exquisite set of bone-handled brushes. The last thing to fall from the box had drifted like a leaf onto the dresser: a glossy photograph of Parva, smiling and made-up to emphasise every single scar. Pen had set her teeth and hissed when she saw it. To her, it was more exposed and traumatic than a skull.

On the corner of the picture, a couple of sentences had been scribbled. Pen had held them up to the mirror to read them.

'Come like this to start, we'll amend as we go. BD.'

Three million people, Pen thought, eyeing the picture, *seeing me like this – no wonder I'm shaking like an earthquake. Parv, how on earth did you ever do this?*

She'd just about managed the foundation, but when her quaking hand nearly shoved a peacock-blue pencil *through* her eye, she put it down and exhaled hard. It felt like her lungs were packed with barbed wire.

'Um . . . Countess?'

Pen started and turned, wondering how long Espel had been watching her. The steeplejill was sitting up on the couch. Sleep had messed up her blonde hair and its random, dandelion strands made the symmetry of her face even more unnerving.

She eyed Pen with a shy curiosity. 'Are you all right?'

'I'm fine, I'm just . . .' Pen tailed off, because she didn't really have an end to that sentence.

Espel's frown said she didn't believe her. She rose and came to stand beside Pen's shoulder, clutching the duvet Pen had thrown over her like a child's security blanket. She hesitated, then picked up a brush and tentatively turned it over in her fingers. 'I don't want to step out of line here or anything,' she said. 'I mean, you're a mirrorstocrat, you do your own makeup – that's your privilege, of course, but it's *Beau Driyard* waiting downstairs. Do you . . . do you want some help?'

Pen nodded and handed her a brush – it was all she trusted herself to do.

She couldn't help tensing when Espel brought the brush to her cheek, and she noticed Espel tense in turn. Then, very gently, the steeplejill eased pigment onto the skin below one of Pen's scars, and started to speak.

'My brother and me, we used to do each other's makeup when we were kids. Well, *he* used to do mine, and then he'd let me smear stuff all over his face and get one of his friends to fix it later. I was only seven. One autumn I won a steeplechase – I was the fastest girl at school, and I was going to have to go up on stage in front of the entire year to get my prize. My brother said he'd help me get ready, but I was so scared I kept jerking around under his brush. When he asked me what was wrong I told him I was afraid of all those people looking at me. Most of my classmates had managed to buy at least a mole or a dimple or *something* original for their false sides, but I was still as symmetrical as symmetrical gets. I was so scared what they'd think, how they'd see me,

172

what their eyes might make me into, that I'd thrown my breakfast up.

Her fingers hovered over Pen's skin with a closeness that stalled her breath, but in the mirror, the half-faced girl was invisible and the brush seemed to float in the air like magic.

'So my bro said to me, "Think of it like this: right now, what I'm painting on you is another face, the one that goes between your face and their eyes. The makeup's a mask, that's all. So you don't need to be scared of how they'll see you, because they won't see you at all."' Espel smiled to herself at the memory. '"The only one who'll see you is me," he said. '"And you can trust me to see you right."'

She'd expertly layered dark blue and red around one of Pen's scars, creating a vivid optical illusion that raised the twisted tissue from her cheek.

A mask. Pen latched on to the idea: *It's Parva they'll see: the most beautiful woman in the world, not me.*

Her breath moved a little easier in her lungs. 'Thank you,' she said, very quietly.

Espel blushed and shrugged Pen's gratitude awkwardly away.

Pen looked into the mirror, at the ghostly floating brush. *You're a mirrorstocrat,* she thought. *You can see yourself. You do your own makeup.*

'Espel?' she said casually.

'Ma'am?'

'How come you don't show up in mirrors?'

Espel actually laughed.

'Give me a break, Countess! I'm only a half-face. I can't *afford* to just go spilling my image into every passing mirror the way you can. Image is essence, after all. Gotta hold on to it.' Espel picked up an eyebrow pencil. 'I was brought up thrifty; runs in the family.'

'The family?'

'For four generations. Ever since my great-grandprofiles were reflected through from the Old City.'

'Like I was,' Pen said.

Espel's lip quirked. 'No, Countess, not like you were – not even close. They were half-faces; you were born in an instant, out of infinite reflections, infinite wealth. My great-grandprofiles gestated over *years* – their originators in the Old City took the exact same pose in the exact same mirrors with the exact same light, time after time, and every time those mirrors retained and remembered a tiny little bit of what they saw.'

Reflections and memories, Pen thought.

Espel sighed. 'Fifty per cent's about the lower limit for consciousness in a Simbryo. When there were enough stored reflections of my great-grandprofiles to make up half a face, that's when they woke up and found themselves here, confused and scared, stumbling away from the mirrors that made them before they could grow any more, remembering only half of who they once were. That's why there aren't any third-faces or three-quarter-faces, only halves and mirrorstocrats. Infinite and sparse. Rich and . . . not so rich.'

Espel looked into the mirror, at the emptiness there. 'I

could,' she said thoughtfully, 'if I tried, I *could* cast a reflection. I could give up a little piece of myself to see myself. I won't lie, it's tempting – but it's also addictive. There are hospitals in the Kennels full of faded men and women who couldn't stop admiring themselves, and I don't want to start down that road.'

Her hand rose to brush the skin on her prosthetic cheek.

'Besides, staying respectable takes pretty much everything I can spare. Ids are reflections too, remember, and reflections ain't free.'

She turned her gaze towards Pen's reflection. She shook her head as she picked up a dark pencil. 'It's strange, I never would have thought—'

She caught Pen's eye, broke off and blushed deeper.

'Never would have thought what?' Pen asked.

'Nothing, Countess,'

'You never would have thought what?' Pen insisted.

'That you'd be scared to be seen,' Espel said quietly. 'I mean, you're a mirrorstocrat. You can see yourself any time you want. You can make yourself with your own eyes – be however you see *yourself*.' Espel pursed her seam-stitched lips wistfully at such luxury. 'What have you got to be afraid of?'

'That maybe how I see myself is how I really am—' Pen said before she thought.

There was a long silence, broken by a long low beeping coming from the desk-monitor.

'That'll be them calling from downstairs.' Espel set the brush down. 'Are you ready?'

Pen stretched her fingers experimentally. They answered her. She looked in the mirror at her stark scars, her inverted image: Parva's face.

'Let's go,' she said.

The digital numbers blinked to 50 and the lift doors slid open. Pen went to step out, but Edward rumbled, 'Ma'am?' in such a pained way that she paused.

He jerked his head at Espel. 'Go and make sure the chamber is prepared for the countess.'

Espel stiffened very slightly, then dropped a curtsey. After much embarrassed protestation, she was wearing a black shirt and trousers Pen had found in one of Parva's seven cavernous walk-in wardrobes, a fact Edward seemed to note with disapprobation as she walked away.

Pen waited. The bodyguard's massive forehead creased until it looked like sedimentary rock, but he didn't speak.

'Edward,' Pen said at last. 'They're waiting for me.'

'Yes, ma'am. I'm sorry, ma'am.' He rubbed his temples with his fingertips. 'This is most awkward, ma'am.'

Pen felt something tighten in her belly.

'What is?'

'Milady's private affairs are her own concern . . .'

'But?'

'The steeplejill girl . . . given her . . . background . . . are you sure she's suitable?'

Pen glanced over her shoulder, but Espel had already vanished around a corner. 'Her *background*? What, have you gotta be posh to be a lady-in-waiting now?'

'I didn't mean for her position, ma'am. I meant for – for . . .'

When some people were uncomfortable they squirmed. Edward went the other way. He froze. Beads of sweat appeared symmetrically on his brow. He was an ice-sculpture slowly melting in the heat of his own embarrassment.

'You must understand, Countess. I don't judge, I like Espel—'

Pen arched an eyebrow. 'I think I just felt the earth shift under the weight of *that* lie.'

'Fine,' Edward admitted, 'I don't like her at all. But what do you expect? I'm your bodyguard; I need to be ready to put two bullets in the brain of anyone who gets within twenty feet of you. *Liking people*,' he said with the sort of curled-lip distaste others might keep for describing animal vivisection, 'is not in the job description. Still, I loathe the girl on a purely professional basis. When it gets out you've taken a half-face for a lover, your fans won't be so moderate.'

Pen felt her jaw loosen. 'When it gets out I've done *what*?' she said, but Edward was still talking.

'She'll get hate mail, death threats probably, and if you two are going to insist on spending any time in public together, then there's a chance some nut-job delusional fanboy will try to blow her head off to prove his love to you, and wind up catching yours instead.' He sighed. 'So you can see why my professional instincts are telling me to stuff the girl in the nearest bin. It's got nothing to do with how ugly she is—'

'She's not ugly,' Pen snapped.

'She's pretty damned symmetrical—'

'So are you,' Pen countered.

Edward flinched. His fingers brushed the two scars on his chin as though reassuring himself they were there. He exhaled slowly. 'Countess,' he said at last, 'sleep with who you want, but please, for my sake, be a little more subtle. Letting her spend the night in your apartments, lending her your clothes – the tabloids will be all over it in about four minutes flat, and after that, the rumours won't ever, *ever* die.'

Pen was ready to laugh, to flat-out contradict him, but she hesitated. It dawned on her that she didn't have a better explanation. She wasn't sure there *was* a better explanation. *You're a celebrity. People are going to gossip.*

And that gossip would give her the perfect cover to keep her lady-in-waiting as close as she liked.

She looked Edward in the eye. 'I don't know if I like you any more,' she said, her tone one of grudging concession.

He shrugged apologetically. 'Technically, *being liked* isn't in the job description either, Countess.'

Pen turned on her heel and stalked off without another word.

Espel was waiting in front of a pair of silver-inlaid mahogany doors, guarded by a pair of armed, black-uniformed men.

'Are they ready for us?' Pen asked.

The steeplejill didn't look at her.

'Espel?'

'What—? Oh! Yes, ma'am. I think so, all set up, the guards say. Only we were late, so Driyard and his team have nipped off for a quick photo-op with Senator Case. There's no one in there right now.'

'A photo-op with a photographer?' Pen asked. 'Isn't that a little—?'

'A little what, ma'am?'

'*Meta?*'

Espel looked nonplussed. 'It's Beau *Driyard.* He's the most celebrated photographer in the city – his pictures can make or break how you're seen,' she said. 'Case wants him on side. He's dead famous.'

Pen smoothed the front of her top. 'Okay, point him out to me when they get back. They tell me I've met him before, but I've got no idea what he looks like.'

Espel smirked at that. 'I don't reckon you'll have any trouble recognising him. Driyard's done well for himself. He sticks out in a crowd.'

The steeplejill went back to looking at the door. She adjusted her cuffs, smoothed her blonde hair down, then adjusted her cuffs again. She was even twitchier than Pen felt.

'What is it?' Pen demanded.

'Oh, it's nothing it's just . . .' Espel broke out into a sheepish grin. 'It's just . . . I'm about to be in the same room as the *Goutierre Device*.' She leaned on the name reverently. 'The machine that makes the whole Lottery *tick*. I mean, I watch the Draw on TV every year, and I read about it in school, but I never thought I'd actually see it *in person*. When you said they were having the shoot in the Hall of Beauty, and that I could come . . . Well, this is kind of a big thing for me.'

She looked so excited, so nervous and so outright *happy* that Pen felt her own fears subside a little. There was something unguarded in the emotion that reminded her of Beth.

An idea occurred to her. 'There's no one in there right now?'

'No, ma'am.'

'Fancy sneaking in a private viewing then, before they come?'

Espel's eyes stretched into tiny blue oceans at the thought. 'By ourselves? The guards'd *never* let us do that.'

Pen looked past her shoulder. The black-uniformed sentries were staring straight ahead, but their eyes kept flicking towards her. She smiled and waved at them. Star-struck grins blossomed on their faces and they waved guiltily back.

'Do you know,' Pen said, 'I think we might be able to persuade them.'

CHAPTER EIGHTEEN

The Hall of Beauty was built on a scale Beth would have called *ludicrous*. Rich purple drapes hung open over forty-foot windows, dwarfing the lights and reflectors already set up for the shoot. Brushed-steel beams arched overhead like metal ribs, making Pen feel like she was in a vast chest cavity – that the palace was a beast that had *inhaled* her.

If the hall was a chest cavity, then the sprawling metal-and-glass machine which dominated it was its beating heart. Pen felt her own breath shorten as she looked at it.

The Goutierre Device, a huge circular array of curved lenses arranged in concentric layers and suspended from the hall's distant ceiling, shone in the early morning light. It looked as though someone had blown up a glass planet and then frozen it just at the moment the tectonic plates had begun to fly apart. In the centre lay the padded leather bench where the Looking-Glass Lottery's fortunate winner would lie to receive their prize, all the lights and all the attention of the city focused on them. For one night, they would be the centre of this reflected world.

Next to her, Espel was utterly awestruck. She turned slowly through a full three hundred and sixty degrees, her arms spread, taking it all in. 'I can't believe I'm actually here,' she whispered. 'Do you have *any* idea how much I want to just jump on that couch right now?'

'I'm guessing that would be frowned upon?' Pen said.

'It'd get me very, very shot by your gun-toting fan club over there.' She jerked her head to where the black-uniformed Chevaliers stood in the doorway. 'You know what? It might almost be worth it, to know what it was like,' she muttered wistfully. 'Just for a few seconds, to have a proper complete aesthetic. Not *this*' – she brushed her prosthetic right cheek with familiar distaste – 'but a full, real face.'

'Where would it come from?' Pen asked. 'I mean, the new face would have to match yours perfectly, but not be a copy of it. That's the whole point right? Where would you *get* something like that? I mean if you were *born* with only' – she gestured at Espel's left side – 'then would the other half even exist?'

Espel looked at her. 'Impressive.'

'Thank you.'

'No, I mean impressively tactless use of "only" there, Countess.'

'Oh.' Pen looked down. 'Sorry.'

Espel snorted. 'I've heard worse. In answer to your question, "Where" is easy – the weather takes care of the "Where".'

'The weather?' Pen was nonplussed.

'Sure – you didn't think brick and slate were the only cloud-cargo, did you?' She wrinkled her forehead. '*Everything* the river reflects in the Old City gets caught up in the cycle.' She spoke with enthusiasm, and also slight impatience, as though this was a kindergarten digest of her pet topic.

'Architecture mostly, sure, 'cause that's what the river mostly reflects anyway, but also boat hulls, motorbikes, post-boxes, stray cats, starlight – always spectacular, when that rains.' She smiled at the memory. 'And faces. The facerains freak you out the first time you see them – the individual drops are too small and quick to notice, but then whole expressions come together in the puddles, or try and talk to you from the gutters before they run down the drain.' She shivered.

'There are more than enough little broken-up features in the water, in the river or in puddles and sinks around the city, to complete any aesthetic. The tricky part is *how* – how to find the right ones, the ones that match. And that is where *that* little miracle comes in.'

Pen followed Espel's pointing finger. Suspended in a tiny steel cage in the very centre of the apparatus, right over the padded leather headrest of the bench, was what looked like an ordinary glass marble, a dark swirl like a storm cloud occluding its heart.

'Goutierre's Eye.' Espel breathed the word reverently. 'Our one and only mirrormap. Folded into that ball are facets in sympathy with every reflective surface in the city, from the river itself to a bathroom window. It sees what they see, reflects what they reflect: a perfect map of London-Under-Glass, in miniature, in real time.'

Pen stepped a little hesitantly up to the marble, and when no one yelled at her to stop, stepped again. She peered into the marble's depths. Seen close-to, the tiny storm-cloud heart was a dense churn and rush of tiny images, each too small and fleeting to properly make out. It was hypnotic.

'Without that little wonder,' Espel was saying, 'they could have everyone in the city panning the river and still they wouldn't find a match. The device just scans the winner, then scans the eye. It's done in seconds.'

The steeplejill's enthusiasm for the machine was infectious, like when Beth spoke about the city.

Pen felt her own lips twitching up at the corners with borrowed awe. 'You're properly into this, aren't you?' she said.

Espel's grin grew wider. She performed a shrug-cum-head-bob of pleased acknowledgment. 'All precipitecture is basically mirror meteorology, and this is by *miles* the coolest thing that's ever been done with our science. Best of all, it's one of a kind. Goutierre disappeared without leaving any notes on how it was made. Watt-Stevens tried to reverse-engineer it back in the thirties and literally went mad – he threw himself off the top of St Paul's—' She whispered the macabre legend of Goutierre's Eye with ghoulish relish.

'THERE SHE IS!'

The words boomed off the metal rafters and rattled the windowpanes. Startled, Pen and Espel turned as one.

The figure in the doorway was built like a praying mantis. He wore pointed shoes of identical shape, but while one was black patent leather, the other was bright red suede. His suit looked like he'd donned it while it was still half made: the left-hand side was an immaculate grey pinstripe, but the right, despite fitting his narrow form perfectly, was cobbled together from scraps of different materials – velvet, leather, even something that looked like tinfoil. His kipper tie glinted at his throat like it was actual fish-scales.

Pen looked at the face above that tie, and started.

'Told you he stuck out in a crowd,' Espel whispered.

Beau Driyard, superstar photographer to the mirrorstocracy, was a dexter – he must have been, because on the right side of his silver seam were the features of an ordinary, middle-aged white man. Unlike Espel though, his prosthetic face didn't mirror his real one at all: it was a patchwork, a stitched-together-quilt of light and dark skin. The lips – which Pen was quite certain had started out life on a woman, even before they'd been coated in glossy red lipstick – parted as he beamed at Pen from across the room.

'*There's* my muse,' he boomed, and crossed the floor in a series of graceful, stick-insecty paces, took Pen's hand, bowed and kissed it.

'My Lady,' he said, 'an honour, as always.'

'Mr Driyard,' Pen managed. 'Likewise. I—' She floundered.

'I know, I know: I've had a make-over. You must barely recognise me!' He grinned like a delighted child and turned his head from side to side for her to see.

'Do you like it? It's not a patch on yours, *obviously*. Patch, get it?' He chuckled. 'But those of us without your natural advantages must make do. Cost me a bloody fortune, especially the ear – apparently they're hard to source at the moment. Still, people are good enough to tell me it was worth it.'

'It's . . . breathtaking,' Pen managed to say. She felt dizzy, queasy. She was sure they'd be able to hear it in her voice, but Beau Driyard seemed not to notice.

'Too kind, too kind, far too kind.' Where the skin was light enough to show it, a blush crept into his cheeks at the compliment. 'Now, we really must get going, so much to do, what with your abduction and return. The drama! I promise you, ma'am, the art you and I will make together today will be extraordinary. The people of London-Under-Glass will love you as never before when they see it.'

He grew briefly sombre and took her face in both his gloved hands. 'I was so relieved to hear you had been returned to us,' he said. 'I had feared that this face, one of our greatest treasures, had been vandalised.'

Pen did her best not to squirm under his gaze. 'Um . . . thanks?' she said. 'The rest of me is fine too, by the way.'

'Fine? Oh no. No no, that won't do at all. Brave is good. Brave works, but *nonchalant* is too far. I'm sure it must have been dreadfully traumatic: ugly symmetrical eyes peering out from hidden faces, hands grasping you in the night—' He shuddered theatrically. '*Terrible.*'

'To be honest, I don't remember too much—'

'Amnesia,' Driyard mused, as though weighing the merits of the idea. 'A trauma so dreadful that it has ripped the memory from your mind. Your very consciousness voids itself and curls inwards like terrified a child. Hmmm. It has potential. It's abstract, but perhaps I can structure a shot that hints at it.' He brightened. 'A challenge! Very well, we shall attempt it.'

He shook her hand warmly. 'You see why I love working with you. Right, now, where's Juliet with that confounded dress? Ah!'

He clapped his mismatched gloved hands and a young half-faced woman appeared at Pen's elbow. She had hair done up in a bun with pins sticking out of it. She proffered a bulging garment-bag with a curtsey.

Pen gave the girl the smile she was starting to think of as the 'Parva Khan special number two' and pulled down the zip on the bag—

—and froze as something familiar glinted at her from the darkness inside. The dress was beautifully, intricately and asymmetrically woven from polished strands of barbed wire.

Pen's heart lurched. Instinctively she jerked her hands away, as if away from handcuffs.

Someone had found her out; this dress was their sick way of telling her they knew that she wasn't who she said she was.

Senator Case's words echoed through her mind: *I've seen the dress they want to put you in. Stunning.*

Was it Case? *Did Case know? Had she known all this time?*

She looked around, certain she'd see black-armoured figures coming for her with machine-guns ready, but there was only Driyard and his assistant looking at her with expectant expressions.

'Well? What do you think?' The patchwork photographer seemed almost breathless. 'It's Sterling and Goddard, *naturellement*. We'd never use anyone else for you, but they've excelled themselves this time. I don't know why we never thought of it before! After all, the story you told, when you were first asked how you received your scars – well, it is almost as famous as the scars themselves . . .'

'It is?'

He knuckled her shoulder fondly. 'Oh, you know it is. "The barbed wire?" – inspired mythmaking, ma'am. Obviously no one believes it *literally*, but it's a lesson, and a fine one: the pain we must endure to be beautiful. It's the best kind of fable, frankly. You're a genuine inspiration!'

Under his mismatched, expectant gaze, Pen reached into the garment bag and lifted the wire dress out. Her fingers felt lumpen, clumsy. She flinched at the touch of the metal.

'Don't worry,' Driyard reassured her, 'all the barbs are fake.' He reached over and pushed one. It had the same colour and shine as the metal around it, but it bent under his fingertip with the pliancy of soft plastic.

'We wouldn't want any accidents. We mustn't tamper with a classic, must we?'

Pen held the dress between finger and thumb, as if it were poisoned. Sweat pricked her skin, and she hoped those around her would put that down to the heat of the lights. She concentrated on the last time she'd seen the Wire Mistress, slashed into ragged lengths in the dust below St Pauls, her sentience fleeing the metal coils, defeated, broken.

She felt a flicker of movement in the wire between her fingers and stifled a yelp.

Driyard and his assistant were looking at her strangely.

The thing's dead, she told herself firmly. *Get a grip, Pen.* 'I think,' she managed to stammer, 'I think I'm going to need a hand with this.'

Driyard wrinkled his nose. He gestured impatiently at Espel, who was back gawping at the Goutierre Device.

'Half-girl!' He snapped his fingers. 'You're supposed to be the countess' lady-in-waiting, yes? Then damn well wait on!'

Pen recoiled at his tone; she wanted to defend Espel, but she was too shaken by the wire dress and she couldn't summon the words. And then the moment had passed and she was shuffling down the short corridor off the hall Driyard's assistant had indicated. She pushed through a door with a cardboard sign on it marked *Dressing Room.* Espel followed.

Pen turned her back and began to struggle out of her clothes. As she reached for her bra clasp her hands grazed the barb-scars on her back and she hesitated. She could feel Espel's eyes on her, two fiery points on her skin that seemed to spread until every inch of her was burning with the steeplejill's attention.

Pen was abruptly and vividly aware that she'd never taken her clothes off in front of anyone before. She swallowed hard.

Really, Pen? Really? After everything that's happened in the last four months you're going to get hung up on this?

Still blushing furiously, she snapped the clasp open, dropped the bra and held her arms up over her head.

And waited.

And waited.

'Espel!'

'What? Oh – yes . . . sorry!'

'Were you staring?'

'No! I was . . . I was . . . just . . .' But Espel didn't finish the sentence and Pen could almost feel the heat of the girl's blush behind her. Pen felt she ought to have been mortified, but instead she felt a completely inappropriate smile tug at her lips. She bit her lip to hide it and coughed.

'Getting kinda cold here, Es,' she said.

There was a rustling like snake scales as Espel gathered up the dress and then lowered it slowly over Pen's upraised fingers. The metal felt almost oily. Pen gritted her teeth as it slithered past her headscarf and over her skin.

Given that it was made mostly of steel, the dress was surprisingly light. It left Pen's arms bare and she was vividly aware of the cool air on her scar-rippled shoulders. Every nerve was shouting at her to cover up, to find a shawl from somewhere.

It's all part of the disguise, she told herself, willing herself to crest the panic, willing the calm to come.

'How do I look?' she said eventually.

'Um . . . I think the word people use is *wow*, Countess.'

Pen's blush deepened. She glanced back over her shoulder and Espel gave her a reassuring, conspiratorial smile.

She swallowed hard.

When she emerged back into the hall everyone fell silent.

Pen looked from face to face, mostly symmetrical, some mirrorstocratic and they all stared openly back. A couple of jaws were actually loose. Pen felt the hot rush of their attention go through her.

Driyard clapped his hands together. Delight was written across his face. 'Let's get cracking.'

'I'm afraid that'll have to wait.' The voice was familiar. When Pen looked around, the hall's sentries were standing to attention. The symmetrically faced, shaven-headed figure of Captain Corbin stood between them, black helmet in his hands.

Driyard was apoplectic. 'Captain, this interruption is quite unforgivable. Senator Case herself arranged this—'

He tailed off as Corbin raised a gauntlet. 'It's on the senator's business that I'm here. And on yours, Countess.' He inclined his head towards Pen. 'You're needed in court.'

'In *court*?' Pen spluttered. 'In court? What for?'

'For quite a show, in all probability.' His voice was tense, but resigned: the particular tone that was reserved for experts the world over who've had their advice ignored by their superiors. 'The Senate, in their wisdom, have chosen to broadcast the trial.'

There was a hollow, cold space in Pen's chest as she asked, 'Whose trial?'

'Why, your kidnapper's, Countess,' Corbin replied. 'We have a confession.'

CHAPTER NINTEEN

Rain – ordinary, liquid rain. Drops slapped against the car window like a million clamouring hands. The Chevalier outriders bent their heads against it, while the coverings of their strange mummified horses spotted and darkened. Rearing into the weather, the surreal towers of London-Under-Glass were hazed out.

Pen barely saw any of it. A mix of fright and excitement fizzed around her skull. Her mind was racing with a thousand questions.

We have a confession. But from whom? If the Chevaliers had found the one who had kidnapped Parva, did that mean they'd found Parva too? If so, why weren't they screaming 'Impostor!' at the top of their voices and clapping handcuffs around Pen's wrists? But if they *hadn't* found Parva . . .

Something stretched queasily in Pen's stomach as she thought, *What can have happened to you, sis, for them to have found your kidnapper, but not you?*

She leaned forward and tried to listen to the conversation Corbin was having with his radio in the front seat.

'Why the rush? The ink's barely dry on the skinny

bastard's confession.' The Chevalier captain squinted through the sheets of rain on the windscreen. The wipers squeaked. The handset crackled enough that it was impossible to tell if the voice coming from it was male or female.

'*Why do you think? They're broadcasting it. The Senate want sentencing as close as possible to the countess' abduction. The more raw the public still are, the more hardline they're likely to be when the decision is handed down.*'

'What do you think they'll push for?' Corbin asked. 'His mouth? His eye?'

Pen shuddered involuntarily, but the radio-voice said, '*That would be a bit lenient, don't you think?*'

Corbin grunted as though lenient wasn't an adjective he'd ever apply to taking someone's eye.

'*He kidnapped a member of the mirrorstocracy, Cap,*' the voice from the radio pointed out. '*I wouldn't be surprised to see the maximum sentence.*'

Corbin exhaled massively as the driver pulled up outside a white art deco building. 'The maximum sentence, broadcast live to the whole damn city, with the Face of the Looking-Glass Lottery in attendance, the person we need to protect. You know what I most love about our dear Senate leaders?' His sarcasm was bitter. 'How tirelessly they work to make my life easier.'

'*Tell me about it, Cap,*' the radio-voice said wearily. '*Tell me about it.*'

A crowd had gathered on the pavement outside, their umbrellas flapping and stretching like batwings as they fought with them against the wind. Through the window, Pen's view was just a thick press of bellies.

Corbin twisted in his seat to look at Pen. 'Ready, ma'am?'

Pen wasn't sure what he was referring to, so she just spread her hands.

Corbin muttered into his radio and the car door was opened from the outside.

'PARVACOUNTESSPARVAWILLYOUPARVAPLEASEOVERHERE-SIGNFORMYBABYPARVAMA'AMPARVAPLEASEPARVAWILLYOULOV ELOVELOVEPARVAPLEASEPLEASEPARVAOVERHERE—!'

It was like stepping under a waterfall. Pen was drenched in sound. She stood bewildered as eager symmetrical faces bloomed before her, blotting everything else out. Their eyes were wide, their grins manic. Some of them were crying while they smiled.

— PARVACOUNTESSPARVAWILLYOUPARVAPLEASE—

Hands reached for her on all sides and she recoiled from them. Something grabbed her by the shoulders and she almost screamed.

'Just keep walking,' Corbin muttered into her ear, frog-marching her into a dark doorway.

—MA'AMPARVAPLEASEPARVAWILLYOULOVE—

The storm of noise ceased suddenly ceased as the heavy door slammed shut behind them. The hallway walls were pitted granite; the floor was tiled in black and white. The place had the cellar-like dankness of old stone buildings everywhere. Espel had accompanied them at Pen's insistence, but she had had to ride behind one of the Chevaliers.

Water plinked off the steeplejill onto the tiled floor as she wrung out the hem of her shirt.

A flatscreen TV mounted on the wall was tuned to a news channel. The sound was muted, but Pen could see the banner at the bottom read *Waterloo Attack*. Men and women in emergency-services uniforms picked their way over rubble, keeping the stretchers they carried level with practised ease. There were prurient close-ups on body-bags and shattered buildings and shattered flesh. One figure sprawled, cradled by broken concrete. He wore a Chevalier uniform bleached grey by dust. He didn't look like he'd been burned by a firebomb or torn by shrapnel; he looked *beaten*, pulverised as though by impossibly strong fists. His legs were broken. His face, a red, perfectly symmetrical mess, had been crushed into carnival mirror concavity. The image changed to the interior of the station: close-ups of walls perforated by bullets, floors scarred by star-shaped ripples of concrete. Underneath the banner-headline, scrolling text summarised: *Major immigration centre attacked. 671 unaccounted for. Garrison Cray claims responsibility for Faceless.* The image changed to show a hoodie- and bandana-wearing figure with the graininess of online footage transplanted to TV. There was something that needled Pen, a sense of familiarity, but her heart was still running like an outboard motor and she couldn't concentrate enough to pin it down.

'Countess?' Something in Corbin's tone suggested he'd said this more than once. 'Shall we?'

Pen looked up and nodded, and followed as he led the way up a sweeping stairway.

'Who *were* those people outside?' Pen whispered as Espel fell into step beside her. Her pulse was still hammering.

'Who?' The blonde girl seemed distracted. 'Oh, they call themselves the *Khannibles* – love you so much they want to eat you up, apparently. They're your biggest fans.' Her cynical smirk was half-hearted, and quickly fell from her face. Her eyes roved quickly over the tiles as though searching for something.

A doorway at the top of the stairs opened onto a balcony overlooking a vaulted stone chamber. Seated in a leather-upholstered chair right at the front, near the wooden balustrade, craggy-faced and severe, was Senator Margaret Case.

'Parva.' She stood to embrace Pen, pressing papery lips to her cheeks. 'Thank you for coming.'

Pen nodded hesitantly, and gave the small, brave smile she thought was expected of her.

'We're all very proud of you.' The senator returned the smile and squeezed her hand. She turned to the two equally craggy and severe-looking men sitting to her right. 'You remember Senators Prism and Spindlethrake?'

'Of course,' Pen lied. 'Senators—'

She didn't like the way they looked at her, smug and possessive, like she was a shiny new car they'd bought themselves. She fought the urge to grimace as she shook their hands. She studied the room below. It was halfway between a courtroom and a film set. There was a polished wooden dock in the centre of the tiled floor, but where there ought to have been a bench for a jury there was a just a wheeled dolly, a TV camera perched on it like a hunting bird.

Pen slowly became aware of a background hubbub in the room. The galleries on the other three walls of the chamber were filling up. Senator Case watched the crowd with an expression of detached satisfaction. The air thrummed with eager murmurs. Many of the audience shot admiring glances at Pen, and she returned their gazes dispassionately. Their faces were a mix of subtle mirrorsto-cratic asymmetry and gaudier skin patchwork like Beau Driyard. Aside from the Chevaliers and Espel, Pen saw no one with a symmetrical face.

When the galleries were rammed to overflowing and the air was stifling with close bodies, Case gestured to Captain Corbin.

'Bring him in,' the Chevalier murmured into his radio. The lights dimmed. The spectators hushed. The old building groaned as the rain lashed the walls. The clunk of a heavy bolt echoed through the chamber.

Pen heard him first, his gait an awkward *clop-shuffle* on the tiles under the balcony. She craned over the balustrade as far as she was able, but it was still long seconds before the condemned man dragged himself into view. She'd been expecting him, but she still felt an uncomfortable thrill of recognition when she saw the man who'd grabbed her in the river, the man who'd begged her for help, flanked by two black-armoured guards. He looked too small in his clothes, as though being a convict was a family business and his grey prison jumpsuit was a hand-me-down. His hair and beard stuck out in a wild tangle. His right arm was in a sling.

He moved awkwardly, dragging his right leg, with his body twisted away from his captors as though to shield himself from them. A few paces behind, a fourth figure emerged: a mirrorstocratic woman in wire-rimmed glasses, carrying a small silver case under one arm. Pen peered at her. It was the doctor from the palace. She glanced at Espel, beside her, and saw the steeplejill couldn't take her eyes off the doctor. Her nails were digging so deep into the balustrade they drew splinters.

The condemned man looked behind him. There was no mistaking the naked fear on his face when his eye fell on the doctor. He limped faster as if to keep ahead of her, his injured leg scraping along the floor as he entered the dock. The doctor smiled gently at him and took up a place by the wall a few feet away, holding the silver case in front of her like a clutch purse.

Another door opened and a scrawny, lawyerly man with a bundle of papers under one arm bustled in. The black robes that fluttered around him made him look like a cross between an old-fashioned schoolmaster and an overgrown crow. When he looked up, seeking approval, his face was asymmetrical.

Senator Case nodded for him to begin.

'Good morning.' The black-robed man acknowledged the crowded galleries curtly before turning to the man in the dock. 'We are here to discuss sentencing in case number

3-23-28: the attempted abduction of Parva, Countess Khan of Dalston, of which by your own admission you stand convicted. Please state your name.'

The wild-haired man's mouth worked for a few seconds, as though he couldn't remember it. 'Harry Blight,' he stammered at last.

'Mr Blight, earlier today you made and signed a full confession to the Glass Chevaliers of the Thirteenth Precinct. I have the text of it here' – the prosecutor patted the bundle under his arm – 'but I am informed you wished to restate it in public. Is this correct?'

Despite the heat of the lights on him, Harry Blight wasn't sweating. His cheeks were dull, as if someone had smeared too much makeup on them. Pen remembered the symmetrical bruises on his face the last time she'd seen him and she gripped the balustrade a little tighter. Someone had made him presentable for TV.

'Yes,' he said quietly.

'In your own time, Mr Blight.'

'I work in the glasshouses.' Blight sounded parched. 'Down by Southwark Bridge. Three months ago, I was recruited into the Faceless by Garrison Cray.'

A ripple went through the crowd. Pen felt her hackles rise.

The Faceless are after you, Espel had said. She saw several expressions set hard.

'Cray himself. Really?' The prosecutor sounded impressed. 'What did London-Under-Glass' most wanted man want with an embankment apple-picker?'

'He . . .' Harry Blight gritted his teeth and swallowed. 'He wanted me to help him kidnap Parva Khan.'

In the wake of this admission the silence in the room seemed to clot, taking on an ugly density. Pen felt her fingers curl around the balustrade. She looked at the crowd and saw her own fury reflected in their faces.

The lawyer leaned on the edge of the dock, an expression of mild interest on his ascetic face. 'Go on.'

Blight whetted his lips. 'He . . . he had a plan to get to her. She went running, most days. Her bodyguards stayed close, but out of sight. She had a panic button.' He spoke awkwardly, and constantly kneaded a spot behind his jaw with his fingertips, as though he was in pain.

'Sometimes she cut inside the greenhouses, through the apple groves. She liked the smell. My job was to wave and smile at her, act like a fan. I was supposed to get her to stop and talk to me, then just let her go, wait for her to come back the next time. She started stopping by more and more. We talked more and more. By the time I offered her the apple, she had no reason to suspect it was drugged. I caught her as she fell. I kept her hands away from her panic button.'

Pen made a little 'oh' sound and exhaled sharply. Senator Case put a hand on her shoulder and the mirrorstocrats around her muttered, asking if she was all right, if she wanted to step outside and get some air. Pen shrugged their concern aside. She felt winded. Her head was full of Parva's bloody handprint in the mirror at Frostfield.

Blight's story didn't fit.

Maybe it will, she thought. *Maybe there's something still coming – something that will make it all make sense.* She tried to still the queasy feeling of wrongness welling up inside her. *Just wait.*

Below her, the prosecutor pursed his lips as though amused. 'A drugged apple for the most beautiful woman in the world? Cray is a romantic, it seems. How did you get her out of the glasshouse?'

'There were tunnels being dug for some new irrigation work. Cray's men extended one to the river and we hid her there until the search passed on.'

'And what did you plan to do with her?' the prosecutor asked, as casually as if discussing the man's plans for the weekend.

Harry Blight hesitated and then said, 'We wanted to d-devisify her.'

A shocked gasp rippled around the galleries as he went on, 'We would never have been able to sell anything we harvested from her face, we knew that, but still, it would've been a strike against the Lottery.' He sounded eager, desperate even. 'But she escaped – she came round early from the dose, surprised us. She swam for it and I chased her. That's when we got picked up.' Spittle gleamed at the corner of his swollen mouth. He started to drool.

Pen looked at his broken face and remembered splashing in the river while the scrawny swimmer reached out to her. The queasy feeling welled up into full-fledged nausea. This wasn't Parva's story. This was *hers.*

'Countess Khan has said she has no memory of these events,' the prosecutor said mildly. 'Can you explain her ignorance?

Harry Blight gave a sickly nod. 'One of the side effects of the drug we gave her is memory loss.'

Up in the gallery, Pen started half out of her seat. 'No—' she started, but for once, no one was looking at her. Espel tried to tug her back to her seat, but she shook her off. Her thoughts tumbled over one another. *There's no way*, she thought. *There's no way—*

There was no way Parva's truth could tie up so closely with the convenient lie Pen had been forced to tell. Harry Blight's confession was false. She looked again at his misshapen jaw. Someone had broken his mouth to put those words in it.

It was a set-up.

To her right, the faces of the silver senators looked grimly satisfied, as though Harry Blight had just confirmed their darkest suspicions. Senator Case favoured Pen with a sad smile and patted her arm. Pen shook her head as if denying it could make it disappear. She cleared her throat, but no words came. She remembered standing in the lift back in the palace, facing Corbin through the doors.

'*He didn't kidnap me!*' she'd protested then.

'*If you can't remember*,' Corbin had said, '*then how do you know?*'

Frantically, Pen scrabbled for something she could say, but nothing came. She was tangled too tightly in the strands of her own lies.

'Please—' Harry Blight whispered the word. He wasn't looking at the prosecutor any more. He was looking at Pen. '*Please.*'

Senator Case stood up and addressed the prosecutor. 'Mr Malachite, I understand this confession has been broadcast, and that the lines have been open?'

'They have, Madam Senator.'

Pen heard the edge of a smile in Case's voice, rather than seeing it on the old woman's face.

'Then perhaps we should hear what the people we serve have to say about this.'

The prosecutor ducked his head and gestured to a woman sitting at the desk by the cameras. She slid one of the controls upwards, and voices began to crackle over the courtroom's PA system.

'. . . *ought to be killed . . .*'

'. . . *disgusting . . .*'

'. . . *take* his *face away. And that'd be too good for him – wanting to devisify a mere girl . . .*'

'. . . *away from this with his life – it's more than he deserves . . .*'

'. . . *Faceless scum. Animal. Ought to be slaughtered like an . . .*'

The voices swirled in the air around Pen, making her head swim. In the dock below, Harry Blight didn't sag, he didn't protest; he just kept looking up at her. He gave no sign he'd even heard the voices.

Please. His lips shaped the word.

'That's enough,' Case said. The speakers in the corners of the room whispered into silence.

'Mr Blight, our fellow citizens don't seem to be inclined towards clemency. I can't say I blame them. You *repel* me.' She snarled the word, and Pen saw the fury erupting from the senator, like a crocodile out of calm water. Even in her panic, Pen felt the warmth from the galleries grow towards the politician's sudden display of emotion.

Case paused and bent for Senator Prism to murmur in her ear, nodded and straightened again.

'My colleagues in the Silver Senate are agreed that the only just punishment is the most severe our laws allow for those' – she paused as she looked at him – 'like you.'

Pen was almost certain she saw an excited flush creep over her schoolmarmish features before she said, 'Harry Blight, you are sentenced to the excitation of your prosthetic side, with immediate effect.' She gestured to the guards below. 'Wake his id.'

Around the chamber a couple of people snatched at breath and murmured.

'*Excitation?*'

'A little *harsh* – I mean, whatever he intended, the countess isn't really harmed . . .'

She cast around herself, looking for the sources of the dissenting voices, hoping they might prevail, but whoever had spoken was quickly shamed into silence by dirty looks from their neighbours. More than one mirrorstocratic face was flushed and eager as they craned over the barriers.

'In your name,' Senator Case leaned over and murmured

in Pen's ear. She squeezed her thigh fondly. 'We're doing this for you.'

In the courtroom below, the black-clad guards seized Harry Blight. They manhandled him from the dock and onto his knees on the floor in front of the TV camera. They twisted his arm behind him and one of them held a gun to his temple, but Blight wasn't struggling. He was slack as an old corpse. His lips moved, but no sound came out.

It was only when the doctor stepped forward and opened her silver box that he started to scream. His shrieks filled the chamber and Pen could feel them inside her chest in the place of air, trying to claw their way out.

The doctor took a syringe of clear liquid from the case. She carefully flicked the bubbles from it as the guard pushed Blight's head to one side, exposing skin as pale as apple-flesh on his neck.

'*Stop!*'

Blight stopped screaming. It was only when every face in the courtroom turned to Pen that she realised the outburst had come from her. Her thoughts eddied like stirred-up water. She groped desperately for something to say. 'I— You're doing for this for me – and – I'm grateful.' She straightened and fought not to gabble. 'But I don't want it. *Please.*' She looked out across the assembled faces, and past them towards the cameras which had already turned towards her.

She exhaled. 'Not in my name.' The words came slow and clear. 'I couldn't live with it.'

There was a moment's silence, then Senator Case, of all

people, started to clap. The rest of the chamber followed her lead. Pen stood bemused in the centre of a storm of applauding hands. When the adulation subsided, Case cleared her throat. 'The Face of the Looking-Glass Lottery,' she said. 'Is she not remarkable? The kindest, the most generous – in every way, she is the best of us.'

Every eye turned to Pen shone with her reflection.

'I wish kindness and generosity could always win the day. I really do.' She seemed to mean it. She raised her voice. 'Mr Malachite, what does the law of Synecdoche say about this situation?'

The lawyer's response was instantaneous. 'An attack on the image of a thing is an attack on the thing itself.'

'Indeed,' Case said softly. 'And you, Countess, *Parva*, you are the image of us – all of us. All of those people you just heard speak. We were *all* victims when this scum attacked you. You wouldn't deny the people of London-Under-Glass, your people, their right to closure, would you? Their right to see justice done?'

Pen's lips moved, but no words came out. Her throat was empty.

We were all victims. She felt her body rebel at the hideous intimacy of that sentence.

Senator Case looked back down at the condemned man. 'Continue,' she said. Harry Blight started to keen. The doctor looked up for approval, and when the senator nodded, she slipped the needle in behind the condemned man's left ear.

Abruptly, Blight's voice cut out. The guards released him, and he crashed face-first onto the floor.

Pen craned over the balustrade. Was he dead? Was excitation the same as execution?

But no. The scrawny, wild-bearded man raised himself onto his good elbow and flopped onto his back. His chest rose and fell. He stirred and groaned.

Then he stiffened, sharply. His back arched. Tendons corded in his neck. Suddenly, he slammed his head back hard into the floor, leaving a vague smudge of blood on the marble.

Pen looked into his symmetrical, seam-split face. His eyes were open. At first, she thought they were just unfocused by the impact, but then she saw one of them close in a half-blink where the other did not. They were moving independently, focusing on opposite walls. His mouth twisted into a mean line as the muscles on either side of it pulled in different directions. He was suddenly disunited, as though the two halves of his sewn-together face were in the grip of separate minds.

Realisation jolted Pen hard. She remembered Espel's words the previous night: *Mirrorskin, grafted on when I was a baby* – and then her own voice: *It's a reflection.*

The id was a reflection, but then so was its wearer. London-Under-Glass was a city where reflections lived.

The ids were alive. Every half-face was sutured at birth to another consciousness.

Wake his id.

Harry Blight's left arm shook, pattering his knuckles against the floor. Gradually it bent. Blight's left hand began to move, jerkily at first and then more smoothly, more purposeful. It crept, spiderlike, up over his chest. Pen could see him flopping his right arm in its sling, but his shoulder had been ruined by a Chevalier bullet, and it could not intercept. Blight's face was hideously distorted now, the left side set in dreadful concentration, the right side stretched in fright.

The left hand reached his neck, fingers spread wide. The part of that conjoined thing that was still Harry Blight tried to scream, but his vocal chords were contested, and only a laboured hiss came out as those fingers closed around his throat.

From the galleries, the great and good of London-Under-Glass watched in silence as the body of Harry Blight strangled both the lives from it, his legs struggling weakly, like a newborn child's.

It took an age until he was still. Pen stared down at the body. A snatch of verse flashed into her head like a poisoned knife: *What immortal hand or eye, could frame thy fearful symmetry.*

She sagged slowly into her seat.

'—*you, Parva. We're doing this for you.*'

The red light on the camera blinked.

Back downstairs in the lobby, Pen peered around the heavy wooden door, watching as the Chevaliers outside herded her fans back. Raindrops splashed off their helmets and shoulder plates as they tried to clear a path from the doorway to the kerb. There was a festive air despite the weather; young girls and boys posed for pictures with the armoured men, holding up magazines on adverts featuring Parva Khan.

Pen set her teeth and tried very hard not to be sick. 'How can they do that?' she murmured. 'How can they act like nothing just happened?'

Espel spread her hands. Her face was clayish. She looked as sick as Pen felt.

'They don't know yet,' she said quietly. She hadn't met Pen's eye since leaving the courtroom. 'They've not been anywhere near a TV. They've been waiting for you.'

The black Chevalier SUV pulled out up front and hooted once.

'Here we go,' Pen muttered as Espel pulled the door back and they both pressed out into the clamour.

'*PARVACOUNTESSPARVAWILLYOUPARVAPLEASEOVERHERE-SIGNFORMYBABYPARVAMA'AMPARVAPLEASEPARVAWILLYOULOV ELOVELOVEPARVAPLEASEPLEASEPARVAOVERHERE!—*'

Through the curtain of noise, Pen's ears randomly filtered individual voices. She staggered, unbalanced by noise, her legs jellied by shock.

'Countess!'

'Parva!'

'Will you take a picture with me?'

'Will you sign my scars?'

This last came from behind her. She turned, drawn by the oddity of the request. All she could see was an arm sticking out from behind a restraining Chevalier, its pink-varnished fingers gripping a ballpoint. As Pen rounded her guard's broad back she saw the girl and faltered slightly.

She was maybe – *maybe* – fourteen, but if so, she was small for her age. She was white as paper, with bright blue eyes. She was wearing a pink T-shirt with *Khannible* scrawled across it in a looping calligraphic font made to look like barbed wire. There was a Parva Khan Official Calendar under her arm, and her cheeks . . .

The cuts were new, angry and red, the pale skin still puffy around them. She was a half-face, so the scars were completely symmetrical, and Pen guessed she was a sinistress, because they were an exact copy of those that Pen knew so well marked the left side of her own face.

Pen remembered the long queue stretching from the doorway of the knife parlour as the girl beamed at her, her eyes goggling out.

'Oh Mago!' she squeaked quietly. 'Oh *Mago!*'

'Your . . . scars?' Pen said. To her ears, she sounded even more stunned than the girl did.

It seemed to take the girl a moment to remember how to speak. 'I had to use up all my Mirrormass and Reflectionday presents for, like, *years*, but my Dad said I could. And . . . and . . . and . . .' she stammered. The question was obviously dreadfully important. 'Do you like them?'

'They're . . . amazing,' Pen managed.

The girl's symmetrical smile stretched even wider and she raised the pen hopefully.

Pen took the ballpoint. It wrote unevenly on the girl's pale skin, and she had to go over it twice. She signed with the same squiggly autograph that was in her passport, and added a couple of scratchy xs. The girl squeaked again with delight, and then bolted.

'Wait,' Pen started, 'you forgot your—'

'Countess?' Espel was holding open the door to the SUV. Rain was dripping off her chin. She looked oddly at Pen and at the ballpoint still gripped in her numb fingers as though it troubled her, then shook it off. Pen dived into the car and she slammed the door shut.

CHAPTER TWENTY

'Countess, welcome back.' Edward loomed by the doors to her apartment like a friendly iceberg. He started forward when he saw Pen's exhausted expression. 'Is everything all right?'

'It's been a draining afternoon for the countess, Ed.' Espel had recovered herself enough to be brisk. 'You watch the trial?'

'I . . . uh . . .' He paled and nodded.

'Then you'll understand why. Give Her Ladyship some space, would you?'

The bodyguard flushed and stepped back.

'Can you call downstairs and tell them not to expect Lady Khan for dinner? They can send something up instead. The countess needs to rest.'

Pen hadn't issued any such instruction, but she nodded her approval. She'd been so strung out with hope and fright, desperate for a confession that might lead her to Parva, and so appalled at what that could mean for her, that now she felt as limp as a popped balloon. She slid bonelessly down onto one of the white sofas, barely hearing the click as Espel closed the door behind them.

'You look like you could use a drink, Countess.'

Pen waved the suggestion away; she was in no mood to fake alcoholism right now.

'In that case do you mind if I do? I mean . . . *Mother mirror*,' Espel swore. 'An *excitation*?' Her voice was blank with disbelief. '*Live on air*? They've never . . .'

The bottle-neck clinked against the glass in Espel's unsteady hand. She slurped at the drink and the ice cubes rattled together.

'Anyone ever tell you, you drink too much?' Pen asked her.

Espel lowered the glass. 'A couple of people,' she said warily. 'From time to time. Why, is My Lady about to join them?'

Pen pinched the bridge of her nose, managed a smile. 'Your Lady isn't,' she said. 'But your friend? She might be.'

Espel swallowed. 'Are we friends, ma'am?'

'Must be,' Pen said. 'I wouldn't let anyone else do my makeup.'

Espel barked, a short flat laugh, but Pen hadn't been joking. She leaned back into the plush white upholstery and closed her eyes. She needed to think, to work out what to do, but Harry Blight's wide, disjointed eyes kept flashing in her mind, shattering any attempt at coherent thought. There was nothing, she told herself, that she could have done to save him.

Nothing, aside from confessing who she was on the spot.

There was a thud that must have been Espel putting the heavy-based glass down on the table, then a sliding sound, something hard moving over wood. Pen didn't open her eyes as she listened to the soft shush of feet across the carpet as the lady-in-waiting came towards her.

'Well then,' Espel's voice came softly from the space above her head, 'friend to friend, I've got to say, Countess, you look terrible.'

'Really?'

'Well no, not really: you look stunning – but by your standards, stunning is pretty damn rough.'

'Like you said,' Pen murmured, 'it's been a pretty damn rough day.'

'Why don't we see what we can do about that?'

Pen felt fingertips slip down the back of her head. She tensed slightly, and then relaxed again as Espel's thumb began to circle the knot of muscle at the base of her neck.

'Espel?'

'Yes, Countess?'

'Harry Blight's id – why did it attack him?'

She heard the parched sound of Espel swallowing before she answered, 'Because it hated him, Countess. It was his inverse, his opposite. His *Intimate Devil*—' She snorted the last as though it was an ancient and unfunny joke. 'Everything about him was its enemy. It was lying in wait, squatting in the dreams it shared with him, envious of his control of his body. When they woke it, it took its chance. He fought it, but . . . it was too strong.'

'And they *sew* these things onto you? Into your mind, your body?' Pen said incredulously. She squeezed her fist until the nails bit her palm. A flesh-memory of barbs. 'How do you stand it?'

'It's the price we pay . . .' Espel tailed off.

'To be beautiful?' Pen asked, remembering Driyard's words.

'No.' One of Espel's hands moved away and Pen imagined her touching her symmetrical face. 'Just to get by.' Her voice hardened slightly, and her fingers tightened on the back of Pen's neck.

Pen opened her eyes and looked up.

Espel was standing behind her, her spare hand holding her steeplejill's knife high. The blade wavered for a tiny fraction of an instant, then flashed down.

Pen didn't think, didn't speak, didn't waste time trying to block the blow. Her arm shot upwards, as fast as if barbed wire propelled it – *shortest distance to target* – her palm crunched into Espel's jaw.

The blonde girl reeled backwards. She knocked a sideboard, and pottery splinters tinkled like shrill wind-chimes as a vase shattered on the ground. Pen tried to rise, but Espel lurched over the back of the sofa and pinned her down. The blade flickered towards Pen's face. Her hands came up instinctively, her palms finding her attacker's wrist. She gripped, tried to twist, but Espel was too strong.

The knife pricked Pen's throat. Instinctively, she swallowed her scream.

Something black nestled against the white upholstery: the panic button Edward had given her was stuck between two of the cushions next to her knee. Pen wanted to reach for it, but both her hands were busy keeping the knife out of her neck. Gritting her teeth, she bent her legs up, twisted her hips towards the sofa back and dropped her left kneecap down hard on the black button.

Espel was oblivious. All her attention was focused on Pen's throat, on the flickering of the pulse she was striving to extinguish. She didn't even flinch when booted feet hammered up the corridor.

'Countess?' There was the thud of a meaty fist on the door. Edward called again, 'Countess Khan?'

Pen's teeth ground horribly. She felt the muscles in her arms vibrating like guitar strings, felt her eyes popping wide. Espel's symmetrical face reddened above her.

'Countess!' The doorknob was rattling now. Espel had locked it and Edward's pounding shook the door in its frame.

Pen's arms burned up and down their length. She imagined how easy it would be to let them slip, to let the blade in.

She looked at Espel. The blonde girl's face was screwed up in concentration, and something that looked like misery, but the knife didn't waver.

I should be dead by now, Pen thought. The steeplejill was strong, her muscles climb-and-scramble-hardened. And Espel had gravity on her side, all she had to do was lean in and the job would have been done. But she hadn't.

Why am I not dead?

Another, louder thud, followed by a shudder, and the sound of splintering wood.

They were both about to die: Pen at the point of the knife and Espel a few seconds later when the door buckled and the bodyguard raged in. The steeplejill must know she had bare fractions of a second to deliver the coup de grâce before they took her, and yet still the killing blow didn't come. Her symmetrical face was crumpled, red and tearful.

Before they take her, Pen thought. In her mind's eye she saw Harry Blight straining against himself, against the murderous parasite they'd awakened in his body.

Thud. Splinter. Crack. The shriek of a door turning on abused hinges. Espel jumped in reflex, the pressure on Pen's throat slackened fractionally and in that frantic heartbeat Pen made a choice.

She dragged Espel's knife-hand sideways and down behind the couch, grabbed the hem of her tunic and pulled. There was a flash of tightly screwed-up eyes – Espel wincing in anticipation of a head-butt – then Pen pressed her lips to hers.

She held her there: steeplejill, lady-in-waiting, friend, assassin. Her pulse thundered through her. The floorboards creaked. She could feel Edward watching them from the doorway.

'Oh – um – I see. I'll—'

Pen could almost hear the blood pouring into the bodyguard's cheeks as he blushed, but she didn't look, clinging instead to the desperate, farcical kiss. Seven more endless, echoing heartbeats passed, and she pointedly didn't look, ignoring Edward's looming presence. She considered making some enamoured noise, then decided against it. Everything was playing out in her ears: the floorboards creaking, more squealing hinges as the door closed, then sheepish splinter-on-splinter scuffles as the bodyguard did his best to make the ruined door latch behind him. Then at last, like oxygen to a drowning girl, came the fading sound of retreating footsteps.

Pen eased her lips back from her would-be killer's, but she didn't release her grip on Espel's wrist. After a moment, the knife thudded onto the floor.

Hesitantly, the blonde girl straightened from the back of the sofa. Her yellow fringe clung to her forehead in sweat-sticky tendrils. She blinked at Pen. She was trembling, her eyes so wide Pen almost felt she could read her thoughts through them.

I'm alive. Mother-fragging-Mirror, I'm alive – what the hell do I do now?

Pen stood, carefully picked up the knife and sat down again. Part of her was braced for another attack, but the aggression seemed to have leaked out of Espel. She slumped down next to Pen on the sofa, elbows on her knees. Head bowed like a condemned woman who's been waiting too long for the axe to fall.

'Well.' Pen's mouth was dry. 'That was . . .'

'Awkward?' Espel volunteered.

'A little understated, but sure. We'll go with that.'

They sat in silence for long moments. Then—

'Why?'

They'd both said the word at once.

Pen gave Espel a long look. 'I think,' she said, turning the knife over her in her hands, 'given the circumstances, I'll let you explain yourself first.'

The blonde girl looked at her, and then searched the ceiling as though looking for a place to begin. 'Well . . . see, I'm a fan—'

Abruptly, Pen began to laugh, bubbling out of her chest like hiccoughs.

'A fan?' she said at last. 'Isn't there usually some kind of ramp-up to this? You know, flowers, chocolates, threatening letters in the evening and dead pets at breakfast, *before* we get to the dagger-in-the-ribs bit?'

'No— I mean, I didn't come here to kill you,' Espel insisted. 'Not at first. I came because I . . .' She threw up her hands as if she knew how absurd it sounded. 'I *believed* in you: the first-ever mirrorborn face of the Lottery. You didn't grow up here. You weren't indoctrinated. I thought that if I could get to know you, if I could show you how things really were here, you'd side with us.'

'Us?' Pen broke in. 'Who's *us*?'

Espel's blue eyes appraised her coolly. 'Who do you think?'

Pen studied the steeplejill. A memory sparked – Espel looking up at her, drunkenness falling away, intense pride lighting her features as she'd said, '*Like you said, Countess, it's my face.*'

'You're Faceless, aren't you?' Pen breathed the name like she was afraid for it to touch her lips.

Espel tongued the inside of her mouth where Pen had hit her. 'You say that like we're a bad thing.'

'You attack immigrants in train stations; I think "bad" is pretty mild.'

'Oh get a grip. We do *not*.' Pen was startled by the contempt in Espel's voice. 'What in Mago's name would be the point?'

'Case said you strip the faces off them and sell them on the black market.'

'Case,' Espel countered, 'is a lying scumbag who has an election in six months and needs someone to blame. What's your excuse?'

'My excuse for what?'

'For not thinking it through,' Espel said. 'I mean, come on, the immigrants caught in those attacks were all half-faces. Offhand, I can't think of a better way to alienate our own fragging constituency – besides, stealing from the city's poorest at the *only* time in their lives they're under heavy guard? Oh yeah, that's every successful terrorist leader's idea of sustainable fucking financing.' She sneered in disgust.

'If anyone in the mirrorstocracy paid any damn attention to what's happening on the street, they'd know that half-faced immigrants have been going missing for years. And we've got sod-all to do with it.'

Some of the heat left her voice. 'The Faceless aren't ghouls who come in the night to rip people's faces off, Countess. Convincing you of that's what I was sent here for.'

'Wait—' Pen hesitated, appalled as her brain finally caught up with her ears. '—*sent?* You weren't sent – I rescued you . . . the slatestorm . . . the rope—'

Espel at least had the grace to look embarrassed. 'Like I said, I believed in you,' she said. 'That pretty much had to include believing you wouldn't let me be cut into some very symmetrical confetti by falling tile.' She shook her head at her luck. 'I just hoped for a connection, the start of a conversation. I had no idea you'd put me on staff.'

The hot-coals sensation of lost control burned in the pit of Pen's stomach. She felt humiliatingly stupid. She eyed Espel, and lifted the knife. 'So if your plan was to win me over,' she said coldly, 'how exactly does the "gut me like a fish in the market" bit fit into *that* strategy?'

'That was Harry Blight,' Espel said.

'Was it?' Pen looked sarcastically around the apartment, as though there was somewhere the dead man could be hiding. 'That's funny, it looked a lot like you.'

'I *mean*,' Espel said with exaggerated patience, 'Blight was what changed my mission. After that—' She hesitated, her voice still filled with disbelief. 'After that little *demonstration,* Garrison said we had to strike back, and I was the girl on the spot. You're the Face of the Lottery. It wasn't personal.'

Pen snorted. 'Ever heard the saying. "The personal is political"?'

'No. Why, you believe that?'

She tested the edge of the blade on her thumb. It was sharp, almost insinuating itself into her skin with the slightest pressure. She remembered it hovering over her throat.

'When the political is a knife severing *my* windpipe, I really do.'

Espel eyed the blade, but when she spoke again she sounded neither scared nor especially apologetic. 'London-Under-Glass doesn't even have a death penalty, did you know that?' she said. 'Legally, they can't kill you. They have to make you kill yourself, and only half-faces have ids to wake. What they did to Harry Blight,' she said bitterly, 'is a punishment they keep just for the poor.'

'That was the first time they've *ever* broadcast an Excitation. Before that they were always done behind closed doors, but the fact that the supposed crime was against *you* —that made them brazen. That minute of film was their way of telling every single half-faced man and woman in London-Under-Glass, "You don't *matter*. You don't *count*." That's how their power works, by convincing people they can't do anything about it.'

Pen glared at her, 'And killing me helps how, exactly?'

'Killing you would have proven them wrong,' Espel replied simply. 'Symbols matter, Countess; you're proof of it. There are good reasons you ought to be dead.'

'So why aren't I?' Pen asked quietly. 'I could have been. You just had to lean in. Why *not* kill me, if it meant that much to you? You could have been merrily martyred by now.'

Espel didn't answer.

'You couldn't do it,' Pen said, 'could you? Even though you had nothing to lose. Even though you knew you were going to die anyway, just for trying, when it came down to it, you couldn't.'

It was a long time before Espel answered, and when she did Pen barely heard her. 'I said I was the girl on the spot,' she whispered. 'I didn't say I was good at it.' She lapsed into silence, staring at the hands that had failed her.

After a long time she asked, 'What about me? Why am I still alive?'

Pen didn't answer. Espel's voice wavered a little as she asked, 'What are you going to do?'

Pen looked into the knife and her reflection stared back. It wasn't really her image she saw in it at all, she realised; it was her face inverted: *Parva*'s face. The bloody handprint goaded her. She was nowhere and she needed help. Parva needed help and she needed allies who knew the inverted city.

The obvious choice was the mirrorstocracy – confess all, and bid them redouble their efforts. But the horror of Harry Blight sprawled on the courtroom floor went through her skin like wire barbs and stopped her.

She thought of something Espel had said: *If the mirrorstocracy paid any damn attention to what happened on the streets . . .*

In her memory, between a pulled-down hood and a tugged-up bandana, a pair of eyes stared out at her. *We're everywhere.* Hadn't Espel just proven exactly that?

She thought of a red handprint on concrete, and then a black handprint on brick.

'*I thought,*' Espel had said, '*if I could get to know you, you'd side with us.*'

For a long time Pen sat listening to the roar and creak of the wind in the steel struts of the tower, remembering a tower in another city, walled only by air and the gaze of cranes' floodlights.

'The Faceless want me on side?' she said at last. 'Then take me to them.'

She could almost hear the sibilants stretch in her mouth as she said, 'I have a proposition for them.'

CHAPTER TWENTY-ONE

Borne on wings of blue fire, Beth burst from the tunnel into the synod's storerooms. She straddled the complex skeins of thermals that interwove like muscle fibres in the sewer-mander's back, her railing couched under her arm like a lance. Her jaw was set: pugnacious and determined.

She had chosen to come this way as a statement of intent, winding her way through the sewers and sub-basements, rather than presenting herself at the old dye-works. She was using the workmen's entrance, the back door, aggressively casual, if you could ever call a girl riding an eighteen-foot incandescent gas dragon *casual*. She was proving to herself as much as to them that this feared place was somewhere she could belong.

She looked at the cracks that veined her pavement-skinned hands. In a flash of memory, she returned to the synod's burning pool, hundreds of yards above on the surface, its chemicals coruscating her, changing her, making her this, whatever *this* was.

In a weird way, she was their child.

Get ready, boys. She swallowed hard. *The prodigal daughter's coming home.*

To her left, the wall reared up endlessly. Oil-drenched pigeons flapped to and from the glowing alcoves, tending the precise constellations of light. As she banked Oscar in towards the wall she tilted her head, trying to take them all in. They extended far beyond the corona that the sewermander's wings cast, above and below, flickering like sputtering candles in the dark.

It was far vaster and more complex than the cloud of semaphoring bulbs Candleman had built to model Fil's consciousness, but Beth could see the relationship: it was like a satellite photograph compared to a hand-scrawled map.

Her breath caught, and she almost laughed at the sheer ambition of it. Now she knew what she was looking at.

The Chemical Synod had bargained and bartered and built themselves the impossible from the scraps sold to them. They had built themselves a *mind*: a mind of a scale and complexity that awed Beth. Candleman's had been a reminder, a simplification. This was the real thing.

Closer, she thought to Oscar, reaching down through the fire to stroke his inner reptilian hide. He dipped his head in acknowledgement. Pigeons squawked and flapped angrily at them, but they had the sense or the instinct not to risk their oily feathers near Oscar's flame.

He brought them in close, hovering next to a shallow alcove about as high and wide as her torso. Inside, nestled like a relic in a shrine, was an intricately sculpted glass bottle. The liquid inside it glowed a queasy yellow; it roiled and scrabbled against the glass as though panicked.

There was a square of paper snagged under the base of the bottle, inscribed with three words in neat copperplate handwriting:

Fear - spiders. Irrational.

Beth took the paper and turned it over. On the reverse side was a stained black-and-white photo of a grumpy-looking kid in a denim jacket. She wondered if this was a 'before' snap, if the kid had looked any less mardy when she'd received whatever the Synod had paid her for her arachnophobia.

Oscar flitted from alcove to alcove, hovering over each like a hummingbird above a flower. Beth found a flask of pink-misted sentimentality, a box of powdered self-regard, beakers of various deep-rooted opinions, all with their own subtle, individual glow. In the fifth or sixth alcove was a conical, flat-bottomed flask, like one you might find in a school science lab. The fluid inside was viscous and metallic like mercury. It clung to the sides as she shook it.

Childhood outlooks, proclivities and memories, the label read. *Complete to sixteen.* And written in a smaller, tighter hand underneath: *Traumatic and unusual, dilute as required.*

Wondering, she turned the paper over and felt a little spark of shock jump up her spine.

Gazing out of the picture at her, his hair as chaotic as a riot and his lip caught in that perpetual cocky twist, was Filius Viae.

She hesitated, blinked. She started sweating. Her fingers twitched back towards the flask—

—and she heard the sharp snaps of Zippo lighter lids being opened close behind her.

'Ahhh, our new voiceless viceroy, come to visssit at lassst.'

She turned, reluctantly leaving the flask where it was. The Chemical Synod watched her from a tunnel-mouth in the opposite wall. As one, they waved to her.

'We wondered when you might wend your way back,' Johnny Naphtha hissed cordially from the apex of the perfect arrowhead formation they stood in. 'What, precisssely purchassess for uss the pleasure of your presssence?'

Beth curled the photo of Fil into her palm and steered Oscar away from the alcove. She urged him over to the synod's tunnel and hopped down onto the bricked floor. She felt the heat on her back slacken as the sewermander de-ignited and scrambled into her hood. He blinked out at the traders, wrinkling his snout at their acrid smell. Beth could feel the rapid tip-tapping of his reptilian heart.

Me too, mate, she thought at it. *Me too.*

She wondered briefly if the link between her and the sewermander went both ways: if the synod would look past her brave face and read her fear in the quailing form of her lizard.

Willing her own heart to slow, she turned to the wall and popped the cap from her magic marker. In fat black capitals, she scrawled her question.

WHAT DID YOU DO TO ME?

The synod turned to read it as one.

'Did I ssay viceroy?' Johnny murmured. 'Perhapss *vandal* would have had more veracity. Notwithsstanding your indifference to the aesstheticss of our ssstoress, the answer to your quesstion iss sstraightforward.'

They unfolded their hands in a gesture of revelation. 'We provided the ssservice purchasssed. What we did to you wass sssimply what wass asssked of uss.'

Beth shook her head firmly. With slow deliberation she wrote on the wall,

HE ASKED YOU TO MAKE ME LIKE HIM

She held out the picture of Fil.

Johnny made a small 'ah' as he took it. The breath was accompanied by the quiet pop of an oil-bubble bursting in the back of his throat.

'I think I ssee the sssource of the confussion. Making you "like him" might well have been the matter of the young massster's mind, but the wordss that left hiss *mouth* were, "*Make her as much a child of Mater Viae as you can.*"'

Beth started as Fil's voice came, perfectly replicated from between Johnny's pitch-threaded lips. The Pylon Spider must have traded them that talent; she wondered what they had got for it.

'And poor Filiusss, whatever he might have believed, wasss not a child of Mater Viae, wasss he?'

Beth could feel a hole opening in the pit of her stomach.

'There isss another rule, Misss Bradley, that musst alwayss be sssatisfied: the equation musst balance. Our transsssactionss musst alwaysss be *fair*. The sssubstrate bought must be of equal value to that which iss bargained with, and what Filiusss sssurrendered for you.' They rubbed their oily fingers and thumbs frictionlessly together. 'Not jusst commodified mortality but ssecuritissed memory as well? Now, that purchassess a far more dramatic transsformation than the petty pickingss Gutterglasss gave up for him in *hiss* turn.'

The synod leaned forward. The oil that covered them reflected the variegated alcove lights so they looked like they had galaxies inside them – they looked like they'd eaten the universe.

'"As much a child of Mater Viae as you can",' Johnny repeated. 'How do you sssupposse we could complete such a complex commisssion?'

With nauseating synchronicity each member of the synod pushed up first one, then the other of his jacket sleeves, waggling their dripping fingers. They pointed up the corridor.

The alcove they indicated had been gouged deeper than the others, and many smaller crevices had been hacked out along the inside of it. Beth walked over to it, picked up the photo lying on its dusty floor and froze.

'We held nothing back,' Johnny said quietly in her ear.

Not taking her eyes from the photograph, Beth put her hand to her face. She felt the needle-like spires through the skin over her jaw. She ran her hand up under her hood where her hair was taking on the rubbery viscosity of insulated cable. She glanced at the bottles inside the alcoves. There were many, many, and they were all empty.

As much like Mater Viae as you can.

The Chemical Synod had put every last drop of Mater Viae they had into remaking her.

She stepped back from the wall. She was still staring at the picture of what she was to become, but something familiar in her peripheral vision snagged her attention. She turned to look at it, and as it came into focus she made a shocked little noise and dropped the photograph.

'I ssuspect that it will quite sssuit you,' Johnny said as he framed her face with his black hands, 'once the change isss complete.'

But Beth wasn't listening. Her heart was clattering against her ribs like a demented railwraith. Unknowingly, she stepped on the photograph of Mater Viae, treading it into the bricks, as she lunged into the next alcove along.

'Wait—' Johnny began, but he broke off as she spun to face him, brandishing the little square of celluloid she'd snatched up. She bared her church-spire fangs in an urban snarl, and the synod, their grins suddenly alarmed, took a step back.

The photo Beth now brandished was of a girl in a scorched hijab. She stood in front of the camera looking terrified but determined.

Only the people you really love can scare you witless enough for true courage, Beth thought. She was scared now – *really* scared – but she would have dug her way out of her own grave to stand beside that girl.

'Ahhh, yess,' Johnny hissed diplomatically. 'We under-sstood you were acquainted with the insssurgent hossst. Alass, our ethicsss dissbar uss from divulging the delicaciess of our dealingsss with othersss—'

But Beth didn't need them to divulge anything; Pen's voice was already echoing back to her from their last conversation: '*Is there a way to go behind the mirrors? To where the Mirrorstocracy live?*'

She pulled her phone out of her pocket, thumbed through the sent messages. The words on the neon-lit screen condemned her.

The Chemical Synod might have a way, but the price they'd charge wouldn't be worth it.

Slowly, her eyes heavy with dread, she turned to read the label on the back of Pen's picture.

Memories. Parental x 2. (Stolen)*

And a little further down, an added note said:

*Hold as collateral for 21 days.
Transfer to project Isis in case of client default through failure to return (Est. 85% likelihood)

Beth lowered the photo slowly. *Eighty-five per cent? Pen, what have you got yourself into?*

Whatever it was, Beth knew where she needed to be. Her hand shook on the marker, and the words came out spidery on the wall.

WHAT YOU GAVE HER. GIVE ME THE SAME

The synod shook their heads. 'Quite imposssssible.'

I'LL

Beth faltered with her marker tip on the bricks. Fear fluttered in her chest at their eager grins, at the price they might claim in her desperation, but this was *Pen*, and there was no time to hesitate.

PAY she wrote. WHATEVER YOU ASK

Another symmetrical head-shake.

She blinked at them in confusion.

'Ass we sssaid, it iss out of the question,' Johnny Naphtha said. 'No matter what you ssssupplied, it would not ssuffice to sssecure you what you sssseek.'

With a snap of lighter-lids and a swish of oil-soaked fabric, the synod turned and began to walk away, past the walls riddled through with their treasures.

Wait! In her panic, Beth actually tried to say the word, but though she almost tore her throat with the strain of trying no sound came out. *Wait—*

She stretched out a hand after them. *Please.*

She watched their retreating backs, her mouth bitter with resentment and desperation and fury. She was shaking. Everything inside her felt heavy and red. She hated them. She hated them so much. For a giddy instant she thought, *I wish every single one of you smug, spiteful fucks was dead.*

Oscar flew from her hood.

The whip of his gaseous tail smacked her back against the wall as he dragged it behind him. He shot like a dun arrow straight at Johnny Naphtha's unprotected back. He lashed his flint-like tongue on the bricks and blue fire exploded in the tunnel.

Johnny spun on his heel and lashed out contemptuously with the edge of his hand. Oscar crashed into the wall and went out.

But the fire remained: flames danced over Johnny's immaculate cuffs, but did not consume them. His gasoline-drenched tie was a brand. He grinned out from the heart of a raging fireball as his four colleagues turned slowly beside him. They extended their arms back towards Beth, a nightmare blossoming of burning limbs.

The fire remained. The *Great* Fire.

Beth scrabbled backwards as images of the last time she'd seen that terrible weapon deployed flashed before her: the Demolition Fields at St Paul's, the synod's burning hands melting through the steel of Reach's cranes.

The five burning men adjusted their cuffs. They took synchronised steps, bearing down on her with stately malice.

'Ssilly girl.' Johnny's voice was cold. 'Foolissh deity. Did you seriously suppose that your sssorry puisssance would prevail againsst ussss?'

All too quickly they were standing over her. Five burning hands reached for her as though in greeting. Beth felt their fire like a weight on her chest, dragging the air from her lungs. She shrieked silently as Johnny Naphtha's fingers curled around her wrist, waiting for the pain and the bubbling hiss of evaporating flesh.

It was only when she opened her eyes that she realised

she'd closed them. She recoiled from the glare as Johnny grinned stupidly at her wrist where he was holding it. The flames washed over Beth's skin, but would not take. Beth stared at his oily fingers and the flames bobbed and ducked under her gaze as though they were bowing.

The Great Fire, she thought. *Mater Viae's greatest weapon.*

Mater Viae's—

Her lip curled as she watched the synod realise their mistake. Whatever properties of Mater Viae's they'd poured into her, they'd made her proof against the Street Goddess' flame.

She snarled silently and wrenched her wrist free. She planted her bare feet and drew everything she could from the deep London bricks. She sucked up the power of church walls as they strained under vaulted roofs, and the power of water torrents crashing through treatment plants, of car tyres accelerating on tarmac, of voltage coursing through cables. She drew it all deep into the core of her. Then, just when she felt like she would burst under the pressure of it, she shoved Johnny Naphtha in the chest.

He flew backwards, his jacket and tie flapping and spraying gouts of burning oil. His fellows, bound to him by invisible bonds of symmetry, sprawled like wind-flattened grass. Their sinuous grace lost, they grubbed about on the floor, trying to stand.

Beth knelt and scooped up Oscar. The little lizard squeaked pathetically, twisting against her palm. His tail was broken. She could feel the little eddies of gas on her skin where he tried and failed to summon his exo-self.

There was still enough energy in her to make her chest ache. She stared at the oil-drenched men who killed through consent and stole through barter. She could feel her loathing for them pounding through her with every beat of her heart. So much fury it seemed impossible to contain, she could feel it overflowing into the floor through her feet. She was shaking, and the world seemed to shake along with her as she reached for her spear—

—which juddered and bounced away from her hand.

Beth hesitated. The world didn't *seem* to shake, she realised; it really *was* shaking. The tunnel was convulsing beneath her, like an earthquake.

The synod were staring at the walls of their storeroom, and Beth followed their gaze. In the space between two alcoves the surface of the bricks was bubbling up, stretching to translucency. Beth could see an organic shape underneath it, squirming and pushing.

With a loud *snap* and a spray of brickdust the caul broke. Dark-red fingers emerged from the wall as through thick mud. A series of snapping sounds told Beth that similar eruptions had taken place around the walls, but she couldn't tear her eyes from this one uncanny birth.

Above the hand, something shoved itself out of the wall: a man's face, hollow-eyed and gaping-mouthed. A brick-red leg emerged suddenly and violently and placed itself uncertainly on the floor. Dark red veins bulged against dark-red skin and then, with an enormous effort, the man dragged himself free of the wall. The brick resealed behind him like putty.

He glistened in the light from the still-burning synod as if he was covered in blood.

The tunnel felt suddenly close and cramped. Beth turned and found herself hemmed in on all sides by the crimson men.

Did I summon you? Beth thought incredulously. Had she somehow called Masonry Men from across the city to her aid?

But they didn't even acknowledge her; their brick gazes were fixed on the Chemical Synod.

Beth took a sharp little breath: she could feel them, she realised; she could *sense* them the same way she sensed Oscar – that little electric thrill beneath the forehead. Using an instinct she didn't even know she possessed, she *tensed* her mind and then threw herself into them – and found herself running through their minds like they were interconnected attic spaces along a terrace, looking out of their eyes as if they were windows. Her perspective on the startled synod shifted with every pair of eyes. She encountered no resist-ance, no foreign thoughts, no new impulses or old memories, nothing but her own rage, choking the space like red dust.

The Masonry Men were empty.

She looked down at them from inside themselves and saw the liquid mortar still clinging to them like afterbirth.

I made them. They're part *of me*, she thought giddily. *They're part of the City.*

Victory and anger swelled inside her. She poured herself back into her little army and attacked.

The front wave of clay soldiers hurled themselves onto the burning men. Johnny Naphtha and his brothers flailed at them in panic and fury, but Beth felt heat but no pain as their hands incinerated brick limbs. She hurled her mindless borrowed bodies at them. Every time she blinked, the sepia photo of Pen was waiting behind her eyelids, behind *all* of their eyelids. The synod stumbled, fell back lashing out at the press of bipedal masonry. Beth advanced on them with her little zombie force, herding them until they toed the brink of their own abyss.

Beth snarled around her church-spire teeth – but stumbled with her next step as her leg gave out under her. She crumpled to one knee. and suddenly realised she was trembling with exhaustion: these few seconds of animating the city had sapped her. Ahead of her, the front rank of brick men began to sink back into the floor as though into quicksand.

Johnny Naphtha's grin widened, a black hole in his burning face, and he sprang forward. Clay bodies smouldered and blackened and burned away under his touch, their brick flesh incinerated where they tried to grapple him. Johnny's brothers fountained outwards in a complex symmetry of flame. When they reached the tunnel walls, they groped into the alcoves.

Beth's stomach plunged. They'd learned fast from their earlier error. There would be weapons they *could* use against her somewhere in these stores.

Their stores.

The thought went through her head like a lightning bolt and with the last of her energy, she pulled her warriors back from the burning synod and threw them at the walls. They barely disturbed the surface as they sank in.

Beth collapsed forward onto her hands.

The synod hesitated a moment, then, as one, they smoothed their burning hair. They almost strutted as they approached.

Beth was so tired she could barely raise her hand. They grinned wider at the gesture; she supposed they thought it was begging, or supplication. She extended her index finger and jerked it to either side.

The synod looked where she was pointing – and froze.

Emerging from the back wall of every alcove, hovering over every twisted glass bottle, every precious, hoarded chemical, was a brick fist.

Beth clenched her fingers and slowly turned her hand to vertical. When her fist fell, the gesture promised, so would all the others.

The synod guttered out. Their suits and eyes and grins were charcoal-grey.

'Desssissst.' Johnny Naphtha sprayed ash from his mouth. His voice was as even as ever, but Beth thought she could detect something pleading in it. 'Our storesss are irreplace-able.'

Beth stared at them. In a few seconds, she wouldn't have the energy to hold her own hand up, let alone five dozen others made of sewer brick.

You know what I want, she thought.

'We cannot sssupply you with the ssubstance your friend requisssitioned' – their own hands were raised, palms held outwards in desperate calming gestures – 'ssimply becausse we do not posssesss it. We had a ssseverely limited ssupply. We ssstrove to analysse it, but the sskill to ssynthesise it remainss beyond usss.'

He hissed in alarm when Beth jerked her hand and said hurriedly, 'Sstill, perhapss there iss a way we can asssisst. The compound we gave the ssteel insurgent came from a cusstomer in part-payment, sssupplementing an aessthetic sssecurity. That cusstomer sstill livess, albeit much transss-formed. We can perhapss' – the shape the synod made before her was cringingly eager – 'refer you?'

Slowly, Beth uncurled her fist, extending her hand out flat. It wasn't until Johnny reached out and shook it, sealing the deal, that she withdrew from the empty minds of the Masonry Men and their brick hands subsided into the walls. Where the bricks resealed, they left ripples on the walls, like scars.

With a flutter of oily wings, a pigeon approached her, a photograph in its beak.

For a second, Beth didn't recognise the subject. It was human, or it looked like it, but she couldn't tell if it was a man or a woman. The person was bundled up in a heavy, high-collared coat. Beth couldn't see much of the face other than a sharp jutting chin and a fringe of dark hair that covered the eyes, but still there was something indefinably familiar about the image.

She froze.

Much transformed . . . sssupplementing an aessthetic sssecurity . . .

A memory surfaced: standing on garbage slopes opposite a woman who wept sour-milk tears from eggshell eyes.

'*What did the synod make you give up?*' she'd asked Gutterglass, demanding to know the price she'd paid for Fil's shabby approximation of divinity. '*What did you used to be?*'

She heard the trash-spirit's voice now, propelled up from her memory by bubblegum and rubber-band vocal chords.

'*Beautiful,*' she'd said.

Beth left the Chemical Synod's store on foot; even as exhausted as she was, her city-steps bore her through the tunnels at an inhuman pace. The synod followed behind her, flowing dark on dark, eager to usher her out.

They gave no sign that they'd noticed when a single redbrick hand had flashed back through the wall behind them and grabbed Filius Viae's bottled memories in its crimson fist.

CHAPTER TWENTY-TWO

Pen leaned out over London-Under-Glass, daring herself, letting her weight hang forward, steadying herself with fingertips and knees on the inside of the window frame. She felt fear and giddy courage rush with the blood to her head. She had a bat's-eye view. The reflected city's lesser towers rose towards her like stalagmites, lights glittering against the darkness like mica.

She waited, for hours, it seemed. The drone of passing cars grew less and less frequent, until the wind cracking in her ears was the only sound. It was deep night, and the streets were as clear as they were going to get. If the most famous face in London-Under-Glass was ever going to be able to walk her pavements unnoticed, it was now.

'Ready?' Espel asked from behind her.

Pen hesitated, then nodded. Before her breath frosted the windowpane, she saw her reflection. Happily, she didn't look anywhere near as scared as she felt.

Espel eased the door open and they slipped out and crept

down the hallways of the sleeping palace with cartoonish care.

'There's a service lift at the back,' Espel whispered. 'To keep unsightly things like laundry and rubbish and stray servants and you and me out of sight. There's cameras and sentries on the lobby 24/7 and I for one don't fancy explaining why we're trying to sneak you out without any bodyguards in the middle of the night. We can leave through the kitchen. There's a nice cosy rubbish chute there we can squeeze out of.'

Silence distilled their footsteps, making them echo loudly in Pen's ears. 'What do we do if someone comes?' she whispered nervously.

'No clue,' Espel whispered back. 'You're the master strategist. This was all your idea.'

'Oh . . . yeah.'

'You could always kiss me again. It worked pretty well last time.'

Pen's heartbeat quickened. For no reason she could think of she felt a flush in her cheeks. She covered with a snort. 'Wishful thinking'll get you nowhere,' she said.

'Actually, Countess, wishful thinking's the only thing that's ever got me anywhere,' Espel replied, and smiled beautifully in the dark.

The kitchen's stainless-steel surfaces glowed green in the emergency exit light. In the reflection of a chrome refrigerator door Pen watched a mouse scurry over lino in another kitchen in another city. There was a rustling behind her, and the *plack* of a lid being prised off Tupperware. Pen turned to see Espel holding a chunk of chocolate brownie with a bite already taken out of it.

'You're taking time out for desert?' Pen demanded incredulously.

Espel's mouth was full, but her expression was eloquent, all hurt innocence: *What?* She had to work her way through the oversized bite before she could answer. 'Sorry, it's been kind of a busy evening, Countess. I've not had time for dinner, and I make bad decisions when I'm hungry.'

'Really? Doesn't bloody show,' Pen hissed. 'I really don't think this is the time and place for a midnight snack—'

Espel broke her off a hunk. 'I am willing to bet this'll change your mind,' she said.

Pen hesitated. Just for a second an entrenched part of her rebelled at the idea of the cake, even panicked a bit – but Espel was smiling as she offered it, and the inhibition broke in a little carefree shiver.

Pen bit down into rich gooey chocolateyness. Stolen midnight-escape brownie, seasoned with a little hysteria was, it turned out, the most delicious thing in the universe.

'S'all right,' she said through the second mouthful. 'A bit too much cocoa—'

Espel smiled. 'I'll make you a better one sometime. You feeling better?'

Another mouthful of brownie and a lungful of air, and Pen had a grip on her hysterics. 'Better,' she confirmed. 'How about you? How's the decision-making?'

'Am I in the palace kitchens, taking a cake-break while leading the Face of the Looking-Glass Lottery to put a mystery proposal to the insurgents who ordered me to kill her?'

'Sure.'

'Then let's assume it's still screwed.'

They wolfed down the rest of the brownie, then greedily sucked the last of it off their fingers.

'You've got chocolate on your lips.' Espel told her.

'So have you. Okay, then. Let's go and meet your terrorist friends.'

The rubbish chute was as cosy as advertised. When Espel dragged the hatch aside a sour fug gusted over them. They stared into it together: it was a throat made of rotten vegetables and wetted with sour milk, and it reminded Pen of Gutterglass, the trash avatar, and that made her think of Beth, and all of a sudden her chest was so tight she snatched at her breath and choked.

From somewhere deep below them, a sound echoed up the shaft: a distant crack of air.

Pen glanced at Espel. 'What was that?'

'No idea – the incinerator, maybe?'

'*Incinerator?*'

'Yeah, there's a trapdoor in the floor of the shaft they use when they want to burn the garbage instead of just sending it to landfill – no need to look at me like that,' Espel added cheerily. 'They only open it when they've got a ton of paper or cardboard or something, otherwise it just stinks the place out.'

'And you're willing to stake your *life* on that?'

Espel gave her a long look. 'What have I done today to give you the impression that hanging onto my life is a big priority for me?'

And with those reassuring words, she hopped onto the lip of the chute, swung her legs round and vanished into the dark. Pen snatched a breath against the smell and perched on the lip of the chute.

Another distant crack of air echoed up and she shot a worried look down the shaft. *Oh well*, she thought. *It's either this, or go back to bed.*

She pushed off.

A couple of heartbeats later, Pen landed in a pile of squashy, overstuffed binbags. She lay back, letting the cool night air wash over her, but Espel wouldn't let them idle.

'Come on, time to move.' She perched easily on the edge of the skip, looking nervously towards the mouth of the alleyway they'd dropped into. 'I'll try and stick to the back ways where I can, but we've still got about three miles of wide-open streets to cover before we get to the Kennels.'

'The Kennels?'

'Yes, Countess.' Espel looked at her, rolling up her sleeves over her wiry arms. 'You didn't think the Council of the Faceless would be holed up in some swanky Tower Hamlets postcode, did you? We're heading to the real badlands tonight. I'm taking you to Kensington.'

CHAPTER TWENTY-THREE

They ran into the night, past the uncanny architecture. Espel set a punishing pace, but Pen found she could keep up. She relished the burn in her chest, the chance to push her body. She glanced over the edge of London Bridge as they crossed the river. Even in the streetlamp light, she could see the water was bloody with dissolved brickdust. Pen faltered; for a moment she thought she saw an eye blink at her from one of the water's short-lived facets.

'*Quit gawping!*' Espel tugged on her hand, but Pen resisted, still staring at the spot where the eye had been. Espel pointed upriver, where a barge puttered under Southwark Bridge. Dark shapes moved on the deck, pausing to bend low over the side. 'They'll recognise you.'

'They're miles away,' Pen protested.

'They're face-fishers,' Espel said, 'panning for cheap treasure. Any idea the kind of eyesight it takes to spot an eyelash floating in the river? And the completely *silly* vision it takes to do it at night? If they look up, they'll see you, and then they'll tell all their friends and we'll be wading through a horde of adoring fans to see the Faceless. So *move.*'

Where they could, they clung to narrow, empty lanes, which forced them to zigzag across the mirror-image of the Square Mile. Back home, this was the city's financial centre. Here, restaurants and chi-chi bars jostled with garishly out-fitted knife parlour pop-ups with kids in sleeping bags queuing outside. Pen shuddered to see them, too excited to sleep, chatting and rubbing their hands together against the cold.

They ran along the embankment, the metal-latticed underside of Blackfriars Bridge passing over their heads. Across the river, the Lottery billboard was floodlit, allowing Pen's mirror-sister to bathe London-Under-Glass in her smile twenty-four hours a day. Exactly as in her own city, the stranded arches and buttresses of the old demolished rail bridge stood clear of the water like the petrified remains of a sea-monster.

They ran until Pen's feet throbbed and she felt little elec-tric shocks jumping through her forearms as she pumped them, and then they ran some more.

Glass and steel gave way to concrete, and then to old red-brick residential streets. Graffiti looped and whorled over the walls, peeling posters advertised rock acts, doorsteps became litter-cluttered. The buildings around them grew weirder, more distorted, their roofs and gables clotted with rained-down masonry. They started to have to hurdle drifts of set mortar where they jutted out into the street.

'Not . . . being . . . rude . . .' Pen managed between gasps, 'but . . . ain't it your . . . colleagues' job to . . . clear this . . . stuff?'

'Good precipitecture crews are expensive – not that us jills and jacks see much of it ourselves, mind.' Espel wasn't remotely out of breath. 'And this borough's dirt-poor. What with the demand from the big East End mansions and the government contracts, neighbourhoods like this just can't hope to afford us. The Royal Borough of Kensington and Chelsea,' she muttered as she vaulted a heap of crushed bits of bollard, 'home, sweet shitty home. It's good to be back.'

'How . . . does . . . anyone . . . get a *car* . . . down here?' Pen asked.

Espel somehow managed to spare the breath for a laugh. 'Cars? You're kidding, right? We can barely afford mascara. We damn sure don't have *cars*.'

The obstacles grew higher, jagged parapets of brick the girls had to scramble over. Espel climbed with an easy control. Her shirt rode up where she reached for an overhang and Pen found herself watching the muscles in her lower back work. It was hypnotic. Pen reached for handholds blind, not wanting to take her eyes from that pale ellipse of revealed skin. She suddenly thought of Espel watching *her* as she'd put the wire dress on her, and her face began to heat up.

She felt her fingers miss their grip a fraction of a second before the bottom dropped out of her stomach. She landed in an inelegant heap at the base of the overhang, chastised by a trickle of small stones that bounced off her head.

'*Countess!*' Espel hissed in frustration from the top of the drift. 'Pay attention, would you?'

Pen blushed furiously and looked hurriedly away from the steeplejill. She found her eyes no more than an inch from the wall.

Pay attention, would you?

The mortar here was unnaturally smooth: fine, evenly spaced grooves ran through it as though it had been cut with tiny teeth. 'Wait, what the—? Es, this can't have just fallen naturally. It's been worked with tools. It's—' She hesitated and then said, 'It's deliberate, isn't it?'

Espel, crouched at the top of the drift, said nothing.

We don't have cars, Pen thought. 'They're *roadblocks*,' she said, understanding at last. The steeplejills and jacks who'd grown up in this poor zone had made it impassable to the cars of the rich – and not just their cars. Pen eyed a chunk of railing spiking from one of the brick drifts and remembered the Chevaliers' strange mounts. You wouldn't get a horse to charge up this street, no matter how well trained it was.

'*Shhh . . .*' Espel laid a finger on her lips 'I have no idea what you're implying – and even if I did, it would be completely illegal.' But there was a wicked smile on her symmetrical face.

A flash of memory brought up news footage of the Iraq war: gunshots crackling in the background as American troops fought house to house. Pen saw the kind of nightmare it would be to take these streets that way. She felt a kind of awed admiration. On the quiet, Espel and her friends had turned this little nook of London-Under-Glass into a fortress.

The rained-down architecture loomed and curved over them like a landscape from a child's nightmare. Espel had just led Pen under the jut of one cliff-like bay window when a fine curtain of dust trickled down in front of them.

'Wait,' the steeplejill hissed, blocking Pen's path with an arm. She bent forward low over the ground, frozen but for a twitch around the eyes, like an animal listening for a predator. Pen felt her heart begin to drum. She tried to listen to, to strain some meaning from the city's soft night-time noise.

There was a scratching overhead. Espel looked slowly upwards, and Pen followed her gaze.

More than fifty feet above them, just poking over the edge of the roof of the house, naked pink and squashy-looking was unmistakably a set of bare toes.

Espel blanched, and Pen barely had time to think, *What, assassins can't afford shoes any more?* before the skinny blonde girl was away, scrambling up the house front with a steeplejill's ease. The ridges of precipitecture soon obscured her. Not sure what else to do, Pen hunkered down, looked up at the suspicious toes and listened.

'Hey.' Espel's voice was all nonchalance as it drifted down. 'What's up?'

The toes immediately shifted, pointing resolutely in the opposite direction from the one the steeplejill had spoken from.

'It's okay,' Espel said gently. 'I won't look unless you want me to.'

A little choked noise came from above the toes, acknow-ledgement in what might have been a girl's voice.

She turned away, Pen thought. *She can't cover her face – that gets you beaten up here – but she doesn't want Espel to see.*

'What happened to it?' Espel's voice was so soft Pen could barely hear it.

The owner of the toes choked back snot. Her answering voice was tear-raw and frightened.

'Sold it,' she whispered.

'Debts?'

A silence that might have included a nod.

'Loan sharks?' A darkness trickled into Espel's voice like blood into water. 'Round here? Tell me who and I'll—'

'No,' the other girl whispered. Her syllables were unsteady, like she was shaking, but whether that was fear or cold, Pen couldn't tell. 'Just . . . skin-taxes. Me ma fell behind and I thought, I thought I could help . . .' She tailed off.

The scuffed tips of Espel's boots appeared next to the toes over the edge of the roof.

'Let me guess,' she said. 'The girls at school didn't think the new look suited?'

Another possibly-nod-filled silence.

'Well, they're fools then.'

A tear-choked laugh. 'You think so?' the voice above the toes asked.

'Definitely,' the steeplejill said. 'Fuck them, and fuck what

252

they think. It's your face. Not theirs, yours. It bears the marks of the choices you made. Be proud of that. I would be.'

'Really?' The owner of the toes sounded like she barely believed that was possible.

'Really.' Espel's voice held no doubt at all. 'With *your* choices? I'd be proud as anything.'

They stood for a while together in silence. Pen watched the toes wriggle in the cold. She heard their owner's teeth chatter, and an embarrassed laugh. The toes shuffled back out of sight.

'So,' Espel said, 'I ask again, what's up?'

'Nothing,' the girl said. She sounded almost shy. 'I'm just looking at the view.'

'Yeah?'

'Yeah.'

'Okay then.'

Pen heard the scuffle and scratch of climbing, more dust trickled and Espel reappeared, shuffling crabwise down over a window ledge.

'Wait . . .' The girl's voice drifted from the roof. 'The way you talk – you must be—? Are you one of . . . one of *them*?'

Espel was close enough for Pen to see her symmetrical smile.

'Go back inside,' she called back. 'Get some sleep.'

The steeplejill dropped the last six feet and landed in a crouch. As she straightened up, her smile slid away. Anger made her symmetrical face as dark as a blood-bruise.

'What was it?' Pen asked, unable to stop herself. 'What did she sell?'

'Eyebrow.'

'Seriously?' Pen's surprise almost made her laugh, but she managed to stifle it. 'That's all? Just an *eyebrow* and she was going to . . . that'd drive her to—?' She looked up into the achingly empty distance the roof.

Espel rounded on Pen, her expression far more violent than when she'd had a knife in her hand. 'Oh, you don't think that's *enough*?' she hissed. 'Hard as it may be for perfect little you with all your perfect little scars to understand, all that girl *had* was her half a face. She needed every bit of it. All right she was never going to be beautiful, but she could get by, she was *okay*.'

She shook her head slowly. 'Not any more. She's ugly now – that's what they'll say, those hyenas she used to call friends. She's slipped below them, and they won't be seen with her any more. She'll be getting whispers and muttered comments and chickenshit anonymous messages online.' Espel's lip curled in disgust. 'The system rolls into action.'

Pen blinked. 'I – I don't understand,' she said.

Espel's expression was almost pitying. 'Why do you think they make it illegal to cover your face, Countess?' she said. 'They *want* us to look at each other like that, constantly judging each other, ranking each other. And we *all* do it too.'

She shrugged, angry and helpless. 'Half-faces can't afford reflections. We can't see ourselves the way the mirrorstocracy do. We have to rely on other people's eyes to tell us what we're worth. And they've turned every pair of eyes in the

254

city into their weapon. Imagine what those eyes are telling that poor girl now.' Espel jerked her head up at the roof. 'That she's *lesser.*' She spat the words. 'That she's *partial.* Imagine how she'll feel every time she sees a billboard of you and it reminds her of what she lacks.

'Why do you think we hate the Lottery so much? Every stamped ticket is a surrender: it's one of us holding up our hands and saying, "I'm not good enough. I'm ugly and worthless."' Her blue eyes were hard in the night. 'Compared to people like you.'

People like you. Pen recoiled hard from those three words, just like she always had. Strands of anger wound themselves around her throat like wires. She wanted to protest, to say, *Of course I know.* She burned to talk of scars and surgery and camouflage makeup.

Instead, she said, 'In the Old City, where I came from, it's the other way around. It's symmetry that's beautiful.'

'I've heard,' Espel said. 'So?'

'So: this thing – beauty? – it's arbitrary. People just make it up.'

Espel snorted, unimpressed. 'Just 'cause something's made up, doesn't mean it's not real.'

'I know,' Pen said. 'But just because it's real now doesn't mean it has to be forever.'

Espel held her gaze for a heartbeat, then her lip quirked. She unslung the bag from her shoulder and yanked down the zip. Stuffed inside were two black hoodies and a pair of black cotton bandanas.

With a little lurch Pen remembered the video Margaret Case had shown her, the two hooded figures and the screaming blank unface between them. Sweat beaded clammily between her headscarf and scalp.

'Careful, Countess. Keep talking like that, people might mistake you for a revolutionary.

CHAPTER TWENTY-FOUR

As they wound their way deeper into the reflected city, they left the roads behind. Canyons of jagged, rained-down brick rose around them, with walls dozens of feet high. They squeezed through narrow crevasses and wriggled on their bellies through tiny cracks in apparent dead ends. There was no glass or metal to reflect here; London had no answer to this place. It existed only here.

The walls around them pressed in tighter and rose higher, shutting out everything but a narrow sliver of sky, even the tallest landmarks. They arched overhead in almost organic curves, like fingers grasping fingers. The masonry was rough, but like the roadblocks, obviously worked with tools.

A shiver of realisation went down Pen's neck. *It's a labyrinth*, she thought.

In the heart of their slum neighbourhood, hidden in the mess of its sheer neglect, the Kennels' steeplejacks had carved out a fastness.

Pen snatched a look up. Dark shapes moved on top of the walls above them. Hooded figures picked their way over the bricks with ease, occasionally silhouetted against the city night's dull burnish. It was too dark to see their eyes, but Pen could feel their gazes on her, accusing her.

Espel looked back at them once and nodded, but didn't say anything. The figures tailed them in silence, like too many shadows.

Espel zigzagged. She took turn after turn after turn, stopping at last in a blank-faced cul-de-sac. She gave a tremulous little exhalation, and, behind them, Pen heard the figures drop into the alley. The crunch of their boots on the gravel was like breaking bones.

'Espel?' she said uncertainly.

'Don't fight it, Parva,' Espel said, still facing the wall. ' It has to be this way.'

Sudden, eager hands reached around from behind Pen and grabbed her wrists and she bit back a cry as her arms were twisted into the small of her back and lashed with slippery-feeling cord. A sour-smelling cloth was pushed over her face, shutting out the world. Hands grabbed her under her arms and under her knees. Her pulse began to slam as she was lifted into the air.

Control, Pen, she thought furiously. *Stay in control.*

Through the cloth, she heard Espel's voice harden into a tone of command. 'Bring her.'

The figures holding Pen began to run.

Pen had no idea how long she was carried, but the acrobatics of her stomach acid told her there were plenty of sharp corners. Panic welled up in her at being powerless, at her lack of control, at the mob of hands that gripped her. She shut her eyes, a redundant gesture under the hood, and told herself, *You chose this, Pen. They're taking you where you wanted to go. It's no different to a car . . .*

It's all you.

At last their jolting progress stopped and Pen was dumped unceremoniously onto dusty-smelling ground. Her hood was dragged clear and she blinked to clear her eyes.

A familiar shudder passed through her. It was a demolition site.

A topography of slain architecture surrounded her. A clutch of houses had been torn down, leaving a wide court-yard, bounded on all sides by the labyrinth. Foundations poked through the ground like the stubs of burned crops and Pen was ambushed by memory – the screams of machinery, brick bodies torn under digger-jaws. The cords seemed to crawl up her wrists as though they were alive.

She shook herself and cast around. This rubble was just rubble: cold, inanimate clay.

Everywhere, perched on the masonry like flocks of carrion birds, were black-clad figures, rank upon rank of them. The light was better in this open place and Pen could see them more clearly. They were all wearing hoodies, with bandanas drawn up over their mouths. They reminded her of the crowd of local estate kids who sometimes clustered around the corner shop on her street, except that she couldn't imagine those kids waiting like this, in disciplined, patient quiet. Only their eyes were visible in their illicitly hidden faces.

One of them sprawled indolently on a pile of rubble like a prince on his father's throne. He shifted and sat forward, staring at her from under his hood. Pen could make out a powerful frame under the jumper. His hands were thick and rough as though from manual labour. Some of the others' gazes flickered towards him for direction. *This must be Garrison Cray.* She felt a prickle on the back of her neck. This was the man who'd ordered her killed.

Well, might as well stand up, then.

That was easier said than done, with her hands bound, but no one tried to stop her and she managed to lurch to her feet. Cray stood too, keeping pace with her, as though in this place without mirrors he was playing at being her reflection. It felt strangely intimate.

When he spoke, his voice was surprisingly youthful. 'What do you want?'

It was a simple question. The answer was simple too. 'I want you to help me find Parva Khan,' she said.

The atmosphere in the yard shifted. There were confused mutterings and a snatch of laughter. The fabric of Cray's bandana shifted in a way that might have suggested a smile underneath.

And then he moved. He crossed the space between them with sinuous speed. His arm moved and Pen's left eye was suddenly blinded, chilly metal pressing against the socket. It took a second for her to refocus her right eye and see the gun barrel receding from her blind spot, Cray's pale fingers curling around the grip.

'Garrison!' Espel's voice was shrill with alarm. Even wrapped up in her hoodie and scarf, Pen recognised her as she started forward, hand outstretched. 'What are you—?'

'It's all right, Espel,' Pen called to her. 'If your boss thinks that his gun is the scariest thing I've ever had against my eye, he's got another think coming.'

The words coming out of her mouth didn't sound like her, Pen realised. They sounded like Beth, cornered and wounded and brave: another not-quite-her to hide behind.

Cray peered at her. His eyes were the same pale blue as Espel's, Pen realised, but on him the colour reminded her of ice rather than sky. 'This will go a lot faster if you don't try to be funny,' he advised.

'It'd go even faster than that if *you* didn't try to look hard,' Pen countered.

Cray snorted, rippling his bandana. There was something wrong with that bandana, Pen realised. The fabric sat too close to the skin.

'Got quite the mouth on you, don't you?'

Pen sucked her reconstructed lip between her teeth, and then she did smile around it. 'Do you like it?' she said. 'It's new.'

Cray's thumb curled up behind the hammer of the pistol and cocked it: an elegant expression of thinning patience.

'You don't want to do that.' Pen forced bravado in past the increasing tightness in her chest. She was dimly aware that her confidence was all she had going for her. She'd delivered herself to him when she knew he wanted her dead and he wanted to know why.

What do you want? he'd asked her. As long as he was curious, she was breathing.

'Shooting me in the face,' she went on. 'Won't that dent my resale value?'

'What?'

'That's what you do to mirrorstocrats, isn't it?' Pen said. The fear made her so giddy it almost felt like courage. 'Strip their faces off them?'

For an awful split second she thought she'd miscalculated. She saw Cray's knuckles pale and every muscle in her locked at the thought of the bullet chewing through her eye and into her brain.

But it never came. Instead Cray lowered his gun and stepped back. 'You've been spending too much time online, Countess,' he said drily. 'It's warping your perception of reality. Jack!' He called back over his shoulder. 'Come and introduce yourself to your fellow uppercruster.'

A lanky figure in green combat trousers stood uncertainly from his rubble perch. 'You sure, Garrison?'

'At present, I can't see any way I'm going to let her Prettiness here leave this place alive, so sure. Go for your life.'

The lanky figure stumbled a little as he made his way towards them. His hand shook as he pulled his hood and bandana away.

Pen started hard. The young man's angular face was seamless, and asymmetric in a way that would've seemed normal to Pen only a couple of days earlier. He had sandy hair and a nervous smile.

'Jack Wingborough,' he said. 'Third Earl of Tufnell Park.' He half extended a hand, which then wilted between them when Pen looked back pointedly over her shoulder at her own bound wrists.

'Or at least I was,' he concluded.

Pen remembered the video Case had shown her, the nightmare basement and the blank face, the ragged, lipless mouth. Her throat dried.

'Then – then who—?' she managed.

'My little brother, Simon.' His mouth tightened into a hard line. 'Auntie Maggie is ever so efficient.'

Pen shivered. 'I'm sorry – I don't—'

'The mirrorstocracy could hardly announce that I'd run off to join the revolution, could they? They needed to do two things.' Jack smiled one of those smiles that is only really teeth and tension. 'Explain my absence, and punish me for it. Having Si in their little film accomplished both – not to mention the fact that with *both* of us out of the way, the Case family stands to inherit. Oh, I snuck as much as I could out, but I'm sure Dad's money is coming in very handy in this election year.'

Little brother, Pen thought, and something curdled in her stomach. Jack Wingborough was a gangly teenager, all angles and acne. How young had Simon been?

'That's the system the Lottery underpins,' Espel said quietly, 'a system that mutilates kids to punish their families.'

'The system you're the face of,' Cray's said. 'So tell me again why I shouldn't kill you.'

'Simple.' Pen forced a calm she didn't feel into her voice. 'I'm not her.'

Cray barked derisively. 'Really? 'Cause you look a hell of a lot like her.'

'Actually,' Pen replied, 'it's her who looks like me.'

The cold eyes narrowed slightly. He didn't understand. He was starting to raise his gun again when Espel whispered, barely audible in the night.

'Mother Mirror merciful be – *that's* it.'

'What's it?' Cray snapped.

'Parva Khan was left-handed.' Espel sounded badly shaken. 'When I was getting ready to go into the palace I watched every video of her I could find. Every autograph was signed with her left hand – but *you*' – she pointed accusingly at Pen – 'you used your right.'

'So?'

'Look at her, Garrison.' Espel said. 'Really look at her—'

'Oh, I'm looking,' Cray said bitterly. 'All I ever do is look at her: on the TV, online, on the train on my way to fragging work in the morning – every minute of every damn day.'

'I know, me too – that's how I missed it. She's so familiar you don't even see her any more. You just assume – you get lost in the scars. But look now – look at her asymmetry.'

From under his hood Cray's eyes stared unblinkingly at Pen, and for long seconds she *willed* him to see.

'Mago,' he whispered at last, 'you're the wrong way round.'

Surprise eddied around the demolition site. Those Faceless figures further back craned in to see, muttering to themselves in shock.

'You're her, aren't you?' Espel came right up to Pen. Her blue eyes were huge. 'Her mirror-sister – the original. You came through the mirror, not *reflected* through, but actually physically here. How did you—?' She faltered, unable even to frame the question. 'Just, *how*?'

Pen said ruefully, 'It doesn't matter—'

'Like hell it doesn't – it's impossible. No one's ever—'

'If "never has" was the same as "never could", Es,' Pen said, 'all of history wouldn't have happened.'

'Just 'cause it's real now, doesn't mean it has to be for ever?' There was a kind of wonder in Espel's voice, and Pen smiled at her.

Cray was eyeing his gun like it was the last thing in the world he understood. He exhaled heavily.

'Let me be sure I've got this,' he said. 'Parva Khan goes missing and you, her mirror-sister, *somehow* come through the reflection to find her. You deliver yourself to *us*, and rather than thank Mago for the stupidity of my enemies, put a pair of bullets in you and take everyone to the pub to celebrate, you want me to help you find the Face of the Looking-Glass Lottery, an institution, lest we forget, that I've spent every waking moment since I was thirteen trying to tear down.

'You're right,' he added, '"how" doesn't matter. What I want to know is *why*? Why in the splintered mirror would I ever do that?'

Pen licked her uneven lips. This was it, her pitch. Behind her back, she clenched her bound hands. 'To tear down the Lottery,' she said, 'you don't need to destroy its face, only its eye.' She held his pale gaze until she was sure he understood.

'Kill me – kill Parva,' she said, 'they'll just find another girl – scar her up, if they're feeling nostalgic – and the whole bloody circus carries on. But I've got access to Goutierre's Eye, the one irreplaceable part of the machine that makes the whole system work.' She jerked her head at Espel. 'She's seen it. She knows I can steal it. Help me find my sister and I promise you, they'll never see it again. No Eye, no Engine. No Engine, and the promise of the Lottery crumbles like a stale cake.'

She watched him struggle with the idea. It was a stretch, she realised. To him – to everyone here, the image of a thing was the thing itself. Parva *was* the Lottery. It was incredibly hard for him to see it any other way.

At last he spoke. 'Your counterfeit countess is quite a find, Sis,' he said to Espel. He nodded over Pen's shoulder and she felt cold metal slide between her wrists. Pins and needles exploded in her fingertips as the bindings fell away.

'Welcome to the Revolution.'

CHAPTER TWENTY-FIVE

The meeting dissolved efficiently and without fuss. The Faceless pulled off their hoodies and bandanas. Shorn of their disguises, they were revealed to be a broad mix of half-faces with various degrees of patching, and even a few mirrorstocrats. Pen watched them in puzzlement, wondering why people apparently so keen to hide their identities should so willingly ditch their disguises while still in full view of one another.

But they used their real names, she realised. *They already know who each other are. They don't need to hide from each other.*

She caught strange, silent exchanges between them as they hurried away into the labyrinth: narrowed eyes, blushes, sudden embarrassed looks away, and then she understood.

Constantly judging each other, Espel had said. *Ranking each other. We rely on other people's eyes.* They'd been raised in the mirrorstocracy's hierarchy and that kind of thinking was stickier than tar. They couldn't help it. Covering their faces wasn't just some directionless gesture of rebellion; it helped them ignore the aesthetics they'd been raised to judge each other by.

It wasn't about anonymity but *equality*.

Garrison Cray was the last to drag his disguise off. Pen bit back a little yelp of shock.

He had no face below his eyes, just a blank sheet of parchment-like skin. His nostrils were elliptical holes, flat to his face. Where his mouth ought to have been, the skin had been razored open and the edges of the cut stitched back on themselves, like a turned-up hem on a pair of trousers. The two sides of his makeshift lips flexed symmetrically around the silver seam as he breathed.

He looked up at Pen, the blue eyes set hard, defiant. Pen steeled herself and met his gaze as though there was nothing unusual about him, even though all around she could feel the atmosphere chill as the other Faceless couldn't help but look away from that blank, symmetrical absence. Even Espel was staring fixedly in the opposite direction.

For a second she thought Cray would speak, but he just turned and stalked away.

A few minutes was all it took for the terrorists to desert their lair, vanishing like water into the maze's cracks. At last only Pen, Espel and Jack Wingborough remained.

The turncoat aristocrat pulled something slippery from his back pocket that glittered in the dim light. He caught Pen watching him as he smoothed it over the right side of his face, then, with a magician's flourish, he whispered, 'Ta da!'

Pen stared. Suddenly, the mirrorstocrat was a half-face. His features were precisely symmetrical – he even had a silver seam running down the centre of his face.

'Did you just – is that– Is that an id?' she whispered incredulously. Harry Blight's jerkily kicking body flashed alarmingly into her mind.

'Mago, no!' Jack said in alarm. 'I'm a sympathiser, but I don't want to *empathise*.' He shot a guilty look at Espel, who was leaning against the wall with her hands behind her. 'Sorry, Es.'

'S'all right, you posh tit. I don't blame you,' Espel said absently, not taking her eyes off Pen.

'Here, there's no reflection – look.' Jack leaned in towards Pen and teased at the seam on his forehead with his fingernail. It peeled back, onion-skin fine, revealing his own asymmetric features again. The seam marked the edge of a half-mask. Where it had lifted clear, Pen could see the mask was a mostly transparent film, clouding to opacity in the few places where Jack's right side didn't quite match his left. They were tiny changes, but it was startling how completely they reconfigured his face.

It was like her camouflage makeup, only infinitely more subtle: a distorting lens to allow him to pass for normal.

'It's illegal as hell, obviously,' he said, 'since the only real market for them is mirrorstocrats on the run – usually from their own governments. Most have it bonded to their skin – it's safer – it means it won't peel off at an inconveniently public moment.' His voice dried slightly. 'But I . . .'

Pen understood. He hadn't yet given up on someday being beautiful again.

'Good luck.' The Third Earl of Tufnell Park clapped her on the shoulder and jogged away up the tunnel.

Espel led Pen back into the labyrinth. It was only when they emerged onto a quiet side street, no more than ten minutes and three corners later, that Pen realised how convoluted the route Espel had taken her in on had been. The endless pathways of the rubble maze existed in a tiny space – an illusion of immensity.

They sprayed clouds of silver breath into the air as they stepped back onto the ice-speckled pavement.

'Espel,' Pen asked at last.

'What.' Espel wouldn't look at her.

'What happened to Cray's face?'

'Skin taxes, just before the election ten years ago.'

'They—?' Pen found herself stammering, even though she wouldn't have believed London-Under-Glass' government could do anything more to shock her. 'They *taxed* his face off?'

Espel snorted. 'Not quite. The rates went up, same as they always seem to just before elections – funny, that, since you vote according your registered features. Cray's family couldn't get the funds together to pay and he was thirteen and stupid and thought he could help them out.' Pen saw the steeplejill's jaw set in the cold streetlight. 'He broke into the Marquess of Finsbury's mansion looking for something to nick . . . His Lordship gave the Chevs leave to help themselves to whatever they wanted off him. He's lucky he's still got his eye.'

His family, Pen thought. *He thought he could help them out.* 'He called you Sis,' she said.

'Yeah,' Espel said. 'I kind of wish he hadn't done that.'

It's your face, not theirs. It wears the marks of the choices you made. Be proud of that. I would be.

'Espel—'

'Yeah?'

'I like you,' Pen said. 'I mention it, because what with the lying, the tying-up and the attempted knifing you might not have got that impression.'

Espel turned up her collar as the freezing wind knifed up the street. 'Come on,' she said shortly. 'We've got a long way to go to get back before sunrise.'

They broke into a jog-cum-scramble over the distorted pavements. Pen felt lighter now. She had allies. She wasn't alone any more, and that buoyed her. She found she liked the feel of the city under her palms, solid and reassuring. The air had turned so cold it felt sluggish, like freezing water, and she relished the way her cheeks burned as her body cut through it.

A dog barked at them as they swung past a shuttered-up corner shop. Pen looked up at the sky, the moon still hung high, a pale sliver crescent and—

A wave of *otherness* crashed through her, so strong that she lost her rhythm and stumbled to a stop. She stood with her hands on her knees, half trembling, and trying not to laugh.

'What's got hold of you?' Espel asked as she came jogging back.

'Oh, nothing much,' Pen gasped. 'I just . . . The moon—'

Espel's brow wrinkled. 'What about the moon?'

'It's – it's the wrong way round.'

Espel squinted skywards. 'No, it's not.'

'I mean, it's the opposite way to home.'

'And that's funny?'

'Apparently' – Pen was just managing to wrench back control of her breathing – 'it's bloody hilarious.'

'I hope you find it quite this entertaining when they're carving you up for parts, which is what they are most definitely going to do if we don't get back in . . .' She tailed off and went very still, her head tilted back, staring at the sky like a cat.

Streetlight etched her outline in orange. Her symmetry made her look uncannily beautiful. Pen followed her gaze. The moon had vanished and dense clouds were gathering over it with impossible speed.

'Wha—?'

The wind redoubled with a sound like something dying. Red dust blew into her eyes and they watered. She felt gravel-like powder trickling down the back of her neck. She inhaled and the musty tang of cement choked her.

'Shit and ugliness,' Espel swore. 'Weatherturn. *Run!*' She dragged Pen down the street as the wind screamed in and whipped up tendrils of ground brick around them.

Pen ran in near-blindness – she had to – opening her eyes more than a sliver dissolved her vision instantly into stinging tears. She had no idea how Espel was navigating as she tugged her harum-scarum over car bonnets and walls and fences.

'Where are we going?' Pen had to spit masonry just to form the question. This wasn't the way she remembered coming.

'We have to find cover!' Espel yelled back. 'Before—' She broke off and dragged Pen hard to the right. Something whistled through the space she'd just left and crunched into the asphalt by her feet.

'—that,' she finished. Pen peered back behind her. Through slitted eyes, she just managed to make out a stone chunk the size of her fist.

'Get in front of me!' Espel ordered. Pen felt the steeplejill come up behind her, close enough that her breath came hot against her neck through her headscarf. She felt a hand pressed lightly against her ribs, another to her hip.

'*Run*,' Espel hissed in her ear, 'and go where I put you.'

Pen half ran, half staggered through the broken streets, inhaling clouds of blood-coloured brickdust. Small stones rattled off her head and rapped her knuckles and she spat in pain but didn't falter. A push to her side and she responded, dancing left without thinking. A heavy hunk of brick cratered at her side. An instant later she felt a tug back and she corrected. She felt rather than saw the impact she dodged. She ran on, and somehow Espel ran behind her, guiding her, a presence of rapid footsteps and scraps of breath, her own guardian ghost.

Panic welled up in Pen then, at not being in control, at not knowing from one instant to the next where her body would step. She almost stumbled to a halt, but Espel barrelled into the back of her and she staggered and was off running again. She forced herself to give way to Espel's touch, *forced* herself to trust. She felt her panic morph into something else, a primal concentration that made her blood pound as her feet flowed over the ground. She was ruled by an urgent instinct – *survive this.*

For a half-instant, in the howl of the wind, she thought she heard a voice whisper, *I will be.*

The terrain under their feet evened out, but they slipped and slid on cloud-strewn gravel.

They could have been running through an alley or pelting up a main street, Pen had no way of telling as they burrowed through the opaque air. Bricks crunched on the ground like a premonition of breaking bones.

She'd *never* run this hard before, not even in the grip of the Wire Mistress. Pins and needles stung and slithered through her muscles, but she gritted her teeth and drove herself on. She knew she was faltering, slowing; any second now she would fail, and she would fall.

Lights burned through the brick haze ahead of her, windows, maybe, or headlamps. Espel shoved her towards them and as they drew closer, a dark archway fuzzed into visibility.

A doorway! Pen threw herself at it. Pain jabbed through her toe as it caught on a step. For a brief moment, Pen flew, then she hit the floor with a bruising *thud.* Everything was black. She tried to push herself up, but her muscles wouldn't answer any more. It was as though her nerves had short-circuited and sparked out. She screwed up her eyes, waiting for the shattering impact of falling masonry, but none came.

The floor was smooth and cold under her. For long seconds she just lay there. She felt Espel's body lying beside her own, intensely hot after the cold night air, and reflexively she curled a little tighter into her warmth. She could feel the steeplejill's breath going in and out. Pen felt a kind of bliss at simply being alive. She could have lain there forever with the girl who'd brought her through the storm.

It took her a long time to notice how the noise of the storm had deadened. Voices murmured and chuckled close by.

'Please bear with us,' a voice boomed over her. The echoes of the artificial crackle of the PA system charted the borders of a vast space. 'The storm has interrupted the power supply to the lights. If you will remain where you are for just a few moments longer we should be able to restore them.'

Espel moved, and an instant later a hand grabbed Pen's collar and pulled. She stifled a yelp of relief as her legs unfolded beneath her. 'Dark's a bit of luck,' Espel muttered by her ear. 'Let's move, quick, before they bring the emergencies on.'

Pen let herself be herded sideways, fumbling through the darkness. Her hands found a wall and pattered along it until she came to a doorway. There was a sudden, coarse smell of bleach and urine.

'In,' Espel whispered, 'and stay out of sight.'

Who can see in this? Pen thought, but she obeyed as best

she could. Her shoes almost skidded on the slick floor. Something hard jabbed into her back.

'Where are we?' she hissed.

'As of midnight?' Espel's voice was taut. 'Immigration Centre South-West One.'

'Immigration *what*?'

There was an echoing *clunk* and the blindness of darkness was exchanged for a blindness of blazing white neon.

Pen squinted as her eyes adjusted, and then she gaped in recognition. 'Bloody hell,' she breathed. 'It's Victoria Station.'

CHAPTER TWENTY-SIX

They were peeking around the doorway of the men's loos on Platform One. The hard thing in her back was the spar of a turnstile. Above them, the vast iron-and-glass roof was folded and crinkled like industrial origami. The platforms were all empty and she could see out over the track-trenches, through the open ticket barriers to the concourse. She could make out inverted logos for Burger King and Marks and Spencer, though the lights were out and the concession booths shuttered.

She felt a brief pang at their familiarity. *Must've ripped off the Old City brands out of nostalgia*, she thought wryly.

She frowned then, puzzled. Just beyond the ticket barriers, a row of booths sat across the middle of the concourse. Uniformed figures sat behind Plexiglas, drumming their fingers and muttering to each other. An occasional nervous laugh rang out. Next to each booth was a green canvas camp bed. Doctors in white coats sat and kicked their heels, chewed on their cuticles and looked anxiously towards the tracks.

Black-armoured Chevaliers prowled up and down nearby, curling and uncurling their hands around the stocks of their machine-guns.

It looked like a cross between a border checkpoint and a field hospital – and it *felt* like everyone in it was waiting for something.

'Espel,' she whispered, 'I go through Victoria Station every other week at home. How come I've never seen this little circus reflected in a shop window or something?'

'During the day it's a regular terminus,' Espel muttered back. 'They only set up the border on nights when they've got a big influx. We were *incredibly* lucky we got in.' She sounded puzzled, suspicious even. 'After the other attacks, this place ought to be crawling with a lot more Chevs than this – especially tonight.'

'Why toni—?'

Pen was cut off by the shriek of brakes and the chunter of steel wheels on track. A lone engine, black and beam-eyed, pulled slowly into the station, dragging a single windowless carriage behind it. The Chevaliers' white chess-knight insignia stood out starkly on the polished black metal. The train was covered in slab-like armour plates. It looked like a prison on rails.

The checkpoint lurched into activity. Doctors readied saline drips and checked surgical tools, Chevaliers jogged in loose formation to meet the slowing train, forming a semicircle around its single set of doors as it stopped. They stood, half crouched, weapons ready.

Their visors were down and Pen couldn't see their faces, but their shapes were *fearful*, somehow.

'New arrivals,' Espel whispered, her voice tense.

There was a *hiss-clunk* of hydraulics and the doors to the carriage slid open. Pen flinched reflexively at the sound, then tried to peer between the black-armoured bodies, to see what it was that could be so dangerous. A soft snow of brickdust trickled down from above her as Espel's fingers tightened on the doorway's edge.

'When half-faces are reflected through for the first time, Chev patrols sweep them up and hold them in internal camps so no one'll have to look at them. They're only half of who they used to be – half of their old memories and faculties. They're disorientated, confused. They can't officially enter 'til they've been processed at the border. The trains visit the camps at night and bring them in.'

Something moved inside the train. Pen's view was obscured by a Chevalier's shoulder-plate. She shuffled sideways for a better look. The figure became clear as it emerged and relief and disappointment mingled bitter at the back of Pen's throat.

It was just a man in a shabby brown suit, his right profile towards her as he walked along the side of the train. He kept his head down, placing his feet with the extreme but not excessive care of someone being watched by twitchy men with guns. 'What's the big deal?' Pen hissed. 'Why's it so important no one sees them?'

'Daddy?'

As the high, frightened voice emerged from the carriage, the man in the brown suit looked around, revealing the left side of his head.

At the exact halfway point on his face, where Espel's seam was on her, his features simply stopped. After his right nostril, his nose rejoined his face in a sharp plane, like dough cut with a razor, his mouth vanished beneath it. His left side was barer than a shop window mannequin, a rough half-oval of skin beneath his sweat-drenched hair.

The Chevaliers crowded the man without touching him, hemming him in with their rifle barrels like they were frightened he was going to flip out and attack someone.

Espel's fingers trembled against her lips. Pen frowned and prised them carefully away. She looked up at her companion. 'What?' she said.

Espel didn't answer. She was staring fixedly at the floor.

'What is it?' Pen whispered. 'Why are they being so rough with them?'

'They're ugly.' Espel's jaw looked like she was fighting some rebellious instinct. 'They're so *empty* – so blatantly incomplete.'

Pen thought about the way even the Faceless had looked away when Cray had revealed the ravaged blank that was his face. It was that lack, that absence of feature that they found so hideous. And the Chevaliers here had none of the seditious group's self-restraint. She could see their fear of the new immigrants in their posture, hear it in their snapped commands.

280

Under the Chevaliers' watchful glares, more figures emerged from the carriage: a middle-aged woman with bleached hair and a tiny skirt, a kid in a baggy Millwall tracksuit and a baseball cap, a younger child in school uniform – the tweed-suited man ran back and wrapped him up in a hug – a businesswoman, and others, two dozen or so in total. All of their faces gave way to nothing at the halfway point. They looked around themselves with their half-mouths agape as the Chevaliers herded them toward the checkpoint. The woman with the bleached hair had a compact, and her single eye searched it frantically, looking in vain for a reflection.

The first immigrant had reached the checkpoint now and Pen could see him shaking his head, raising his hands, pleading in confusion. Behind the Plexiglas, the border official stared fixedly over his shoulder as he jotted down details, and then gave a curt nod.

A Chevalier gestured with his gun, pointing the man towards one of the camp beds and he collapsed onto the canvas and allowed his limbs to be secured with leather straps.

A spider of unease walked up Pen's spine. 'Espel, what are they doing?'

Espel looked at her. Behind her pale eyes, Pen saw guilt, relief and horror struggle with each other. 'Obeying the law,' she whispered. Her fingers were resting absently on the artificial right side of her face. Her id.

An image leapt unbidden from Pen's memory: Espel,

sitting drunkenly in her borrowed palace apartment. *My id might not be pretty, but it does its job, keeps me legal.*

Pen knew, quite suddenly, exactly what the doctors were there for.

Cosmetic – she heard the jingle in her head – *prosthetic, completing your aesthetic* . . .

Crouching beside the camp bed, a young male doctor pulled on surgical gloves with the sharp, efficient movements of someone not allowing himself to feel. In the bed, the brown-suited man's single eye roved frantically from the doctor's face to his hands as he tapped air bubbles from a needle, and then slid it in behind his patient's ear. Instantly the muscles in the man's half-face sagged into paralysis, the eye revolving to rest looking at the bisected nose. As the doctor moved to delve into his medical pack, Pen saw drool glimmer on the brown-suited man's lower lip.

'Dad!' the boy in the school uniform shouted, his fear made to sound strangely hollow by his half-mouth. He tried to start forward, but he was caught around the midriff by a black-armoured arm.

The doctor lifted something flat from his pack and peeled plastic from the top of it. Pen felt a terrible pressure squeezing her heart as she leaned out to look.

It was a half-oval, made of some kind of fabric; it had the suppleness of thin rubber but it shone dully like tarnished steel.

Metal shrieked over concrete and Pen jumped and almost swore. The man in the bed was struggling, his limbs jerking in their restraints in defiance of the slack expressionless of his face. He'd managed to drag the bed an inch across the floor. A curt gesture from the doctor and two Chevaliers pinned him back down on the bed. Pen heard a low gurgling sound – a cry of fear, trapped in a chest with no lips to give it shape – but the man couldn't turn away, couldn't even roll his eye to watch as the doctor fitted the silver half-mask snugly over the right-hand side of his face.

The doctor pulled an oddly shaped tool from his pocket and ran it swiftly down the centre of the patient's face. A series of sharp clicks filled the air, and when the doctor moved aside, Pen could see a row of neat metal stitches bisecting the man from hairline to chin, joining the metal mask to his skin.

And then the metal on the man's face started to move. Ripples ran across its surface like a breeze over a pond. The metal stretched and warped into a new topography, shrinking and tightening in some places and sagging into fulsomeness in others. It bulged towards the bridge of the man's nose and opened like a seam to continue the line of his mouth. A crater sank to mimic his eye socket.

Only when the shape was complete did the colour arrive: it billowed in like ink through water, eddying until it settled and the man in the bed was utterly, perfectly symmetrical. The new eye blinked and rolled in its socket until it was staring furiously across the steel-stitched border at its rival.

The man's left hand, secured in its leather cuff, curled into a fist.

'Now,' the doctor barked. One of the attendant Chevaliers grabbed the patient's head and pulled it hard to the side. The doctor stabbed another syringe in behind his *left* ear. For a second, Pen saw the id's eye stretch in outrage and pain, she watched it panic as it scrabbled to hold onto its newly granted consciousness, then, inevitably, the lid slid over it like night-fall. The man in the bed blinked and shuddered, and when his eyes opened again they moved in unison.

The guards holding the tweed-suited man relaxed visibly and began to undo his restraints. The doctor dabbed delicately at his seamed brow with a handkerchief.

But all Pen could think of was that baleful second mind, its instant of wakefulness and the ferocious, territorial hate of its stare.

Images came to her without warning: wicked tendrils, barbs glinting like steel thorns, lashing round her face, alien predatory thoughts seeping through her scalp. And somehow in that moment, the gleaming metal of the wire was also the metal of *stitches* – stitches like those down the middle of the man's face, like Espel's, like Harry Blight's, as he'd lain kicking weakly on the floor of the courtroom, throttled by a parasite consciousness.

Parasite.

'Dad!' The young boy sounded so relieved to see his father stand. The doctor looked over at him, shrugged and then nodded to the Chevaliers, who let the boy run towards the bed. The doctor was already lifting another of the half-masks from his pack.

Pen thought of it crawling and pressing on the kid's skin. *Parasite.* The word seized her throat and squeezed. It wasn't involuntary when her muscles fired; Pen *decided* to run.

'Stop!' Her yell echoed massively in the space. 'You can't!'

She pelted up the platform towards the gates. An armoured figure spun towards her shout, his rifle already set into his shoulder. There was a crack, and a bright tongue of muzzle-flash lit the air. Granite chips flew from the wall a foot from Pen's face. A second Chevalier dragged the gun away and bellowed at him to cease fire. Pen didn't break stride. Footsteps pattered rapidly behind her – Espel, swearing as she pounded after her.

Pen crashed through the open ticket barrier with her arm outstretched. 'Stop!' she cried raggedly, lurching to a halt in the midst of a crowd of Chevaliers, doctors and bemused half-faced immigrants. Desperately she tried to drag in enough breath to speak. 'You – you – can't—' she gasped.

The boy and the doctor who stood over him both gaped at her. From here Pen could clearly see the words INVERSE DEPICTOR (20) stencilled on the doctor's pack.

'C-C-Countess Khan?' A Chevalier – an officer, by the silver chevrons on his upper arm – stepped carefully between the doctor and Pen's outstretched, trembling fingers. He pulled off his helmet. His grizzled, near-symmetrical face was incredulous.

'What . . . excuse me, ma'am, but what are you doing here? And who is *that*?'

Pen glanced over her shoulder. Espel was about a foot

behind her. She gave Pen a lethal look from under her blonde fringe. *What the hell are you doing?*

Pen didn't know; all she knew was that the thought of this kid being sutured made it feel like someone was wringing her heart out. 'You can't stitch him to that thing,' she stammered. 'I won't . . . I'm . . .' she faltered, and then realised there was only one thing she could say. 'I'm the Face of the Looking-Glass Lottery and I won't let you.'

'Ma'am?' The Chevalier officer wrinkled his brow, looking both confused and more than a little pissed off at whatever fates had decided to dump a lunatic celebrity into the middle of his operation. 'I'm sorry, but *what*?'

'You can't.'

'We have to.'

'You can't.'

'Excuse me, My Lady, but it's the law.'

'You *can't*.' Pen just repeated it stolidly, raising her chin like it was a weapon. She had only her face and her name to bargain with.

The Chevaliers' gun barrels were starting to twitch like predators' muzzles. The black-armoured men shifted slightly, subtly and unhurriedly putting more of their bodies between Pen and the half-faced boy on the bed.

'I'm sorry, ma'am,' the officer said, and then added, ' I know that your recent experiences must have been . . . traumatic, but I'm going to have to ask you and your associate' – he barely glanced at Espel – 'to accompany Sergeant Price here.' He spoke slowly, giving her the kind of nervous, sympathetic smile you might reserve for the lady in the old folks' home who talks to the petunias.

No, Pen thought, *no, you can't think I'm crazy. This doesn't work if you think I'm crazy. But then—* She licked her dry lips as she considered her behaviour, looked at the black helmets and realised every one of them would hold a stitched face. *What else could you think I was?*

'My Lady.' The sergeant the officer had indicated, a heavy-set Chev with a breastplate curved to accommodate his paunch, stepped forward and offered her his hand. 'With me, please—'

Thunder boomed outside and falling masonry rattled against the roof. Pen felt like a cornered animal. She *could not* let this happen, but she couldn't think of a way to stop it.

The sergeant took off his helmet. He had a kindly enough face. His right cheek was patched with a few expensive freckles. 'If you'll just come with me, ma'am, and we'll get you back to the palace when the storm abates.'

Another wave of thunder shook the sky, and the whole station reverberated. The very floor seemed to shudder—

No, not *seemed*. It *did*.

The concrete *was* trembling under their feet, and it didn't stop shaking when the thunder subsided. Pen felt her teeth clatter together as she staggered. The Chevaliers and immigrants fought for balance, staring downwards in baffled fright. Pen felt her throat narrow. Whatever this was, they didn't understand it either.

The floor shivered like the skin of a drum. Ripples moved under the polished surface, distorting it into almost recognisable shapes.

The sergeant tracked the disturbances with his rifle. 'What—?' he murmured as one of the shapes ghosted towards him. 'What in Mago's name—?'

Splitting the stone like water, a grey hand speckled with cement scree burst upwards and seized the sergeant's ankle. He bellowed and squeezed the trigger. With a deafening rattle-roar the weapon unloaded into the spot between his feet.

Pen leapt back from the noise. She lost her balance and the floor jarred through her spine as she fell. Eye-level with the ground, she saw the last of the bullets chip splinters from the surface of the granite tiles. They didn't penetrate.

She blinked and her breath came in fast gasps. The grey hand was gone. For an instant she thought that she'd imagined it – that the *sergeant* had imagined it; that somehow they'd both fallen victim to some storm-induced psychosis.

But then he screamed, 'Oh Mago, oh Mother Mirror,' he yammered desperately. 'My leg!'

It was sunk into the solid concrete up to the shin.

'Oh Mago, the *weight*—' His symmetrical face was utterly bloodless, his lips spittle-flecked. 'I can feel it crushing . . . It's *crushing* my *foot*—'

'You'll be okay, Price.' The officer's voice was panic-stricken and not at all reassuring. 'We'll get you out. We'll – uh . . . we'll—' He fumbled for his radio.

288

The sergeant howled in pain again and Pen's heart shuddered, but her pity turned into fear as the floor rippled again, an inch from her face.

She scrambled upright. The Chevaliers, Espel, the doctors and the immigrants all backed into a close little knot around her and the sergeant. The fug of their sweat choked her.

In the spaces between their bodies. Pen saw shapes cruising under the surface of the floor, effortless as hunting rays, they described a predatory circle around the trapped crowd. The Chevalier sergeant moaned.

'Everybody stay very still,' the officer ordered. 'Just keep still.' He fumbled for his radio. 'Command, this is South-West Border Team One, over.'

'*Come in South-West One.*'

'Command, we are under attack, repeat, under attack. Send immediate back-up.'

'*Negative, South-West One. Storm's too heavy. Back-up not available until abatement.*'

'Command, I have no idea how, but we have the Face of the Looking-Glass Fragging Lottery here. Send back-up, right now!'

The hesitation on the line was audible. Then, '*Stand by.*'

The sergeant had lapsed into a feverish muttering. Right next to Pen, the man in the brown suit trembled. His eyes darted from the floor to his reflected son, then to the dark archway that opened onto the street and back again. His symmetrical expression was sick with fright. 'We *can't*,' he whispered.

He grabbed his boy around the waist, lifted him bodily in one arm, and with a terrified howl, hurled himself towards the station's open exit.

Pen counted his footsteps by the echoes they cast into the silence. He managed five before the creature struck.

It breached the floor with sickening grace, leaping, its shadow bleeding over the running man's back. The creature was man-shaped, naked and skeletal, wrapped in a concrete skin that dripped from it like liquid. Its hollow-cheeked face was like a skull. It howled silently and brought its crooked, too-long fingers down on the man's shoulders. It dragged him down like a leopard pinning prey. The man didn't cry out but his child shrieked as they fell. The floor opened liquidly around them as they hit it, and the boy's scream was cut off abruptly as it closed over them. A rippling scar marred the concrete where it had sealed over.

The air dissolved into thunder as the Chevaliers opened fire.

Panicked, they poured ammunition into the floor, trying to get at the four-limbed shapes that rippled its surface. The immigrants shrieked at the noise and broke, chasing hither and thither like startled deer. Pen found herself running too, without even thinking. The shattering noise galvanised her muscles. She couldn't stand still. She could feel her heart lodge in her throat. She stared desperately at the floor for signs of breaching fingertips.

The floor in front of Pen erupted. She froze in terror as the creature surfaced. With widespread arms, fingers hooked like claws, and a mouth set in a silent, sickening howl it came for her.

There was a sharp rattle of gunfire. Sparks flew from the creature's side and it stopped. It shuddered as though hurt, though the bullets had barely chipped its flank.

The creature's head turned on its neck with organic smoothness, and Pen looked where it looked. Twenty feet away a Chevalier was lowering his gun from his shoulder, clumsy with fright.

The creature jagged sideways. It didn't run, it *slid* friction-lessly through the surface of the tile, careering into the Chevalier and grabbing him like a rag before plunging him backwards into the station wall. Pen saw the Chevalier's legs twitch spastically and then stop, sticking out of the other-wise unbroken brick.

The creature turned back towards her.

Pen stared at it for a heartbeat – its cavernous ribcage, grey concrete muscles flexing over its bones, fingers spread wide, a fine, flexible webbing of cement stretching between them. Then with a serpentine flex of its spine, it dived back into the floor.

Something yanked Pen backwards by the collar. She yelped and spun, her fists held up in useless pugnacity.

'*Countess!*' It was Espel, her face taut with disbelief. 'Do you want to make fragging tracks or *what*?'

The steeplejill half pushed, half dragged her until her legs started working again. They ran. The main exit was perhaps fifty feet away across the lethal concrete. Screams blended with the gunfire as those around them were picked off, but the grey figures themselves made no sound as they burst upwards, tangling their emaciated limbs with their victims and bearing them under.

It's the immigrants, Pen thought. *They're only going for the immigrants.*

Only the new arrivals were being hauled alive underground. The tracksuited girl was dragged down screaming, but half a second later her head broke back through the surface, bobbing and gasping as the once-solid floor lapped at her chin. She drew breath to shriek again, but grey fingers clamped over her half-mouth and yanked her back with terrible strength.

The Chevaliers were ignored, or where their desperate rifle-fire stung the creatures, disposed of with imperious brutality. The trapped sergeant was bellowing incoherently, jamming new clips into his gun and pumping them out at any patch of floor he could see moving. As Pen watched, one of the creatures sprang up behind him, seized his chin and twisted his neck to an impossible angle. He dropped, a sack of twitching meat. Pen heard the crack as his falling bodyweight broke the bone in his trapped leg.

Pen's heart lurched for him, but she didn't stop running. Her feet kicked into a fallen rifle and even as she stumbled she bent and gathered it up, cradling it clumsily like an armful of firewood. They were almost there, almost out. The archway yawned hugely in front of them and beyond it she could hear the crash and clatter of the storm and see the flickering chunks of brick falling through the sodium dusk. Espel was five yards ahead now, despite her shorter stride, her head low like a greyhound—

—but then she was breaking, yelling, skidding as she fought to turn. Beyond her, Pen saw the grey stone on the inside of the archway flex.

A grinning figure stepped smoothly out of the stone, shedding mortar.

Desperately, Pen tried to brake too. Her heels slid under her and she reeled backwards. Time took on a nightmarish slowness as she fell. She watched the grinning man reach back into the inside of the arch. The cement-etched muscles in his forearms stood out as he gripped, and the wall *moved*.

Pen's breath caught. He was *dragging* the wall. There was no sound, no shriek of rending concrete; in his grip the masonry was as pliable as cloth and he pulled it across the arch like a curtain. She watched in horrified awe as the doorway narrowed and vanished.

Espel wasn't so lucky as to fall back; her momentum was too great and she over-balanced forward. The grinning creature gathered her eagerly in its stony arms. It braced her against its chest, lifting her feet from the floor. Pen saw the wall ripple around it as it backed slowly into the concrete where the doorway had been. Espel kicked and spat like a child in a tantrum, her blue eyes wide with terror. She screamed.

There was a weight on Pen's chest: the Chevalier rifle. She

lurched to her feet, threw herself across the few feet that separated her from the steeplejill, swinging the weapon around in a tight arc. As the muzzle fell over the eye socket of the grey monster, she fired.

The roar of the weapon split Pen's skull. The recoil nearly took her arm out but she clung to the trigger for dear life. The creature's mouth gaped in silent agony. It threw its arms wide and Espel crashed forward into Pen. The floor cracked hard into her head before she even knew she was falling.

Stars erupted and the world swam dully. She heard an explosion as if from a long way off. Her head lolled sideways and she saw a ragged hole ripped in the wall. Black-armoured figures poured through it, past her, firing at the floor: fat, slow projectiles from heavy guns which bored deep before exploding and ripping up the ground. Pen heard more dim detonations and shrapnel buzzed past her face like flies.

Another bolt of dizziness rocked her head back. Espel was warm and heavy on top of her. The steeplejill was pressing her down, protecting her body with her own. Over Espel's shoulder she could see the grey man, its face still howling, its half-submerged arms still thrust wide as if in an embrace.

Pen felt a jolt of recognition and stared at the thing's right arm in disbelief, struggling against the darkness that seeped in at the corners of her vision. Carved into the inside of the concrete man's right wrist was a design she recognised: city tower blocks, arranged to form the spokes of a crown.

'Parva!' Espel cried. 'Stay with me!' But Pen could barely hear the words. Blackness welled up and she let it take her.

III

THE LOOKING-GLASS
LOTTERY

CHAPTER TWENTY-SEVEN

'Parva! Stay with me!'

A monster had Espel in its grip. She kicked and struggled and cried. Wiry grey arms bound her, trapped her, dragging her backwards . . .

Pen felt the weight of the gun in her hand. As slowly as the blonde girl was receding in front of her, her own muscles moved slower yet. She swung the weapon around. Its muzzle eclipsed the creature's stretched grey eye.

'Pen! Stay with me!' a familiar voice called to her.

She fired.

Espel fell, bearing Pen to the ground with the slow inevitability of an avalanche.

'Pen . . .'

Pen looked over the steeplejill's shoulder. The monster half-submerged in the wall was a girl. Grey-red blood oozed, slow as cement, from the ruined eye socket, over a face Pen knew as well as her own. The girl in the wall seemed to be trying to focus on Pen, to meet her eyes with her own, but the blood meant she couldn't focus. She tried to reach up to clear it, but the wall trapped her arm, sealing around it just above a mark shaped like a tower-block crown.

'Pen,' she whispered. 'Stay with me.'

'Beth?' Pen croaked. The hammer and echo of machine-gun fire died slowly in her ears, replaced by the soft hum of electronics and the *shush* of distant traffic through a window. She felt soft, warm sheets over her.

'Beth? Who's Beth?' a dry voice asked.

Pen opened her eyes.

She was lying in Parva's bed, back in her apartment in the palace. She was wearing pyjamas. Her hijab was gone, and there was a thick, sticky dressing on the back of her head where it had struck the ground.

The lights in the room were out, but the city glow seeping in around the curtain outlined a tall, thin figure sitting patiently on the edge of her bed. The figure reached out and flicked on the lamp on the dresser, illuminating her wrinkled face.

'Who's Beth, Parva?' Senator Case asked again.

'Senator?' Pen squinted in the sudden light. Awareness of her situation crashed in on her: she'd been found without bodyguards, miles from the palace in the middle of the night, loudly trying to flout London-Under-Glass' border laws. Groggily, she tried to think of a plausible explanation. 'I—'

'Maggie.' Case corrected gently. 'And save your strength. Your new lady-in-waiting told me everything when I interviewed her an hour ago.'

'Maggie – I – she did?'

'Indeed.' Case smoothed her already immaculate grey suit. It must have been before five in the morning, but she showed no signs of having been roughly woken or hurriedly dressed. Pen wondered if she ever slept.

'Espel told us about you waking from a nightmare in the middle of the night – how you kept repeating, "They're all looking at me, I have to get out," over and over, how she tried to persuade you otherwise, but eventually had to settle for following you and how you wandered apparently aimlessly for hours, and she managed to guide you to shelter in the immigration station when the slatestorm struck.' She paused. 'I must say, a number of very expensive eyebrows were raised around here when you appointed a former steeplejill as your lady-in-waiting, but it's lucky you did. I doubt anyone else would have had the instincts to guide you safely through that kind of weather. We all owe the ugly little thing a debt.' She pursed her lips, as though the idea of being in debt to a half-face amused her.

Pen stretched slowly. 'She said that? That I . . . freaked out?'

Case nodded, her lined face set in a sympathetic smile. Pen looked at that smile and remembered the undone face of the man in the video. Jack Wingborough's voice echoed in her mind.

Auntie Maggie is ever so efficient.

There was no sign on her face at all of what she was capable of. Even her eyes were kind.

'It's all right,' Case said. 'You think you're the first of the Lottery's Faces to have a little wobble? It's completely under-standable.'

'It is?'

'Of course. *Of course*,' she said soothingly. 'It's our privilege that we of the mirrorstocracy can see ourselves in the mirror; one of the gazes that defines us is our own. But it is still only one out of thousands of pairs of eyes that we encounter in our lives. And for the Face of the Looking-Glass Lottery, that effect, that *dilution* of our power to decide who we are, is multiplied a thousandfold again.'

Case smiled and shook her head. 'Who amongst us, faced with the prospect of stepping in front of the cameras on Draw Night, would *not* be afraid of losing ourselves in all those gazes, of having them pin us like a butterfly to card? Who wouldn't fear that after that they would never be free?'

Case laughed. It sounded genuine. 'There have been six Lottery Faces while I've held office, and without exception they've all been terrified of their first Draw Night. Admit-tedly, they did not all express their anxiety quite so dramatically as you have, but still. You shouldn't worry.'

The amusement in her voice dried up, shrinking like a puddle on a hot pavement. 'We can't have you running off again though, Parva,' she said, 'so I'll tell you what. I'm going to tell you a story – one I didn't tell any of the others, because I think you need to hear it more than they did, and because . . .' She hesitated. 'Well, because we have enough in common that I think you'll understand.'

Her brown eyes locked onto Pen's. 'The story is about a little girl. Let's call her' – her lip quirked – 'Margarethe. She grew up with her mother in an estate in the Old City, Kylemore Close in Newham – perhaps you remember it from the days before your mirrorbirth?'

Pen shook her head, although she knew the place well enough.

'Ah well.' Case shrugged. 'Margarethe's mother was very young. She was a bright girl, kind, and very resourceful. You would have liked her, I think. She was only sixteen when Margarethe was born – she was already pregnant with her when she came to London from Gdansk, although she did not know it at the time. Margarethe's mother had no parents in the Old City, she was alone, so she set about doing what she had to do to look after her little girl. They grew up together, Margarethe and her mother; they were each other's best friends. On her first day at school, Margarethe cried when her mother left her, and then she sat glumly in the classroom like it was a prison cell, hating the seconds as they passed. Every day for two years she sat at her desk and prayed to be free.'

'And then one day' – her voice didn't waver by so much as a semitone – 'her mother's colleagues came for her. There was a hammering at the door, and shouting, and the sound of cheap wood splintering, and suddenly a place that had always been safe simply wasn't safe any more. Margarethe was only eight, and at first she didn't understand what the big men with knives who crashed into her kitchen were shouting about. She was very frightened, of course, but she tried to tell them that they had it wrong; that her mother was a good person who would never have cheated them like they were saying she had. The men didn't listen – she didn't have the *power* to make them listen. Perhaps, Margarethe thought, her mother would be able to explain.

'But Margarethe's mother didn't protest. She didn't even look at the men; she just looked at Margarethe and she was crying, and she said, "Darling, if you love me, then run."

'So Margarethe ran: she ran and she ran, as hard and fast as she could, to prove to her mother how much she loved her. She darted between the swearing men, dodging the huge hands that reached for her, and sped out of the door and down the stairwell and into the maze of the estate.

'She didn't stop until she came to a place where she sometimes played: a narrow, weed-choked space between the backs of buildings where washing hung out of windows overhead, and where someone, years before, had dumped an old patina-splotched mirror, propped against a wall. The mirror sat opposite a window, and on bright summer days Margarethe would stand between them, transfixed by the images that stretched like paperchain cut-outs into the reflections on either side. She stood like that now, tearful and scared, just *hoping* for something to happen and— Well, I'm sure you can guess what did.'

Pen nodded, but didn't speak.

'Margarethe's mirror-sister took a different but similar name and the two girls became fast friends, united by common experience and divided only by the width of a mirror-pane. Even when the newly minted mirrorstocrat was adopted by a rich New City family, she would sneak back to that spot and to the girl she'd been sundered from. She kept faith with her sister for years.

'Neither of the sisters ever saw their mother again. The men never came for Margarethe in anything other than her nightmares, and neither did the council or the police. There was no one to tell her to go back to school; she finally had the freedom she had wished for in the classroom, but those last few seconds in her home had already shown her that freedom was a chimera.

'You couldn't really be free, she'd realised, because there are too many other people in the world: people who might mean you harm – people who can knock you off the path you want to walk on. The clockwork metaphor is a cliché, admittedly' – Case winced in apparent embarrassment – 'but it's a cliché for a reason: we are all cogs, and the only way you can control yourself is to control all the other cogs that interlock with you, and so control all the cogs that interlock with *them*, and so on. True freedom is predicated on absolute control.' She stated it simply, like it was an obvious fact.

'Margarethe's mirror-sister had by now grown into a powerful young woman, and she knew she would become more so in time. So even though it was risky and her new family didn't approve, when she was sixteen she snuck back to that place between the towers one last time, and she made both of the girls she saw in the reflection a promise. She promised that she would be free, for both of them. And if total control was what was needed, then that was what she would seek.'

She shrugged self-deprecatingly. 'It's an impossible task, admittedly, but we stumble and we strive and we approximate success as best we can. Now, you may be thinking, "What is the old bag bleating about?" but I think you can probably see my point?'

Pen didn't respond. Case rubbed her shoulder fondly. 'I think you understand how important control is, Parva. I can see it in you. I think it was the *loss of control* that really scared you last night, but you don't need to be afraid. We're on your side: me, the Senate, the mirrorstocracy, the whole of London-Under-Glass is behind you. It's my city, and I've seen to it: this is the biggest and most tightly managed publicity campaign ever seen this side of the mirror.

'You don't need to be afraid of their gaze, Parva. Let them look. We can control how they see you. The only thing waiting for you tomorrow night is their love.'

She gently lifted Pen's head and plumped the pillows, then pulled the duvet further up over her. Pen stiffened as the old woman leaned in and kissed her scarred forehead.

'Get some rest. It's only a day until the Draw, and we need you as well as you can be.' She stood. 'We've kept that steeplejill of yours waiting outside – she's been *terribly* eager to get in to see you, hopping from one foot to the other.'

Case arched an eyebrow and then smiled like a parent who thinks they're cool. 'You have yourself a good one there,

I think, Parva. I like her. But if this . . . *thing* you two have is going to continue, I think we'd better give her a raise. Enough so that she can buy herself some freckles and possibly a dimple or two. Just to keep it respectable, you know?'

Pen felt her gorge rising behind the smile she returned. 'I'll ask her about it.' She kept her tone light. 'After all, it's her face.'

Case laughed, though Pen wasn't joking. She hesitated, her hand on the door handle. 'Parva,' she said casually, 'we're all grateful to Espel's quick thinking last night of course, but it is . . . regrettable that the only shelter available was the station. I don't know how much you remember about the Faceless attack.'

'The Faceless attack?' Pen said sharply.

'That's right,' Case said evenly. 'They bombed the place out – the Chevaliers were heroic, but because of the storm, they arrived too late to stop the terrorists' racist onslaught. It claimed the lives of every one of the new immigrants. A terrible tragedy, a terrible crime.' She paused. 'I have personally spoken to every one of the Chevaliers and medical staff who survived the attack, and they all agree that that is what happened. Just as they all agree that they never saw the most beautiful woman in London-Under-Glass last night. As far as they were concerned, she must have been tucked up in her bed here in the Shard, where she belongs.'

Pen swallowed hard under Case's gentle but unblinking gaze.

'In the name of control?' she asked. Her voice sounded thin in her ears. Case smiled thinly but said nothing.

'I don't remember anything about a Faceless attack last night,' Pen said at last.

'Of course not,' Case said. 'How could you? It was miles away.'

She opened the door. Outside Pen saw Espel, nervously shifting from foot to foot. She was back in the black blouse and trousers Pen had lent her – and Pen couldn't help but notice that despite having been the one nearly snatched by the concrete-skinned creature, the half-faced girl wasn't getting the pillow-fluffing treatment. She looked haggard, but just about together.

The steeplejill ducked her head low to the senator. Given Espel's disdain for formality, Pen could only conclude that she was very, *very* afraid of the old mirrorstocrat.

'Your mistress is awake,' Case told her. 'Look after her, the way you always do.'

CHAPTER TWENTY-EIGHT

As soon as the door closed, Espel rooted in her pocket and threw something to Pen. When she looked at the small, cold, surprisingly heavy object she started: nestled in her palm was Goutierre's Eye.

She stared in astonishment for a few seconds before she realised the marble's core was dull and motionless and there was a bloom of small cracks on one side.

'Where did you get it?' She turned the thing over, examining it.

Espel smiled slightly sheepishly. 'From my mum,' she said. 'Reflectionday present. It's a toy, Countess – official merchandise. I took it with me everywhere. It won't fool anyone for long, but it's the right size and from a distance . . .' She shrugged. 'I thought it might be useful to have something to switch the real eye for.'

Pen squinted critically. 'Be better without the cracks.'

'Well, I'll go back in time immediately and tell my ten-year-old self to be more careful, shall I?' Espel said tartly. She dropped herself onto the edge of the bed and eyed the closed door. 'So what did Case say to you?' she asked. She drew her knees up under her chin and hugged them.

'Same as she said to you, I expect,' Pen said. '"You weren't there, you didn't see anything. Any resemblance last night may have born to anything except another Faceless terrorist attack is purely coincidental, and likely the product of my overstressed mind this close to Draw Night." Oh, and she told me to give you a raise.' Pen looked up from picking the skin off her scarred cuticles, a cheap little self-demolition she hadn't indulged for months. 'Am I even paying you?'

Espel managed a smile. 'Not as such, no. Been meaning to talk to you about it, but things kept coming up.'

'Things like killing me with knives?'

'And saving your arse from a brick storm.'

'Well, if you will let trifles distract you . . .' Pen mocked an indifferent shrug.

Espel's smile staggered over the line into a laugh. For a moment it felt like they could have been anywhere, they could have been home. Two friends, sitting on a bed in the middle of the night and laughing.

Except it was different, Pen thought, watching the way Espel's face broke into symmetrical dimples. She'd never looked at anyone like that, not even Beth. Beth was safety. Beth *was* home, Pen knew her better than anyone. Being with Espel was different, charting the lines and shapes of her felt like discovery, it made something nameless and exciting swell inside Pen's chest.

Eventually, Espel's smile faded. 'Those . . . things, last night . . .' she said, and trailed off. Her eyes were glassy.

Pen recognised that expression. She'd worn it herself: the look of someone's whose world was breached. The reality she'd always accepted was leaking out of it like air pressure from a crashing plane. The masonry-skinned man who'd come so close to taking her was as alien to Espel as Espel had once been to Pen. She'd been stolen, if only for a few seconds, by something *other*.

Pen threaded her fingers between the steeplejill's. The scars on the back of her hand stood out as she squeezed sympathetically. 'People,' she said quietly, 'not things.'

Espel looked up. 'You *know* them?'

'Not them, exactly, but their like. Yes.'

'Tell me,' Espel demanded.

The hunger in her voice startled Pen, but she knew where it had come from: these things had almost killed her and now she was determined to understand them. Pen flinched a little from the intensity of her stare, but started, 'I saw them once in the Old City, at St Paul's. There was digging and I – I saw them die. Those ones were just people – civilians, I suppose – but I think the ones that attacked last night were soldiers. They were disciplined; when they swam under the floor they held *formation*. I think they had a mission – they were very specific about what they took.'

'The immigrants,' Espel said.

'Whatever they were after, the new arrivals had it,' Pen agreed. 'They snatched them, but they didn't kill them – you noticed that too, right? The Chevaliers, the doctors, them they killed, but they carried the immigrants away alive and whole, back under the – under the . . .' She tailed off, staring at the raised lesions on the back of her hand. She exhaled a little 'oh' of realisation and rocked back hard on the bed.

'What is it?' Espel asked in alarm.

'The floor,' Pen said softly. 'When they dived back into it, it didn't seal properly. It rippled' – she turned her hand in front of her – 'it *scarred*. I couldn't see it on the news reports about the other stations' attacks because their floors had been wrecked by explosives, but last night—'

'So the floor rippled,' Espel said. 'So what?'

'So . . . I saw the bathroom where Parva was snatched – the floor was scarred just like that.' She exhaled hard, as though that could push off the weight she suddenly felt on her chest.

'That's why they took her – they were looking for new arrivals. Those things have got my sister.'

And suddenly her mind was with Parva, being dragged under the floor of the reflected bathroom, concrete flowing close over her skin like thick water. Pen shuddered at the terror she must have felt.

'Grenades,' Espel said.

'What?'

'Grenades. You said the other stations on the news were wrecked by explosives. Last night, when the reinforcements showed up, the Chevs were packing these launcher-things, grenades. When they fired them they kind of . . . *burrowed* into the ground before they went off. Don't you see? They came prepared. They knew what they were fighting – they'd done it before. Mirror-*fuck*,' she swore. 'Have we just found ourselves in the middle of some kind of secret war?'

A secret war. Pen thought. *That's a bad habit.*

Espel was already digging in her pocket for her mobile phone 'I have to warn Garrison,' she said. 'We've got people looking for your sister right now. What if one of them finds her, and those things along with her? Goutierre's Eye or no, it won't be worth them getting buried alive for.'

Espel went to stand up, but found she couldn't because Pen's fingers were clamped hard around her wrist. In Pen's other hand the replica marble glimmered as she turned it in the light of the table lamp.

'What did you say?'

'I said, Eye or no Eye, Garrison has to call off the—'

'Eye, or no eye,' Pen echoed her. '*I*.' She exhaled hard and released Espel's wrist. 'I am so bloody stupid – no, scratch that, *you* are so bloody stupid.' She levelled a finger at Espel. 'I'd never heard of Goutierre's bleeding Eye until three days ago. You're the one who's been collecting souvenirs since you were *ten*—'

'What are you talking about?' Espel demanded.

'The Device, the Lottery Device. Think about it. How does it work?'

'It scans the winner, and then the Eye checks every mirror in the city for matching—' She broke off and stared at Pen.

'Can you operate it?' Pen asked. The steeplejill nodded hesitantly, and then with more certainty.

'They show it close up on TV every Draw Night – I've watched them do it every year.'

Anticipation was a layer of thin ice just below Pen's skin. 'Then we know how to find her,' she said. 'The girl who shares my face.'

CHAPTER TWENTY-NINE

Beth's efforts at being inconspicuous were a little hampered by the cats.

They'd started following her just after she passed Finsbury Park tube, hopping over garden fences and slinking out from behind bins. So far as she could tell, they were just ordinary London strays, not Fleet or Wandle or any other member of Mater Viae's feline honour guard, but they trailed in her wake in Hamelinesque procession, single file with their tails held daintily high. By the time she passed a Turkish bakery on Green Lanes and cut through a business park, she couldn't see the end of the line.

Luckily, it was the middle of the night and there was just a handful of people on the street, a reasonable percentage of whom were drunk and wearing T-shirts and so would be most likely to put the sight of her feline entourage down to hallucinations caused by alcohol or hypothermia or both. She still drew some stares and pointed fingers, but she kept her hood up and her head down and hustled onwards. The insulated cable of her hair felt slick on the back of her neck.

The synod's photo was still curled in her fist. She didn't know why she'd taken it from their stores; it wasn't like she needed a reminder. The image was branded on her mind.

Pen, she said to herself, over and over, filling the space between her other conscious thoughts: *Pen*.

She'd heard rumours, but she only knew she was close when she noticed the backstreet she was walking down was better lit than its neighbours. The streetlamps sprouted more densely from these pavements. Close to, she could see the cement caking the bases of many of them was fresh. She peered into the bulbs, and in the midst of the orange glow she saw oscillations of light and shadow that might have been fingers.

She smiled and pressed on, her retinue of cats padding silently after her. Soon they began to pass statues standing incongruously outside newsagents and next to flyer-plastered phone boxes. They were all facing the same way, and she followed their stone gazes with her own.

Rising beside the railway was a squat concrete tower. Its architecture was rough, a brutality of cheapness rather than design, but two things set it apart from the other tower blocks that rose above the skyline. First, every single one of its windows was dark, and second, the concrete yard that surrounded it was dotted with stone bodies. A surrounding army hemmed in the tower.

A change in the wind brought the rich, sour scent of garbage to Beth's nostrils. Gutterglass was under siege.

She hefted her spear in one hand, curled Pen's photo in

the other and set off at a run. Shouts of alarm and anger followed her across the yard. Some of the stone bodies blurred towards her, but none of them could touch her. Her bare feet slapped on the concrete, growing faster as she drew the essence of London into her body. The synod's divine toxins continued to work in her; she could feel her physiology changing moment by moment.

Ahead of her, a Pavement Priest in a pitted iron punishment skin launched himself at one of the tower's ground-floor windows. The glass exploded as a giant fist made of rusting radiators burst outwards. The metal statue took the punch full in the chest and stopped cold. The clang as he hit the concrete echoed over the city.

The fist retreated back into the tower.

Beth altered her trajectory, sprinting for the empty window frame. *Have to hope that I'm harder than a Pavement Priest*, she thought. *Or that Glas is happy to see me . . .*

Given how she'd left things with Mater Viae's former seneschal, she didn't think *that* was very likely.

She leapt, and sailed through the window like a circus performer. She landed inside with much less of a bump than she'd expected, the ground releasing a rich stink of decay as it shifted and squashed under her.

She rose to her feet. The room was waist-high in rubbish: orange peel, bits of white plastic, smashed furniture, circuit boards, stacks of mouldering paper, shoes decayed to the point where only the soles were left. Beth crouched, her spear high, waiting for the attack: any of these rubbish-dunes might be hiding a blade made from a broken car door, or reshape itself into an eggshell-eyed face that would spit rusting nails at her with bullet-like velocity.

Minutes came and went, and there was no attack. The sea of garbage remained quiescent. Beth drew in a shuddering breath and waded towards the door.

The corridors were equally filled with trash. Beth couldn't force her way through it and instead had to clamber over it. She was painfully aware that every second out of contact with the masonry weakened her, but Pen's name just kept spinning round her mind, goading her onwards. She reached the emergency stairwell and began to scale the trashslide that covered it like a mountaineer.

She was impressed; she'd heard the rumours that Gutterglass, under attack on all sides, had found the landfill fastness north of Euston too vast to defend and had relocated south, towards the city's centre – but she hadn't realised the trash-spirit had brought the dump *with* it.

Beth guessed that for Glas, this was the equivalent of some aristocrat moving out of their stately home and trying to fit all their old posh furniture in a one-bedroom flat.

Must feel cramped, she thought.

She rose through storey after storey, reaching down through the chaotic mulch of rotting meat and crushed lightbulbs and Thames knew what else to brush the concrete floor with her fingertips. She could sense a spark of consciousness through her outstretched fingertips, but it was diffuse: Glas was obviously here – and equally obviously in no hurry to manifest. One other thing was certain too: the old spirit knew she was here.

She kept climbing.

The top floor was a little less choked with rubbish, and Beth was able to walk upright. Wide windows opened onto a million sparks of the city night.

Perched on the stripped casing of an old washing machine, knees tucked under chin, apparently admiring the view, was a figure cowled in black plastic. Beth heard the cheep and chitter of rats.

'Here comes the source of all my joy, who brought me all my woe.' The voice, reedy and sing-song, was squeezed from washing-up-bottle lungs and rubber-band vocal chords, belying the power of its owner. 'But what she doth intend with me, only the seas and the streets do know.

'Well' – the voice became wry – 'perhaps the seas, the streets and the occasional attentive trash-spirit . . .'

Gutterglass turned and regarded Beth with eggshell eyes set in an almost featureless papier-mâché head. Fingers made of empty cigarette lighters held up a phial of transparent liquid. 'Looking for this? No need to look so surprised, My Lady. The synod's pigeons may be soaked in their chemicals, but they are still *pigeons*.' The seneschal nodded towards the roof, and somewhere in the shadows something cooed. 'They still talk. Unlike some people I could mention.' There was a bitter twist to the trash-spirit's tone. 'I've been waiting for you.'

Beth eyed Glas uneasily. *My Lady?* she thought. She scanned the rubbish until she found a discarded door from a bathroom cabinet. She turned its mirrored front towards Glas and raised her eyebrows questioningly.

Gutterglass snorted. 'Yes, that used to be home.' The eggshell eyes peered into the glass and stubby fingers smoothed nonexistent eyebrows. 'I was a doctor, and then a scientist. I wanted to know what lay under the surface of things.' There was a chittering commotion under the black plastic sack. 'So I did what scientists do: I theorised and I conducted experiments, and one of them brought me here.' Glas looked at the phial. 'This one, to be precise. It's a compound of three common, overlooked waste chemicals. I've always been good at making things from what other people throw away.

'I believe I'm the only person ever to make that particular journey – at least I was, until a few days ago. On it, I met *her* . . . or perhaps' – a rip in the papier-mâché curled like a smile – 'perhaps I mean *you*.' The eggshell gaze took in her cable-hair and her architectural skin.

Beth shook her head firmly. Gutterglass didn't contradict her, but the papier-mâché smile remained.

It curled tighter when Beth popped the cap off her marker and wrote on the mirror.

'What was . . . a scientist doing under . . . the thumb of a god?' Glas read the message good-humouredly, head tilted to one side. 'Oh, Miss Bradley, what do you think I was doing? Who better than a scientist – an explorer? I'd spent my entire life looking for the thing just beyond the edge of my understanding, and I found it in her: an infinity of it. I fell in love.'

Glas' voice was as wistful as the makeshift materials would allow. 'How could I not? But' – split-pen fingers tossed the phial and caught it – 'you didn't come here for a personal history, did you?'

Beth smeared away the writing from the mirror-surface. She curled her other hand tightly around Pen's picture. *Please have an answer*, she thought. *Any answer.*

Steeling herself, she turned the mirror around.

'What do I want for it?' Glas sounded genuinely surprised. Then the hidden lungs wheezed out a laugh. 'Oh, My Lady, you've been spending too much time with Johnny Naphtha. Is that what's got you so wound up? I'm genuinely curious. What did you think I'd ask you to give me? Or did you stalk up here with Filius' railing in your fist because you thought you'd have to *fight* me for it?'

The binbags stretched like black wings as Glas spread arms made of unwound coat-hangers. The trash-spirit accreted towards Beth on a tide of insects, and Beth stiffened in shock as Gutterglass embraced her.

'You poor, naïve goddess,' the reedy voice wheezed into her ear. 'What could I possibly ask you for? You're already doing everything I could ever want you to do – *becoming* everything I could ever want you to be.' Glas stood back and looked at Beth fondly.

'You look so much like her. So much.' An old sponge tongue wetted the lips to keep them from crumbling as they flexed. 'And even if there were something' – another shrug, this time sadder – 'one does not *bargain* with one's gods.'

Glas offered Beth the phial with the shy smile of a child giving its mum something it'd made for her. 'You can take it. All you need to do is *command* it of me.'

Beth stiffened at the word. There was something triumphant in the eggshell eyes. Glas had seen her flinch, and knew she understood.

'After all, I've made much bigger sacrifices for my religion.'

CHAPTER THIRTY

'Can't sleep, Countess?'

The elder of the two guards in the Hall of Beauty sounded concerned, but there was no suspicion in his voice. He clearly had no idea Pen had been out of the palace tonight.

'Nerves,' she said, as if admitting a secret.

The man's seam-split face creased indulgently. He looked in his sixties, and his grey stubble peppered his chin perfectly symmetrically.

Pen smiled back at him. She was more comfortable playing up to his paternal smile than to his younger colleague's gawking admiration. 'It's my first year.'

'You'll be golden,' he assured her. 'How could you not be? You've got everything you need right there.'

Pen ducked her head. 'I just hope I don't forget what I'm supposed to say, or swear in front of the camera, you know? All those *people* . . . I was wondering—' She looked up at him from under the edge of her hijab, shy but hopeful. 'Could I get in, to practise? Just to get the feel of the place – I won't touch anything.' She jerked her head over her shoulder at

Espel with what she hoped was the right amount of impe-
riousness. 'That way my lady-in-waiting could go over my
speech with me.'

The guard hesitated, but then he winked at her. There it
was again, that trust; that sense that a face so familiar
couldn't be anything but a friend. 'Can't see any problem
with that,' he said. 'Long as you don't tell anyone.'

In the dark, the Goutierre Device was a sleeping monster.
Its panes of glass glinted in the moonlight that shone
through the chamber's vast windows, hanging in the air
like fangs, ready to fall on any unsuspecting sacrifice. Tiered
seating had been erected around the machine like benches
in a Roman circus, from which the privileged few would be
invited to watch the beast feed.

The second the doors closed behind them, Pen saw Espel's
posture shift; the slight deferential hunch she'd maintained
slid off her like water. Pen wondered whether her own shape
had changed too. Had her deception inhabited her muscles
as well as her voice? Had she been standing more and more
like her mirror-sister?

Espel crossed to the control panel, her feet silent on the
thick carpet, raised her voice and said, 'That's good, Countess,
almost there, but it's "My Lords, Ladies and *Gentlemen*". You
mustn't forget the gentlemen, else they get terribly upset.'

While she was speaking, she snapped her fingers at Pen
and pointed to the leather-clad bench at the centre of the
device.

'Ah . . . "My Lords, Ladies and Gentlemen",' Pen said, trying to remember the speech she'd watched Parva practising on film. She matched Espel's volume, eyeing the narrow crack between the double doors as she hopped up onto the bench. Goutierre's Eye hung over her, the tiny sun around which the manifold glass lenses turned in their orbits.

'Welcome to the Draw for the – uh . . . two hundred and fifth?'

'Two hundred and fourth,' Espel corrected her

'Two hundred and *fourth* Looking-Glass Lottery. We are joined by . . . Uh, no, sorry. Can we go from the top?'

'That's okay, Countess,' Espel announced encouragingly. 'In your own time.'

Pen dropped her voice. 'Well?' she murmured. 'Can you work it?'

'I think so.' Espel's answering whisper fizzed with excitement. From where she was lying, all Pen could see was a crowd of backlit silhouettes caught in the overlapping panes of glass.

'The interface for calibrating the Eye is more complicated than it looks on TV,' Espel whispered. 'I'm going to need a little time.' She raised her voice again. 'Oh, Countess, really now, there's no need to cry.'

'*Cry?*' Pen hissed dangerously.

The manifold silhouettes shrugged. Pen ground her teeth together and then twisted her throat to choke out the closest sound she could make to a sob.

'Hey, *hey*,' Espel said soothingly. 'It's okay. Remember,

everyone's rooting for you. Let's just pause for a second. Take as much time as you need, ma'am'

'You're having way too much fun with this,' Pen muttered.

The half-dozen shadow-Espels stuck out half a dozen shadow-tongues. There was a faint tapping of computer keys as the steeplejill programmed the device.

'So tell me,' Espel whispered, 'what did Old Lady Case want you to give me a raise for?' She sounded almost casual, like she was just making conversation, but there was a very slight edge in her voice.

'Gratitude, mostly,' Pen replied. 'For keeping me out of the weather.'

Espel hissed a suppressed laugh. 'And what else? I can't see gratitude moving Maggie Case to much.'

You're wrong, Pen thought. Being grateful for who and where she was moved the old mirrorstocrat to the most terrible things. Pen was very, *very* afraid of Senator Case's gratitude.

'What else?' Espel repeated.

'She'd heard the rumours about you and me being . . . um . . . together,' Pen said. 'She wanted you to buy some more features – "make it respectable". Her words,' Pen added hurriedly, 'not mine.'

The tapping of the keys faltered for a heartbeat, then resumed. 'Huh,' Espel said softly, and then a few keystrokes later, 'too ugly to date the Face of the Looking-Glass Lottery, hey?' She snorted in a way that was almost a laugh. *Almost.* 'Well, I suppose that's not news to anyone.'

'You're not ugly.'

'Oh no, I *am* ugly, Countess,' Espel corrected her flatly. 'If ugly means anything, it means me. Beauty may be in the eye of the beholder, but all the beholders are agreed, and I ain't got it. And, you know what?' she said. Her whisper took on a hard, angry edge. 'That's fine. I don't *want* them to think I'm beautiful. What I want is for it not to matter that they don't.'

There was silence, filled only with keystrokes.

Pen looked up. Above her, the ultimate beholding eye glittered in its shaft of moonlight. Her throat was tight. *Say it*, she scolded herself.

'I get that,' she whispered. 'I really do. But . . . just a point of fact, one small detail . . . and this can matter as much or as little as you like—' She paused to steady her voice, though it wasn't insincerity that made it tremble. 'As far as beauty goes, there's at least one beholder who thinks you have very much got it.'

The silhouettes in the glass went very still. Pen could hear her heart slamming in her ears.

At last Espel spoke. 'Don't move. It's ready.'

A switch was flicked, and over her head Goutierre's Eye began to rotate in its cage. A beam of white light tracked slowly from Pen's right ear to her nose and back again. The device was scanning her, *seeing* her. It was a strange relief, to be seen like that, unfiltered by envy or pity or revilement or lust or expectation, just to be *seen* as she was.

The Eye spun faster, silent and frictionless in its cage. The stormy ribbon at its heart shifted, spreading as though by centripetal force. Its flurry of images scattered across the inside of the little orb, millions of fragmented faces pressed up against the glass like eager children. Even though she knew it was impossible – they were all far too small – Pen could swear she could make out their features, their piece-meal eyes and noses and smiles, crow's-feet and laughter lines. Her heart began to trip. She refused to blink, desperately scanning for that one familiar face. A droplet of sweat ran past her reconstructed ear.

The Eye spun faster still, galaxies of reflected faces whirled and rushed inside it. Pen felt her own eye stretch, striving hopelessly to see them all. Her eyeball dried out, started to itch, but she *would not* blink. She saw reflections caught in taps and windows and puddles and raindrops and hubcaps and corneas and spoons and the impossible churn of the Thames and—

—it was infinitesimally brief: a flicker of recognition, felt rather than actually seen: an after-image of a girl in a green hijab was burned onto her eye.

The hum of the machine died. Above her, the glass orb slowed to a halt.

'Did we get it?' Pen demanded. 'Did it work?'

Espel was hoarse. 'We got it.'

Pen scrambled from the bench. There were three screens set up above the control podium where Espel stood. Two of them showed scrolling white text against a black background, but the third held an image of a face. It was distorted, rippling as though cast onto water, only the left side had been captured – and that was grainy where it had been blown up to fit the screen.

Even so, the face was unmistakable – and unmistakably alive. It even looked like Parva was smiling.

'Hello, Sis,' Pen whispered. Her throat was tight and full. It was only when she tasted salt on her rebuilt lip that she realised she was crying. 'Where are you?'

Espel answered her. 'The Kennels.' The steeplejill sounded rueful. 'We were less than four streets from there a few hours ago.'

'Can you find the place?'

Espel nodded. Pen let out a slow breath and smudged away the tears with the heel of her hand. 'Good.' She slipped back between the glass panes and took hold of the cage where Goutierre's Eye was still swinging. She slipped the catch and the glass sphere tumbled into her hand. She slid the replica marble in its place.

When she turned, Espel's gaze was quizzical.

'I made a promise,' she whispered with a smile. 'A member of the Faceless did find my sister for me, after all.'

She looked at the precious, unique thing nestling in her palm, then slipped it into her pocket. 'Come on. What are we waiting for?'

Espel paused. She looked frightened and Pen wondered what could possibly scare this lean, hungry girl who built towers from falling masonry and went suicidally undercover in the palaces of her enemies. Then she remembered the way Espel had talked about the Masonry Men; that shudder when she'd called them *those things*. Tears shivered in her eyes, waiting to fall.

'Listen,' Pen said, 'you don't have to come. I know what happened last night was—'

'Shut up,' Espel whispered. She laid her fingers gently against Pen's mouth. 'Shut up with that right now, *Milady*. Of course I'm fragging coming. You won't even get out of the building without me. We'll go and hand-deliver our arses to a bunch of concrete-skinned kidnappers who can walk through walls and snap our necks like stale biscuits and that's . . . *fine. That's* not what's bothering me . . .

'It's just, before we do—' She stepped forward. Pen felt a jolt of anticipation below her breastbone. Espel was close enough for Pen to breathe in her exhalation. ' I need to know if you really *meant* . . .' She faltered.

Pen took a chance.

She put her hand on top of Espel's and slid it from her lips down onto her neck. The fingers fluttered as her pulse hammered under them. Pen put her hand over Espel's temple and wound her fingers into her hair. She hesitated for a fraction of a second and kissed her.

Espel inhaled sharply. There was a terrifying, paralysed moment, when Pen was certain that Espel was going to push herself away, and then that breath came out again and the steeplejill's lips gave way under hers. They held the kiss for long moments, Pen's heart loud in her ears, and then Espel stepped into her.

Her body was close and warm. Her fingers stroked along Pen's collarbone, then rose and gently traced her scars, leaving sparks in their wake. Pen came up on the balls of her feet, pushing herself deeper into the kiss, tasting the salt on Espel's lips, smelling the soap on her skin and the dye in her hair, seizing onto every detail.

She had no idea how long they stood like that. Pen pulled back only when she started to feel lightheaded. It was an unutterable relief to see Espel's grin mirrored in her own.

'If I turn around now,' Espel whispered, 'and there's a bunch of Chevs watching us, I'm going to be sorely disappointed, Countess.'

Pen shook her head. 'Just us,' she said, and it sounded like a promise.

'So, does this mean you're into girls?' Espel asked.

Pen felt a flash of panic then – an almost irresistible urge to deny it, to take it back – but then she realised she didn't know if it was panic or elation; she couldn't tell the difference. She felt like a sprinter who'd been crouched on the starting line for so long she'd ceased to believe that she'd ever get to run, but she was running now, really flying and she didn't want to stop.

She started to laugh, she couldn't help it. Espel looked mortified until Pen laid a gentle hand on her neck and kissed her again.

'It means I'm into you,' she said softly as they parted. They were forehead to forehead, the cool metal of Espel's seam resting against Pen's scars. 'If I decide it means anything else, I'll let you know.' Her lips were still tingling, even the rebuilt one. She had no idea how that worked, but she knew she liked it. The tingle turned into a tremble which spread through her limbs until every muscle felt like a strummed guitar string.

This, she thought, *is how it's supposed to be.* The part of her that wanted to deny, to run away, to lock this moment up and forget about it – that was still there, still pushing at her, but she pushed back fiercely.

We're about to go and hand-deliver our arses to a bunch of concrete-skinned kidnappers who can walk through walls and snap our necks like stale biscuits, she thought, *so I ought to at least have this.*

Another laugh burst up from her chest and she bit her lip to trap it. 'Come on,' she said. She jerked her head at the door. 'Before they think we've started making out on the Device.'

Pen felt a flush of pleasure at the wistful look Espel threw the padded leather bench.

'Later,' she smiled, a little startled by how naturally the promise came to her; at how easy it was to make. 'Definitely later.'

CHAPTER THIRTY-ONE

'You sure these'll fit?' Pen asked as she caught the holdall Espel had thrown to her.

'Yours fit me well enough, don't they?' Espel gestured to the black shirt Pen had loaned her. Beside her bare feet was a small heap of leather and tin she'd already dug out of the holdall. She went to turn away, but then a mischievous smile crinkled her tattooed cheeks. She straightened, looked Pen in the eye and began very deliberately to unbutton her clothing.

'Hang on— What are you—?' Pen's protestations faded as Espel wriggled out of her trousers. The waistband of her knickers had slipped very slightly, showing a smooth, pale hip. Pen bit her lip, but she didn't turn away. Espel's gaze was direct, an eloquent invitation to look; she knew exactly how hard Pen's pulse was stampeding right now and she was enjoying it.

The sight of Espel's pale skin made her want to touch it, to feel its texture against her own. She felt like maybe she should have been surprised by that, but she wasn't. It was as though a muscle in her chest that she'd held tensed for so long she'd forgotten it was there had suddenly relaxed, and now she could breathe like she'd always been meant to breathe.

What am I going to tell Mum and Dad? The thought made her falter. She fingered the glass Eye in her pocket. *Let's cross that bridge when we've managed to rebuild it from its charred remains, hey, Pen?*

'You gonna try yours on then?' Espel's gaze was challenging.

'You've seen it all anyway.' Her voice didn't even tremble, but when she pulled her T-shirt up over her face, she held it there until she felt her flush subside.

She shivered as she felt the eyes of the first girl she'd ever kissed linger on her scarred skin.

'Not like it's ever gonna get old.' Espel sighed. 'I only wish we had time to do something about it.' She look she gave Pen was like she was storing her up. 'Okay,' she said, with a wistful smile, 'take temptation away.'

'For now,' Pen said. Espel's wistful smile became a grin.

As it happened, the spare steeplejill armour didn't fit Pen particularly well. Despite being roughly the same height and build as her, Espel was noticeably narrower in the limb and the leather sleeves were tight around Pen's elbows, almost trapping them in an awkward half-hug, like she was doing the Robot. At least her brown fabric messenger bag didn't look too out of place, strapped tight over her shoulder. Inside it were Goutierre's Eye and the precious second phial of the doorway drug, her passage home.

In contrast, Espel wore her armour like a tiger wears its stripes. It made her more powerful, more graceful, more forcefully *herself*. Pen enjoyed seeing her like that, not faking it as a servant or conflicted as a terrorist, but in her element, equipped for the art she'd spent more than half her life perfecting.

'We're a little tight on exits,' she remarked wryly to Pen as she started pulling coil after coil of blue nylon rope from the kitbags she'd lugged up to the apartment, then connecting each length to the next with metal clasps.

The main lobby was out of the question – they wouldn't be allowed to leave without a full Chevalier escort, which would start getting awkward right around the time that Pen was reunited with the girl she'd spent the last three days pretending to be. Their previous rat-run through the kitchen was ruled out on account of the dozen pastry and sous-chefs who would by now be sweating over eggs and croissants for the hundred or so resident members of the mirrorstocracy who were expecting their Draw Night morning breakfasts.

'Happily, for a jill, this place hasn't got two doors, it's got twenty thousand.' Espel flipped the latch and shoved the window open. The air was crisp and cool after the previous night's storm. Dawn painted London-Under-Glass' towers in colours of molten magma. A few figures moved across the roofscape, dressed as they were. Distance and perspective made the jacks and jills slow as they swept and sorted through the fallen brick.

'Now, remember what I told you.' Espel put a hand on Pen's shoulder. 'We need to move *fast*.'

Pen felt her stomach plunge, apparently trying to get a head start on her. She eyed the drop. 'I know,' she said. 'We need to spare Lady Leytonstone the sight of my face over her morning coffee—'

'*Deprive*,' Espel said. 'We need to *deprive* her of the sight of you, at least to the extent that she won't be able to recognise it.' She snorted. 'If someone does spot us, mind, we can only hope it *is* Lady L. If she's awake this early it'll be because she's not run out of ouzo yet. She'd see at least three of each of us and put it down to a trick of the weather. Hey! I've not connected your rope yet—'

Pen was leaning out of the window. The glare coming off the glass roof of the station hit her like a wall of light. She hung there, weight poised on her hands against the windowsill, just on the tipping point of her balance, her boots barely scraping the floor, daring herself to breathe. Her nostrils were full of the scent of concrete dust, her ears the clang of machines.

Espel's protestations had long since faded away by the time she dropped herself back inside.

She met the steeplejill's gaze with steady eyes.

'Mago, girl,' Espel murmured. 'Where'd you get your head for heights?'

Pen's lips thinned. 'Somewhere there wasn't any rope, only wire.'

Espel clipped Pen's harness into place and fed the vital

umbilical of rope through the loops. She hefted the soft rubber counterweight in her palm for a second, clipped herself to the line and then threw it out of the window. As the line slithered over the sill Espel stood by the window and spread her arms.

Pen didn't let herself hesitate. She stepped in close to Espel and breathed in the scent of sweat and leather and soap. It smelled right, *human*. She made herself surrender as Espel's arms folded around her.

'I've got you, Countess,' Espel whispered to her. 'Let me know you're ready. Just say when.'

She gave a fractional nod, barely more than she could have managed with a steel cage around her. 'Call me Pen,' she said.

Espel didn't comment; she just tipped backwards and bore them out into the light.

CHAPTER THIRTY-TWO

The two girls followed an illicit path through the streets of London-Under-Glass. It wasn't long after dawn, but the pavements were already filling up with commuters, their heads down and chins tucked against their chests as they breathed little webs of frost into the air.

The meandering route was frustrating, but if any of the pedestrians saw Pen, there would be what Espel called a *ruckus*. A ruckus apparently was three full stages up on a *fuss* and only one step below a *riot*. At best, they'd have to wade through adoring crowds as thick and clinging as heavy mud; at worst, word would get back to the Chevs . . .

Fortunately, Pen knew how to hide them. She had learned under the Wire Mistress's brutal tutelage how secret spaces could open up in the heart of the city. Alleyways and court-yards and low, accessible rooftops could all be navigated to avoid busy streets. The reversed city's rained-down masonry helped them: the deeper they delved into the architectural thicket of the Kennels, the more they were able to sneak behind opaque globs of precipitated brick and stone.

Pen dragged Espel by the hand. They were a needle, their path a thread that stitched London-Under-Glass' hidden places together.

'We're almost there,' Espel said at last. 'It's the next street over. Countess— Pen, are you okay?'

Pen wasn't sure. She had been looking around herself for the last few minutes, trying to work out what was familiar about the swollen buildings that currently surrounded her. It felt a bit like something she'd once glimpsed from the corner of her eye.

She let go of Espel's hand, and dropped back a few paces, trailing her fingertips over the wall of the alley. Weeds grew from cracks in the brick dunes under her feet. Pen marvelled at the way neglect made neighbourhoods anonymous. Despite the weird architecture, she felt like she could have been sneaking with Beth around the back of a Hackney terrace, looking for a good place to leave a tag or a scribbled verse.

Longing for home, for her best friend, winded her. There was a ragged wound where she'd torn herself away from that life. Right now, the other edge of that tear felt so close it was almost unbearable.

She sucked in a breath and let the winter air chill the water in her eyes until it no longer felt like tears.

When she was steady again, she walked over to join Espel. The steeplejill leaned against the wall, peeking out of the end of the alleyway. Sounds filtered in from the street, young voices raised in shouts and raucous laughter.

'That's the place,' Espel whispered triumphantly. 'Looks like it's a school.'

Pen froze as she came up behind Espel. The sense of familiarity made sudden sense. *Glimpsed from the corner of an eye*, she thought; *reflected in window-glass.*

The helpful reverse-lettered sign was irrelevant; even swaddled in rained-down masonry, Pen would have known Frostfield High anywhere. A tide of stitched-faced, blue-uniformed students was pouring through its gates for the new day.

'You're sure that image was current?' Pen whispered, her throat dry.

'Last twenty-four hours for definite,' Espel confirmed. 'Why?'

This doesn't make any sense, Pen thought. *Why would they take her, only to bring her back?*

'You got any brilliant ideas for getting us across that street?' Espel's identical brows raised either side of her seam. 'Because at least six of those kids have *Khannible* rucksacks.'

Pen didn't; she was about to suggest they just flat-out run for it when a familiar laugh stopped her voice in her throat.

It was light, utterly carefree. She hadn't heard that sound in so long she barely recognised it.

She spun around and pressed herself against the wall, looking up the street in the direction the laugh had come from.

Trudging over the uneven pavement towards them, scars immaculately made-up and underlined in dark makeup, was

Parva Khan. She had her arm slung around the shoulder of a redheaded girl and her head was bent to whisper in her ear. Whatever she was saying, they were both finding it hilarious.

Pen stared in incomprehension. Parva Khan, the Face of the Looking-Glass Lottery – on the busy street, she should have been like a magnet in a bowl of iron filings, but the people she passed barely gave her a second look.

It was only when Parva gave her a companion a playful shove and turned her face fully towards Pen that she understood.

A silver seam ran from the edge of the girl's green hijab to her chin.

Disappointment curdled in the pit of Pen's stomach like rotten meat. This wasn't her mirror-twin – this wasn't the girl she'd spoken to through the glass. This was a half-faced stranger. All right, she looked enough like Pen that perhaps she had begun in one of her reflections – but that could have been at any point in her life. Or maybe she just had a really good plastic surgeon. The scars the girl so proudly displayed were mostly likely an affectation, the work of some knife-parlour pop-up. Maybe even the headscarf the girl wore was—

Pen froze. *The headscarf.* She stared at it until her eyes ached. It was the scarf her parents had given her when she'd come out of hospital, the one that had been burned and stamped into the snow in the playground of Frostfield High.

It was the scarf Pen had been wearing in the derelict bath-room the day Parva was born.

'Es,' she said quickly, 'there—'

'I see her,' Espel sounded as confused as she felt. 'But isn't she—?'

'I don't know. I have to talk to her. Create a diversion.'

'*A diversion?* What do you want me to do, breakdance?'

Pen hesitated. 'Can you?'

'Not even close.'

'Well . . . do something else, sing, or scream "fire!" or any-thing,' Pen begged. 'Just distract her friend – just for a minute, please.'

She didn't give Espel a chance to argue; she just shoved the steeplejill into their path as the half-faced Parva and her redheaded friend approached the alley. 'HEY – excuse me, ladies,' Espel said loudly as she barrelled between them. She spread her arms, made herself as big as she could, trying to block the redhead's line of sight to her companion.

'Uh – there are important precipitecture works taking place. The whole side of the street is structurally unsound, *very* dangerous—'

The girls stared at the strange steeplejill.

'What?' the half-faced Parva started. 'Precipitecture? But everyone else is—'

Her protest ended in a yelp as she was dragged into the alley by her wrist, pushed against the wall and had a hand clapped over her mouth.

Pen held her there for a second. Everything about her was

symmetrical on either side of the silver seam. Her scars, her pores, everything, except . . .

Around the girl's brown eyes, the tiny red filament cracks of capillary were slightly different.

She remembered Jack Wingborough with the distorting half-mask pressed to his face.

The only real market for them is Mirrorstocrats on the run from their own governments. Most have them it bonded to their skin – it's safer – it means it won't peel off at an inconveniently public moment.'

Most of them have it bonded to their skin . . .

The girl's eyes were wide. Pen pressed a finger to her lips and the girl gave a shuddering little nod before Pen lowered her hand, and then hissed in excitement, 'Mother Mirror! *Countess Parva Khan?* What are you—? I'm – I'm a *huge* fan.' She proudly brushed her fingertips through the air over the makeup-lined scars on her right cheek.

'They're lovely,' Pen said. 'The best I've seen. I . . . I was just passing and I just – I wanted to tell you that.'

The girl beamed incredulously.

Pen said apologetically, 'Sorry for all the spy-movie stuff. I'm trying to stay incognito, hence the somewhat unfortunate wardrobe choices.' She gestured to the steeplejill armour she was wearing and gave the half-faced girl a conspiratorial smile.

'What's your name?' Pen asked.

'Aisha.'

Pen swallowed what felt like a boulder of air, but her smile stayed on as she said casually, 'Great headscarf too, Aisha.' The name was like brambles in her mouth. 'The colour's wonderful. I'd totally love one like it.'

The half-faced girl blushed with pleasure, and Pen could almost see her imagining telling her friends that the Face of the Looking-Glass Lottery had taken a fashion tip from her.

'Could you let me know where you got it?' Pen asked.

'Oh sure, I . . .'

It wasn't until Pen saw confusion cloud the girl's face that she was certain. She'd only seen that expression once before, but it was one she would never forget. It was the look her father had worn three days and a lifetime before, when Pen had asked him why he'd moved to Wendover Road – the look of someone reaching inside themselves for a memory that had been scoured away.

Aisha – the girl who had been Parva Khan – swallowed. A symmetrical frown crinkled her skin. 'I'm really sorry.' She sounded genuinely distressed. 'I just . . . I can't remember. It's completely gone out of my head.'

Pen nodded. Her gracious smile hurt her cheeks. 'Don't worry about it – I just wondered.' She paused and looked out of the alley-mouth. 'New at school?'

The girl looked at her incredulously. 'How could you possibly know that? I only started here yesterday.'

'You walk like a new girl,' Pen said, as if it were a real explanation. 'I'm good at reading people. Were you . . . were you happy, where you were before?'

342

Aisha-who-had-been-Parva scuffed her feet. 'It was okay,' she said in a voice that suggested it really hadn't been. 'It's early days, but this is better.'

Pen remembered the mercury-coloured solution her parent's memories had made. She looked into those oh-so-familiar brown eyes and wondered what bottled memories this girl had drunk to replace those stolen from her.

Johnny Naphtha's oil-slick voice whispered back from inside her memory: '*Thisss potion iss highly proprietary,*' he'd said as he'd placed it into her hand. '*Itss preparation iss a ssecret we have sssupplied to only one other persssonage.*'

But somehow, that secret had travelled to this side of the glass.

Pen drew in a shuddering breath. Confusion and relief and fright and loss and other emotions she didn't even know the names of jostled in her chest. Then a violent energy seized her. For a moment she was almost overwhelmed by the urge to scratch the symmetrical face away with her fingernails, to peel back the distorting mask, to beg her mirror-sister to remember what they'd been through together, to remember *her*. The desire screamed its way up from her chest—

—but then she thought of the girl's carefree laugh, and she trapped the urge before it could become action.

'*It's early days.*' The voice in her head sounded just like hers. '*But this is better.*'

'I'd better let you get on,' Pen said. 'It's only your second day. You don't want to be late.'

'Look, it's been such a total honour—' the girl started.

Pen waved that away. 'I know it's an ask, but do you mind keeping quiet about this?'

'Incognito, right?'

'You got it.'

The girl ducked her head in acknowledgement, until all Pen could see was the green headscarf, then she ran to rejoin her friend.

'Aisha!' Pen heard the redheaded girl say. 'Where did you go? One minute there was this mental steeplejill all up in my face and the next, you weren't there any more.'

'Oh—' Aisha's voice faltered for a second. 'I thought I saw someone I recognised, but it wasn't her.'

'Well,' Espel asked as she slipped back beside Pen, 'are we done?'

Grief was a thread being drawn tightly through Pen as she answered, 'Yeah, we're done.'

Espel looked out at the street. 'So that girl . . . is she—?' She tailed off.

'Is she what?' Pen asked. Espel didn't reply. 'Es? Is she *what*?'

It was only when Pen looked up that she saw Espel was frozen. Her expression was a tight mask of fear, and she was pointing.

Pen followed the line of her finger. On the street, unnoticed amongst the agglomerations of rained-down materials, right under the feet of the students, the pavement rippled in a four-limbed shape.

It was only visible for an instant, then it vanished. When it returned, a split second later, it was pointing at them. The squat hump that was its head swayed slowly from side to side, distorting the concrete, as though it was sniffing for them.

They were watching her, Pen thought. Cold fear blossomed at the base of her skull.

'Run,' she whispered. Espel sprang like a greyhound from a trap, Pen tearing after her, back down the alleyway, the way they'd come. The ground shifted as the creature surged after them.

Pen's blood pounded in her ears, artillery-loud. The armoured jacket was stiff and clumsy and she frantically ripped it open. Her messenger bag flew out behind her, dragging her like a parachute and she clawed it back to her side.

Espel ran beside her, breathing raggedly. Fear sparked through Pen with every footfall. Every step felt like it invited the grey man's grip.

'*Pen!*' Espel shrieked as a hand the colour of clay erupted from the wall in front of them, fingers splayed like spiders' legs. It groped, grotesquely blind. Pen seized Espel by the scruff of her neck and yanked her under the forearm that followed it. They didn't even break step.

More quiet explosions, more *traps*.

Hands grasped at them from all directions, reaching from the walls. Pen didn't have the breath to scream. She hurled herself despairingly at the thicket of limbs. Concrete fingers touched her skin; they were as warm as flesh. She spun off one thick forearm and hit another. Mortar glistened on them like afterbirth. She fell to her knees and started dragging herself on her elbows through their fingers like they were wire – like they were *barbed wire*. They hemmed her in, their hands on her mouth, stopping her breath, burying her alive in the open air. She hissed and kicked and clawed at them in panic. Soft clay lodged under nails like clotted blood.

Clear sweet breath rushed suddenly into her lungs: she was through!

She scrambled back to her feet. Espel stumbled along beside her, blood seeping from the side of the steeplejill's neck. The edges of the wound were stained with clay finger-prints.

Pen remembered the sinuous speed of the predators in Victoria Station. *Why haven't they caught us up yet?* she wondered.

They ran for ten more unhindered breaths, perhaps forty strides, before Pen risked a glance over her shoulder.

The masonry men had broken from the walls, blinking brick-dust from their featureless eyes like sleep – but there were too many of them. The narrow alley couldn't contain them all, and in their eagerness to thrust themselves free they'd emerged *into one another*. Their arms were thrust through the concrete of each other's wrists; knees burst through thighs and teeth through shoulders: a nightmare clot of torsos and limbs and heads. They grimaced in pain, their innards churned by the intruding bodies of their fellows.

Hope filled Pen as she ran.

But then a dark shape shifted in the heart of the mass. As if driven by some predatory instinct, a single Masonry Man burst outwards in a spray of bloody brickdust. Pieces of clay and concrete bodies fell around him, torn open by his escape. There were sudden and terrible gaps in skin, revealing grey arteries and grey organs. Gouts of thick cement oozed from wounds. Pen could see their throats working as they screamed silently.

The escapee threw his head back in a soundless, grief-stricken howl, even as he gave chase.

Pen and Espel put their heads down and sprinted, but the precipitecture drifts slowed them. Exhaustion burned in Pen's muscles like fever and the world shuddered and shook in time with her breaths. She snatched a sideways glance – Espel was horribly pale. Blood seeped through her fingers where they were clamped to her neck.

From a nearby street, Pen heard the growl of an engine. *A car*, she thought muzzily. *Open road*. It was a slim chance, but Pen wore Parva Khan's face and the driver might let them in. She grabbed Espel by the forearm and dragged her round a corner towards the sound.

They burst onto what looked like an empty road, then a cloud of exhaust engulfed them as a black blur tore past. Tyres screamed like agonised animals as the blur braked and resolved into an SUV which skidded to a stop. There was a white chess knight stencilled on the door that faced them.

The door opened and Pen stared in utter disbelief as the shaven head of Captain Corbin emerged over it. A squad of black-armoured figures boiled out of the vehicle behind him, all hefting squat grenade-launchers.

Espel ran towards them, her instinctive distrust of Chevaliers utterly obliterated by her terror of what hunted her, but Pen found herself slowing. She eyed them uncertainly.

How can you be here, now – how could you know?

There was no chance this was a coincidence.

A tremor rippled under Pen's feet and she heard a soft explosion behind her, then the grating sound of concrete feet on asphalt. Corbin grabbed a weapon and aimed it over her shoulder. She wondered how close the monster was, how far she could dive, if she'd be able to evade the fireball that would blossom out from the stricken creature.

But then Corbin spoke, and the word he used sat strangely in the mouth of a man holding a grenade-launcher.

'*Please*,' he said. He sounded desperate. 'Please. Let us take her.'

'*No.*'

Pen felt her heart slow. She saw Espel stiffen in shock. As one, they turned.

The creature stood only yards behind them, its concrete-coloured ribcage flexing silently as it drew deeply on something that couldn't have been air. It opened its mouth onto a tunnel-like throat. Pen could see the effort as it fought to distort its throat into something that could speak. '*She knows.*' The voice was high, almost inaudible: a whistle of

348

air through concrete. The thing spoke in draughty gusts, and Pen found herself straining to hear it. '*The agreement is breached.*'

'Please,' Corbin repeated. 'Please – we need her. We'll . . . we'll give you as many others as you want, but let us keep her.'

'*The agreement is breached.*' The thing was as intractable as its flesh. '*There can be no return.*'

The Masonry Man opened its arms as for an embrace. The wounds where it had ripped itself clear of its fellows still oozed concrete. Pen watched the liquid progress down its forearm, running in the channels between protruding veins, over the device of the Towerblock Crown.

'*She must attend my mistress,*' it wheezed. '*Take her above, or I will take her below.*'

Pen looked back at Corbin. All the blood had fled his seam-split face.

'I understand,' he said.

CHAPTER THIRTY-THREE

They drove back to the palace, and Parva Khan smiled on them every inch of the way.

She beamed out from billboards and bumper-stickers and posters pasted against walls. She flickered on TV screens glimpsed through front-room windows. Men bundled up against the cold perched on stepladders, hung bunting and fixed flags over their doors, all printed with Pen's reverse image. On the street, greetings were exchanged on gusts of steaming breath and smiles passed back and forth like gifts between strangers. It felt like all of London-Under-Glass was adorned with her scars.

Even strapped into the back of the SUV, the shock at finding Parva and fear of the Masonry Man's chase still vivid in her mind, Pen could feel the buzz about the reflected city. It was the day before Draw Night. The Looking-Glass Lottery was about to have a winner.

It was close on midday, and the palace's crenelated shadow fell across the surrounding blocks like a claw. Security had obviously been stepped up for the big night: half a dozen guards, bulked massively by their heavy armour, stood by the entrance, drumming their fingers on their machine-guns. Mounted Chevaliers urged their black-shrouded horses up and down the street. A pair of vast plasma screens had been mounted on the metal framework on the front of the palace. They beamed Pen's mirror-sister's smile down over the little square below.

'Now, Countess . . .' Corbin looked back at her. 'Are you going to walk in quietly, or are we going to have to stage some kind of accident?' He looked a little sick as he spoke, like a man threatening his own daughter, but he also looked scared enough to be capable of anything.

Pen didn't answer. She was horribly aware of Espel on the seat beside her and the guns holstered at her captors' hips. When the door was opened, she got out slowly.

'Countess! Welcome back!'

'Countess Khan, always a delight.'

They cast slightly puzzled looks at her outfit, but their confusion didn't impact their eager smiles. Pen returned those smiles carefully, listening to Corbin's footsteps, close behind hers. She could see in his shadow how his hand was casually resting on his belt next his side-arm. In the polished floor, Pen watched her reflection walk alone to the last lift on the right.

The doors hissed open, Pen stepped in, and this time Corbin did join her. When Espel moved to follow, a black-armoured forearm blocked her way.

'Just the Countess,' Corbin said.

Pen saw the muscles lock up in Espel's symmetrical face. She was very, very scared, and Pen didn't think it was for herself.

Pen reached past the Chevaliers and laid her hand on Espel's breastbone, just where her leather and tin jacket opened up. The warmth of her skin through the cotton was startling.

Pen made the promise looking right to her eyes: 'I'll find you at the end of the day.'

The lift doors slid shut slowly, eclipsing the girl who'd believed in her.

The Chevalier spoke into his radio. 'This is Corbin. We're in the elevator.'

'*Understood*,' the answer crackled back.

A mechanism whirred into life behind the stainless-steel walls. There was a clunk, like something locking into place under the floor, and a hiss as hydraulic clamps released. Pen's stomach lurched upwards.

The lift was going down, and fast – but only the floor was moving. The lift cage itself dwindled above them, dangling forlornly at the limit of its cable.

The lift was never meant to descend this far, she thought. *This is a jury-rig.*

The light from inside the lift-car diminished quickly, but Pen could still make out the shaft's steel supports where they fed into the concrete of the Shard's foundations. The walls were so smooth that it almost looked like they weren't moving at all, but Pen kept her hands clamped close to her sides. Judging by the surge in her stomach, they were dropping so fast that the passing concrete would strip her fingertips bloody if she touched it. Neither she nor Corbin spoke.

The light gave out long before they hit the bottom. The foundations felt impossibly deep and cold, like an ancient grave sunk into the bedrock beneath London's clay. The weight of the city seemed to concentrate itself over her with terrible potential. By the time they slowed she was desperate for light and barely holding in the panic.

At last the platform slowed and clicked to a halt. A rough tunnel stretched into the dark in front of them. Meagre illumination etched the cracks around a closed door at the far end.

'I don't have to threaten you again, do I?' Corbin's tone was pleading.

She must attend my mistress.

Compelled by a curiosity so much worse than her fear, Pen started walking. To distract herself from the man and the gun behind her, she studied the tunnel walls. They were rippled, almost organic-looking, and with a little thrill of understanding Pen saw that the undulations in its surface were thousands of overlapping handprints: the shaft had somehow been *pushed* into existence by an army of miners.

Sounds came to her, muted by the concrete, so quiet that Corbin's booted footsteps almost drowned them out: low, staccato noises punctuated by sudden pauses. Pen strained to listen. There was something familiar about them.

It was only when she realised the pauses matched the frequency of her own ragged breaths that she knew what she was hearing: voices. Dozens of voices, crying.

Memory burst over her.

Barbed tendrils undulating like insect legs, dragging her through the maze under St Paul's. Agonised voices crooning to her. The Wire Mistress' claws in her scalp, in her mind, dripping itself through her like slow poison.

The Wire Mistress.

She slowed, sucked in by the terrible gravity of memory. Every step pulled her deeper into the past.

'*She must attend my mistress.*'

At the end of the tunnel, a loud *crack* stopped her in her tracks.

It had come from behind the closed door, deafeningly loud, but it wasn't the volume that froze her muscles. It was the fact that she'd heard that sound before, echoing up from the rubbish chute in the kitchen. With a sudden, cold certainty, she knew it wasn't an incinerator.

On the ground in front of her, the handprints dappled together like ripples on water. A Masonry Man breached from the centre of the distortion, his arms outstretched. Pen jerked back hard, but the intruder wasn't reaching for her. Instead, he plunged his emaciated hands into the wall and dragged the concrete aside like a curtain.

The crying grew instantly louder as a tiny niche was uncovered in the wall. A man in a dusty brown tweed suit crouched protectively over a young boy in a school uniform.

The space was too small for him to stand up fully, and it had no light source. The captive man blinked as the weak glimmer from the tunnel caught his brand-new seam. His child continued to sob, oblivious. His features gave way to empty skin at the halfway point.

Pen stared uncomprehendingly at the little family from Victoria Station.

The father moved fast, trying to put himself between the grinning, skeletal jailor and his son, but the Masonry Man just shoved him contemptuously to the ground. The child screamed once as concrete fingers closed on his wrist, and then fell silent, his eye wide in terror.

'Wait!' the man yelped. 'Please – I'll—'

But whatever threat or promise he was going to make was lost as the Masonry Man dragged the tunnel wall back into place, sealing him back into darkness.

Without turning its concrete gaze on either Pen or Corbin, the Masonry Man pushed through the metal door at the end of the corridor, yanking the stumbling child after it. Corbin gestured to Pen. The air was like hot clay in her throat as she stepped into the room beyond.

Something crunched underfoot. Pen looked down and saw broken bottles and flasks covering the floor; fragments in all shapes and sizes. The dregs that clung to them glinted like mercury. The sea of shattered glass stretched out into the darkness as far as Pen could see.

The room's sole source of illumination was a lamp on a desk that sat in a little island of clear space near the door.

A solitary figure sat there, bent over a stack of paper as though in study. The lamp was set so that Pen could only see one of the figure's hands as it flicked absently at the corner of a page. A heavy-based tumbler sat next to it. The Masonry Man dragged its kicking, jerking captive onto a tarpaulin spread in front of the desk.

The child found his voice again and shrieked almightily. The figure behind the desk started and tilted the lamp towards its visitors. It was only when she peered out from behind her paperwork that Pen recognised Margaret Case.

'For Mago's sake, can't you see he's terrified?' Case snapped at the grey-skinned man. 'Let him go. Just . . . get out of my sight, would you? I'll deal with it from here.'

The Masonry Man's grin didn't diminish, but he let the boy go. He arched like a diver and plunged back into the floor.

'Case,' Pen started, but the mirrorstocrat ignored her and dropped to one knee in front of the trembling boy.

'I know,' she said softly. 'I know, I know. They're scary, I know.' She looked into his single eye, her wrinkled face open and empathic. 'But listen to me: I promise he'll never touch you again. It's over. You've been incredibly brave, all right? Your father's going to come in here in a moment and it will all be over. You were so, so brave.'

It was her best reassuring headmistress voice, and against all expectation it worked. As the boy's cries quietened, Pen wondered if, somewhere in the jumbled half of the memories he retained from the Old City, he'd once had a teacher just like her.

'Look at you, you're shaking.' Case went behind her desk and took something from a drawer. 'Here, drink this. It'll help.'

The small bottle caught the light from the desk lamp as she held it out. The liquid inside glinted like mercury.

Pen drew in a breath, to scream, to protest, to try to warn the child, but a black-gauntleted hand clamped under her jaw, holding it shut. She tried to struggle, to elbow Corbin, but he slid his other arm under her shoulder and locked her up with humiliating ease. She made sounds in her throat, but they were too quiet. The boy was too scared, too enraptured by the glimmer of the elixir he'd been offered. He didn't even look round.

Pen could only watch as the half-faced child tilted the bottle to his mouth. Little gobs of liquid ran out of the imperfect seal of his half-lips. They dribbled over the empty skin of his unreflected side, carving runnels in the dirt that caked it, and splashed onto the tarp with flat *plack plack* sounds.

He hesitated, uncertain, and Case moved fast, as fast as Pen had with her parents, sliding a gentle hand behind the boy's head and easing the bottle away. The boy gave way pliantly. He stared into space.

Case sighed. Pity and distaste warred on her face as she looked at the child. *As ugly as they come.* Espel's description of the immigrants flashed back to her. *Blatantly incomplete.*

'Corbin,' Case said, 'let her go.'

The grip on Pen eased and she tore herself free. She spun, hawked savagely, and spat at Corbin's face, but he didn't even blink as the spittle hit his eye. She tried to claw at him, to kick him, rage fountaining through her. He fended her off absently, his face ashen.

Pen turned and ran to the little boy; she dropped to her knees in front of him. 'Hey,' she said to him urgently. 'Hey.'

He looked at her, but his single eye showed no recognition, no sign he understood her words. He was like a half-finished doll. Pen felt something heavy drop into the pit of her stomach.

'What . . . what did they make you forget?' she said quietly.

'Everything,' Case said softly. She slumped against the edge of her desk. 'Corbin, could you take this one? I'm tired.'

Corbin's jaw tightened. He stepped almost respectfully around Pen.

'Don't use your own,' Case told him. She pulled an automatic pistol from another desk drawer and handed it to him. 'Here. This one doesn't leave the room.'

The boy didn't even flinch as Corbin levelled the gun at his head. He couldn't remember to be afraid.

Pen felt the world lurch around her. Much too late, she tried to move. 'Wai—'

The shot ripped all sound from the world. Pen was close enough to feel the heat of the bullet, the warmth of the blood. She recoiled, lurching to her feet and staggering backwards. She kicked bottles and heard them clink through the buzzing in her ears.

The glass.

The shot.

That percussive *snap* of air and explosive—

Now, she knew exactly what the sounds she'd heard echoing up into the kitchen had been. And she knew that there had been a sound like it for every one of the bottles strewn on the floor.

Pen screamed at Case, at Corbin, shrieking at them as senseless as an animal. She dragged in high, hysterical breaths.

It was a long time before she managed words.

'*How— How* could you—?'

'What else would you like us to do with them?' Case snapped back. 'Shelter them? Free them? Turn them loose on the street? They can't even remember how to *eat*, Parva. Mother Mirror, pull yourself together, would you? *This*' – she shook the bottle – 'is all of him. You understand? There was nothing left in that body but muscle reflexes.'

Her voice was flat, expressionless, but her eyes were bloodshot and pouched deep. It wasn't that she didn't feel it, Pen realised. It was just that the part of her that felt it was screwed down so hard it was dying.

Absolute control.

Corbin knelt and began rolling the body up in the wet tarpaulin.

'Bring in a fresh tarpaulin, would you?' Case told him. 'I thought we were done, but she keeps demanding more. They're lasting less and less. You—'

Resentment burned in her face as she looked at Pen. 'Follow me.'

Pen could barely feel her legs. When she tried to walk, she almost fell. Corbin left off rolling up the corpse to support her, but she hissed like a cat and raked her fingernails across his face. Three bright red scratches appeared on each of his cheeks. He fell back, staring at her.

Case looked at them both, snorted in disgust and stalked away.

'I'm surprised you've got the guts to do all this yourself,' Pen called after her.

'You think it's got anything to do with guts? How many people do you think I can afford to have find out about this?' Case looked despairingly about her. She kicked bottles out of her path with her expensive shoes. 'Such a fucking mess,' she muttered.

She looked back over her shoulder. 'Are you coming or not?'

Pen didn't move.

'What are you going to do then, just stand there? For how long? There's only one way out of here, Parva, and when I leave, the lift comes with me. Besides' – her voice hardened – 'she wants to meet you.'

She. And again, Pen felt it: the press of that terrible curiosity. She went reluctantly to Case's side and together they left the desk's little island of light behind them, and pressed out into the chamber.

Pen couldn't tell how big the space was. The walls returned no echoes. The ceiling could have been ten or a hundred feet above. It seemed an endless sea of bottles.

'They came for *me*, didn't they?' she said quietly. 'Last night, the only person the Chevaliers were there to save was me.'

'And they killed twelve of our allies.' Case's voice tightened a fraction on the word. 'A pretty little tap dance I had to do down here to explain it. I worried she might not listen, but happily she has an unsentimental attitude to her clayling brood. I was given one more chance to look after you.'

Look after you. Pen felt another, deeper chill at the phrase. Gradually, she became aware of city sounds, very quiet: the growl of engines and the gurgle of drains, hooting traffic, even something that might have been music. Perhaps the same trick of acoustics that had allowed the gunshots to echo all the way to the kitchen was carrying the noise of London-Under-Glass back to her. In the darkness ahead, she saw two pinpricks of green light.

'I can't believe you were so stupid,' Case snapped under her breath. 'I told you – *I told you,* we couldn't afford to have you running off again. I gave you every chance to be her. You could have been *happy.*'

—every chance to be her. 'You knew.' The shock was draining from Pen. She felt sick and heavy, like she'd swallowed liquid lead and it was setting in her belly. 'You knew who I was all the time.'

'Of course I did.' She sounded nonplussed by Pen's surprise. 'I didn't know how you'd done it, but I knew – of course I knew. Who else could you have been? I *grieved* when your mirror-sister was taken. I did my best for her.'

361

Pen thought of the difference between Parva, subsisting on a fake set of memories in a school in Kensington, and the boy rolled in the tarp.

'Well, what a thing it is to have your favour,' she snarled, but Case didn't seem to notice the sarcasm.

'I knew who you were the moment you walked into my garden,' she said. 'But still, your face was as perfect as hers and I thought – how could I not think – the Mirror has brought her back to me? You seemed content to play your sister's part, so I was content to let you. There was a chance . . . we could have *made* it true.' Case licked her lips.

'*She* wanted you, of course. She was *very* curious to know how you'd managed to come here. But I made a deal: I – I bargained with her. I told her that if she gave me just a little time, I could get that secret from you without violence.' There was an awful pride in her words. 'I was in control.'

'*Control.*'

Pen froze. The voice had come out of the dark ahead of them, and it was not human.

It had coalesced from the edges of the sounds of the traffic and the water and the drains and the distant music, carried in waves that filled the hidden expanse of the chamber and reverberated deep inside her skull, closer and more intimate than the sounds of which it was made. In her life, Pen had heard one other voice like it.

Soundlessly, her lips made the words: *I will be.*

Glass crunched on the floor. The green pinpricks of light

shifted and drew closer. They were, Pen realised, the right space apart to be eyes.

'*Control*,' said the city-voice. '*That was our agreement, Margarethe.*'

The eye-lights drew closer, revealing more of the face of which they were part.

The woman was old. Her skin was cracked, scaled in interlocking paving stones. The folds around her mouth were rows of terraced houses. Road markings lined her eyes and cheekbones like makeup. Her irises glowed the luminous green of traffic lights. Her skirts were lost in the darkness, but they rustled like estuary tides.

And then, a fraction of a second after seeing her, Pen *felt* her.

She inhaled sharply as that face rushed outwards to envelop her. Scale and distance dissolved: every road that lined the woman's intricate face was long enough to walk down; every rooftop was wide and solid enough to shelter her. Pen was immersed in and surrounded by that presence: a sense of place so raw and pure it was like being in love. She was standing in the labyrinthine city of the old woman, feeling the warmth of its streetlight on her face—

—and then it was over, and she was back facing a decrepit woman with cracked skin, in a room full of murder and glass.

Mater Viae gave her a smile filled with church spires. '*If you can't control her*' – though her lips did not move, her voice carried – '*you can't keep her.*'

Case didn't look at her as she offered up the bottle of distilled memory. Mater Viae grasped at it eagerly and Pen shuddered when she saw her fingers. Pressing skeletally against the inside of her skin were the outlines of cranes.

The City Goddess gulped at the silvery liquid in the bottle. When she'd drained it, she briefly closed her eyes in bliss. Case and Pen were plunged into a darkness that eased when the lights lit up in the windows of that city face.

'Please—' Pen recognised Case's expression as she spoke to the goddess. It was the same look she saw in the mirror every day, when she put makeup on her scars: the look of someone bound to something they hated. Case's city *was* concrete and glass and brick – everything she loved lay in the palm of that crane-boned hand – and Mater Viae could turn it against her with the sparest thought.

'Please,' she begged. 'Just a little more time.'

'*Time*,' Mater Viae echoed. She turned the green wash of her eyes on Pen.

'*I remember. In the flood and chaos of my new memories, I remember.*

'*I remember believing in you when I was taken. When the grey men dragged me through the floor and the earth filled my mouth and yet somehow I still breathed. When I was so, so scared, I remember believing you would come for me.*'

The voice changed, became familiar; not in tone, but in rhythm and inflection. Pen stiffened against the sickness she felt as she realised the Goddess was speaking from Parva's memories.

364

'*Even when they made me drink. Even though I thought it was poison. Even though I believed I was going to die. Even though I knew there was no way you could, to the end, I still believed you'd come.*'

There was a note of delight as she said, '*And you did.*'

And then, abruptly, the sense of Parva slid away.

'*There is no more time, Margarethe. I remember her. I remember being her, and being one who knew her better than anyone else in the world. I remember gazing back through at her through the mirror from this prison. She doesn't want your lottery. She doesn't want your fame. She has what she came for, and she has no more reason to stay.*'

Her expression became one of desperate need. Streetlights burned in the cracks of her face, lighting her like a Hallowe'en lantern. '*I will not risk letting her slip. She will leave for good, and I will lose my chance. I must have her secret. I must. I must.*' The words were an eager shriek of wheels on a road somewhere inside her.

'*I must know how you came here. I must know—*

'*—is there a way back, to my child?*'

My child. Pen's heart lurched as suddenly *everything* – the bottles, the Masonry Men attacks, the kidnapping of the immigrants – finally, it all made sense.

Johnny Naphtha's words slithered greasily back to her: *Nothing you possess is so potent as a parent's memories of those they have borne. They are the wellsprings of hope and obsessions of even the sanest of men.*

How much more intense might that obsession be for a

Goddess? A Goddess whose *name* meant mother, who had been trapped between two mirrors and then awakened to find herself stranded in another world, cut off from the child she loved – a child who was her home and her very nature.

How long had it taken her to realise what had happened? That the place she so cherished was somewhere she'd never been, somewhere she could never go, that her memories of that place belonged to another. What might she be willing to do to keep those memories from fading?

Pen felt a pang like a broken rib. She looked at the shattered bottles, the evidence of a homesick Goddess' addiction.

'How long?' Pen breathed. 'How long since you were caught between the mirrors?'

The highways that were the Mirror-Mater Viae's lips curled as if in contempt, but she did not answer.

'*Where is the pathway?*' her city-voice demanded. '*Where is the fissure that leads between cities? I do not remember it, so your sister did not know. Tell me, how can I go home again?*'

Pen's mouth was arid. She thought of Parva and gritted her teeth. 'You can't,' she said.

Mater Viae sighed. '*I must know. I must. I must remember it for myself.*' The light of her eyes made Case's skin sickly as she turned to her. '*Bring another dose, Margarethe.*'

'Please—'

With a little jolt, Pen realised Case was speaking not to Mater Viae, but to *her*.

'Please, Parva, just tell her. Tell her where you came through – it won't make any difference. She will have her way.'

But Pen shook her head, tight-lipped. She had only her obstinacy. She could feel barbs in her skin. Her hands were starting to shake. All she could do now was resist.

Case's face screwed up in fury. 'PARVA!' she screamed at Pen.

Pen flinched back half a step, and in her bag two glass objects clinked together. Before she could stop herself, she shot the bag a guilty, desperate glance.

Case read her expression, and in that heartbeat Pen knew her body had betrayed her.

Then Case lunged for the bag.

'Wait, *wait*—' Pen scrabbled for the straps, but the mirror-stocrat had already torn it from her. Pen felt her heart beating in her throat as Case rooted inside. Her mouth set in a hard line as she withdrew Goutierre's Eye, and for a desperate moment Pen thought Case might stop there, but then she reached back in and took out the phial of the doorway drug.

Grey fingers articulated like cranes to take the slender tube. The clear fluid inside glowed green under the Goddess' scrutiny.

'Well? Is that it?' Case asked. She was still staring at the glass sphere in her own palm. 'Can we take her back?'

Mater Viae's voice was as soft as rain on rooftops. '*Do what you will with her. I no longer care.*'

CHAPTER THIRTY-FOUR

All the way up through the gloom of the lift shaft out into the brittle light of the lobby and then back into the mirrored seclusion of the main elevators, Pen didn't say a word. She hugged herself as though her arms were all that were holding her together. Part of her didn't feel like it had left that nightmare chamber; that part was still deep underground, frozen at the moment when Mater Viae had taken her only way home.

Case stood a little behind her, Corbin's gun held idly in her hand like it was the most natural thing in the world for a member of the Silver Senate to go armed. Perhaps because of her nonchalance with it, no one challenged her. Pen was only vaguely aware of how fast the broken slave from the basement had slipped back beneath the surface of the reflected city's chief bureaucrat.

At last, when they reached the door to her apartments, Pen turned to face her captor. 'All those people,' she said quietly, 'didn't they mean anything to you? Didn't you ever even *think* about saying no?'

Case gave her the greyest smile. 'Oh, I said no. Once.'

Pen parted her lips to ask what happened, but then closed it again. She *knew* what had happened. She could see the pain of it in every line of the old woman's face. Case had been punished.

Parva – the only mirrorstocrat Mater Viae had abducted amongst who knew how many half-faces, her sister, the Face of the Looking-Glass Lottery – had been taken to teach Margaret Case obedience.

The only mirrorstocrat ... But that didn't make any *sense*, Pen realised suddenly. Half-faces had only half the memories of where they came from, so surely the homesick deity in the basement would have needed far more of them to feed her addiction to those memories. There was no reason for her to have preyed so exclusively on them, *unless* ...

Shock was an icy hammer-blow as Pen understood exactly what Case's bargain with Mater Viae had bought her: no victims amongst the mirrorstocracy. Case had sold double the number of her citizens to the predatory Goddess to keep the handful she cared about safe.

The senator regarded her. If she knew what Pen was thinking, she didn't let it show on her face. 'Get some sleep.' she said. 'You're needed in makeup in six hours. The cameras roll in eight and I don't want you looking haggard.'

Pen's fingers crooked into claws. From somewhere, new fury bubbled up into her heart. 'I will not perform for you, Senator. Your mistress' – she saw Case wince slightly at the word, but she was too angry to even enjoy her discomfort – '*drank* your Parva Khan. I won't replace her for you.'

'She was—' Case began to say.

'SHE WAS MY SISTER!' Pen screamed.

Case didn't flinch; she waited patiently, as though pausing for the ringing of Pen's voice to fade from her ears, and then spoke with a chilly distaste. 'I think you're wrong. I think you will go before the cameras, Parva. There are techniques of persuasion that won't impact how you look.'

For a second, Pen had no idea what she was talking about. Then she almost laughed. 'Torture?' She pointed at her own face. 'You do know where these came from?'

'I know the fable you – your sister – told about the barbed wire, if that's what you are referring to—'

'You still think it was a fable?' Pen hissed. '*Think* about where we just came from. Think about what *you just saw*.'

Case's gaze twitched back and forth in incomprehension across Pen's face. Pen just stared back, marvelling at how completely the old woman had sealed off the secret shame in the basement from the rest of her thoughts.

Pen kept looking into Case's pale eyes and she saw the moment when that seal cracked. 'You mean it was—?'

'Every word of it,' Pen said. She stood straighter, opened her chest out. Contempt filled her voice. Defying this woman had become like breathing. 'So what do *you* think you can threaten me with?'

For half a heartbeat, Case looked shaken, then that old unflappability closed over her features, smooth as thick oil.

'I'll have to think of something,' she said. She threw Pen's empty satchel back to her and then wrenched the door open. 'Sleep well, Countess.'

The second Pen heard the key turn in the lock, she fell heavily against the door and started clawing at it like she could scratch her way through it. Barbs of splintered wood lodged under her nails, drawing blood that smeared on the grain.

Shaking, she spun, crossed the room in three quick strides and threw herself bodily against the window – but the reinforced glass had been built to withstand chunks of falling brick. It didn't even flex as she threw herself at it again and again, demented as an insect.

She didn't stop until her legs went out from under her and she collapsed to her knees. She dashed her arm fiercely across her eyes and stared at the window. It was a bright, cold afternoon in the reflected city and Parva stared out of the glass at her, vague as a ghost.

Maybe, she tried to tell herself, *maybe this is better, for her at least.* Maybe there was some part of her mirror-sister left that *was* still her, and for that fragment perhaps, it was better not to remember. Pen tried, but she couldn't make herself believe it. There was a sob like a boulder lodged under her ribcage and she couldn't get it out.

She closed her eyes and saw their faces: Parva, and her mum and her dad and Beth, Beth most of all, whom she'd snuck away from without a word. She loved them all so much, and she was never, ever going to see any of them again.

She delved into her leather satchel and took out the last thing inside. The brick eggshell Beth had given her trembled against her palm. Beth would never know why her best friend had left her. Pen's fingers closed slowly over the fragile, precious thing, moving beyond her control. She watched from inside herself in a kind of absent horror as her fingers squeezed and the shell cracked. The baked clay shards bit into her palm and she treasured the pain even as she grieved for the memory they represented.

She couldn't rein in her thoughts. She pictured the Goddess in the basement, squatting in the foundations of the inverted city. She saw her own hand shaking and remembered the junkie-palsy in Mater Viae's crane-boned fingers.

Tell me, how can I go home again?

Empathy invaded her like a parasite and she recoiled from it. She tried to push it away but it clung to her. In her mind's eye she saw the Lady of the Streets, cut off from home, from everyone who loved and hated her, from everyone who knew her at all, from everything that made her *her*.

Shudders wracked Pen, and she started to sob, the tears coming in great gouts. She curled up on the floor, trying futilely to still herself. She tried to grit her teeth, but they just clacked against each other. She fought to ride out the shudders, her skin vivid with the memory of wire.

It took a long time for her muscles to shake themselves quiet. She let her head loll sideways against the floor. Her hair was sweat-sticky under her headscarf and her eyes felt like pebbles in her skull. She was exhausted. Her mind was a blank.

Gradually, she became aware of a thought like a buried ember in the spent fire of her brain.

I will not perform for you, Senator.

Hours must have passed, because outside the light through the windows was dimming and the cloud-wrought towers burned with sunset colours.

I will not.

Pen tested her legs, and was relieved to find that although she couldn't really feel them, they uncurled under her. They were knackered, but they were her own. She drew in a long breath, and stood.

She staggered to the window. It was only when she'd tried the handle twice that she noticed the welts of shiny metal around the frame where it'd been welded shut. Case wasn't fool enough to leave her the same escape route twice. Outside, someone was singing, chirpy at the onset of Draw Night. The glass made his voice reedy.

Trapped, away from everyone who knew her. She looked down at the river, at the evening fire reflected there. It touched a memory.

I will . . .

She took off her headscarf, folded it carefully and placed it on the floor beside her, then pulled off her boots and her socks. More purposeful, though still not hurrying, she walked into the bathroom and ran the tap. She exhaled.

Bismillah, she thought.

She washed her hands, the way she'd been taught, the way she had for years: left over right and right over left, three times each. Her right palm throbbed in the cold as blood and fragments of eggshell trickled down the paths marked by her scars. She cupped her hands under the tap and scooped water into her mouth and breathed it into her nose. She washed her face and scrubbed at her forearms and dragged her wet palms back over her hair. She worked at the dirt and fluff that had somehow got stuck to her feet and when it was gone she washed them twice more. About halfway through the second time, she began to feel calmer.

She pointed at the ceiling and recited in Arabic the affirmation she'd learned when she was a little girl. Her voice was calm. She didn't stumble over it. Whatever else it was, it was a part of her. Rituals were important.

Back in the living room, she rewrapped her headscarf. She looked out of the window and, after a brief moment's hesitation, she turned to her left instead of right towards the fading sunset.

She inhaled deeply and lifted her hands beside her head. She filled her mind and herself with the words as she spoke them, and felt the force of them drive the fear out of her.

'Allahu akbar,' she said.

When she'd finished the final rak'ah, Pen stood up. She felt taller. The air moved more freely inside her. Her shape felt more like her own. She rubbed her fingers over her thumb tip, but she didn't scratch her cuticle. Her hand was itching to hold something, to *make* something.

Her eye fell on the makeup box on the dresser. She picked it up and took it to the window. Her hand trembled, but that was just eagerness – *energy* – stampeding through her. She wrote quickly, the nub of the eye-pencil squeaking over the glass. In a place where image was everything, the window held the image of London-Under-Glass, Case's city, and Pen wrote over that image in jagged black letters until, at last, with the last of the energy that infused her she hurled the pencil down.

Heart hammering, she stepped back and read her handiwork.

Above rooftops like wave-crests
Behind a mirror like a sea
Beyond the eyes of anyone I ever knew,
I am still me.
In this city or any other.
In my breaths and my choices, in every word I utter and every
*   thought I think, in love, or in wire, in desperation or fear,*
*   in my own skin.*
Always,
I. Will. Be.

She settled herself cross-legged on the floor. Her hands, cupped in her lap, were finally still. The last light faded out of the sky. She heard car-horns far below. The guests for the ceremony would be arriving about now, she guessed, done up to the nines in the asymmetric designer evening wear she'd seen splashed across the magazine covers. They'd have brought their families, everyone no doubt giddy at the thought of meeting the Face of the Looking-Glass Lottery. Pen smiled, a tentative expression. A risk. Just for herself.

So sorry to disappoint.

The beeping from the computer startled her. She didn't move for a long time, but the beeping just went on, a high, repeated tone as polite and insistent as a tax collector leaning on a doorbell. Finally, more curious than anything, Pen went to the monitor on the desk.

The words *Incoming Call* were flashing in reverse script on the screen. Pen hit a random key, and a little thorn of anger stabbed into her heart as Case's face materialised onscreen.

'Countess.' Her voice came through the computer speakers. 'I trust you slept well.'

'Bugger off, would you, Senator?' Pen said sweetly.

'You're due in makeup. Please come down to the fiftieth floor.'

The bolt clunked back in the door.

'Nicely timed.' Pen was unimpressed. 'Did you have someone waiting on the end of a phone to unlock it when you said that?'

Case ignored Pen's scorn. 'Please come down to the fiftieth floor,' she repeated.

Pen eyed the little camera set into the monitor frame, snorted and shook her head.

Case stared back. There was no recognisable emotion on her wizened face. Without another word, she stepped away from the camera.

Pen hissed. The thorn in her heart was suddenly huge.

With Case out of the way, Pen could see the room behind her. It was the little dressing room just off the Hall of Beauty where she'd struggled into the barbed-wire dress. There were two other people in there along with the senator.

The first, on her knees on the floorboards, was Espel. Her arms were behind her back, and the way her shoulders were strained made it look like her wrists were tied. She stared at the camera. Either side of her silver seam, her eyes were huge with panic. Tears ran symmetrically down her face, their tracks conditioned by the identical topography of her cheeks.

The second figure was Corbin. He stood over her in formal black uniform, silver braid criss-crossing his shoulders. He had one hand woven tightly into Espel's hair, and with the other he held a silver syringe pressed to the side of her neck.

What do you think you can threaten me with?

I'll have to think of something.

Case's tone didn't change even a little. 'Please come down to the fiftieth floor,' she repeated.

CHAPTER THIRTY-FIVE

'*Steady now, Countess*,' Case's voice buzzed from the tiny speaker in Pen's ear. '*Wait for your cue.*'

She stared up the corridor towards the lights in the Hall of Beauty. Beau Driyard's speech echoed hollowly back to her as he warmed up the crowd. Someone she'd never heard of had introduced someone else she'd never heard of, who'd introduced someone whose name she'd seen on a couple of tabloid front pages, who'd introduced Driyard, and now he was introducing her. Each time, the cheers of the spectators seated in the hall had grown louder: a crescendo of celebrity.

'. . . had the privilege of working with many times in the past,' Driyard's voice swelled to a suave, but faintly lascivious climax, 'to bring you the images of her extraordinary story. The Face of *your* Looking-Glass Lottery: my Lords, Ladies and Gentlemen, Senators and honoured guests, please join me in welcoming: the Countess of Dalston, *Parva Khan!*'

The crowd in the hall exploded into hysterics.

'*Do please join your public*,' Case murmured.

With small, resentful steps, Pen obeyed, wobbling in her vertiginous heels. Her scars stood out starkly on her face, emphasised by carefully applied makeup. The barbed-wire dress rustled and hissed as she moved as though it was alive.

She glanced down at the phone Case had given her. On its screen, above the discreet inverted message reading ǝɔɐlq ɔɐll ɐ ui ssǝɹƃoɹd, she could see Espel on her knees. Corbin stood behind her with that wicked needle pressed to her neck. Both of their seam-split faces were bent away from the camera, towards the dressing room's tiny TV screen. It was an image-circuit, a closed loop: what Corbin saw on his screen would determine what Pen saw on hers.

Pen's eyes were drawn inexorably to the point of that needle. She could see Espel's fear; she could taste it like a thin trickle of poison down the back of her throat.

We're doing this for you, Parva.

Pen's skin remembered the fond squeeze of Case's fingers in the courtroom, and her own fingers curled at the memory of a time when even that simple motion had been beyond her.

Intimate Devil . . .

Harry Blight's torn expression flickered behind her eyelids when she blinked.

The cheers broke over her like storm-swells as she crossed the threshold to the hall. She paused and rocked on her feet. Some trick of acoustics had held the sound in check until she stepped through the door.

A spotlight dazzled her. She squinted through the glare.

In the temporary stands, the spectators were on their feet, howling and whistling gleefully. Lamplight refracted through the hanging panes of the Goutierre Device, crowding the room so much so that it took a moment for Pen to realise how few people were actually there – perhaps three hundred at the most. Every face in the crowd was either mirrorstocratic or heavily patched. The Lottery's contestants might be London-Under-Glass' poor, but that didn't mean they got to see it live. Case sat towards the middle of the fifth row, dressed in a demure midnight-blue gown, her face lit by the same passion as everyone else's in the hall. Guards in full dress uniform stood in the wings, Edward amongst them. Cameras crouched like avian predators on their dollies to the side of the stands, their red lights staring out at Pen, transmitting her to the reflected city's electorate, cut, framed and controlled.

Leaning on the lectern in the centre of the chamber, Driyard grinned at her and extended a hand. His silver seams glittered as if they'd been polished for the occasion; maybe they had. When she leaned in, he gave her a kiss on the cheek she didn't even feel and then left the stage.

The cheering showed no sign of stopping.

'*Smile for them, Countess.*' In the stands, Case's lips barely twitched around her own rapturous smile as she delivered the instruction. Her hand rested on her breastbone as though out of emotion, cupping the tiny mic. '*Surely they deserve it, even if I don't.*'

Pen placed the phone on the lectern. Espel's eyes pleaded

at her. Her lips parted and she cleared her throat to speak, but Case's voice buzzed sharply in her ear. '*Not just yet. Let us make our venerations.*'

So Pen just stood, stiff and smiling as a mannequin, drenched in their adulation. In spite of everything, she felt it lift her. The power of their attention tugged at her like a current in water. She could *feel* the gaze of the millions of viewers watching her on TV; all of their trust in her, all their hopes to win flowed through her. She could feel the muscles around her mouth twitch to pull her smile wider. It was as though her face was trying to shape itself more closely to their expectation. She clamped her lips tightly together, asserting control.

She heard Case's voice, and she wasn't sure if it came from her earpiece or her memory.

'*We can control how you are seen.*'

Control, Pen, she told herself. *Stay in control.*

But she wasn't in control, panic whispered to her: Case was.

'*That's enough,*' the voice buzzed in her ear.

Pen raised her hands, scarred palms outwards, and the crowd quietened. She swallowed against an arid throat and began to speak.

'My Lords, Ladies and—'

She hesitated. On the phone screen, Espel's mouth moved. It was a subtle motion, if it hadn't been for months of practise watching Beth mouth things, Pen might not have been able to read it:

What have I done? the steeplejill mouthed. With the tiny freedom allowed her by Corbin's grin, she was shaking her head.

What have I done?

Pen stared at the screen. *What have you done?* she wondered. *What do you mean? What have you done to* get *here? What have you done to deserve this?*

And then, quite clearly in her mind, she saw Espel perched on the edge of the kitchen rubbish chute, her mouth still stained with stolen brownie, grinning at her.

'*What have I done today to give you the idea that hanging onto my life is a big priority for me?*'

Pen stared out at the sea of eyes and cameras. She looked back at the Looking-Glass Lottery, at everything Espel despised.

On the phone screen, Espel and Corbin were both transfixed by Pen's hesitation. She thought she saw the arm that held the syringe tense. Espel's blue eyes, the same eyes as her insurgent brother's, flickered towards the camera.

Do it for me, Espel mouthed.

Pen was plunged into confusion. She clutched at the lectern for support.

Doubt whipped her mind Do it for me? Do *what* for me? What did Espel mean? Pen snatched at her breath. She could feel the dress crawling on her skin. She looked back at the phone, but Espel's gaze had returned to the dressing-room TV.

The red lights burned on the cameras. Hundreds of intent faces watched. They were all waiting for her.

We're doing this for you, Parva.

Pen straightened slowly and cleared her throat. 'My Lords, Ladies and Gentlemen,' she said. 'Senators, honoured guests—'

In the fifth row, she saw Case relax slightly.

'—and most of all, every single one of you watching this live across the city: welcome to the Draw for the two hundred and fourth Looking-Glass Lottery.' She smiled. 'I don't think we've been properly introduced. My name's Parva Khan—'

Laughter and cheers exploded out from the audience. Pen felt her breath come quicker as they hit her. She waited for them to subside.

We're doing this for you, Parva.

Do it for me.

She looked directly into the camera.

'—but I am not the Countess of Dalston.'

Case stiffened like she'd been electrocuted. Pen's eyes flickered to the phone screen, but neither Corbin nor Espel had moved. They were both staring open-mouthed at their TV. Was that a smile at the corner of Espel's mouth? Pen couldn't be certain.

'I'm not the girl you know by my name' – she looked back up at the crowd – 'although I loved her as dearly as you do. Find a picture, *any* picture of her, now. Look at it and look at me. *See the difference.* She's my inverse, my opposite – my mirror-sister. I'm afraid I've lied to you,' she said. 'And I am not the only one.'

383

Case's face was as white as a snake's underbelly. Her lips were moving furiously, her voice was buzzing in Pen's ear, deadly desperate threats.

Pen didn't listen.

'They were lying when they told you the Faceless had been kidnapping the new mirrorborn from train stations. They were lying when they told you the Faceless kidnapped Parva Khan. Harry Blight was an *innocent man*.' She let that sink in.

'Parva and the people from the train station and every other immigrant snatched off your pavements have all been taken for the same reason: they, like your grandprofiles, like your parents and like a lot of you too, came here from another place. Before this city there was somewhere else they called home, somewhere that they loved.

'They were taken by an enemy who needed that love, who drank them dry of it, and left them as good as dead. And that enemy is *not* Garrison Cray.'

Case was on her feet, screaming at the technicians behind the cameras to cut the transmission, but those same technicians were just staring at Pen and the red lights kept burning.

Pen raised her chin, 'Senator Margaret Case' – she spoke the name clearly – 'made a deal with that enemy.'

She felt a grim satisfaction as hundreds of accusing eyes turned towards the wizened mirrorstocrat.

Case pleaded with them, begging them not to believe the words coming from the very face she'd worked so hard to get them to love, to *trust*. Pen could see their expressions;

384

she could see them trying to reconcile that trust with her confession: *I've lied to you.* Their faces were contorted, as if that paradox was causing them physical pain.

'She sacrificed Parva Khan, and thousands like her, to that enemy. She'll tell you she did it to protect you.' Pen looked down at the phone on the lectern, at Espel's unreadable face. 'But I don't think that's what you would have wanted.'

Someone in the audience screamed and Pen looked back up sharply. Case wasn't pleading any more; she was standing tall and sighting Pen down the length of Corbin's service pistol.

'Shut up!' she was screaming. 'Just SHUT UP!'

There was a crack that made every bone in Pen shudder. Her hands moved instinctively to her forehead. The fabric of her headscarf was wet. She waited for the pain to come.

Then she saw that Case had rocked back on her heels, the gun falling slack to her side. The old mirrorstocrat stared in astonishment at a spreading patch of darkness on her shoulder. The men and women in the rows behind her were cowering, hiding their heads beneath their arms. Their expensive sleeves were patterned with glistening red.

Pen looked around in slow disbelief. Behind her, Edward was lowering his pistol. His eyes were wide at what his bodyguard reflexes had made him do. The gun barrel started to shake in front of him.

Five more shots split the air – Pen heard them; they were almost surreally distinct. A Goutierre lens shivered into splinters. Edward spasmed as if being electrocuted and then collapsed. The Hall of Beauty dissolved into screams.

Pen ducked her head and ran without thinking. Her heels slipped on the floor and she kicked them off. She stumbled and fell to her knees next to her former bodyguard. His head was turned away from her and Pen's heart lurched as she saw the symmetrical red crater that blossomed from the back of it.

Behind her, soldiers in ceremonial dress were shooting and shouting at one another as the great and good of London-Under-Glass scattered like startled livestock.

'*Corbin*,' Case's voice crackled into her ear, gritted and thick with pain, '*wake the steeplejill's id.*'

Pen grabbed Edward's pistol, though it burned her fingers, and pushed herself off the floor. She hared down the corridor towards the dressing rooms, dancing her bare toes between the splinters of broken glass. She overshot the door and slammed her shoulder painfully into the end of the hallway. Screaming in fear and frustration, she hurled herself at the dressing-room door.

The door wasn't locked, and Pen fell into the little room. Espel was lying on the floor, kicking and jerking. Corbin knelt behind her, fumbling with the bonds that held her wrists. He looked up at Pen as she entered, and started. He reached for the holster at his belt – but his fingers groped empty air. Case had never given him his pistol back.

He paled and lurched towards her. Pen raised Edward's gun and yanked backwards on the trigger.

The noise was hideous. The gun jerked itself out of her hands and clattered to the floor. The recoil felt like someone shoving a screwdriver into her wrist. Corbin's legs slid out from him and he hit the floor hard, clutching at his ribs. His mouth stretched like he was trying to scream, but all he could manage was a liquid gurgle. Bloody saliva bubbled out over his lip.

For a fraction of a second, Pen stared at him, frozen by the noise and the violence of what she'd done to him. Then Espel spasmed hard, and Pen dropped to her knees beside her. The silver syringe lay on the floor, its plunger depressed. The tip of the needle was red.

Gently, Pen rolled Espel over. The blonde girl's tattooed face twisted and contorted as the muscles in it pulled in opposite directions. The tendons in her neck corded as both of the minds in her fought against the plastic ties binding her wrists.

'Did I do it right?' Pen shouted desperately at her. 'Was this what you wanted?'

Espel's lips rippled back from her teeth, but the strained noises that came from her throat could have been anything.

'I'm so sorry,' Pen whispered. Horror made her feel light, dizzy. She had no idea what to do. Corbin made dreadful wheezing sounds. A dark stain was spreading through his uniform, just over where his lung would be. His legs kicked weakly under him, but he couldn't stand. He appealed to Pen with his eyes.

She set her teeth and looked away, but she couldn't block

out the pattering little wheezes he made as he fought to manage his breath: 'P-p-p—'

She stood and grabbed Espel by the collar of her jacket, dragged her up until her feet were under her and propelled her towards the door. The steeplejill's thrashing legs were forced into some semblance of coordination as she overbalanced, and she staggered in an ungainly reel in front of Pen.

They found the Hall of Beauty abandoned. Edward's body lay where it had fallen, but Case and all the other soldiers were gone. Pen's gaze lighted on Goutierre's Eye, swinging like a pendulum over the leather bench. Bullet-shattered lenses hung around it, jagged as fangs. She dragged Espel past it, tucked Edward's gun under her arm, reached up and slipped the all seeing sphere from its cage.

'Made you a promise,' she whispered to the back of Espel's jerking head as she barrelled her onwards out of the Hall.

Shrieks and cries echoed up the corridor from the direction of the main lift shaft, so Pen herded Espel the opposite way. She slammed the butt of the pistol into the button for the little service lift and, gloriously, the door slid open immediately.

Inside the lift, Espel's legs went from under her and she started to kick and jerk. Pen could see her shoulders straining fit to tear themselves out of their sockets as her arms worked against the cuffs. She threw herself on top of the steeplejill's body, trying to restrain the awful chaos of her limbs.

The moment the lift reached the ground, Pen was hauling on Espel's collar, swearing and pleading and cajoling. For a horrible moment she didn't think she'd be able to get the steeplejill moving again, but then she threw her weight into it and felt the resistance disappear as the blonde girl and her newly awakened passenger staggered onwards.

Got to keep her running. It was all Pen could think about, though her own legs and lungs were beginning to burn. *Got to keep her moving.*

They crashed through the kitchen. Roasted poussin and ramekins of peas and tall glasses of shrimp mousse flew and shattered in their wake. The half-faced chefs and wait staff didn't scream; they watched Pen in shocked silence. Their eyes flicked from her gun to the tiny TV hanging over the counter, still showing the silent, ruined spectacle of the hall.

Pen crossed the last few feet towards the rubbish chute in four short steps. Grunting with effort, she hurled them both headfirst into its maw.

CHAPTER THIRTY-SIX

For a sickening, frictionless second, Pen lost her grip on Espel's collar. She imagined the steeplejill getting stuck and her id-consciousness smashing their collective brains to a bloody smear on the metal shaft. She scrabbled and just managed to snare a handful of Espel's clothing as they tumbled onto their faces into filth and black plastic, but she didn't hesitate; she staggered over the uneven binbag terrain, but she managed to keep her forward momentum, hauling Espel after her.

Keep her moving, keep her moving. As long as she kept Espel's body off-balance, the twin consciousnesses inside it couldn't make it battle itself.

They raced out of the alleyway and through the dim arches of London Bridge Station. It was deserted – everyone was home in front of the TV. Pen hesitated briefly as the entrance to the tube station yawned, but horror at the thought of being trapped underground gripped her and she barrelled them back out onto the street instead. She split left on a whim. The frost on the pavement blistered the soles of her bare feet. The winter night chilled the metal dress to freezing point on her skin. Her ears were full of her own harsh breathing and her heart leapt and stuttered in time to the disjointed footsteps of the divided girl behind her.

Keep moving, just keep her moving.

But when they crested the rise that led up to the bridge, she stumbled and almost stopped dead. She managed to keep her balance, even as she stared in amazement at what was crossing London Bridge.

Marching towards her in a ragged wave, hooded and scarved and equal, *gleefully* flouting the law, was a huge crowd of Faceless, many brandishing bottles that spat oily orange flame. The silver painted legends on their black banners caught the streetlight: *Not by your Eyes!* they read, and *Our Gaze and No Others!* and a little less obliquely: *Fuck you, I am beautiful.*

Pen gaped at their numbers. There were hundreds, no, thousands of them, many more than she'd seen in their Kensington fastness. They cheered and roared their slogans, but it was the sound of their feet that sent a shiver up the back of Pen's neck. Their steps drummed on the tarmac as if they would shake the bridge itself into the river below.

Hush spread across the bridge as Pen pulled Espel out onto it, and the Faceless stopped cold. For a moment, as she ran towards them, Pen thought they'd stopped for her, their Counterfeit Countess, but as she drew closer she made out their eyes, visible in thin strips of bare skin above their scarves. None of them were looking at her.

She heard a crash like metal footsteps behind her, and felt something fall into the pit of her stomach as she looked back to follow their gaze.

Less than a hundred yards from the south end of the bridge, a line of Chevaliers stretched across the street. Their opaque visors shone with reflected streetlight and they held their rifles stiffly across their chests.

Pen had run straight into the middle of no-man's-land.

There were no warnings, no calls to disperse or surrender. The armoured police stood in eerie silence. Then, the crackle of a radio whispered through the air, an officer barked a one-syllable command, and with a sound like a thousand bones breaking, the Chevaliers set their guns to their shoulders.

Pen ran on, pulling Espel after her. Her heart skittered and skipped and she could feel all the muscles in the core of her squeezing together. She was ten paces from the first of the Faceless crowd. Her feet felt like blocks of ice as they slapped on the ground. *Five paces.* She heard another shouted order behind her, something that sounded sickeningly like '*Stop them.*'

The crowd in front of her began to churn like boiling liquid. Frantic black-clad bodies pressed themselves back against those behind them, trying to escape. Now she was close to them she saw they mostly weren't wearing hoodies after all; their faces were swaddled in improvised disguises made of torn bedding, scarves, old clothes.

They aren't Faceless. It came to her in an instant as she ran.

At least – they weren't before tonight. These people were here because of her. What she'd said had shattered the image of the glass republic, its fragile self.

They're here because of me.

A single voice shouted in alarm in the heart of the crowd; the sound echoed off the brick-laden clouds, creating bizarre acoustics. A shrouded figure erupted from the press of bodies with its arm outstretched. Its fingers closed around Pen's wrist and jerked her forward. She overbalanced and stumbled and stomach acid bubbled harshly into her mouth as she fell, dragging Espel down behind her. The cold pavement thudded up through her bones.

She couldn't breathe, her lungs clawed at air. She stared up at the man who'd pulled her, and he stared back. His veil was a torn and tattered flag. A familiar scarred smile rippled on the fabric over his throat.

A gunshot shattered the night.

The Faceless man's head snapped hard to the right, like it had been punched. Liquid jetted from his temple into the streetlight. He swayed on his feet for a second, then he crumpled. He lay where he fell, terribly still. His eyes, inches from Pen's, were like marbles.

Screams split the crowd. The protestors ran, bolting in all directions. Unable to flee through the thick press of their fellows, some of the Faceless charged the police line, hollering incoherently. More shots, more screams. A boot grazed Pen's ear as it stamped down. Pen tore herself from the dead protestor's gaze and threw herself over Espel, covering the steeplejill's flailing body with her own. An unruly knee knocked the wind out of her, but she managed to cling on. She threaded her hands into Espel's sweat-soaked hair and gritted her teeth. It took all her strength to keep the divided girl from slamming her head back on the kerb.

Gunfire echoed off the sky.

The thicket of legs around them was thinning. Pen dragged her eyes from Espel's and looked up. Shrouded bodies were falling around her. The Chevs weren't indiscriminate; they tracked the protestors who wore black hoodies and bandanas – the bona fide Faceless uniform – and split their skulls with carefully aimed shots. Terrified protestors hurled their firebrand bottles at the marksmen and, as Pen watched, an armoured figure was engulfed in sooty orange fire.

'Not by your eyes!' a protestor bellowed.

Pen scrambled to her feet. She tried to pull Espel with her, but her fingers were numb with cold and Espel was thrashing so hard she couldn't keep a grip.

'Help me!' she screamed into the chaos around her. 'They woke her id! Help me—'

But no one heard her over the boots and the shots and the screaming. A succession of petrol bombs flew like close comets, falling short of the Chevalier line, and shattered flaming on the pavement. At first Pen thought they'd missed, but then she saw the palls of oily smoke begin to roll across the bridge and the staccato rattle of the gunfire faltered. Rifle barrels wavered uncertainly as the marksmen struggled to draw a bead.

Protestors charged, bellowing obscenities and brandishing their banners like clubs. One Chevalier struggled to bring his rifle to bear, but veiled figures swarmed him under, swinging placards with bone-breaking force. Suddenly there was a gap in the line and the Faceless boiled through it. Pen saw them move, indistinct and wraithlike through the smoke. Some simply fled down side streets, but far more hurled half-bricks at the office-block windows that refused to reflect them. They shattered the images that kept them out, and their victorious shouts mingled with the sound of breaking glass.

Pen grappled with Espel. 'Help me!' she begged, but no one was listening.

A breeze stirred hairs that had slipped her headscarf. The smoke began to drift across the bridge and Pen eyed it anxiously – its cover wouldn't last long, and the crowd had thinned. In a few seconds the sharp-shooters would have a clear view again, and she and Espel would be horribly exposed.

A gunshot rang out – this time behind her. She turned her head and saw a streetlight tinkle into fragments. Another shot came and another bulb shattered, then another, then another, each in time to the gun's report. Someone had obviously reached the same conclusion as Pen.

Shrouded figures flitted around her, vague as shadows at dusk. Her eye lighted on a big man in a dark hoodie. He raised his pistol towards another streetlamp and she saw his ice-pale eyes narrow as he sighted along the barrel of the gun.

'CRAY!' she screamed at him, 'CRAY, HELP ME! IT'S ESPEL!'

He jerked around to face her. For a moment he stared disbelievingly at her, like he'd just seen her step out of a television screen. Then he was running towards her, elbowing and punching his way through the crowd.

'It's Espel,' Pen said as he reached her. Her throat dried, but the Faceless boss didn't even look at her. He dropped to his knees beside Espel.

'Sis,' he whispered, his voice taught with fright, 'what happened, are you hit, are you bleeding—?'

He faltered when he saw the cuffs binding her, red gumming the white plastic where they'd cut into her wrists. Tentatively, Cray put his hand on Espel's shoulder and pulled her onto her side.

He recoiled hard when he saw the muscles warring in her face.

'*How?*' His voice was flat.

'It was me,' Pen told him. 'It was because of me. Case did it because I . . . because of what I said. I'm— I'm so sorry.'

When Cray looked at her then, there was nothing in his eyes, nothing at all. He lifted his gun and pointed it at her forehead.

Pen didn't flinch. 'Please,' she said quietly, holding his gaze. 'We have to help her.'

For a long moment, Cray eyed her down the barrel of his pistol. Then he moved with sudden purpose. He tucked his gun into the waistband at the back of his trousers, bent and took Espel's lapels in both hands. With a grunt of effort, he dragged his sister bodily off the floor. Her feet jerked and twitched in the air like a hanged woman's.

'Hey—' He spoke gruffly and his head dipped from side to side as both of his eyes sought Espel's left one. 'Hey, I'm here, okay? I've got you. I love you, Sis. Okay? I love you.'

Pen couldn't be sure, but she thought Espel's thrashing eased fractionally.

Cray dropped to one knee, turned his struggling sister in his grip and jammed an arm under her chin. He jabbed his other elbow into the back of her neck and started to count under his breath. Even without the streetlight, Pen could see the tears blotting into his bandana. Gradually, Espel's jerking slowed and she went limp. For a dreadful second, Pen thought Espel's brother had suffocated her. But then she saw the slow rise and fall of her chest under her jacket. The divided girl's muscles reunited in unconsciousness.

'Jack,' Cray was shouting into a mobile phone, 'I need you. North side. *Now*.'

He heaved Espel's prone form onto his shoulder and stood up. 'Come on,' he said to Pen. 'We have to get her out of here before . . .' His voice tailed off.

'Before what?' Pen asked.

'That.'

She followed his gaze.

Hundreds of armoured Chevaliers were swarming down the approach from the train station. At this distance they looked like beetles, their armour glinting like a carapace, but they were closing fast. They carried short, ugly machine-guns with flaring muzzles: indiscriminate wide-burst weapons.

Bravado left the rioters like a tide going out. At first in ones and twos, then fives and sixes, then finally as a single dense mêlée of arms and legs, the veiled figures fled back across the bridge.

The Chevalier machine-guns deafened Pen as they opened fire.

She ran with the crowd, weaving through the protestors, dragging in painful breaths. Cray, just ahead of her, was more direct; he bulldozed up the centre of the road, slapping obstructing rioters aside with his spade-like hand. Espel bounced unconscious on his shoulder. They were almost at the far end of the bridge before Pen risked a look back. She watched men and women fall to the blaze of suppression fire like cornstalks in a hurricane.

She collided with a knot of bodies: the protestors in front of her had stopped running. She tried to sidestep and wriggle through, but there was no way between them. They were pressing back into her, trying to flee back the way they'd come.

Towards the gunmen? Pen thought in panicky bewilderment. She shoved at the protestors and they shoved back. Even in their hunted terror, she saw their eyes widen as they touched the cold metal of her dress and looked at her properly. She tried to look past them, to see what could have turned them around.

All around her, bodies churned in a slow, suffocating

vortex as those fleeing from both directions clashed. Her arm was snagged between two figures moving opposite ways and her elbow bent the wrong way. Pain flared through it and she just managed to pull it back in, even as hooded figures lost their footing and stumbled under the crush.

Pen heard a crunch and a choking scream as an off-balance foot caved in a cheekbone.

She gritted her teeth and clawed the figures away from her. She threw herself forward in her fake barbed-wire dress, forcing them to flinch. She used those fractional hesitations, those tiny spaces, to wriggle her way to the edge of the crowd. She grabbed the post of a shattered streetlamp and pulled herself up onto the bridge's balustrade.

As her eyes rose above her neighbours' heads, she saw what they were running from.

A line of mounted Chevaliers was advancing from the north end of the bridge, urging their bandaged-up horses at an unhurried canter. They held thin black lances high, the butts resting in their stirrups. At a signal from the officer in the centre, they reined in their steeds.

The officer surveyed the swirling mass of trapped protestors, inscrutable behind his dark visor. He raised one gauntleted hand. Below him, the men and women in the crowd were screaming.

The officer let his hand drop.

The Chevs pulled cords at the necks of their mounts and, as one, the black bindings fell away. Pen heard a gasp, and only a heartbeat later recognised it as her own.

The horses snorted and tossed their heads, the fog erupting from their nostrils glittering in the air like diamond dust. They stamped, and the impact of their hooves on the pavement chimed like bells. The horses blazed with reflected streetlamp light: perfect living sculptures of mirrored glass.

Lance points fell in a breaking wave. With a clatter like vast windchimes, the Glass Chevaliers charged.

The protestors broke and fled as best as they could. Those at the sides of the bridge jumped into the water, or else were shoved over by the terrified throng. For most, though, there was simply no time.

The glass cavalry smashed into the crowd with sickening force.

Where the lance points struck flesh, Pen saw blue electricity arc. The victims dropped sharply, spasming onto the ground in the path of the horses. Some of them were churned into a bloody meal of bone and cloth under the weight of the glass hooves, but others . . .

One of the horses reared up over a fallen Faceless, and Pen hissed in shock.

She could see the cowering protestor reflected in the glass of the horse's belly, between the straps that held the rider's saddle in place. His image ran slick through the curved, distorting panes of the Chevalier mount's flanks. Pen was close enough to make out the seam that divided the prone man's face.

I can't afford to just go spilling my image into every passing mirror the way you can, she remembered Espel saying. *Image is essence, after all . . .*

And that essence, Pen realised, was being ripped from the prone man by the mirror-mount's skin. It was a thief of images: a reflection-vampire.

The man shrieked like his heart was being torn out of his chest, his screams so loud that even with all the other cries that plagued the night air, his was the only voice Pen heard. His hood sagged horribly over his left cheek, like it was caving in. Flesh-coloured vapour boiled over his bandana towards the rearing horse.

Then, as sharply as if they'd been switched off, his screams cut out and he slumped back on the tarmac. The gap between his hood and his scarf was half-filled by a plane of tarnished mirror, and half-filled by nothing at all.

The Chevalier wheeled his mount and urged it deeper into the crowd, but the flesh-coloured reflection still spilled through its flanks. In the midst of it, something like a distorted eye blinked.

Pen reeled. She had to cling to the lamppost to keep herself from falling. Desperately, she tried to peer between the running bodies.

What if they've fallen? she thought frantically. *What if he's dropped her? How will I know?* In their hoods and masks they all looked the same.

But then her eyes found Espel, still spread across Cray's shoulders like an absurd cloak. The Faceless boss had somehow slipped through the cavalry line and was pounding

401

along the opposite pavement towards the bridge's northern end. As Pen watched, a Chevalier wheeled his mount and spurred it after them. Pen leapt down from the balustrade and started to run.

Cray was quick for a big man, *very* quick for a big man with an unconscious teenager draped on his back, but the glass horse was immeasurably faster. Pen had barely made it halfway across the road when blue lightning flashed out from Cray's spine to the Chevalier's lance.

Cray's back arched violently. His toes scraped along the pavement as every muscle in his body tensed. Then he crashed forward onto his face. Espel rolled limply off his back and sprawled in the gutter. The Chevalier yanked hard on his reins and his horse reared, the organic glass of its hide flexing. Lying in its shadow, Cray began to scream.

Pen's legs burned as she drove them harder. Spittle flew through her gritted teeth. She ran herself between the horse and its prey, her arms spread wide, blocking the line of sight between Cray and the mirror-mount's lethal hide.

In the curves of the horse's belly she saw her own reflection begin to flex and ripple. She raised her hand to her eyes. Her fingers guttered like a flesh-hued flame, but there was no pain, just a gentle feeling of heat, a fizzing over her skin. The glass horse's eye was stretched wide; its blunt teeth ground in effort. Pen's image flowed through all of its surfaces, but no matter how much she gave it, she still felt no loss.

Infinite reflections, she thought, awed and sickened. She, like a mirrorstocrat, was immune. The mirror-mount was a weapon designed for the half-faced alone.

The horse's front legs crashed back to earth and Pen threw herself flat. She sprawled over Cray's prone form, just missing its glass hooves. Its rider struggled to position his lance, then hurled it aside and groped instead for the pistol strapped to his thigh.

Pen felt Cray's arm shift under her. The Chevalier was still fumbling with the straps on his holster when Cray, screaming obscenities, leaned out from behind Pen and fired.

The Chevalier's visor exploded inwards. He slid sideways from his saddle and hung, his legs tangled in his stirrups. Pen stared, utterly frozen. The man's face, framed by the jagged plastic of his shattered helmet, was a bloody crater.

The horse whinnied against the sudden weight on its right flank and wheeled away, dragging its rider with it.

Pen felt like a firework had gone off inside her head. The gun was still loud in her ears. She felt like she should be yelling herself hoarse, but all she could do was stare. Everything felt distant and muffled.

Cray got his feet under him and crouched in front of her. She gazed at him incuriously. He said something, and it took her a moment for her to make sense of the words.

'Thank you,' he said again, and Pen nodded numbly. Reflexively she shook his hands off her.

The skin crinkled around his eyes in a way that might have been a smile. 'Come on.'

Pen helped him lift Espel's unconscious form out of the

gutter. Now she wasn't struggling, it was easy; the steeplejill was almost frighteningly light.

An engine growl became audible over the sound of the carnage further up the bridge and headlights washed over them as a battered saloon pulled up onto the bridge. Pen stiffened, ready to fight, but Cray held up a hand.

'It's okay.'

The car's brakes squealed. The driver's door was open before it had stopped moving. A familiar gangly figure emerged.

'When I say I need you *now*, Jack,' Cray said testily, 'it's normally safe to assume I mean *before* the fragging riot cops show up.'

'Oh *goody*,' Jack Wingborough snapped back. He jerked his head at the mêlée still churning further up the bridge. 'Do let's discuss this now. I can't think of *anything* better we could be doing . . .'

His sarcasm faltered as he watched Pen and Cray hoist Espel onto the back seat. Pen scrambled in beside her, while Cray jumped in the front.

'What happened to Es?' Jack demanded as he slid back behind the wheel.

'I put her out,' Cray said shortly.

'Why?' Jack asked, but his voice was hoarse, and the pallor of the skin visible in the rear-view mirror said he already knew.

Jack threw the car squealing into reverse, spun it into a 180-degree turn and stamped on the accelerator. The battered saloon leapt forward like a startled cat. The shouts and sounds of gunshots and the light of burning petrol faded behind them.

Pen watched as Cray looked back. She saw him take in all the ordinary people who'd adopted his image, who, just for one night had become him. He pulled his bandana slowly aside. His makeshift mouth was anguished. She knew he would always believe he'd betrayed them.

'Where am I going?' Jack demanded. 'Garrison, give me some bloody pointers.'

'St Janus,' Cray said. His voice was flat.

'You bloody fractured?' Jack sounded incredulous. 'You want me to take a girl with a woken id to a *military hospital*? What are we supposed to do, just give ourselves up?'

Cray didn't answer.

'Garrison, *please*,' Jack said. 'I'd walk under a mirror-mount for her – you know I would – but there's no way they'd treat her. They'd take one look at her, cut the cuffs off her and let her throttle herself. There's no way for her to have been split that isn't an official punishment. She's *marked*.'

Marked, Pen thought. On the seat next to her, Espel's symmetrical features were still at rest. Streetlamps painted tiger stripes over her through the car's windows as they drove. Red blotches marked her skin where the muscles under it had contorted, where they would again when she woke. *Branded. Scarred.*

Pen slumped into her seat. Tears surged up in her throat and she swallowed them back. She sought inside herself for something, anything that could galvanise her against the despair that was welling out from the core of her. She felt a flicker of anger and she concentrated on it, cradling and stoking it like an ember.

She remembered the bullet wound in Corbin's chest; she remembered his desperate, trembling failure to speak. A shiver passed over her as she realised she'd probably never know if he'd died there.

She battened herself down as she started to tremble. *I will not pity you*, she told herself. She fixed the little half-faced boy in her mind, the blank look in his single eye before Corbin shot him. *I am not sorry*, she said inside her head, over and over again, hating the way it made her feel like a liar. *I am not sorry.*

Pain spread through the back of her left hand and she looked at it. She'd gouged bloody lines across the tangle of scars with her right.

In the front seat, Cray and Jack were still arguing.

'I know one of the nurses at St Janus—' Cray's voice was quiet, almost like he was trying to convince himself. ' He could—'

'One nurse? It would take an army of doctors, round the clock, *for the rest of her life.* And even then . . . You know I don't want to say this, Garrison but she's—'

'Shut up,' Cray told him.

'Mate, *please*.'

'No, I mean, *shut up*. I'm trying to listen.'

The young mirrorstocrat fell silent. Cray bent his earless

head, and Pen strained to listen too. At first all she could hear was the engine and the hiss of the tyres on the tarmac. Then, very distant but growing louder with alarming speed, came a sound like wind-chimes.

'Jack,' Cray said simply, '*floor it.*'

Pen looked back through the back windscreen just as six glass horses galloped from a side street and thundered after them.

CHAPTER THIRTY-SEVEN

The battered saloon lurched forward as Jack stamped on the accelerator. Through the rear windscreen, Pen saw the Chevaliers react, goading their horses to greater speed. The chime of their hooves on the road almost blotted out the engine's roar.

'They can't catch us, right?' she asked. 'I mean, this is a car. They're only on *horses*—'

Cray was frantically winding his window down. He had his gun out. 'WHAT ABOUT THEM LOOKS LIKE NORMAL HORSES TO YOU?' he yelled over the blast of air. He pulled himself half out of the car, leaning like a windsurfer, and started shooting.

The glass horses seemed to gallop ever faster, eating up the road with their ringing hooves. The beasts burned with reflected streetlight, growing brighter and brighter, until Pen couldn't look at them straight. The lamps they left in their wake were dark, as though they were leeching the energy they reflected. Their hooves blazed and blurred under them like shooting stars.

They were closing.

At some hidden signal, the Chevaliers bent low over the necks of their steeds. Behind each of them, a second black-clad rider became visible, each holding a long-barrelled rifle. They aimed with practised ease from their jolting mounts.

Pen threw herself flat over Espel as the rear window dissolved. Glass splinters sprayed over her, nicking the back of her neck. The wind screamed in through the gap.

'New plan,' Jack shouted to Cray over the roar. 'No place like home!'

Cray fired off one last, futile shot and slid back inside the car. Jack spun the wheel and the saloon veered left. A rippling column that might have been the reflected Centrepoint appeared and then vanished behind them.

Pen levered herself up. The wind rippled her headscarf against her face and she clawed it back. The architecture blurring past on both sides was growing more clotted as they sped further west. Jack swerved the car around the low brick drifts that stretched into the road, but the mirror-mounts jumped them like fences on a steeplechase without breaking their charge. The passenger-side mirror exploded into fragments as a bullet hit it.

'*Little close, Jack*,' Cray grated.

'Righto!'

Jack jinked the car into a series of tight corners, and stomach acid leaped into Pen's mouth. They straightened up along a narrow side road. A fraction of a second later, three Chevaliers tore around the corner behind them, but they'd taken the turn too fast. The horses veered sideways as their riders wrestled with their reins. Hooves scrabbled on concrete as the mirror-mounts fought for traction. Their lips peeled back from their slab-like teeth as their glowing glass legs tangled. The horses screamed strange, crystalline screams as their momentum overcame them.

One of the beasts skidded flank-first into the front wall of a newsagent. A fraction of a second later, its fellows collided with it. With a brittle shriek of glass the horses shattered into fragments.

'Mother Mirror, Jack – where did you learn to drive?' Cray shouted.

'Benefits of a private education,' Pen heard the grin in the young mirrorstocrat's voice. 'I totalled three Porsches before I was fifteen.'

The air howling through the shattered rear window was cold enough to hurt Pen's face, but she didn't dare look away. Even as the heap of armoured bodies and broken glass dwindled behind them, she saw the three remaining horses eased around the turn by their riders. One by one, the lights around them flared, stretched to touch their hides and went out. The vampiric steeds blazed as they accelerated up the centre of the road. They were closing the distance with sickening speed.

'We can't outrun them!' Pen shouted as they swerved into another turn.

'I know.' Jack tore the scarf from his mouth. He sucked in tight concentrated breaths. 'But I can take my wheels places they can't force their hooves. *Please, Mago*,' he murmured fervently. 'Just one more mile.'

Eight-foot dunes of precipitecture were rearing in front of them now, bristling with broken railings and jagged spurs of scaffolding. Jack's face flushed as he wrestled the car around them, on two wheels as often as four.

'*Just a little further*,' he was muttering under his breath to the car. '*Just a little further*.'

Pen tried to listen past the sound of the wind and the engine until at last she realised there wasn't anything else to hear. 'I can't hear hoof beats!' she shouted jubilantly over her shoulder. 'I can't hear—'

Her voice was obliterated by screaming tyres as the car slipped sideways. The window filled edge to edge with brick. Pen just managed to curl her body around Espel as the car scraped to a halt along the wall.

The vibration of the grazing metal shuddered through Pen's skeleton. Cray was up and out even before the sparks struck by the fender had landed. He ran around the back of the saloon and shoved the boot open.

'Jack—' His voice was tightly controlled. 'How long have we got?'

'Five minutes, maybe ten.' Jack worked breathlessly beside Cray. He was pulling something that clanked from the back of the car. 'I can't see them getting those bastard horses past Cadogan Street, but I don't know how fast they can run in their armour.'

'No chance you lost them?' Cray asked.

411

Jack just snorted. 'I think we left a trail of rubber on the road half an inch thick. *Damn*, I miss my old car.'

Pen felt gelatinous, like her bones had dissolved, but she managed to clamber out of the car's uncrumpled side. She hooked her arms under Espel's shoulders and pulled her out. Her body came limply. Her tattooed face was still slack.

'Bloody hell, Cray,' she said incredulously. 'What did you do, put her in a coma? Is she ever going to wake up?'

'I put her down deep. She's got another half an hour or so, maybe a little less,' Cray replied. 'The two of you need to be a long way away by then.'

Pen looked up. From where she now stood, she could see what Cray and Jack had taken from the boot – a pair of short assault rifles with stylised chess knights stamped on the handles. The contraband weapons clicked as they jammed clips into them.

'The *two* of us,' Pen echoed hollowly.

'You'll manage,' Cray said firmly. 'My sister never did eat enough, and I reckon you're stronger than you look. Squat down, let her drape over your shoulders. Just carry her like a sack of coal.'

He pointed towards a crack in the rippling brick wall of the cul-de-sac. It had been mostly swallowed by precipitecture and it looked more like a crevasse in a mountain than the narrow lane it was.

'Get going. Jack and I'll give London-Under-Glass' finest something to think about. Should buy you a bit of time.'

Pen gave him a flat stare. 'You'll be killed.' Her tone said all that was needed about the acceptability of this solution.

'That's right.' Cray ducked under the strap of his rifle. Jack was already scrambling up a rise in the precipitecture, aiming over it like a rampart.

'I'm not going to just—'

'Yeah, you really are,' Cray interrupted her. His bandana had slipped and there was a wry twist to his homemade lips. 'Do you know how many men I've killed, *Miss* Khan?

Pen stared at him and sullenly shook her head.

'Neither do I, but I do know that my hand didn't shake the last time I pulled the trigger, get me?' He lifted his chin fractionally, took in the space around him and exhaled slowly. He almost looked proud. 'This has been coming for a long time. Believe it or not, having the Chevs gunning for me is not a new experience for me. If they get me this time – fine. *But not her.*'

Anger whipped into his voice like a sudden icy wind as he looked at Espel. 'Not her,' he repeated. 'My sister's not like me – she's the *opposite* of me. She's never hurt anyone.' Tears ran, one by one, his meagre face giving them up reluctantly. He started to talk faster; his words ran into each other, but he didn't stutter and he didn't blink. 'She *couldn't* hurt anyone. I told her to kill the Face of the bloody Lottery and she couldn't. She was the best steeplejill in the Kennels, and she had a future, but she came and worked for me, because she believed in me, and she believed in you too, and now she's sharing her body with psychopath because of a choice you made, so will you *JUST GET GOING*!'

413

The last three bellowed words echoed off the surrounding walls and Pen jumped as he slammed the boot closed. For all that Cray sounded furious, his eyes were pleading.

Under the entreaty of those pale blue eyes, Pen bent and let Espel's motionless form drape over her. She stood straight. The weight was bearable. She looked at Jack, who was lounging on the rubble, rolling a cigarette. 'What about you?'

The young mirrorstocrat shrugged. He put his roll-up aside and palmed a half-brick from the drift beside him. With a flick of his wrist he sent it spinning into the air and in one smooth motion brought his rifle to his shoulder and fired. The brick erupted in a satisfying spray of powder.

'Tell you what,' he said returning to his roll-up, 'if you're a better shot you can take my place.'

Pen stared helplessly at the two of them for a moment, then, bent slightly under her burden, she took a couple of steps backwards. The strange shadows of the inverse city closed over her. Cray scrambled up the side of the drift to Jack's side. They muttered to each other in rapid whispers and took turns taking drags on the cigarette.

The last thing Pen saw before she turned away was them pulling their bandanas up over their mouths: like bandits and like equals.

Pen moved through the alleyways at a kind of fast stagger. Espel wasn't that heavy, but she was dead weight and she kept slipping, pulling her off balance. She could feel sweat running between her shoulder blades, even in the unforgiving cold of the steel dress.

Warehouses loomed either side of her, their rain-augmented architecture spilling onto the street. The air smelled faintly of smoke and petrol. The walls were scorched. Faceless slogans looped in still-drying spray-paint on the brick and Pen felt a sudden pang for Beth when she looked at them. It looked like London Bridge wasn't the only district that had seen protests.

Clouds of broken glass glittered like nebulae on the street. Every reflection – every image that excluded the half-faced population – had been shattered.

Pen felt a movement on her shoulder, out of rhythm with Espel's breathing. The divided girl's right ankle was beginning to twitch.

Half an hour, Cray had said. *Maybe less.*

Definitely less, Pen thought. It was a struggle to swallow. Scraps of remembered phrases flitted through her head as she watched that foot, the right foot, the *id's* foot, slowly rotate.

'—*she's sharing her body with a psychopath*—'

'—*because it hated him, Countess*—'

'—*it takes an army of doctors, for the rest of her life*—'

An army of doctors, and Espel had only her, exposed and helpless on a freezing street corner. They had to find a place to hide.

For a second, Pen thought she heard glass hooves chiming on asphalt, even though here in the confines of the Kennels it should have been impossible.

Of course, *the Kennels* . . . She did know of one hiding place here. She set Espel gently down for a moment and then scrambled up a precipitecture drift. The warped skyline of London-Under-Glass became visible above the rooftops. Sirens reached her on the wind. Away to the east, across the river, the clouds glowed with reflected fire. The reflected city was burning.

Pen chewed her lip, waiting until she was sure she had her bearings. It wasn't far. She skidded and slid back down to the street and was just reaching for Espel when the sound of machine-guns froze her.

It echoed back up from the way she had come. She listened, paralysed, her heartbeat slamming painfully in her chest. Bursts of gunfire answered each other for a couple of minutes and then stopped. Pen eyed the street behind her and a bead of sweat trickled over her temple. Was that it – was that all there would be? She hadn't heard any cries, but maybe she was too far away for that. She closed her eyes and pictured Jack Wingborough and Garrison Cray. She hoped they'd walked out of that cul-de-sac alive, even though the odds were three to one. She realised with a pang that she'd probably never know.

Stick to the plan, now that you've got one, she told herself. She lifted Espel back onto her shoulder and lurched deeper into the claw-like architecture of the Kennels.

CHAPTER THIRTY-EIGHT

CHAPTER THIRTY-EIGHT

Rained-down bricks piled up like earthworks against the outer wall of Frostfield High, so there was no need to climb in over the gates.

'Not even for old times' sake,' Pen murmured. She eyed some skilful graffiti across the road and rationed herself half a smile. She gripped Espel tightly with both arms. Over the last few streets the steeplejill's struggles had grown more and more intense.

Pen skidded down the rubble inside the wall, but kept her balance. She peered through the dim backwash from the streetlights. The layout of the warped buildings exactly mirrored that at her own school, and she felt a stab of relief when she saw the orange tape bandaging the junior block.

The abandoned bathroom was as cold as its counterpart in her own city, and it smelled of the same must. The chill from the lino numbed her bare feet. She groped in the familiar place for the switch and the halogen tubes in the ceiling flickered on, their bluish light somehow sucking even more heat from the room. Pen's eye fell on a rust-brown stain beside a rip in the lino, smeared into the shape of a hand.

She couldn't help looking in the mirror. A girl in a barbed-wire dress and dusty hijab, with makeup running over her scars, stared back at her from a place she'd never set foot in again. *Home*.

Pen stifled the thought as soon as it rose.

As gently as she could, she laid Espel down. When she caught sight of the steeplejill's face, the pain was like all of her ribs breaking.

Espel's teeth were gritted, the eyes on both sides of her seam stretched and staring, wide as madness. Veins stood clear on her forehead under sticky strands of blonde hair. Under her jacket, Pen could see her arms straining against the cuffs that kept her from strangling herself.

Pen knelt beside her. She tried to take the weight of Espel's head. 'It's— It's—' She tried to say *okay* – it was all she could think of, but the lie was too big and its sharp edges caught in her throat.

Desperately, she tried to think of something – *anything* – she could do to ease the girl's pain, but what was there? The instant she'd – *they'd* – awakened – Pen felt sick as she corrected her thought – a brutal territorial struggle had recommenced inside Espel's skull, a fight for the one thing everyone ought to be able to call home. Garrison was right: Espel was trapped inside her own body with a psychopath, and it was because of Pen. Es's 'intimate devil' was awake; it knew her, and it wanted to destroy her. It was her inverse, her opposite.

418

Opposite.

Time seemed to run slow, slower than freezing water, as slow as glass, as Pen turned the idea over in her mind. She looked into the mirror and saw the scarred girl reflected there, the face that wasn't hers, not really. She met the blue eyes Espel Cray shared with her brother. Garrison's words kept playing in her head, but it was she who spoke them aloud.

'My sister's the opposite of me,' she breathed.

It was a strand of hope, cobweb-fine.

Pen pressed her hands to Espel's temples, trying to hold her still. She sought the steeplejill's left eye with both of her own, just like her brother had done on the bridge.

'Listen to me, Es,' she said. 'Please, listen to me. *Parva* was my inverse, remember? She was the opposite of me. Please, please lie still.' Pen was starting to gabble, she could feel her own desperation reaching up to choke her. She struggled to slow herself, to make herself make sense.

'She was my *opposite*, but she didn't hate me, not at all. So maybe – *maybe* – your id isn't born to hate you either. Maybe it's only fighting you because you're fighting it. So . . .' Pen felt the barb-scars tug at her scalp. She had to force the words out of her throat. She knew how terrible a thing this was to ask.

'Stop.'

She swallowed hard. 'Stop fighting it. I know you can feel it in there with you. I know how scary that is, but stop. It's not its fault – it's not *her* fault. Stop.' She dashed away her tears and refocused both her eyes on Espel's right.

'Both of you,' she pleaded, 'stop.'

For a terrible second Espel's head strained against her grip, and then went suddenly still. The blue eyes roved, frightened, as though searching for a coming attack, but the breathing was easier and the muscles stayed slack.

Pen watched them for long minutes: the girl who'd believed in her, and her terrible, blameless passenger. Her eye lighted on the mirror, on the glass. An idea occurred.

At first she recoiled from it – it was too terrible a risk; what if she was wrong? Harry Blight's contorted features flashed in front of her exhausted eyes. She sat back on her haunches and looked around the abandoned bathroom, searching it for other ideas, but nothing came. Out there in the night, a battle was raging for control of the inverted city. Who knew if she and Espel would have any friends left on this side of the mirror by sunrise? And even if they did, even if Jack and Cray had somehow survived, neither of them had had the first clue what to do with a girl with a woken id. The Chevs would be hunting for them; they'd find them eventually and a stray bullet could kill Pen, leaving Espel trussed and waiting for her captors.

It was a sliver of a chance, barely even a wish's chance.

Actually, Countess, Espel's voice and secret smile drifted up from a remembered darkness, *wishful thinking's the only thing that's ever got me anywhere.*

She stood and crossed to the abandoned stalls. The screws in one of the door handles were loose, she remembered, and it took only a moment to work it free. She weighed it in her hand, shooting little looks back at Espel. Both blue eyes looked nervously back.

Pen gripped the loose handle like a wrench, turned and smashed it into the bottom corner of the bathroom mirror, and again, and again. On the third strike, a fragment of mirrored glass the size of her palm flaked from the wall. She gathered it up.

Both sides of Espel seemed to recoil as Pen knelt back beside her.

'I'm going to free your hands, okay?'

They just stared at her as she reached around behind Espel and began to saw at the blood-crusted plastic that held her wrists.

Neither arm moved as the cuffs frayed apart and Pen let out a breath she didn't know she'd been holding. Pen eased both arms out from behind Espel and laid them on the floor. She sat back on her haunches and watched the divided girl.

'What now?' she muttered, mostly to herself.

Espel's right shoulder twitched. Pen started forward, but she held herself when she saw how slow, how *tentative* the movement was. Very gradually, Espel's right hand started to rise. Her left eyed rolled to watch it, but the corresponding arm stayed still.

For a moment, the right hand seemed to hesitate over the open front of the steeplejill's jacket, then, slowly, as if trying not to startle a frightened bird, it descended towards the left.

Pen watched open-mouthed, as Espel's right hand took

her swollen, cuff-scarred left wrist and gently started to rub feeling back into it. After a few endless seconds it let go and laid across Espel's stomach. Then, just as tentatively, Espel's left hand began to massage the tender skin on the right wrist.

At last, the divided girl rested her hands on her stomach. She said nothing. Pen wasn't sure that she could, but she was breathing evenly. Both eyes closed.

Pen breathed out the kind of quiet, tentative breath that doesn't want to disturb the world. She shuffled backwards on her bum towards the wall with the sinks on it. One of the pipes that ran over the chapped brickwork was warm. For a second she thought about pulling Espel over too, but she didn't feel she could disturb her.

Relief broke over her in a wave, pulling exhaustion along behind it.

Have to stay alert, she told herself. *Stay awake.* But the tiredness settled like silt in her limbs, and she couldn't bring herself to move away from the warm pipe.

'Good night, Es,' she breathed, before her eyelids fell.

CHAPTER THIRTY-NINE

Pen woke to the soft sound of someone trying to cry quietly.

Her eyes opened instantly. Weak daylight was visible through the dusty windows. She looked across the floor to Espel, but the steeplejill was lying where Pen had left her; eyes open, staring at the ceiling, blinking slightly out of time every now and then but otherwise intensely still. Little clouds of condensation rolled in the air above her mouth.

Pen rolled away from the pipe. She'd drooled in the night and the cold had cracked her lips under the moisture. The sobbing sounds continued. They were coming from behind her, from the mirror.

Pen stood stiffly. Her eyes were sticky and she felt as if her bones had frosted. She looked into the reflection.

The source of the sobbing sounds looked barely human – she was so small, so tightly curled in on herself. She sat against the far wall of the London bathroom, her arms wrapped around her knees and her face buried behind them so that every inch of skin was covered. The only thing to identify her was the cloud of frizzy red hair.

423

'Trudi?' Sleep made Pen's voice croaky. 'What are you doing here?'

The sobs stopped. Trudi's pale, freckled face rose from behind her denim-covered kneecaps. Pen watched her shocked eyes as they looked back into the mirror, then predictably moved to stare at the empty space where Pen should have been standing to cast that reflection, and then back to the mirror again. Trudi's mouth began to work silently.

'I—' She blinked. 'I . . . Am I—?'

'Don't look away,' Pen said quickly, trying to keep her tone soothing. 'You aren't mad. Your mum didn't spike your Coco Pops this morning. This is really happening. What are you doing in here?'

'I-I-I—' Trudi stammered, still staring, unable to believe what she was seeing, but seeing it anyway. She answered the question on reflex. 'I come here to be alone.'

'Because being alone hurts less when there's no one around?' Pen said. She didn't blink as she held Trudi's gaze. She didn't like knowing how the other girl felt. She resented the surge of empathy. 'When did Gwen cut you loose?'

'After I . . . After you—' Trudi was trembling now. 'She said she was disgusted with me.'

She didn't say a word to stop you, though, did she? Pen thought. She remembered the flush in Gwen's perfect cheeks as Trudi set fire to her hijab. She remembered the audience she'd helped arrange, and swallowed back a little angry bubble.

'What is this?' Trudi breathed. 'Some kind of Dickensian guilt thing?'

'Yeah, I'm the ghost of Christmas Shut-the-fuck-up-and-listen.' Pen's voice snapped around both rooms as her patience gave way.

Trudi flinched. 'Parva, I'm s—'

'I'd love to have the time to care,' Pen cut her off. 'Want to make it up to me? Get your phone out.'

Trudi obeyed, not taking her eyes from Pen's as she rummaged in her bag.

'Send a text to this number.' Pen recited the digits from memory. Trudi's fingers trembled and she typed them in. 'Tell her "Pen's in the mirror", and tell her where. Tell her to come now, and tell her . . .' Pen felt her throat constrict. 'Tell her my harmony is very much fractured.'

'Tell who?' Trudi asked.

'A girl you used to know.'

Trudi didn't question her further, but when she was done keying the message in she stared in chagrin at her phone screen.

'What are you waiting for?' Pen demanded.

'No signal.'

'THEN FIND ONE!' Pen shouted it at her through the glass.

Trudi scrambled to her feet. 'I really am sorry, Parva,' she said quietly. Pen didn't answer, just watched as she fled into the corridor.

Pen hugged herself, feeling the fake barbs of her dress. She paced over the lino. She thought about seeing Beth again, and the anticipation fizzed in the back of her throat. She wished she had some way of telling the time. Four transits of the narrow room and it already felt like hours. Pen scratched at her cuticles and muttered to herself under her breath, trying to get straight what she'd say to Beth: how she was sorry she'd left, how she couldn't come back, how – and the pit of her stomach began to squeeze – how there was someone far worse coming in her place.

And goodbye.

She snatched a breath. Goodbye would be the last thing she'd have to say.

She was so distracted she didn't notice at first that Espel was fidgeting.

She scrambled to the steeplejill's side in alarm, scared the fragile truce in the divided girl had been broken, but neither hand moved to cross the border marked by the silver seam. They just twitched and pattered on the floor. Espel's head rolled first this way then that, her neck craning as though she was trying to see. Pen followed her frantic gaze and froze.

Just visible through the tear in the lino, next to Parva's old bloody handprint, the concrete floor was trembling.

It was a tiny vibration, a minuscule fraction of a point on the Richter scale, but it was definitely there, and it was getting stronger.

Fear galvanised her muscles. She gathered Espel to her and lifted her in her arms, ready to flee. But she hesitated. She looked back into the reflection of the empty London bathroom. She imagined Beth arriving, finding no one there. She agonised, torn between the mirror and the door.

Espel stirred against her.

They aren't looking for you, Pen thought.

She hefted Espel's slight body across to the last toilet stall on the left and kicked the door open. She sat the steeplejill on the closed toilet seat, frantically trying to arrange her legs so they wouldn't show through the crack at the bottom of the door.

'They aren't looking for you,' Pen told her. 'You don't have anything they want. Stay quiet – stay still. Whatever happens, whatever you hear, stay still.'

She looked back at the rip in the lino. She didn't know what had brought Mater Viae's clayling soldiers abroad, but she couldn't shake the bone-deep feeling that they were coming for her. It had to be – there had to be something about the doorway drug or her mirror-sister's memories or, or *something* that had drawn the Lady of the Streets to hunt her again. Espel had been born in the reflected city. She'd never even seen the home Mater Viae craved.

'You don't have anything they want,' she repeated, desperately wanting to believe it. The expressions either side of Espel's seam were unreadable as Pen stepped out of the stall and pulled the door closed. She exhaled hard.

'*Okay*,' she whispered. She turned, and screamed.

A dark figure gazed at her through the rust-splotched mirror. The irises in its eyes glowed softly, the green of traffic lights. Pen recoiled from the rooftops that overlapped on its cheeks like scales, from the black cable hair that coiled over its ears, from the church spires that showed between its lips as it mouthed: *Pen*.

No sound, just the shape of her name.

Pen started hard. And now she saw the black Chemical Brothers hoodie the girl wore – and she saw it *was* a girl. The architecture of her face made sense in a new and familiar way.

'Beth?' she said, in utter astonishment.

She ran over to the mirror, put her hands on the glass. Beth did the same, keeping right by the side of Pen's reflection.

Why? she mouthed.

Tears spilled out of Pen's eyes and splashed on the sink. 'No, B – please just listen. I'm sorry, okay, I'm so, so sorry. But there's no time—' It felt like everything she had to say to Beth was compacting up hard in her throat, churning together, making it hard to breathe. She could feel the tremor in the floor through the lino now. The halogen tubes rattled in their ceiling fittings. 'Mater Viae' – she saw Beth start at the name – 'she's—'

There was a soft explosion in the floor behind her, followed by the sound of footsteps.

Pen turned slowly. The Masonry Man stalked towards her, its cadaverous ribcage swelling and shrinking in time to something that wasn't breath.

'*Come*,' it said in its frail draught-voice. It extended a hand. '*Come*.'

Pen stumbled backwards. The barbs in her dress scraped over the mirror-glass. 'No,' she said.

The clayling creature took another step, and then it hes-

428

itated, looking past Pen into the mirror. Suddenly it looked uncertain. '*Mistress?*' it breathed.

Pen's pulse slammed as she looked back over her shoulder. Beth was staring into the bathroom, although the light of her green eyes never touched it, rebounding from the silver and glass in her world. Her throat was straining; Pen could read the words off her lips.

Pen, what is it? What's wrong?

She couldn't see the concrete-skinned predator, only the fright written on her friend's face.

The Masonry Man looked confused for a moment. It studied Beth and then, in a shockingly human gesture, it shook its head. Pen heard concrete sinews grind in its neck. She steeled herself as it, less sure now, it resumed its advance.

'It's all still you, Pen,' she whispered.

Whatever happened, wherever it took her, she told herself, that would be true.

The stall door banged open behind the Masonry Man and Pen jumped. Mater Viae's servant turned with a sinuous, liquid grace.

With halting steps, Espel walked into the bathroom. Pen watched her in dry-mouthed astonishment. She walked the way a baby walked, concentrating first on one leg, and then the other. The steeplejill watched each foot as it moved, both sides of her divided face set in fearful concentration. With awe, Pen saw Espel overbalance and correct herself, as though the bathroom lino was a high-wire. Espel's eyes flickered back and forth, and Pen wondered at the extraordinary negotiation, the *collaboration*, that must be taking place behind them.

Run, she thought, incredulous hope rising in her. *Get away.*

But then Espel opened her mouth. 'Mmmee—' The word was stretched, the lips and tongue not quite coordinated, but it was completely comprehensible. 'Iiit's m-me.'

Her jaw worked silently for a moment, then she spoke with more confidence. 'I hhave it. I know whaaat you're looking for. She t-told me. Sh-she gave it to me. C-come and g-get it.'

'Es, no!' Pen shouted. 'She's lying—'

The Masonry Man hesitated, daintily poised on the balls of its concrete feet. Its pupilless eyes fell first on Pen, then on the disturbing presence of Beth in the mirror, and then it turned back to Espel and took a step forward.

Pen heard the sound of a lid being spun against a screw thread, and then a *flick*, like water hitting glass. There was a change in the air pressure behind her, a breeze, as though someone had opened a window. She tried to push off the mirror behind her, to get between the clayling and Espel, but her fingers groped nothing but air. Much too late, she tried to run.

Grey hands clamped around her chest, their pavement scales crushing and bending the barbs on her dress. She struggled, but the arms that held her were as strong as cranes.

'*Beth, no!*' she tried to say, but in her desperation Beth was squeezing her so hard she couldn't draw the breath and it came out as a shapeless wheeze. Pen felt herself dragged backwards. She felt London air on her cheek. Liquid edges of mirror-glass entered her field of vision as they rushed back towards each other.

Espel moved into the doorway with that slow, extraordinary gait. The Masonry Man took another step towards her, its hand outstretched like a welcome. The gap in the mirror was a tiny porthole now.

'Es,' Pen gasped. She caught one last glimpse of Espel's blue eyes over the creature's shoulder. They were focused. Then the mirror sealed noiselessly, and all Pen could see in it was a dusty bathroom and her own, horrified face.

CHAPTER FORTY

Pen sat at the Bradleys' kitchen table, slowly turning Goutierre's Eye in her fingers, gazing into its storm-occluded heart. Somewhere in that rush of images, she knew, there was a facet in sympathy with that reversed city bathroom mirror. *Right now*, she was looking at a picture that could tell her what had happened to Espel, only she couldn't see it. She couldn't *see* it. She stared until her eyes ached, but without the rest of the device, without Espel's expertise to wake it, the dark cloud at the heart of the eye remained quiescent.

Es.

The memory of that grey hand reaching for Espel was like shards of broken glass in her heart.

She'd turned on Beth as the mirror closed, hammering on skin like architecture with her fists, screaming at her to reopen the glass, to send her back. Beth had gazed at her in confusion that had shifted into silent horror when Pen finally managed to force an explanation past her sobs. Beth had scrambled for her phone and Gutterglass was already brewing more of the doorway drug, but it was a fragile and time-consuming process and until it was complete Pen could do nothing but chew her reconstructed lip into ribbons and stare into the clouded glass.

Please, she whispered inside herself to the only girl she'd ever kissed, *please be all right. Please hold on.*

A scraping sound behind her drew her gaze. Beth leaned against the doorway, looking at her with those glowing eyes. She came and sat down opposite Pen, and the cats followed her across the floor with a ceremony wholly at odds with their Goddess' stripy pyjama trousers and ragged Faithless T-shirt. Oscar was curled up on her shoulder, exuding an air of slight reptilian smugness even while he snored.

Pen glanced at the digital clock face in the microwave. It burned green: 3:23 *a.m.* Beth and her dad had retired only four hours earlier. It had taken all day for Pen to recount what had happened to her.

'She'll be okay.' She said it aloud, trying to force certainty into herself with her own voice. 'We'll go back, we'll find her.'

Beth nodded and smiled encouragingly. *We.* She mouthed the word and pointed to both of them. Pen stiffened slightly as her lips opened on church spires, but she tried not to let it show.

It's all you, B, she thought. *They just rearranged you a little bit.*

She wished she could be like Beth's dad. When he'd opened the door to them that morning he'd stood staring open-mouthed at his daughter's sheepish smile for a full thirty seconds, but then he'd embraced her fiercely.

'And I just bought you that electric toothbrush too,' he'd muttered with a laugh that was worth five times more for being forced, and ushered them inside.

Pen was proud of Paul Bradley for that, but he hadn't seen what she'd seen. It must have been tough for him to see the face he'd given his daughter swallowed up by city streets, but at least when he looked at her, he didn't see a basement floor covered in empty bottles.

We'll find her, Pen told herself again. *We*. Beth had always been the other half of that word.

Pen steeled herself, and then stretched out her spare hand on the table. With a grateful and slightly surprised smile, Beth took it. Their fingers interlocked, skin to skin, scar to scar.

It's all you, B.

'Oh lord.' Mr Bradley ambled in blearily, tying the cord on his dressing gown. He eyed the feline brigade on his kitchen floor. 'This is because I told you couldn't have a kitten when you were eight, isn't it?' He yawned around the back of his hand and said. 'You two never were much for keeping conventional hours, were you?' Beth squeezed Pen's hand a little conspiratorially.

'Well,' he said, 'if we're all up, I may as well make cocoa. Would you like some, Parva?'

Pen considered how distraught Mr Bradley had looked the previous day when she'd told him she wasn't hungry.

It appeared he'd gone to the same school of crisis-management as her mother, and had learned the same universal strategy: combine heat, sugar and dairy products in the magnitude required until evil is defeated. Paul had started off with a relatively mild mug of sweet tea, but then, as Pen told her story, he'd rapidly escalated, finally reaching the point where he had all the ingredients out for a DEFCON One banoffee pie. He'd looked totally at a loss when it became apparent that neither of the two girls was in the mood to eat anything.

'That'd be lovely, Mr B,' Pen said carefully. 'Thank you.'

Mr Bradley lit the gas under a saucepan of milk and then joined them at the table. His eye fell on the glass marble in Pen's hand.

'Parva, you know you can stay here for as long as you'd like. You *know* there's nothing either of us would like more—' He hesitated, and rubbed at the stubble-speckled skin of his neck. 'But . . . you are going to trade that, right? I mean, you've still got two weeks on the deadline you agreed with the synod. Your parents' memories – you can get them back.'

Pen looked at the little sphere – the window she couldn't see through. The window she'd *never* be able to see through. It shouldn't have been a hard decision.

'I'll—' She broke off, staring at the hob.

Tendrils of blue fire were curling out from under the saucepan.

Beth jerked her head round to stare at Oscar, but the sewermander just kept snoring and for once the burning gas wasn't reaching for him. Instead it twisted and writhed its way through the doorway into the hall, towards the front door.

Pen looked at Oscar, looked back up at Beth's softly glowing eyes, then she gave a startled yelp and scrambled after the flames. Beth and her dad both raced after her.

The skeins of fire were threading themselves under the brass flap of the letterbox, staining the metal where they touched it. Pen yanked the door open, swerved round the tail of the fire and ran into the freezing street. She halted there, astonished by what she saw.

Fine threads of blue flame were pouring from every house on the terrace. They pooled together in the middle of the street, like tributaries joining a great river. A fat tongue of azure fire warped and surged in the air above the road.

On Beth's shoulder, Oscar woke and started to keen. Pen watched the muscles tense under the little lizard's skin, but the flame stemming from the house barely flickered.

'Mr Bradley,' she said, her voice very cold. 'Get your car.'

Without a word he ran back inside for his keys.

'Beth—' Pen turned and felt the green light of her best friend's gaze on her face. 'She's coming.'

Beth swallowed, and nodded. A procession of cats emerged from the doorway, the iron railing balanced across their backs. Beth seized it in one hand and then dissolved into a blur like petrol on the wind as she started to run.

Paul's Volvo chuntered up to the kerb and Pen jumped into the passenger seat.

'Follow the fire,' she said. He stamped on the accelerator before she'd pulled the door shut.

They had to dodge cars and pedestrians fleeing the other way as they swung out onto Hackney Road. The heat from the fire brought out beads of sweat on their heads. Pen's heart slammed as she peered through the windows on either side. Stray cats slunk from alleys and from under parked cars. They walked with an unnerving, stately pace, hundreds of them, far more than Beth had ever commanded. They turned down Bishopsgate and Pen glimpsed a white enamel sign. The black letters on it were in no language she knew. They veered around buses and taxis and awestruck gawkers. Paul clung to the wheel like it was a life raft, wrestling with it to keep them out of the torrent of fire pouring down the centre of the road. He stood on the accelerator again, keeping the tip of the flame, its blind, wormlike nose, in sight. The Shard rose above the city's lesser towers as they approached London Bridge.

'Oh no – oh mercy, *no*,' Pen whispered to herself.

There were no lights on in the northern side of the Shard. The glass that ought to have covered the side of the enormous skyscraper was no longer there. When Pen looked through the space it had left she didn't see exposed, empty office cubicles. She saw distant, rippling towers, some of which were still on fire. She saw London-Under-Glass.

The skein of fire climbed sharply as it reached the South

Bank of the Thames and rose over the low roof of London Bridge Station. Dozens of other fiery snakes breached the skyline alongside it, all converging on the Shard.

For an instant, she thought the flames would push through into the inverted city, but just before they reached that mirror-marked border they suddenly blossomed, splashing against some invisible barrier. The flames unfurled symmetrically, igniting massive wings.

Huge dragon shapes, outlined in blue fire, wheeled in the air over London.

A figure in striped pyjama trousers and a faded T-shirt stood on a bollard outside a construction site next to Borough Market. Londoners ran screaming past her, Londoners of flesh and of glass and of stone, but she didn't flinch. Mr Bradley's face was pale as he pulled the car up beside his daughter and got out.

Beth acknowledged neither her father nor her best friend as they came to stand beside her. Her eyes were fixed dead ahead, on the absent glass of the Shard. The lights of which were only an echo burned bright in the architecture of her face.

Grey figures erupted from the road like sharks from water, their thin bodies landing with deadly poise, and behind them, in the heart of the tower, something moved.

At first, all that was visible was a pair of green eyes, a mirror to Beth's own, then a shimmer of skirts that caught the light like estuary water.

The lady of the streets smiled her church-spire smile as

438

she stepped into the road in front of the Shard. Pen saw her ribs swell as she drew in a deep breath. She looked at Beth and frowned around her smile, as though pleasantly surprised. Then she turned her gaze east, towards Canary Wharf.

Mater Viae looked at her right hand and curled her fingers. Across the river, the cranes grasping at the sky over St Pauls began to move.

ACKNOWLEDGEMENTS

Once more, I'm hugely grateful to the team that made this with me: The peerless Jo Fletcher, Nicola Budd, Lucy Ramsey, Alice Hill, Tim Kershaw and everyone at Quercus; Don Maass, Cameron McClure and all at DMLA. Extra special thanks to Comrade-Conspirator Amy Boggs for building me up, talking me down and taking no prisoners as my agent.

Thanks also to Sam Miles, Emily Richards, Den Patrick, Darren Hartwell, James Smythe, Kim Curran and Helen Callaghan for helping me make this a better book, and especially to Shahd Fouda for coming to the aid of a stranger in need.

As always, love and gratitude to Sarah Pollock, David Pollock, Barbara Pollock and all my family.

Finally to Lizzie Barrett, wife, thank you for your patience, your presence and your love.

I remain in awe of, and in debt to, those authors mentioned in the previous volume. To their number I would like to add Ursula le Guin, John le Carré, Frances Hardinge and Lewis Carroll. In the writing of reflections, conspiracy and counterparts, I have never known their equal.

Beth's and Pen's stories conclude in

Our Lady of the Streets